Hailed by the *Los ...* ... the masters of the ... van de Wetering i... acclaimed mystery ... Adjutant Grijpstra and Sergeant de Gier of Amsterdam's Murder Brigade. Filled with unusual characters and exotic settings, laced with humor both subtle and broad, and starring a pair of detectives who are excellent company indeed, these books are absolute bliss for the most discriminating of mystery lovers.

"A rare combination of good character development, intellectual content, humor, exotic settings, and coherent plots... These are not unfeeling, hard-bitten cops. They are sensitive, personable men of whom we grow very fond. They seem like real people and it is as much to find out more about them as to see what new plots or settings van de Wetering can come up with that we eagerly await each new book."

The Armchair Detective

"He is adept at turning a plot that can leave one guessing."

The Chicago Daily News

"What makes this series so engaging is that the policemen are as quirky and complicated and human as the criminals."

Washington Post

Also by Janwillem van de Wetering:

THE
RATTLE-RAT

Janwillem
van de Wetering

BALLANTINE BOOKS • NEW YORK

Library of Congress Catalog Card Number: 85-3681

ISBN 0-345-32872-8

This edition published by arrangement with Pantheon Books, a division of Random House, Inc.

Printed in Canada

First Ballantine Books Edition: August 1986

NORTH SEA

Ameland

Anjum
Engwierum
Dokkum
Franeker
Dingjum
Leeuwarden

FRIESLAND

Bolsward
Joure

The Hague
(Den Haag)

Amsterdam

Rotterdam

THE NETHERLANDS

GERMANY

BELGIUM

mmmmm *The Great Dike*

PREFACE

The Netherlands is known as a small country, but what foreigners usually don't know is that even this little speck on the map is divided into eleven provinces. Ten of these parts of a greater whole have been interdependent for centuries, but the eleventh province, Friesland, in the northwest, has liked to keep free of interference. It refused blind obedience to the government in The Hague to the south—and, as this tale will show, it is somewhat on its own today, still stubborn, separate, and in spirit proudly free.

Friesland has its own language, not a dialect, with grammar, verb conjugations, spellings, and sounds different from the Dutch language, which is spoken across its eastern frontier and south of the Great Dike that now connects Friesland with the province of North Holland and its capital, Amsterdam. Friesland's other frontier is the sea. The color of the sea reflects in Frisian eyes, the clear blue of valiant Vikings.

When Roman, Spanish, French, and German armies in turn overran the Netherlands, Frisian guerrillas fought them fairly, one hand clasping the Bible, the other a deadly weapon. Foreign tax collectors never had a good time in Friesland. Seafaring, cattle-farming (the raising of the famous black-and-white cows), superior toolmaking, and the growing of high-quality vegetables are profitable occupations. Why share the gain with useless hangers-on from abroad?

The world is becoming smaller; in time even Frisians had to give in to their neighbors, a little. Differences, however, are still obvious. If the Netherlands is clean, Friesland is cleaner. If the Netherlands has good dikes, Friesland has better dikes. If the Netherlands has few murders, Friesland has almost none.

Now what would happen if a Frisian was foully killed in wicked Amsterdam?

The Amsterdam Murder Brigade, led by its old commissaris, would go after the killer, with a vengeance, for the commissaris was born in Friesland.

A commissaris is a high-ranking officer; there's only one higher rank in the Municipal Police—chief constable. Under a commissaris work chief inspectors, inspectors, noncommissioned officers such as adjutants and sergeants, and constables first-class or second-class. The Netherlands outside the cities is policed by the State Troopers, with military ranks; then, to complicate matters a little further, there's the Military Police, sometimes known as the Marechaussee, which guards frontiers, protects the Queen, and disciplines the fighting forces. In case of a crisis—and a murder is a Dutch crisis—all policemen work together and their territories overlap.

DOEKE ALGRA, BORN IN MENALDUM, FRIESLAND, TWENTY-eight years ago, was experiencing feelings of extreme happiness. He had been uplifted by such euphoria before, when, on his father's lap, he was watching doggies. There were never any doggies, but their mysterious absence was part of the happiness. Doeke Algra, Sr., at that time filled with the strength of his young adult life, had to work hard for a living and liked to relax after dinner, and little Doeke preferred to jump and wriggle. He could sit still but only if there was a Purpose. "The doggies will be coming by the window in a minute," father Algra would say and cuddle his offspring, and together they kept looking through the narrow window of a lowly laborer's cottage set between gnarled willow trees, and enjoyed each other's warmth while the doggies didn't come.

Protective warmth—that had returned for a few moments while Constable First-Class Algra looked over the water of Amsterdam's Inner Harbor from Prince Henry Quay. Policeman Algra, detailed with the uniformed section of the Red District Station, wasn't on active duty at that moment, somewhere between 2:00 A.M. and five minutes later—or perhaps he was, for a cop serves the community twenty-four hours a day, and Doeke was therefore equipped with his gun and identification, although he wasn't dressed in uniform. He wore a leather windbreaker and tight jeans. The pistol was hidden under his armpit. The plastic ID, adorned diagonally with the red, white, and blue of the Dutch flag, stating clearly that the bearer was official, hid in the breast pocket of the windbreaker. His ever-ready social conscience hid in a haze of Frisian jenever, a herbal variety of Dutch gin, the vaporous remnants of a fair number of drinks poured till half an hour ago in Jelle Troelstra's bar. Troelstra was Doeke's guardian and the owner of a brown hole-in-the-wall at the Old Side Alley. Whenever Doeke was stricken by homesickness, he visited Jelle.

"*Jûn,*" Jelle would say then, meaning "evening" in Frisian and nothing at all in Dutch. After that they would converse in their very own lingo, a remedy against the pains of having to live elsewhere. Jelle was the listener, sharing Doeke's lament in silence. Doeke would complain, about Amsterdam's vicious vice, about the coarseness of its public women and the violent greed of the quarter's black pimps. While Jelle listened he made the earthenware jar of jenever gurgle: first and last glass on the *hûs*. At times Jelle, the comforting provider of liquid solace, sweated, for he still suffered from swamp fever; and sometimes he would rub his thigh where an old gunshot wound hurt him. He had contracted the fever in the tropical hell of New Guinea, and the shot was fired by a mounted Cossack. Both Jelle and Doeke were martial Frisians, but Jelle no longer discussed his violent quest, for he had fought on the wrong side—which was the right side a long time ago, as he had honestly believed during those far-gone days. He had been a sergeant in the Netherlands SS Legion during World War II, and had defended the flanks of a German transport against irregular Russian troops, galloping on the snow. Jelle had once fought for Greater Europe and was rewarded with hard labor, building a road through the jungle of a useless colony. Doeke was still fighting for peace in Amsterdam's inner city and wasn't rewarded at all.

All human bravery leads nowhere; Jelle had known that truth for a while; Doeke still cherished ideals. Doeke didn't know that Jelle had been a well-meaning traitor. He didn't know either that Jelle had been born in Hallum, a village close to Doeke's own Menaldum. When asked, Jelle would place his origins in Anjum, a small town well away from the truth. The farther the better. Doeke knew no one in Anjum.

The exiled Jelle comforted Doeke, who served humanity abroad. The barkeeper's silence soothed the younger man.

Jelle's patient quietness and the jenever's glow now warmed Doeke's soul from a hot point in his stomach; ambling about, he had reached the Inner Harbor, where nothing was in view except an expanse of gray, swelling water. The gray movement reminded him of shreds of fog that had caressed the windows of his parents' little house, in the dreamtime when he was secure in his father's embrace.

There he stood, legs apart, hands on his back, staring peacefully across the low, slow waves.

Something should happen now, Doeke thought, something pleasant. Perhaps he expected a glorious vision. Alcohol releases brakes, liberates happy insights that will flame from the soul and burn away the daily pain.

When exactly did he see the floating fire? Doeke couldn't remember later on, when he had to admit, somewhat sillily, while being interrogated by detectives, that his perception had been rather foggy, due to his abuse of herb-flavored liquor.

Something was burning, the sharp flames cutting through the fog, and the something was moving along with the slow swell of the waves. Doeke had been raised religiously, and remembered that the Dear Lord, in early times, was known to walk on water; there had also been a burning bush of brambles, and angels were about, carrying burning swords. It was therefore quite believable that Doeke associated the happening of that night with heavenly instruction, and that he hadn't immediately thought of an ordinary fire. A fire on a ship? No—he was focusing now—on a small boat.

Why would a dory be on fire?

Doeke sobered a little and attempted logical thought. He remembered that he was still a constable first-class, even now, early on a day off, dressed in civilian clothes and unfortunately rather drunk. Whatever was happening there could not be in order and he would have to make a report. Where was a phone?

At the Central Railway Station. Doeke ran, with long elastic jumps. The burning dory was still visible from the Inner Harbor Quay. Doeke swayed, but he kept running, and the alcohol diluted in his tall, muscular body. He dialed the local alarm number in the station's telephone booth and reported, succinctly and to the point, mentioning his name and rank and the booth's telephone number. The sergeant in charge of the radio room at headquarters, at the Moose Canal, only had to press a button. The State Water Police answered at once and the sergeant over there pressed another button. A patrol boat crewman grunted in reply. Doeke's telephone rang within three minutes.

"Yes?" Doeke asked.

"That's understood," Doeke said. He was running again, still swaying a little. Ten minutes later he jumped down from the bridge at the Harbor Building, overlooking Admiral's Quay, and almost missed the flat gray patrol boat, because he was still far from sober. The sailor policemen steadied their colleague. The engine of their craft murmured with quiet energy.

"Inner Harbor," Doeke said.

The boat cut through the murky water, underneath the bridges of the Open Harbor and the Front. The sailor policemen had greeted Doeke with a slight display of helpful friendliness, but weren't too hopeful, for they expected a false alarm. A fire on the water? Noticed by a drunken constable of the shore? They would see what they wouldn't see.

"Now where is the disturbance located?"

Doeke's finger slid vaguely across the chart. "Well, here, maybe? I was on Prince Henry Quay—here, I would say. A dory, I thought, with flames spouting up, some black smoke too—quite a cloud."

They looked about in vain, some thirty minutes. Doeke was taken back to the shore, on the Singel, where he lived in an attic. "Pleasant duty," Doeke said formally, and the sailor cops said good night.

What could the disturbance have been? Lightning? There had been a thunderstorm earlier in the day. Some soft thunder, in the outskirts of the city. Warm summer weather—didn't that sometimes lead to sudden electricity bursting from low clouds? The sailor policemen didn't think so, this time. Destructive youth? Boys like to light matches. A floating box stuffed with burning paper? Or maybe a vision, after all? Doeke had been fairly active and had slept little for a few days. Extra hours of duty, long hours of study for his upcoming sergeant's exam. Add a few hours of serious drinking, the hurt of a recently broken engagement, a visit to a most attractive and most unhelpful whore—tensions not broken by proper relaxation—so what do you see? Fire on water?

The sailor cops wrote the unsubstantiated phenomenon in their report and a note was filed in the radio room of Municipal Headquarters. The night changed once again into day.

Waling Wiarda was up early and out for a walk—not on his own time, for Waling was working. A chief of the Department of Public Parks goes for walks in his line of duty, to check the growth of the city's living greenery. While walking, Waling recited a poem. In the cracks of rocks that form the quay walls were supposed to (*oh, wild and wondrous glory . . . of flowers, splendid . . .*) grow some extraordinarily tall mountain-ash berries, which were weakening the mortar. City official Wiarda, dressed in khaki municipal corduroy, tried to remember the rest of the Flemish poet's wordplay, but the lines wouldn't come to mind and he hummed musically instead, visualizing the flowers' glory. The waterworks engineers shouldn't complain so much, Chief Wiarda thought. So the mountain-ash bushes were six feet tall, and their roots were unsettling the rocks, so what? The quays had been around for hundreds of years, they would last a while longer. *His* duty was to make sure there was still some natural life in this godforsaken town. More wildflowers, more fresh leaves, *pom-pom* (he was humming again), *the wild and wondrous glory*. Flowers would raise the spirits of the citizens. By encouraging the city's greenery he was doing good work. The chief stooped to admire a large cluster of golden dandelions, not of the common variety. Strong stems, shiny leaves. Very nice, right? But just look at that mess floating in the harbor. Ah, another report to be drawn up, bristling with understated sarcasm. Stinking garbage, torn plastic, all in the wrong colors, unmentionables glued together, cubic yards of disease breeding filth, and—well, why not?—a burned-out dory. A dented aluminum wreck, eight feet long, pushing its prow stupidly against the smooth rocks, damaging the blooming bushes with its inane destructive bashing. Wiarda lowered himself carefully, finding support by holding on to the ashes' branches. Maybe he was a provincial, talked down to by the city slickers, but in Friesland, his home, such degeneration would not be allowed, and thanks to him, the country bumpkin, prepared to work for the country's worst part, it wasn't as bad here as it would certainly be without him. He would never give up fighting against filth. This very day he would type out his umpteenth report and deliver it personally to City Sanitation.

"Sanitation," snarled Wiarda. That department was the sloppiest of them all; he wouldn't be surprised if they had dumped this rubbish themselves.

"*Himel*," groaned the chief, invoking heaven in his own language. Wiarda was a devout Christian. What could he have done that heaven punished him now by providing a glimpse of the awful contents of hell? The punishment was still going on. Wiarda, frightened out of his surface calm, felt his feet slip, and saw his well-polished boots dip into the dirty slime that surrounded the dead dory. He clawed his way up and staggered about on Prince Henry Quay.

A motorcycle cop came by and stopped to see why Wiarda was waving. The policeman lifted his orange helmet and held a hand behind an ear. "What's that?"

"Corpse," babbled Wiarda. "Blackened, down below."

They looked together, brother officials, attached to safety by the wild mountain-ash and their own clasped hands.

"I'll pass it on," the cop whispered.

The Water Police patrol arrived again, in another vessel, manned by other sailor cops, the Municipal Murder Brigade showed up in an old model Volkswagen, and marked police cars spewed constables who placed striped fences to hold traffic off. A black limo arrived too, filled with well-dressed gentlemen who had brought equipment to document the event on film and videotape.

What did they all see? Human remains in a blackened aluminum rowboat. The dory was lifted on a pickup truck and taken to Headquarters. Doeke Algra was awakened by detectives, and wrote his report, sitting next to Waling Wiarda, supervised by Adjutant Grijpstra of the Murder Brigade and supplied with coffee by his assistant, Sergeant de Gier.

"It doesn't have to be murder," the adjutant said.

"They do meet with accidents, you know," the sergeant explained. "There's no telling what people will get themselves into. A fisherman, maybe? An open can of gasoline? A cigar lit with a careless match?"

Doeke and Waling didn't think so, Doeke because of the floating fire that reminded him of the fears of his holy early youth, and Waling because he couldn't forget the hollow eye sockets of the partly burned skull that had stared at him in terror from the semiliquid filth of this damned city's waterways.

"No?" Grijpstra asked, rubbing the almost white stubble that covered his heavy head. "What a coincidence that both of you are Frisians. I am too, you know. My parents came from the port of Harlingen."

"Three compatriots in full agreement," Sergeant de Gier

said, adjusting the ends of his full cavalry-style mustache. "I would like to join you, but I was born in Rotterdam."

Why he had to state his origins, de Gier didn't know; perhaps he wanted to defend himself against a sudden trinity of those who think differently.

Doeke Algra, Waling Wiarda, and Henk Grijpstra looked at de Gier with mutual contempt.

"*It Heitelân*," Wiarda said solemnly. Doeke bowed his young head. Grijpstra smiled benevolently. Constable First-Class Algra and Chief Wiarda were allowed to leave.

"Murder?" Grijpstra asked, lowering his bulk, neatly covered by a three-piece suit, dark blue offset by thin white stripes, on a rickety chair. "Is that what they were saying?"

De Gier shrugged his wide shoulders. "You don't speak Frisian?"

Grijpstra admitted his ignorance in silence.

"*Heit* means 'father,'" de Gier said. "Never heard a Frisian suspect cry in his cell? So *Heitelân* means 'fatherland.' How come you don't understand your own language?"

"Don't be trivial," Grijpstra said. "Who cares about unnecessary details?"

Sergeant de Gier stretched his tall body, arranged his thick curls, and carefully knotted his silk scarf inside the collar of his tailor-made denim jacket. The sergeant had just turned forty; the adjutant had celebrated his fiftieth birthday some years ago. Grijpstra rubbed ash off his knees. "No murder," he prayed aloud. The prayer wouldn't be answered, as he knew; his cynicism was well established by a long career.

"You know what I like about the start of this case?" de Gier asked. "That we don't have to do much for a couple of days. All we do now is wait. I'm getting better at waiting. Will you join me for coffee once we've talked to the doctor?"

Grijpstra nodded. "Somebody will be missing somewhere."

"There were some teeth left in the skull," de Gier said. "Teeth are excellent identification. Fit them into the physical description of the missing person and you know Who is Who."

"And catch the other 'Who,'" the adjutant said.

"The 'Who' who did it," the sergeant said.

But it wasn't quite that simple.

2

"HASTE IS A DISEASE," THE PATHOLOGIST SAID. HE RESEMbled a bird, not a nice sort of bird. A picker of corpses, de Gier thought, a neurotic crow, half lame, hopping about at an angle. To keep his balance, the doctor slanted his large, pointed head, while he peered at his visitors.

"So what is it now?" the pathologist asked, studying his watch. "We're about to close here. What do you want to know?"

"Whether you're getting somewhere," Grijpstra said patiently, "with your study of the person burned in the dory."

"That mess you sent in?" the pathologist asked. "It should be here somewhere." His little claw lifted plastic covers. "Burned bones and scorched parts of a skull. A man. Getting along—late fifties, I would say. Five feet nine, if he would stand up straight, but he didn't, it seems. Laborer type? Farmer on an acre and a half? Pushing a wheelbarrow for a living? There are a few inches of spine here and there, rather bent." The doctor gestured desperately, flapping his arms as if he were ready to fly off. "Uneducated guesses, dear sirs. If you want concrete information, you'll have to deliver a concrete corpse."

"Clothes?" de Gier asked. "Shoes?"

The pathologist attempted to straighten his head. "Not my department. I take care of the temporary body. Whatever isn't body has been sent to your lab."

"Teeth?" Grijpstra asked.

"Teeth is body. Over there. In the little bag."

Grijpstra looked. "Could that be gold?"

"A lot of gold," the pathologist said. "Bridges, caps, what have you, but I'm not a dentist, you don't even employ a dentist. You cut costs, you know."

"A permanently bent-over laborer at minimum wages with a golden mouth?"

"Listen here, Adjutant," the pathologist croaked, "don't expect deductions. I'm not paid for deductions, I'm paid for cutting corpses."

De Gier shivered. The remnant of the skull stared at him, for the sockets still existed, surrounded by charred bone, covered with soot. How, the sergeant thought, can someone who isn't there be staring at me?

"Is sir unwell?" the pathologist inquired.

De Gier's hand, covering his mouth, trembled. "I'll never get used to it, never, never. He's gone and he's here, minding my business while I mind his. What's a skull? The head of death? Is death alive?"

"Beg pardon?" the pathologist asked sharply. "Are we philosophizing, perhaps? We're scientists here, I'll have you know. I show you facts: a spine bent by hard labor, expensive artificial dentures glued to rotten roots. I supply debatable data, pulled from test results compared with computerized experience. A dead laborer in his late fifties with gold in his mouth. That's all you'll be getting here. Discuss illusionary reality with representatives of the longhaired disciplines, if you please."

"Doctor," Grijpstra said. "We fight on your side. Now tell us, please, was the subject murdered?"

"Behold"—the pathologist's claw shot up—"a telltale photo."

The photo was a study in gray, spotted in places.

"What do I see?" asked Grijpstra complainingly.

"Rear of the skull, my dear ignorant Adjutant," the pathologist said. "As far as it was available of course, for a good deal was burned, but here, see here? A round hole can be observed here, near the edge."

"A bullet hole?" de Gier asked. "Can we have the picture?"

"Don't ask me for conclusions!" the pathologist yelled. "*You* draw conclusions."

"And I'll take the teeth," Grijpstra said. "Do accept our thanks."

"Sure," a laboratory assistant said an hour later. "Could very well be a bullet hole. Entered through the back of the skull and left through an eye socket. Guessing again. We don't mind doing work for you, but you have to bring in more observable objects."

"Small-caliber," said a ballistics expert who had been called into the room, "but that doesn't limit your choice. Even fully automatic assault rifles use point-twenty-two-caliber nowadays. But the subject was shot, I think I can go that far."

"Clothes? Shoes?" the sergeant asked.

"He was dressed," the lab assistant said. "Subject didn't die in his nothings. These ashes, in this here tray, were some textile once, and those ashes, in that there tray, undoubtedly were leather. But what kind of textile and what kind of leather? I wouldn't know."

"And in the other tray?" de Gier asked.

"An orl," the assistant said. "Can't you read? Isn't that what it says?"

"In judo practice," de Gier said, "I've learned some degree of containing my lower feelings, but I have learned more. I know how to break laboratory assistants into little pieces."

The assistant smiled in a servile manner. "That tray contains the remains of a ballpoint pen, Sergeant, low quality, a giveaway, printed with some advertising. The text has been burned off, except the letters forming the word 'orl.'"

De Gier took the tray.

* * *

"Now what?" Grijpstra asked in the canteen. He answered his own question. "Now nothing. You're right. We wait." He stirred his coffee slowly. He pointed across de Gier's shoulder. "Look, there goes Jane."

De Gier turned round. His head turned back again. "That wasn't Jane, and you're eating my piece of cake."

"Aren't I clever?" Grijpstra asked. "Every time, I manage to manipulate the other—even when *you're* the other. And to think that I trained you. It's quite simple, really. Jane is attractive. You're interested in attractive women. When I say 'Jane,' you're bound to stop watching your plate."

"You could have asked for cake if you wanted some," de Gier said. "I would have bought you a piece of cake."

"Ask," Grijpstra said, and flicked the word away. "Why take the easy way out? Isn't stealing more intelligent than begging? Are we going to do anything else but wait? What would you like to do? Teeth or the orl?"

De Gier came back with another slice of cake.

"Not that it matters much," Grijpstra said. "I always trace clues quicker than you do."

"All the same to me," de Gier said.

Grijpstra flipped a coin, caught it, and slapped it against his wrist. "The queen is orl."

The queen was up. "Orl for you."

"Easy little job," de Gier said. "You go ahead. As soon as you give up, you can go to the commissaris's room and I'll be waiting for you with some interesting information."

"Yes?" the commissaris asked. The commissaris hadn't come up with anything useful yet. He sat, impeccably diminutive in his antique swivel-chair behind his huge desk, which stood on lion legs. The opening door caused a draft that made the leaves of the begonias tremble on the windowsills. With small, narrow hands on which the transparent skin covered white bones and blue veins, the commissaris beat down papers that wanted to escape. He looked up nervously, alarmed by the breeze. "Close that door. Hello, Adjutant, sit down."

Maybe the commissaris had thought of a useful connection. The report mentioned Frisian names only. Algra and Wiarda. The commissaris considered himself to be Frisian. Hadn't he been born in the northern town of Joure? He had left Friesland as an infant, but once Frisian, Frisian forever.

"The Frisian case," the commissaris said. "Right. You've come up with something?"

De Gier had entered in Grijpstra's shadow. The adjutant and the sergeant placed their material on the commissaris's desk. "Teeth," Grijpstra said. "Orl," said de Gier.

"I'll adhere to order of rank," the commissaris said. "Report, Adjutant."

"The corpse's teeth," Grijpstra said, "checked by an expert. My dentist says that these small charred objects are the remains of a fully restored set of teeth. Very well done. Very expensively done. A most efficient construction, attached to a few roots. My dentist estimates that the restoration cost a small fortune, a laborer's yearly wages, more likely a multiple thereof. Our pathologist insists that the corpse is that of a laborer who pushed a wheelbarrow. A contradiction, perhaps? Conflicting facts that may shed some light?"

Two streetcars, passing each other in Marnix Street, below, greeted each other with a harsh clamor of bells. Grijpstra was still talking, or so it seemed; his mouth was moving.

"What was that?" the commissaris asked.

"A wealthy pusher of wheelbarrows, sir?"

"Who?" the commissaris asked.

"I thought we didn't know."

"I meant the dentist," the commissaris said, "who makes his living in the mouths of millionaires. There can't be too many millionaires' dentists about."

Grijpstra's blunt index finger turned a page in a small, crumpled notebook. "According to my tooth-puller, there's only one," the adjutant said, "and his answering machine informs that he's out of town today. Tomorrow I'll see him."

"Show him the teeth and he'll remember the name of our corpse. Tomorrow will do. Haste is often unseemly. What does the sergeant have to tell us?"

De Gier smiled.

"Let's have it, de Gier."

"*Orl*," de Gier said, "is *horloge*, without beginning or end, and because I found those letters on the molten remains of a ballpoint found in the corpse's boat, I visited the watch dealers of the Inner City. At the fifth I was lucky. That seller of clocks runs a store in Haarlemmer Street, and gives a free pen to each customer who spends some money—with a high minimum, for even ballpoints aren't free."

"Don't tell me," Grijpstra said, "that you're about to tell us something solid."

"Aren't we lucky," de Gier asked, "that the watch dealer is a tightwad who remembers the names of the clients to whom he gives free ballpoints?"

"You do have something," Grijpstra said, and frowned.

"Douwe Scherjoen," de Gier said. "Name of the corpse."

Grijpstra thumped his thigh. "Don't jump to conclusions."

"Frisian name?" de Gier asked. "Right?"

Grijpstra shrugged. "Wild guess. Tomorrow we'll know. Just let me see that super dentist."

"He'll come up with the same name."

"Tell us all," the commissaris said gently.

"Mr. Scherjoen," de Gier said, "bought an expensive watch last week. It broke down the next day. He returned it to the store, insisting on a fast repair. He should have picked it up this morning, but he didn't show."

Grijpstra whistled a fairly complicated tune.

"What was that?" the commissaris asked. "That sounded most despondent."

"Mahler, sir. Fifth Symphony. Majestic but doubtful. The trumpets make a statement, but the other instruments don't believe it yet."

"And then," de Gier said quickly, "this Mr. Scherjoen was described to me as a man in his fifties, farmer type, who spoke little Dutch and preferred to express himself in the lingo that Frisians use for private communication. Also," de Gier said quickly, "subject walked bent forward, as if pushing a wheelbarrow, and the watch dealer informed me," de Gier said, falling over his words, "that Scherjoen wore an expensive-looking suit and carried a well-filled wallet."

"The hell with you," Grijpstra said.

"The hell with subject," de Gier said, "and I'm almost sure that he can in fact be found in hell at this moment, and that he got there by being shot and subsequently burned in an aluminum dory seen last night by Constable First-Class Algra, and found this morning by Chief Wiarda."

"A Frisian," the commissaris said. "And where does subject live, or rather where *did* he live? Has he got a wife? Did you talk with her?"

"In the village of Dingjum," de Gier said. "What a name. Dingjum. The watch dealer gave me the address. I telephoned, and Mrs. Scherjoen says that her husband is away on business and that she doesn't know when he'll return."

"You left it at that?"

"Yes, sir."

"Did you tell her she was speaking to the police?"

"No, sir. I gave her my name and said I would phone again."

"Older lady?"

"A middle-aged voice. She said *doeg* before she hung up."

"Meaning what?"

"Meaning 'good-bye,' didn't you know, sir? You're Frisian, aren't you? Born in Joure? I do remember that you mentioned that fact a few times. Frisians aren't like us, you said, they're better."

"Of course, Sergeant. Poor lady."

"Not necessarily," Grijpstra said. "So what has de Gier given us so far? Ill-assorted balderdash? Unchecked coincidences that might just fit?"

The commissaris caressed his stomach. "Unless your tooth-replacer comes up with the same name, Adjutant."

The dentist came up with the same name the next morning.

"Easily recognizable work, Adjutant. The best of the best. My talent, for all to see."

"The price?"

"A lot of money."

"But who do the teeth belong to?"

"To one of my clients."

"Scherjoen?" whispered Grijpstra.

The dentist pulled an index card from his filing cabinet. "Douwe Scherjoen, yes indeed."

"Can you describe your client?"

"Smallish man," the dentist said. "Looked even smaller, for he stooped a bit. Energetic, however. Nasty little devil. Growled every time he had to pay, which was before each visit, for I rather mistrusted him. Unpleasant individual, with a mean little face."

"Paid cash?"

"Notes of maximum denomination, taken from a leather purse attached by a brass chain under his waistcoat. The man has been murdered?"

"Yes."

"Messy lives," the dentist said. "Don't pay attention. I give them my best work, I spend a hundred hours on their miserable jaws, and they rush out and get themselves killed."

"Would you have a look at my teeth?" Grijpstra asked.

The dentist looked. "You can close your mouth now."

"Can you fix that?" Grijpstra asked.

"No."

"What about your superior talent?" Grijpstra asked.

"What about your miserable wages?" the dentist asked. "Any more questions? Will you be leaving now? I still have a few things to do."

⦀⦀⦀ 3 ⫽⫽⫽

"BUT, DEAR," THE COMMISSARIS SAID, SHAKING HIS PHONE.
"Dear?"

The telephone said nothing.

"Are you still there?"

"I am," his wife said, "and so are the Belgian endives.
You ordered them, remember? You absolutely had to eat
baked Belgian endives tonight. Any idea about the *price* of
Belgian endives?"

"We could eat them tomorrow," the commissaris said.

"Tonight. Once they're out of the freezer, they can't go
back."

The commissaris looked for support in the glowing end
of his cigar, and in the begonia flowers on the windowsills;
he also glanced at the encouraging smiles on the lions' heads
above his chair. He stood next to his desk and tried to skip
airily onto its top. He didn't jump high enough and knocked
his hip. "Ouch."

"Did you hurt yourself?"

"And to think," the commissaris said, "that I was once a
prizewinning gymnast. I flywheeled around the bar, and then
swung onto the mat, and bowed, and straightened up to my
full athletic length again, and didn't the audience applaud?"

"Does it still hurt?"

"No," the commissaris said, "but I do have to go to Friesland, really. It only takes two hours to drive there. A compatriot was shot there—can't have that, you know. I've got to find out what's what."

"You're coming home for dinner. Send Grijpstra."

"He's got something else to do, too."

"Send *somebody*," his wife said. "I'm hanging up now. You'll be home at seven. I'm not bending over a hot stove all day for nothing."

The telephone clicked. The commissaris sighed. He extended a small finger and dialed two numbers. "Dear?"

"Sir?"

"Have Grijpstra called. He should phone me." The commissaris waited. The phone was quiet. "Dear?"

"Sir?"

"Is that understood?"

"You didn't finish your request."

"My request is quite finished."

"No," the soft female voice said. "You never said 'please,' so I'm still waiting, as is customary these modern days."

"What are you?" the commissaris asked. "A communist? A feminist? I gave you an order. I don't have to say 'please.'"

"I'm not your slave."

"Please," the commissaris said, "dear."

"Thank you," the secretary said. "I won't insist that you call me 'miss.'"

"Is that so?" the commissaris asked. "The new rule allows for exceptions?"

"I think you're a dear, too," the soft voice said. The telephone clicked.

The commissaris watered his begonias, while reflecting. They were right, he thought in between his reflections. They were abused, yelled at, repressed, underpaid, and overworked. It had to come to an end, but why today? Today he wanted to go to Friesland. He looked out the window. A splendid day. And today he had his new car, he hadn't even

driven the miracle yet, the silver car, delivered to Headquarters' yard only that morning, now gleaming in the sunlight. To take that car to the Great Dike, to make it whiz
along twenty straight miles. How pleasurable that drive would
be.

The telephone rang.

"Grijpstra here," the phone said. "The teeth belong to
Douwe Scherjoen from Dingjum, so that subject is the
corpse."

"Where are you now?"

"In a café, sir."

"And de Gier?"

"I've just met him here."

"Go to Ding-whatever," the commissaris said. "There'll
be State Police out there. Let them know you're around. It's
our case, but they might give us a hand. You know where
Ding-whatever is?"

"Not yet, sir."

"You might hurry a little," the commissaris said, "and you
might take de Gier for company. Is that understood?"

The telephone was quiet.

"Are you still there, Adjutant?"

"Our car is malfunctioning," Grijpstra said.

"What's wrong with it now?"

"It's mainly the clutch, sir," Grijpstra said. "It's got a
click in it, and the second gear seems to have gone altogether,
and the exhaust isn't attached properly—it sort of bangs
about—and the brake doesn't brake."

The commissaris sighed.

"Sir?"

"In the lot here," the commissaris said, "you'll find a new
silver Citroën. Brand-new, Adjutant. Don't let de Gier drive
it. You can come here and take my new car."

"But you haven't even driven it yet, sir."

"The key'll be with the doorman," the commissaris said
shrilly. "I'll tell him it's all right. I'll be ringing off now,
Adjutant. I'll back you from here."

"Upset, was he?" de Gier asked.

"He seemed a little unhappy," Grijpstra said. "Rheumatism in the legs again, perhaps."

"Did he complain about pains?"

"No, but he sounded that way."

"As long as he doesn't retire ahead of time," de Gier said. "We musn't strain him."

"We're supposed to be in a hurry now," Grijpstra said, "and the Volkswagen has to be fixed. Maybe it can still get back to Headquarters. There's a lot the matter with it these days. You think it can still be repaired?"

"What do you mean?" de Gier asked. "Our trusted steed?"

"The garage sergeant keeps wanting to throw the car away."

"Never," de Gier said. "I'll have Jane work on the fellow again."

"Jane doesn't want to know you anymore."

"She shares our duties."

"You're asking too much from Jane," Grijpstra said, "and you give her too little. You've got to entertain that girl in town first, and then try to get her to your apartment. Not the other way around. And don't make her pay for the entertainment."

"The pathetic whiner hasn't been crying on your shoulder, has she?"

"Whiner?" Grijpstra asked threateningly. "You didn't really use that expression, did you?"

"Pathetic female," de Gier said, "and she didn't even fall for my proposition. She never went to my apartment and she never bought me dinner. It was raining that day. My apartment is nice and dry. It was the end of the month. I was short on money."

De Gier was allowed to pay for the coffee. Grijpstra left the café and waited in the car. De Gier scowled as he got into the Volkswagen. "Listen," Grijpstra said, "if we want to keep this car, you have to be nice to Jane. You have to change your egocentric attitude—before we take off to Dingjum."

"I've no idea where that could be."

"I'll try to find out, while you prepare Jane for the garage sergeant's perverted desires. Is that understood?"

"May your bowels swell up with smelly vapors," de Gier said.

"Please?"

"Don't get polite on me."

"I'm always polite," Grijpstra said. "And when I am, I can order you around. Yes? Please?"

"Some vehicle," de Gier said. "At what speed is the super Citroën traveling now?"

Grijpstra glanced at the speedometer. "Maximum legal speed."

"Might she be capable of traveling at twice the maximum legal speed?"

"Easily. According to the numbers on the speedometer, she could get close to multiplying the restriction by three."

"That's hard to believe," de Gier said.

"Do you believe me now?" Grijpstra asked.

De Gier leaned over. "You sure that gadget is accurate? I hardly hear the engine. Kick that gas pedal a little more, will you?"

"Like this?"

"Better," de Gier said. "The commissaris did say that a bit of a hurry would be in order. This nice straight dike goes on forever. Scherjoen's eye sockets are still staring at me. Get me away from that terror. He'll keep disturbing my thoughts until we crack the case. We still don't know anything. The sooner we get to Friesland, the sooner we'll know. There's a killer about."

"But why was the subject killed in Amsterdam?" Grijpstra asked. "I can understand that the corpse bought his watch there, and he might select the capital to have his teeth replaced, but why should he get himself shot in Amsterdam?

Frisians are strong, pure people, from a free and clean environment. How did get our corpse get involved in the capital's mental and physical pollution? What's behind all this, eh?"

"Aren't you Frisian yourself?" de Gier asked.

"I am," Grijpstra said.

"You're neither strong nor pure nor free nor clean."

"I grew up in Amsterdam," Grijpstra said. "Only the core of my being is still untouched, but Scherjoen stayed within the freshness of a blessed country, and he still got shot and was burned as well."

"I don't want to talk to his widow," de Gier said. "That's not my thing at all. You can talk to her."

"I'll take care of the whole case," Grijpstra said. "I don't want you to get involved in any way at all. I don't even want you to drive this car."

"Do you hear something?" de Gier asked.

Grijpstra heard a siren. The siren screamed closer.

"That's a good motorcycle," de Gier said, looking over his shoulder. "Just look at her go. A Guzzi. I used to ride BMWs. They never went that fast."

Grijpstra slowed down and aimed for the breakdown lane. The motorcycle parked and the cop walked toward the car, slowly and at ease, pulling a notebook from the side pocket of his white leather coat.

Grijpstra dropped a window.

"Would you please get out?" the cop asked. "On the other side? The lane is rather narrow. Any idea how fast you were going?"

De Gier had gotten out already. Grijpstra slid across the front seats and joined the sergeant. Together they looked down on the cop, who seemed rather slender and had painted lips, mascaraed eyelashes, and varnished fingernails.

"You're a woman," Grijpstra said.

The cop studied the adjutant's identification.

"Adjutant?" the cop asked, and offered Grijpstra her hand. "Corporal Hilarius. What's your hurry?"

Grijpstra looked out over the Inland Sea, where swans

bobbed on the waves, fluffing their feathers and slowly moving their slender necks. Beyond the birds floated a fishing boat with a yellow-coated crew bending over the railing, lifting an eel trap. "How nice," Grijpstra said. "I could watch this forever."

"But we're hard at work," de Gier said helpfully. "Destination Dingjum, a most serious matter. Murder, I'll have you know. We're hot on the trail."

"Murder in Friesland?" Corporal Hilarius asked, pulling off her helmet and freeing flowing golden curls. The helmet was orange. Grijpstra began to tremble. The yellow of the fishermen's coats, the helmet's bright orange, and the resplendent shade of the girl's hair—were they not contrasts, completing each other? The corporal's low, hoarse voice became a part of the moment. Moments sometimes inspired Grijpstra. He wondered whether he would be able to show the sudden abstract harmony in one of his Sunday paintings. Can a sound be shown in color?

"The murder was at our end," de Gier said, "but the corpse lived on yours. We follow indications that will take us to your province. We're about to interview the dead man's wife."

Policewoman Hilarius knew about the burning dory, that was front-page news. So was cattle plague.

"The dike is blocked farther along, you can't see it from here. There's a line of traffic, stalled for a few miles. The disease is rampant in the south, and we're trying to keep it from killing our cows. All trucks and vans are being checked to make sure they don't transport animals. You'll never get through."

"We are in a hurry," de Gier said. "Maybe you can guide us along."

A black dot buzzed down out of a cloud. The motorcycle's radio came alive. "Seventeen? Over."

The corporal grabbed the microphone from the Guzzi. "Seventeen here."

"What are you doing there?" the helicopter asked. "Give

the Citroën a ticket and make your way to the north end of the dike. Maybe you can get something moving. Please?"

"We're in a bit of a hurry," de Gier said, smiling with perfect strong white teeth. His soft brown eyes glowed pleadingly. His muscular torso bent toward the girl. "Our commissaris's instructions. He wants us to get through with this, the quicker the better."

"*The* commissaris," Grijpstra said, "who was interviewed in the *Police Gazette* last week. The top sleuth who never fails. That's *our* commissaris."

The corporal stepped aside and spoke into her microphone.

"Understood," the loudspeaker on the Guzzi answered. "Park the Citroën against the dike, beyond the bicycle path. Over and out."

Corporal Hilarius stopped the traffic with an imperative gesture, and de Gier drove across four lanes and parked in the manner requested from above. The helicopter grew in size. Grijpstra and de Gier ran toward the blue-and-white egg, now setting down gently. A little door slid aside, and a leather-clad arm beckoned invitingly.

"Heights frighten me," Grijpstra said, "and we aren't really in all that much of a hurry."

But the pilot's arm pulled, and de Gier and the corporal pushed. De Gier thanked the lovely biker. The corporal answered hoarsely that the sergeant was welcome. De Gier jumped up, the little door snapped shut, and the chopper lifted away and cut through low clouds. The pilot pushed a handle and the machine fell through the next hole in the vapors. The pilot pointed down, shaking his head in disgust at the crawling mess below. Traffic at the end of the dike had tied itself into a snarl. "Dingjum?" the pilot yelled. Grijpstra and de Gier nodded and grinned, the adjutant fearfully, the sergeant cheerfully. The dike ended underneath them. The blues of the North and Inland seas gave way to fertile greens, changing again to the pink and brownish red of dwellings. "Franeker," the pilot yelled. "The most rustically beautiful village in all of our land." The helicopter vibrated into a muddle of dark gray shreds of clouds. Grijpstra no longer looked; he felt he was dying in dirty cotton wool. He did look after a while, because even fear has its limitations. Was he reborn? He was, in the clear emptiness of an uncluttered sky, and there below—hurray!—waited the beloved earth, and the helicopter touched that earth softly with the metal tubes that protruded from its little belly, set itself down, and rested.

The pilot saluted. De Gier was outside already, and caught his tumbling superior. The helicopter wafted away and pointed its round nose southward.

Grijpstra expressed his liberation in a short series of jubilant curses.

"Weren't we in a hurry?" de Gier asked. "You kept saying that, and I passed the message to the goddess on the bike to make her believe in our haste. If she hadn't, we would have a ticket now, and three times the maximum legal speed is an inexcusability that will even drag you into jail. You would have lost your license. Ever met an adjutant-detective without wheels? I saved you again."

They were on a meadow, at the center of a circling flock of sheep. One sheep was male, and was even now veering off to attack. "Shoo!" Grijpstra yelled. The ram didn't listen. He was in charge of the meadow and aware of an opportunity to show off to his wives. Horns lowered, the ram chose Grijpstra for his target. "Help!" Grijpstra yelled.

De Gier helped. He jumped the ram from the side, pulled a front and a hind leg, and rolled smoothly over the enemy, holding him down.

Grijpstra climbed a fence, groaning. De Gier jumped the fence after him, one leg forward, one leg to the rear, arms stretched, head straight.

"And now?" Grijpstra asked.

De Gier pointed at a State Police sign displayed under two lime trees that had grown into each other, their branches cut artfully into a raised square, shielding a low building.

Grijpstra gathered his thoughts, straightened his bulk, stepped through the door, and beckoned the sergeant to follow.

A corporal welcomed his colleagues from the south. Grijpstra stated the purpose of his visit.

"Are you in charge here?" de Gier asked.

"Lieutenant Sudema is in charge, but the lieutenant has the day off."

"So you're in charge."

The corporal wasn't sure. He left a message on the telephone's tape recorder and invited his guests to join him in his Land Rover. He locked the station's door. The journey took them to a greenhouse. A tall man in faded overalls was packing large tomatoes in small plastic boxes. "Lieutenant Sudema," the corporal said.

Grijpstra explained his presence.

The lieutenant filled another three boxes. "Douwe Scherjoen?"

"Yes."

"Our Douwe. In an Amsterdam dory? Shot and burned?"

"His skull looked at me," de Gier said. He curled his fingers around his eyes and dropped his head a little. "Like this, but worse, of course, for he was staring at me from some distance."

"Subject wasn't known to us," Grijpstra said. "Do you have something on subject here?"

The lieutenant stacked his boxes. "Mrs. Scherjoen is a good friend of my wife, Gyske. The tax detectives have been after Douwe for a while; they were about to bring charges, and if they had, he might have been in serious trouble."

"Do you personally know the tax detectives who are working on subject's case?"

"Please," Lieutenant Sudema said. His long dark eyelashes flicked up, and cold light flashed from his steely blue eyes. "Please. I don't want to know them."

"Was Mr. Scherjoen hiding income?"

"You understate," Lieutenant Sudema said. He guided his visitors to two chestnut trees behind the greenhouse. A small house was hidden under the trees. Gyske Sudema poured tea in the house while the lieutenant changed into a spotless uniform. Gyske was tight underneath, in leather pants, and well-filled above, in a taut white blouse. Her face was noble and her eyes sedate. De Gier was much impressed. So it was true about the beauty of Frisian women; he had heard tales, but then he had heard a lot of things.

"Our Douwe is *dea*?" Gyske whispered in sorrow.

"So we may assume," Grijpstra said, and explained about the orl and the expensive teeth. De Gier wanted to comfort Gyske and tried to prove that nothing can ever be proved conclusively, that there might be an incorrect turn of deduction somewhere, that what seemed to have happened might be altogether off. "*Dea* or not *dea*?" Gyske Sudema asked.

"*Dea*," said de Gier.

Gyske's sadness became anger. "They can have the *sjoelke*. Douwe is a *smjunt*."

"Who?" asked Grijpstra, suddenly aware of possible suspicion. "*Who* can have our Douwe?"

She pointed to the floor. "The *helliche duvels*."

"Oh, those," Grijpstra said.

Gyske talked on for a while.

"Mrs. Sudema," Grijpstra asked, "what are you saying?"

Gyske switched into Dutch. "I'm saying that Douwe was no good. He was a chauvinist, too. I won't miss our Douwe." Tears ran down Gyske's high cheekbones. "Now Mem will be free."

"Mem?"

"*Mem* means 'mother,'" Lieutenant Sudema said. "Mrs. Scherjoen's first name is really Krista, but she's rather motherly, you see, so everybody calls her Mem."

"Krista, as in female 'Christ'?" de Gier asked.

"Yes," Gyske said. "Christ suffered too, to redeem the sins of all of us. Mem suffered to redeem Douwe. Same thing. Douwe was as bad as all of us together."

"Douwe is *dea*," de Gier said, glad that he could comfort

the young woman after all. Gyske looked unsure. "Is Douwe punished now?"

De Gier wasn't certain. "Is death a punishment?" He tried his best smile. "But he has been taken away from us; death did remove the subject. If the subject was bad, the removal would be all to the good."

"Douwe has to be punished," insisted Gyske.

"I wouldn't know," de Gier said. "Do you? What denomination do you belong to, ma'am?"

Gyske was Dutch Reformed. "And you?"

De Gier was nothing. "Of nothing," he added as clarification.

Lieutenant Sudema fastened his belt and arranged his pistol. In his uniform he was even more handsome.

"On foot, by bicycle, or by car?" the lieutenant asked. "Would you prefer to walk? A quarter of an hour? We can talk on the way. The Scherjoens live in a stately mansion just outside the village, on the most magnificent estate of the region. The *landhûs* dates back centuries."

Lieutenant Sudema marched next to de Gier. Both were equally tall. Grijpstra ran after them, an unacceptable situation. He pushed between the two men. "What is a *sjoelke*?"

"An asshole," the lieutenant said. "A grabber for himself. One who never thinks of others. A sour self-spoiler. A *sjoelke* is a *smjunt*."

De Gier looked up at the splendor of elm trees that protected the path. He pointed out a variety of natural beauty. "Great land you have here."

"Over there is a forest of beeches," Lieutenant Sudema said. "Douwe wanted to cut the trees down. He had no need of beauty. Look there, see that oak on the meadow? That oak is dead, the cows have been ripping the bark. When there's a tree in a meadow, we take the trouble to protect it with a little fence; too much trouble for Douwe."

Grijpstra admired a cluster of hawthorns and a moat in the shadow of alders. "Why cut beeches? Don't they hold the silence? Isn't silence healthy for the mind?"

"You know what a foot of beech board sells for?" the lieutenant asked. "Beeches are thousand-guilder notes."

"A little grabby?" asked de Gier. "Our Douwe?"

"To him it was all green," Lieutenant Sudema said sadly. "But he preferred the green of money." He grinned ferociously at his joke.

"The tax detectives," Grijpstra said brightly, for he was now enjoying the walk; his slow-moving weight kept the others back. "Did they come up with some proof of evasion?"

"Not yet," the lieutenant said. "Good for Douwe."

"You've changed sides?" asked de Gier.

"Tax"—the lieutenant spat the word—"is even worse than Douwe. I don't wish tax-hounds on the worst of us." He shivered. "The country's curse."

"Right you are," said de Gier. "They clip my wages. Forty percent it was, last month." He shook a fist. "Must I be punished because I work? Must lazy officials in The Hague fatten on the spoils of my labor? Is it my fault that bums on welfare sneer at me through café windows while they swill beer at my expense?"

"You must be Frisian," the lieutenant said with pleasure.

"*I'm* Frisian," Grijpstra said. "He's a mere Dutchman. I'm in charge of this case. He's a mere tourist."

"We detest taxes here," Lieutenant Sudema said, "and we always have. We prefer to be free of the greed of others. We pay for the foolishness of the other provinces. Are they ever grateful? Sales tax! Bah! Ever try to buy a tomato in a store? I exchange mine; barter is the only decent commerce. I swap my tomatoes for sole. My brother fishes from Midlum. We keep our profits here. *Gjin* sales tax, *nèt* income tax." He blew a bubble of spittle.

"I really like your language," said de Gier. "So you *nèt* like us?"

"Dutchmen have to be about, too," the lieutenant admitted, "but not at our cost."

The sheep that had been running along with them on the

other side of the moat had reached a fenced bridge and now pointed their long snouts through its boards. Grijpstra touched one of the woolly faces but pulled his hand back when a coarse tongue licked his fingers. "Filthy beast."

"Do they belong to Douwe?" de Gier asked.

"Douwe dealt in sheep," the lieutenant said. "He used to export cows, but all cows are registered now by computers. Sheep can't be identified, they look too much alike."

"Look at that," Grijpstra said. The mansion was worth admiring. It stared back through large clear window-eyes, gazing over a majestic lawn protected by beeches reaching out their branches. A wide flight of stone stairs flowed easily up to freshly painted, oversized doors. Red bricks framed the large open windows, three on each side, with another row on the first floor, under a thick straw roof. Intricate latticework shielded a veranda that surrounded the house, adding color from blossoming vines. A bent-over old woman was raking the shiny gravel of a path around the lawn. She looked up.

"*Good mid dei, Mem*," the lieutenant said.

The woman tried to smile. "You bring bad news, don't you, Sjurd?" Her wooden clogs scratched across the gravel as she moved away from the three men; the rake fell from her hand.

De Gier picked up the rake. Grijpstra introduced himself and the sergeant. Mem didn't see their outstretched hands. She pushed silver hairs away from her forehead as her light brown eyes receded between tightening wrinkles. Her gnarled hands plucked at her coarse skirt. "Is Douwe *dea*?"

"Perhaps," Lieutenant Sudema said, but his head nodded.

De Gier produced his handkerchief, but Mrs. Scherjoen didn't cry.

"Colleagues from Amsterdam," the lieutenant said.

She took them inside and offered them coffee poured from a jug that had been waiting on the stove. The kitchen was spotlessly clean under low, blackened beams. "Mind your head," Mem said, but it was too late. De Gier rubbed his curls. "Did you hurt yourself?" Mem asked softly.

"No ma'am. You have children?"

She poured coffee. "No."

She lifted the lid of a cookie jar. "How did it happen?"

"A shot," Grijpstra said. "So we think. It didn't show too well."

Mem didn't understand.

"He was burned too," Grijpstra said, lowering his voice, smiling his apology sadly. Lieutenant Sudema touched Mrs. Scherjoen's shoulder. "Mem," the lieutenant said, "we're sorry, Mem."

"The *duvel*," Mrs. Scherjoen said, "he's got him now. Douwe was always frightened of fire. He dreamed about flames that came to take him. I had to wake him up then and make him turn over, but the flames would return and he'd yell and yell. He was afraid of the devil."

Lieutenant Sudema coughed. "Yes."

"Thank you for the coffee," Grijpstra said from the door. "We'll come back another time—tomorrow, will that suit you? We have a few questions."

"Gyske'll be along soon," the lieutenant said. Mrs. Scherjoen didn't hear him. Sudema got up and walked over to Grijpstra. "I'd better stay. Could you tell Gyske to hurry over? I'll join you as soon as I can, in the café perhaps. My corporal will take you there, you must be hungry."

Grijpstra and de Gier walked back to the village.

"Even here," Grijpstra said, waving an arm. "How can that be? Within the peace of unspoiled nature?"

"Even here, what?"

"The *duvel*," Grijpstra said. "And a marriage that was no good. Couldn't Scherjoen be nice to his wife? She's a great person, it seems to me."

De Gier studied wildflowers growing at the side of the moat.

"I was nice to my wife," Grijpstra said. "In many marriages, at least one partner is good. She released me. Douwe could have given Mem her freedom. The bad side lets the good side go."

De Gier ambled on.

"Hey," Grijpstra said.

"I'm confused," de Gier said. "Your comparison isn't clear. You mean you're a good side?"

"Aren't I?"

"Let's do some work," de Gier said.

"You work," Grijpstra said. "I'll enjoy the walk."

"I thought I was just going to be company."

"You're here," Grijpstra said. "You can talk to me."

"Right," de Gier said. "Douwe Scherjoen was no good. A selfish grabber. Bought and sold for cash and evaded taxes. Had his good times in Amsterdam while his wife slaved at home. A fortune in his mouth, and his wife is the maid, the gravel raker, the free help in his mansion. Douwe is too much of a skinflint to build a little fence around a glorious oak. But he did know he was bad, for the devil pursued him."

"He dreamed about pursuing flames," Grijpstra said. "*My* dreams are quite pleasant."

"Are we discussing you?" de Gier asked. "Have you been shot and soaked with gasoline and burned and made to float with the garbage? Was it your skull staring at me in the pathologist's cave?"

"Why was so much violence applied?" Grijpstra asked. "The war is over. You're too young, you don't remember recent history, but Frisians can be quite violent. The resistance was fiercer here than anywhere else in the country. German soldiers were often shot and burned."

"I remember the way Douwe's skull looked at me," de Gier said. "From the hereafter. He begged me for revenge."

"Leave the hereafter for later. We're looking for the tangible present. What was the motive? What living entity benefits from subject's death? Who had the opportunity to knock him off? No mysticism, Sergeant."

"The hereafter *is* now," de Gier said pleasantly. "Let me work from my own angle." He stopped and took a deep breath. "The air here is clear. But evil is about. The tax detectives are lurking even here, and they know something; maybe they'll tell us. We're out of our depth; if they're Frisian too, maybe they won't tell us. Everything is different here, the locals even think in another language."

"I'm well within my depth," Grijpstra said, "and I'll get into this slowly. Life is slower here." He smiled at a sheep ruminating in high grass. "I may have some lambchops soon, and Frisian fried potatoes and some of the lieutenant's fresh tomatoes. I'll find suitable quarters while you fetch the commissaris. In order to pursue our investigation properly, we'll need permission from local authority. The commissaris can call on whoever is in charge here, and then he can stay to help. He's Frisian too. Once we're both into this, the job'll be easy."

"You don't need permission. Scherjoen was killed in Amsterdam, and we're on a warm trail. Our pursuit is proper police procedure."

"Fetch the commissaris."

"I'm going back and I won't return," de Gier said. "I'm no good to you here. I'm from outside."

"All right, all right," Grijpstra said pleasantly. "You can stay around. It's always nice for somebody like me to have somebody like you around. And you can have a good time. It'll be a holiday for you."

Evening fell slowly, and thick sunbeams crossed loosening clouds. Beech branches embraced the quiet landscape. A cow lowed sleepily, and a farmer on a slow bicycle lifted a greeting hand. Grijpstra's fingers wobbled in response.

They reached the station. "Hello," Grijpstra said. "Corporal, if you please, would you take Mrs. Sudema to Mrs. Scherjoen and my sergeant to the dike. Our car is out there and he has to return to Amsterdam."

"Right now?" the corporal asked. "Don't you two want dinner?"

"The sergeant is pressed for time."

"Not at all," de Gier said. "I'm a tourist here. I would love some dinner."

"Back in a moment," the corporal said. "The café is across the street."

Grijpstra ordered lambchops. "For two," de Gier said.

The corporal came back with the lieutenant.

"Is Mem feeling a little better?" Grijpstra asked.

"Yes, Adjutant, Gyske is taking care of her."

"Pity she has no children."

"Douwe was her child," Lieutenant Sudema said. "He was too jealous of competition. Amazing that she could put up with the *sjmunt*."

The corporal shook his head. "They do like to be abused."

De Gier said that women may perhaps sometimes like to be abused, but that he, for one, would never abuse them.

Grijpstra's nostrils widened. "And Jane?"

"Sharing is not abusing."

Grijpstra explained the perfidy of the sergeant's plans for Jane. "But she didn't fall for it," he concluded.

"They don't very much, nowadays," the corporal said. "It's not as easy as before."

"I've got to do the cooking," Lieutenant Sudema said. "Gyske works half days and I work full days, and I still have to do the cooking. I rather like cooking, but there's the washing up, too, and putting the dishes away. If they gain, we lose. I can't yell at her anymore, either."

"I never yelled at my wife," Grijpstra said. "Why should I? She was deaf, and the TV at full volume."

"You do yell," de Gier yelled. "You yell at me. You're known as the yeller."

Grijpstra asked the lieutenant to please ask the corporal to please take the sergeant to the dike, right now.

De Gier had to finish his coffee.

"Bit of a bastard," the corporal asked, steering the Land Rover along narrow dikes, "that adjutant of yours?"

"A fine fellow," de Gier said. "But never tell him I told you that."

"And a bit of a bastard," the corporal said. "The lieutenant is another, but he's been easing up a lot. I can thank Gyske for that."

"If we don't bend, they'll break us," de Gier said. "Take that Scherjoen, for instance. He didn't want to bend."

The corporal was taller than de Gier, and wider. His chin resembled a granite rock. "They don't just want to break us," the corporal whispered.

"Are Frisian women more fierce than ours?"

"I won't say more," the corporal said.

"They might be listening in."

The Land Rover parked behind the Citroën. De Gier slid behind the sleek car's wheel, and the Citroën flashed away.

⫼⫼⫼ 4 ⫼⫼⫼

THE COMMISSARIS, WANDERING ABOUT HIS ELEGANT OFFICE, was not content. A Frisian dies. In Amsterdam. What was the next move? Would he go to Friesland? Why look far away if it happened here?

Because there was this new car and he wanted to drive along the Great Dike? He could indulge himself, but there was also the necessity to sniff about here. He could delegate the local search to his very best men and take off himself. The commissaris pushed out his thin lips. He attempted to whistle.

"The other way round," he mumbled sadly. His best men were enjoying themselves in Ding... Dingjum. And bothering the widow. He got up and wandered over to his desk, looking for an article in the *Police Gazette*. "Instructions for Superior Officers." He read the relevant passage. *Make sure your temperament, skills, interest, and competency fill the job*. Wasn't he supposed to be good at interviewing old ladies? So why wasn't *he* interrogating Mrs. Scherjoen?

His leg glowed and hurt. He rubbed the painful spot, not too hard, for that would increase the trouble. Suppose he went home and immersed his painful body in hot water spiced with herbs? He might as well; maybe this wasn't a day for work.

He limped to the corridor. The uniformed girls in the computer room looked up. "Sir," they said. "Ladies," the commissaris said. He was given a chair. He thought. The policewomen waited.

"Douwe Scherjoen," the commissaris said.

"Adjutant Grijpstra asked us to check him out, sir," a constable first-class said. "There's nothing on Scherjoen."

"How good is your computer?" the commissaris asked.

"Our computer," the constable first-class said, "knows everything."

"So what would the computer tell us if you activated it with the key words 'Friesland' and 'crime'?"

"Too much, sir. It would tell us about all the wrongdoings of all the Frisians, it would go on forever."

"And what if you limited it to Frisian crime in Amsterdam?"

"It would still go on and on."

"Let's see," the commissaris said.

The constable first-class typed in the two words. The commissaris watched the screen. A small green square trembled.

"Well?" the commissaris asked.

"The computer is searching, sir. It will tell us about its findings any minute now, at incredible speed."

The little green square trembled.

"Well?" the commissaris asked.

The constable first-class pressed a few buttons.

"It's broken," a constable said. The constable first-class stared at the girl. "Down," the girl said nervously. "That's what I meant. Honestly. The computer is down."

"Not broken?" the commissaris asked.

"Just down," the constable first-class said. "It'll be up in a second, it just fell down a little."

"When will it be up again?"

"It could take a while," the constable first-class said. "This does happen now and then. I'll phone and the supplier will send an engineer. He may be busy for an hour or longer— it does take longer once in a while. Maybe the terminal is down too, then we'll have to wait a little while longer."

The commissaris was back in the corridor. He used a wall phone. "Can you find me that Frisian detective, what's his name now? Fokkema, maybe?"

"He's in Spain sir, on holiday, with sick leave added. Detective Fokkema may be away for a while."

"Any other personnel of Frisian origin around?"

"I wouldn't know, sir, did you try the computer?"

The commissaris was back in his room. He thought. Frisian. Frisian what? By happenstance a Frisian cop sees something, and a Frisian park official sees something too?

He picked up the phone.

"Please, dear, Constable First-Class Algra of the Red District Station, and afterward I'd like to speak to Chief Wiarda of Municipal Parks."

His secretary couldn't find either party; Algra had gone off somewhere and Wiarda hadn't yet returned.

They won't know anything either, the commissaris thought; he thought a little further. Frisian convicts, locked up in jail somewhere? Who could locate Frisian convicts? The computer? Hurriedly he changed thoughts. The new thoughts were pushed back by something else again, burped up from memory. "Jelle Troelstra," his memory kept repeating.

"Who?" the commissaris asked.

"You know," his memory insisted.

"I don't."

"SS?" his memory asked.

Right, the commissaris thought, for now he did remember. A limping SS man at large. In 1945, that was a long time back now. Troelstra had fought on the Eastern Front, had been released from duty because of serious wounds, had returned to Friesland just before the liberation, and was wanted afterward by the Dutch police on charges of treason. Traitor Troelstra. The suspect didn't want to be shot, so he hid with relatives, and was seen by neighbors. The neighbors alerted the local police, and Troelstra fled to Amsterdam, where he hid again, this time in a girlfriend's house, at the Old Side Alley. Tired of being hunted, Troelstra asked the girlfriend to phone the police to tell them that he would be ending his life, but would like to talk to someone first, a qualified authority preferably. The commissaris was an assistant inspector at the time and answered the call in person. He took a streetcar. The girlfriend opened the door. Jelle was in bed, with a German pistol in his hand. Jelle Troelstra, ex-hero. The commissaris nodded. Not a bad chap at all, rather an idealist, but on the wrong side, of course. Misdirected loyalty. Hitler, a devil masquerading as an angel, Troelstra saw that now. And subject hadn't committed atrocities, because he was a decent fellow, quite incapable of evil deed.

He listened to Troelstra in those late days of 1945, and encouraged him somewhat, telling him he wouldn't be shot, that he might still live a useful life and that the punishment would be bearable, since subject was turning himself in. Self-confessed traitors were sent to the colonies then, to New Guinea, the enormous island in Indonesia's utmost East, a Dutch possession still, and much in need of roads. Subject would have served there and been returned in due course.

The commissaris picked up his phone again. "Dear?"

"Sir?"

"Please, Jelle Troelstra in . . . Anjum. Try to locate the man. If he isn't listed, try any other Troelstra in Anjum and ask where we can find Jelle. Is that understood? If you please?"

"You said it at the beginning, sir. One 'please' will suffice."

"At your service," the commissaris said. "You're welcome."

The phone rang. "Yes?"

"Mr. Troelstra lives in Amsterdam, sir. He's on the line now."

"Mr. Troelstra?"

"Yes," a gravelly voice said.

"You're alive," the commissaris said. "I'm pleased to hear that. It's me, the policeman who fetched you in '45. Your girlfriend called and we had a talk. Do you remember?"

"And you're a commissaris now?"

"And I would like to talk to you."

"I've got a café," Troelstra said. "In my girlfriend's house. She left last year, for good, because of cancer. I'm still around for a little bit."

"May I visit? Will that be all right?"

The two men observed each other attentively, in the dark narrow barroom. "Jenever?" Troelstra asked.

"If you please," the commissaris said, "and one for you too."

Their glasses touched and tipped. The jar tipped for the second time, but this time the commissaris merely sipped and Troelstra followed his example. The commissaris liked the café; all of its contents dated back many years, to a tangible past. He caressed the stem of his tulip-shaped glass.

"You were polite to me," Troelstra said. "I remember that. A little human decency and understanding, there wasn't much of that around then, but with you it stuck. It kept me going in New Guinea, if I wasn't down. I got pretty ill there."

"Were you sent home ahead of time?"

"Malaria," Troelstra said. "It gets you by spells. We all had it, and when the fever went down we were back at work."

"Bad, was it?"

"Not too bad," Troelstra said. "Have you come to fetch me again? War crimes are never forgiven, but I didn't commit any crimes. I fought the Soviet Bolsheviks. It would be okay now, but in those days it wasn't done yet."

"I came for some information," the commissaris said, "about a Douwe Scherjoen."

"He doesn't come to this bar."

"The name is known to you?"

"I've heard of Scherjoen," Troelstra said. "This place isn't set up for Frisians only, but they all know who I am, and when they come I speak our language, not that I talk a great deal; they prefer me to listen."

"I was born out there, in Joure," the commissaris said.

Troelstra nodded. "You said that last time, so I could trust you some. You told me I should stay alive. Tell me again, why did I have to stay alive?"

'Because there's a point to living."

"You still think so?"

"I was young," the commissaris said. "I put it a little simply. You were young too. I got through to you, didn't I?"

Troelstra's hands pushed his sunken cheeks further inward. His calm eyes stared at the visitor. "This Scherjoen, was he the corpse in the paper this morning?"

"Yes," the commissaris said. "He was shot in this neighborhood and burned afterward, in a dory, or so we think; there wasn't much left of him."

"Sometimes," Troelstra said, "it doesn't pay to try and outthink the others." He grinned. "There are too many of them. What rule did he break?"

"We don't know much yet." The commissaris put his glass down after a carefully measured sip. "We do know that the deceased lived in Dingjum, could spend money, that's about it. What do you know?"

"He sold sheep," Troelstra said, "to Morocco, Turkey, Algeria. Frisian sheep. More than are ever officially counted in all of Friesland. Sheep look a lot alike. There's too much administration these days, but maybe the sheep still slip through."

"But he never came here?"

"Other sheep dealers come here, and they talked about him. The dealers like to visit the Red Quarter. Leeuwarden, our capital, used to have a nice quarter of its own, but now they have to slide down the Great Dike, all the way down to Gomorrah here. Here we can satisfy most any desire."

"In our lower regions?" the commissaris asked. "And what did Douwe's colleagues have to say about him?"

"They didn't like Douwe."

"Jealousy?"

"Of course," Troelstra said. "But maybe more than just jealousy. Douwe wasn't too straight. Broke his agreements, or changed them later on, not quite what Frisians expect of each other."

"Would any of your clients be a shooting man?"

"I am a traitor," Troelstra said, "but I don't really like squealing too much."

"Scherjoen was shot from the rear."

Troelstra lifted the jenever jar. The commissaris nodded. He had lunched lightly and the strong gin made his body tingle. His leg no longer hurt; on the contrary, the usually sensitive nerves seemed to be alive with calm energy. How enjoyable it would be to be just a little drunk forever. Doesn't alcohol addiction exclude all other desires? The thought wasn't new to him. To simplify life's motivation should be an excellent short-term goal. Whoever is interested in alcohol can afford to forget about everything else. Any new day begins with the necessity to drown the hangover, and once that's done time flows on joyfully again. It wouldn't work out in the end, he knew that too, but the idea was still exciting. To realize the wish would be easy enough. He could retire and get up late and go to bed early and be smashed in between. With a bit of discipline, the change shouldn't be hard.

"One more?" Troelstra asked.

"No, thanks."

"Coffee, freshly made?"

"If you please."

Troelstra handled his coffee machine with the slow, exact movements that are the result of long practice.

"How old are you, Troelstra?"

They shared the same age.

"You know," Troelstra said, "I once shot a prisoner in

Russia, from the rear. The Russian never knew what happened to him. He was talking to a tree, and the next thing he was out."

"No!" the commissaris said, shaking his head in disbelief.

Troelstra nodded thoughtfully. "He had gone mad. We were out on patrol. I was in charge of the squad. Frisian boys, every one of them. There were hardly any Frisians fighting for the Germans, but the few that went out there were under my command. Good fellows, steady, courageous, supermen, all specially picked for SS training. We were liberating the world. Civilian Russia was the worst place I had ever seen—starving people in hovels, suppressed by a terrible system; we didn't know then that we were making it even worse. Suddenly there was that Russian soldier behind us, with a rifle, hand grenades on his belt; quite a young man still, and he had lost his mind. He was yelling at us and pointing at the clouds. We took his weapons and he never noticed. He was singing by then. We tried to send him off, for a prisoner would slow us down; we were about to attack."

"Yes," the commissaris said.

"I was the sergeant," Troelstra said. "I was supposed to know what to do. My men were looking up to me. The Russian was stamping on the snow, screaming some ditty, frothing at the mouth, eyes popping out of his head. We were close to the enemy, and he was giving our position away."

"Yes," the commissaris said. "I could have some more coffee."

"Java Mocha," Troelstra said. "Too good a brand for this place but I'm getting too old to make a profit."

"Yes?"

"I took that Russian along," Troelstra said, "with my arm around his shoulders, friendly-like, I was his older brother. He pulled away and ran into the trees; when I found him again, he was talking to an oak."

"You shot him?"

"Yes."

"And that's the way Scherjoen was helped out?"

"I wouldn't know," Troelstra said slowly.

An old man shuffled into the café, in a dirty raincoat and frayed trousers. "Jelle, a lemonade today."

Jelle poured soda, holding the gin jar in his left hand. The old man studied first the jar, then his own trembling hands, clutching at the counter. "Yes, go ahead."

The gin joined the lemonade in the tall glass. Jelle lifted the jar but didn't replace it. "Right," the old man said. The jar tinkled again. The man drank. He put the glass down. "Aaah," the man said happily.

"I only meant," Troelstra said to the commissaris, "that things are often not quite what they seem. So I betrayed my country. Maybe I did. Maybe it wasn't meant that way."

"You meant well?"

"Things had to get better, didn't they?" Troelstra asked. "And they got worse. Isn't that the human way? We mean well and we become active and we go down even further."

"In the beginning . . ."

" . . . there was God." Troelstra scratched his chin. "But where did He go? I sometimes think about that a bit."

The man in the dirty raincoat rattled his glass. "Same again, Jelle." Jelle poured from bottle and jar. The man's toothless smile widened. "Nice day today."

Troelstra and the commissaris said that the old man was right.

"It's all so easy," the old man said, "but I keep forgetting, and it takes a few glasses to remember it again. To keep it easy can be rather tricky."

"You generally succeed?" the commissaris asked.

"I've got a strong character," the old man said. "I never stop trying. No matter what they do to me. They won't knock me over."

"Let's have the bill," the commissaris said.

Troelstra looked out the window. Shadows moved through the street, dating back to a far past. Comrades-in-arms? A dying Russian? Wild men, with bones through their noses?

An assistant inspector who didn't handcuff the traitor and took him to Headquarters in a streetcar?

"That won't be necessary," Troelstra said. "I still owe you. You kept me alive. I could experience a few good moments. New Guinea is beautiful, there are some fine birds out there, colorful, with long tails, and flowering shrubs that grow nowhere else. The voyage, there and back, tropical seas, palm trees on beaches, going on for miles. And the café here at the end, I don't mind doing this."

"Scherjoen?" the commissaris asked.

"Can't help you there."

The commissaris didn't catch on at once. He wondered whether he should ask.

"Is there something else you can help me with?"

"Last week . . ." Troelstra interrupted himself and looked at the old man, who was smiling and occupied with rolling a cigarette. "Would you mind moving up?" he asked the commissaris, who got off his stool and followed the coffee cup that Troelstra slid across the counter.

"Last week," Troelstra said softly, "two heavy boys came here to have a few. A certain Ary, small chap and bald, and a certain Fritz, big fellow with a tuft of stiff hair on his big head. Southern types, from the Belgian border. I had some sheep dealers too, well away in the bottle. A Friday it was, when there's the cattle market in Friesland and they had collected some cash, safely tucked away in the purse. The Frisian purse is chained to the neck. It's all cash with us up north, we don't believe in checks and such. We're a bit silly that way."

"Frisians aren't silly," the commissaris said.

"Maybe they are sometimes. Carrying cash into this district? Cash that comes from evading taxes should be well hidden, I believe." Troelstra smiled. "It's silly to pay taxes, of course, especially when the money leaves the country. Hasn't everybody always been after our profits? The Romans, the Spanish, the French, the Germans, we kicked them all out, and then came the Dutch."

"And you were fighting for United Europe?"

Now why did I say that? the commissaris thought. Here he wants to tell me something and I have to argue.

"United Europe," Troelstra's eyelids dropped. "That's the dream. Why shouldn't it come about some day? All together and still apart? America has done it. Why don't we do the same? The State of Friesland, and the State of Germany, and the State of Russia, and so on and so forth? United above our troubles?" He poured more coffee.

"You're too early," the commissaris said. "It'll come if we grant ourselves time."

Troelstra held a finger alongside his nose. "That's what I think now, but I'm still not sure. Maybe the urge to fight is too strong in us. Maybe it's part of human nature. Ever seen little kids play? They'll always invent weapons and bang away at each other. Have you ever seen little kids play peacemaking games?"

"Well..."

"Take the movies," Troelstra said. "I fought too, I know how bad it is. Creep up to a Russian camp and see the enemy eat, or sleep, or shit in a quiet corner, and you still have to mow them down. That can't be right. So why do I go to see future air vessels destroying each other, with humans in them, eh? I enjoy watching that destruction. So how can that be? If it isn't right, I mean?"

"About that bald Ary," the commissaris said, "and Fritz with the tuft."

Troelstra closed one eye. "You don't know either, right?"

"I don't know," the commissaris said.

Troelstra laughed dryly. "Nobody knows, I think. Maybe we just do what we were planned to do, maybe we have no say. I read the paper. There's war all over the place again. Same thing all over."

The commissaris waited.

"Right," Troelstra said. "Here's a fight for you. Ary and Fritz were watching my sheep dealers and licking their chops. Suppose each dealer was carrying some twenty thousand in cash, and you hit them all—then you have a year's good wages. That's hardly enough if the risk is a few years in jail. Ary and Fritz had just come from jail."

"So?"

"So," Troelstra said, "they discussed better possibilities and I listened in a bit, for they kept ordering refills. On the cattle market in Leeuwarden..."

"Hey, hey," the commissaris said. "And the subjects are professionals?"

"Bank robbers," Troelstra said.

"But listen here, at the Leeuwarden market there'll be hundreds of dealers, and there are only two of them."

"It can be done," Troelstra said. "Each dealer has a purse, and if you pull the copper chains, they'll snap. Herd them together..."

"Thanks." The commissaris felt for his wallet.

"No money." Troelstra crossed his arms.

The commissaris put down a note. "Not for me, for your customer over there."

The old man in the dirty coat laughed gratefully. "It's really quite easy."

"You're sure now?" the commissaris asked.

"Have a few drinks with me, sir, and you'll know for yourself." The old man waved an all-explaining arm. "Drink your ignorant self to the center where the mystery lives. Once you see it, everything becomes clear."

"And can you stay there?"

The old man winked. "Follow me."

"I'd rather go alone."

"The method is the same," the old man said. "I'll guide you a bit of the way."

"Perhaps later," the commissaris said, and escaped through the door.

ⅢⅢ 5 ⅢⅢ

DETECTIVE FIRST-CLASS SIMON CARDOZO, TEMPORARILY
serving with the Murder Brigade, objected to the easy small
talk of his more established colleagues, standing around him
in the Headquarters canteen. His colleagues looked down
on Cardozo. He was small in size and sitting down. He also
looked down on himself. A more powerful and larger-size
Cardozo talked to the little one, for he had split himself in
two, to simplify the situation, and was engaged in dialogue.

Little Cardozo complained. He was not treated with
respect, so he told Big Cardozo. Take this Douwe Scherjoen
case, for instance. Was it acceptable to have to look at a file
dropped casually on his desk? "Have a look at this," Grijpstra had said. "Do something," de Gier had said. And gone
they were, to flirt with Jane, no doubt. Jane was important.
Jane was abused too, but at least she was treated with respect.
She was told good things about herself so that the stupid girl
would go to make eyes at the garage sergeant so that the
Brigade's old Volkswagen could be repaired again. But he,
Little Cardozo—who had to do real work, who had to gather
data that would unmask a murderous unidentified madman,
who subsequently had to arrest the merciless criminal, and
subsequently had to prepare a charge that would hold up in

49

court—he, Little Cardozo, had a file dropped on his desk. "Do something, Cardozo."

"Now, now," Big Cardozo said.

"Don't belittle me," Little Cardozo said. "I get enough of that from *them*. They hang out in some pleasant province, enjoy the sights, live off the fat of the land, while I, the stupid sucker, the shit-upon, under risky circumstances, unprotected . . ."

"Now, now."

"You keep on saying that," whined Little Cardozo. "And I don't feel well, either."

"Do your job," Big Cardozo said. "Commit yourself to doing. Don't stew over the actions of others. If you do, you'll isolate yourself and your productivity will suffer."

"Why don't *you* do something," Little Cardozo said, "instead of reading that idiot article in the *Police Gazette* to me? That's theory for morons."

"You fret," Big Cardozo said. "So you're still temporarily with the Murder Brigade? So what? You want to be fixed? Whatever is fixed can't move freely. Move away, float lightly through the city, think of a theory and find some facts that'll hold it up. Aren't you lucky that you can finally work alone? Others hold hands while they stumble about, but you, carried by your very own cleverness, make your individual moves, relentlessly closing in on the culprit who cowers in darkness."

"Now, now," Little Cardozo said.

Both Cardozos joined and got up. The unity left the canteen. It was about to do something. What had Cardozo in mind, while he slouched out of the canteen indifferently, under his untidy uncut curls, in his crumpled corduroy suit, loosely swaggering down the corridor? Coughing. Sneezing.

Just for a moment the unity split again so that Little Cardozo could tell Big Cardozo that he was suffering from flu. He might go home. Nobody would miss him. A temporary Murder Brigade member, left quite alone?

Big Cardozo leaned on Little Cardozo. "Get going."

Cardozo had to take a leak. The foaming ray of liquid that connected him to a tiled wall in the toilet made him think of water. His lighter's flame reminded him of fire. The combination of the two associations evoked the file photographs of the remnants of Douwe Scherjoen. Where were the remnants found? In a dory. The dory had been confiscated and should be somewhere in the building.

He found it, stored in a basement corner. The brand name was still visible. LOWE. Cardozo deciphered the serial number pressed into a small copper plate, welded inside the bow. The dory looked old. Would he find out who sold that brand of boat, in a remote past, to some forgotten client? How many times would the dory have changed owners in between? Stolen? Given away? Lost and found? Where had it been found last? In the Inner Harbor. He checked the large wall map near the main entrance of the building. The Inner Harbor ends at Prince Henry Quay. Cardozo's roaming finger rubbed pink quays, extended into blue water. Boats are moored to quays.

He caught a streetcar. He walked up and down all quays, and boarded all vessels attached to the quays. Had anyone lost a dory?

"Not me," a skipper said, "but over there, in the corner where the garbage floats, there used to be a dory, and it isn't there now. Filched by the boys who come here to annoy us. Useless dory, damaged, no good to anyone. It was tied up with a bit of red wire."

So far, so good. The dory in Headquarters' basement had some red wire attached to the bow. He thanked the skipper.

"Righto," the skipper said.

Cardozo sat on a rotten post. He was the killer. He absolutely loathed Douwe Scherjoen. He closed his eyes to darken his view, so that it might be night, cloudy, pitch black all around. He had shot Douwe a few minutes ago, but he wasn't quite done. Douwe's corpse was in the way. Had he committed murder in a frenzy of hatred? Probably not. Angry amateurs will shoot a man in the chest. He had shot Douwe intelligently, according to a premeditated plan, from the rear, of course. Was the dory so that he wouldn't have to drag the corpse a great distance?

Or had fate played tricks on him and complicated the scheme? Fate's often unreasonable chaos may upset the best of plans. Very well, the dory was here, but he hadn't brought a sufficient quantity of gasoline. No, he hadn't thought of bringing any gasoline at all, and would have to find it now, but where? Suck it from a car's tank through a tube? Where would he get the tube? Nobody ever carries a tube. Had he ripped it off a cookstove somewhere? Cookstoves are found in kitchens. Was his kitchen close by, in his home?

Close by. Cardozo opened his eyes. His gaze wandered over the long row of houses on Prince Henry Quay. There would be a number of side streets too. If the suspect lived in the neighborhood, Cardozo was now faced with a multitude of suspects. Add to that all the skippers of the vessels moored nearby.

Was he getting anywhere? He was getting hungry.

At this stage of an investigation, any point is a starting point, Cardozo thought as he tripped over the high threshold of a small Chinese restaurant called Wo Hop. Mister Hop caught his prospective client and guided him to a table. Cardozo read the specials on the menu. Fried noodles. Fried rice.

"Fried noodles," Cardozo said. "Beer."

The restaurant consisted of a bare room furnished with plastic chairs and tables. Neon light reflected from Hop's shaven skull. The other customers were longhaired louts with skin diseases, silently picking scabs when they weren't coughing or sneezing. In the back of the room, young Chinese men in loud shirts conducted a conversation in which nouns were musically stretched, and then abruptly swallowed. Cardozo noticed their crewcuts and staccato movements. Karate types, he thought.

So I can start anywhere, Cardozo thought. What would

a sheep dealer be doing near the harbor? Delivering sheep for transport to the Near East?

The noodles arrived in a bowl. Hop dropped off a pair of chopsticks and a glass of beer. The bottle's label was Chinese. Would Chinese buy Frisian sheep? From Dingjum? From New Zealand more likely, thought Cardozo. There should be no food shortage in China now. They probably wouldn't need any foreign sheep at all.

He ate and drank, without tasting much. When Hop presented the bill, Cardozo noticed the man's cold eyes, like slivers of ice. Even the glow of Hop's golden canines was cold. Scherjoen had also been equipped with golden dentures. Could that line connect? Why should it? Cardozo thought.

He wandered through the neighborhood. The memory of Wo Hop's presence wandered with him, bathed in neon light. Cardozo couldn't understand why he couldn't lose Hop's image. What more could the Chinese be than a bit player in gray clothes, vertically adorned by old-fashioned suspenders like those worn by laborers in antique pictures? The owner of a small-time eating place, a retreat of footsore junkies and Chinese sailors, a hardly exotic migrant like so many, chained to their marginal establishments, saving hard-earned guilders that might, one faraway day, buy them a return ticket to Hong Kong or Singapore, home cities that their spirits had never left. Cardozo walked a little faster and managed to leave Hop behind. He stopped a few minutes later to stare at a car. Why? Perhaps he was tired and had to rest his eyes on an interesting object. Why interesting? Because it was a new Citroën, of a model that the commissaris had been talking about. Because Cardozo had seen Grijpstra and de Gier leaving Headquarters' courtyard in the commissaris's new car, waving airly, ordering him to "do something" from an electronically dropped window. Was this the same car? There wouldn't be too many new silver super-Citroëns about. Cardozo walked around the car. No, this had to be a different vehicle; it bore a white oval sticker marked FR. Dutch cars were marked NL. What would FR mean? Friesland. The sticker was unofficial, marking fervent national feeling, claiming independence for a province absorbed by the country. FR, meaning "free." All nonsense. Frisians also had their own money that not even Frisian stores would accept, and their own postage stamps, equally without any value. Amazing, that unquenchable desire to be cut off. His brother Samuel had read him a newspaper article on the problem. "Pathetic," Samuel had said. "We don't go about wearing an embroidered *J* on our chests." Samuel did wear a golden star of David on a chain around his neck, and collected Israeli stamps.

Free? Cardozo thought. Who is free? I'm not free. I jump when others pull my strings. "Do something, Cardozo."

The Citroën, parked half on the sidewalk, fronted a health-food store. Cardozo went in. "Has that car been here long?"

"What of it?" snarled the woman behind the counter. She had been constructed of large bones, covered by a square cloth slit by a blunt knife to leave a hole for her thin neck. She had to push matted hair away to squint at this party who offended her by his presence. "A poison sprayer," the woman screamed. "Oh, I know the type. A juggler of genes. An injector of hormones. Ha! Our greedy farmers. They wear their little caps and pretend to bring us the gifts of the earth, but they swindle us out of our money and buy capitalist cars and obstruct the sidewalk and I can't even park my bike, does anybody ever think of me?"

"May I use your phone?"

Cardozo burped. The food displayed in the dim store made him unwell. Cracked plastic pots were half-filled with moldy grains. A bowl had been filled with a jelly crusted on top. Sickly-looking mice scurried about on a shelf.

The store had no phone.

Cardozo walked back to Wo Hop's restaurant, where more junkies leered at each other in noisy despair. Cardozo sneezed with them. The young fighting Chinese were still nervously conversing; their singsong was louder now, even less in harmony with the trumpeting of the addicted. "Phone?" Cardozo asked. "Go grab," Wo Hop said, translating freely from Cantonese. He pointed. Cardozo walked through the cold light. He dialed Headquarters and passed along the Citroën's license plate number.

"Can't check that for you right now," a girlish voice said. "The computer hasn't come up yet."

"Up from where?"

"From being down."

Cardozo caught a streetcar back to Headquarters. The computer room's young ladies were politely unhelpful. "I've got to know," Cardozo said, wandering away. In the Traffic Department, another screen showed another little green square, trembling quietly. It was on view again in the Road Tax Department, and he found it once more in the Department That Hauls Wrecks. Cardozo knocked on the commissaris's door. He rattled the handle.

"Maybe the chief isn't in," a bass voice said, rumbling from a large chest covered by a tight T-shirt. "Would you do me a small favor? Won't take a minute. In the sports room. Do come along."

"No," Cardozo said.

The sports instructor's long, hairy arm clasped Cardozo's shoulders. "Colleague, break your restraining ego and serve others for a change. Here we are, would you mind taking off your shoes?"

Other large and strong men waited, kneeling around the judo mat. "This, colleague," said the sports instructor to Cardozo, "is an Arrest Team. They learn from me. Today we demonstrate Sudden Unexpected Attack. Mind joining us for a moment?"

The sports instructor put on a duck-billed cap.

Cardozo smiled shyly. He scratched his ear. The instructor addressed the team. "Please pay attention. This colleague will now suddenly and unexpectedly attack me."

The hand that scratched Cardozo's ear attached itself to the bill of the instructor's cap. The headgear dipped over the instructor's eyes. Cardozo's other hand clenched and hit the instructor's belly, twisting as it thumped. The instructor bent forward. Cardozo's fist slid up and slammed against the instructor's chin. The instructor bent backward. He kept bending backward because Cardozo's ankle hooked around the enemy's shin and pulled it forward. The instructor fell on his back. Cardozo fell too, twisted free, and yanked on the instructor's wrist so that his whole heavy body turned over. The instructor rested on his belly, with arms stretched out. Cardozo lifted the arms, joined the wrists, and attached them with handcuffs.

"Like this?" Cardozo asked.

The instructor groaned.

"I'll free you," Cardozo said, "as soon as I can locate my key." Cardozo was emptying out his pockets. "Now where did I put it? In my hankie, perhaps? No. In my wallet?"

"Does anyone happen to have a handcuff key?" Cardozo asked the kneeling, attentively watching Arrest Team members.

The team shook their heads.

"Here it is," Cardozo said. "In my new belt. Nifty belt, eh? See this zipper? Hides a secret slit to keep things in. You never thought of that, did you now?"

The team nodded their heads in amazement.

"Anything else I can do for you gents today?" Cardozo asked.

"You, get out of here," the instructor said.

The commissaris had arrived in the meantime. "There have been complaints about you," the commissaris said. "You've been causing some trouble. What trouble were you causing?"

"I'm sorry," Cardozo said. "I was only trying to be of help, and I did come up with something useful. I found the dead man's car, or so it seems for the moment."

The commissaris's small fist bounced on his desk. "I want confirmed facts."

"Our confirmation device is down, sir, but the car was

parked asocially, half on the pavement and under a 'no parking' sign. Would you have a photograph of Mr. Scherjoen? I would like to show it around in the area where I found the car."

"No," the commissaris said.

"Where can I obtain a photo?"

"Grijpstra?" the commissaris asked. "He stays in Friesland now. I just had a call to that effect, from the chief constable of Leeuwarden, Lasius of Burmania, a nobleman from up north. Grijpstra has been given the use of a house at the Spanish Lane in Friesland's capital. I'm not sure why. There isn't much I'm sure of these days. I'm an old man."

"Not at all," Cardozo said. "How do I get to Friesland?"

"My car is gone," the commissaris said. "De Gier will bring it back, but that'll be tomorrow. I don't want de Gier driving my new car, he's a reckless speeder. Not that it matters. Nothing matters much these days."

"Does your leg hurt?" Cardozo asked.

"Should it?" the commissaris asked. "I'm on a diet of Belgian endives. My wife says I'm very fond of Belgian endives. I would rather be driving on the Great Dike, but I'm short of a car."

"What are Grijpstra and de Gier doing in Friesland, sir?"

"Grijpstra," the commissaris said, "is in Friesland because he's a Frisian. His parents were born in Harlingen, just north of the dike. I should be there because I'm a Frisian too. I was born in Joure, a little farther inland. De Gier is in Friesland because he drifted after Grijpstra."

"Wasn't Scherjoen murdered here?"

"That's an effect," the commissaris said. "We're looking for causes, Cardozo. The present hardly matters. Think with me now. Scherjoen has been described to us as an inferior being of a devilish nature. He even parks his car asocially. A ne'er-do-well, this Douwe. It's a first attempt at constructing a theory, but we have to begin in the past."

"But you've only just heard that Scherjoen is an asocial parker."

The commissaris sighed.

"Is your leg hurting badly?"

"You want to hear the truth?"

"Why not?" Cardozo asked.

"I was trying to construct a theory that would take me to Friesland, because I've a new car. I wanted to race it on the dike. Fate got in my way again. My theory was designed to satisfy my selfish longings. But I could still be right. If Douwe is no good, he started by being no good in Friesland. Suppose Frisians wanted to be rid of Douwe and did that here. Couldn't that be possible?"

"Why not in Friesland?"

"It's pure out there," the commissaris said. "And messy here. Another misdeed here might attract little attention."

Cardozo rolled a cigarette.

"And if the misdeed is Frisian-related," the commissaris said, "the inquiry should be Frisian too, for only we Frisians know the depth of our own soul. Grijpstra and I will be the most suitable sleuths."

Cardozo lit his cigarette.

"Grijpstra hunts out there," the commissaris said, "and I drive up and down the dike, to keep contact at over a hundred miles an hour, that's what I had in mind."

"And I would be hunting here?"

"Yes," the commissaris said. His phone rang. "I'm on my way, dear," he said, and replaced the phone on its cradle. "Have to go home now, to eat Belgian endives."

Cardozo coughed and sneezed.

"You should go home too," the commissaris said.

They waited at the elevator together.

"The elevator broke down," a passing constable said. "Everything is down these days, but the elevator got stuck upstairs."

The commissaris and Cardozo walked down the stairs together. Cardozo limped a little. "Are you imitating me?" the commissaris asked.

"I fought the Arrest Team, sir."

"You lost? So why did they complain to me?"

"I sort of not-lost, sir."

"I'm in a bad mood," the commissaris said. "You must excuse me."

"Tomorrow you'll have your car again, sir."

"True," the commissaris said. "Visit me again tomorrow, my spirits should be up."

Waiting at the streetcar stop together, they felt better together. "Bald Ary," the commissaris said, "and Fritz with the Tuft, in Friesland too. Yes, things may be looking up."

His streetcar came first. Cardozo waved good-bye.

||||| 6 /////

THE COMMISSARIS, WHO HAD ONLY JUST GOT OUT INTO THE new day, looked fresh in the early sunlight. His light gray three-piece summer suit contrasted pleasantly with the luscious colors of the begonia flowers in the windows. His small head, under the last few hairs neatly combed across his gleaming skull, rose energetically from the collar of a starched white shirt that held a bright blue tie clasped with a large pearl set in silver. He related his adventure with the barkeep Troelstra and the possibility of future charges against the criminal Bald Ary and his mate, Fritz with the Tuft.

Cardozo listened.

De Gier came in. "*Moarn*," he said.

The commissaris and Cardozo questioned the sergeant soundlessly, from under raised eyebrows.

"*Moarn*?" de Gier asked. "Haven't I fattened the vowels sufficiently? Is my accent blurring my meaning?"

The commissaris's and Cardozo's eyebrows were still up.

"Can I sit down?"

"We are accustomed here," the commissaris said, "to wishing each other a good morning first. After that we can sit down."

"But I did wish you a good morning," de Gier said. "In

the Frisian language. You're Frisian, I believe?" He held up a small black book. "My dictionary, the word is listed." He held up a multicolored book. "And this is a novel, or rather a bundle of Frisian stories, called"—he read the title—"*We're Out of Condiments at Home, and Other Stories,* in Frisian, that is."

"Sit down," the commissaris said.

De Gier sat down. "Excellent stories, sir, and all connected. About a lady. A Frisian lady, about the suffering she gets herself into out there. In her stories she calls herself Martha. Literature is interesting, don't you think? Truthful and schizophrenic. We split ourselves, allow the split part to grow and change its name."

"Goïnga?" Cardozo asked, taking the book away from de Gier. "Is that her real name? Sounds like Hungarian-Finnish to me."

"Frisian is very foreign," de Gier said, "but understandable to me. Even more, because the novel is female. I've been studying the female mind for a while, and she won't escape me, not even in a foreign language. Most of the words I can guess, and the few exceptions I've looked up. There's some confusion about the negative, which they express as positive, but once you've turned it around again, there's nothing to miss."

"Our linguistic wonderboy," the commissaris said, "and the eternal victim of his fantasies about the miracle of Woman. Did you return my car?"

"But sir," de Gier said, "there may be a female suspect. This book is filled with clues."

"My car? Is it here?"

"Yes sir. It was too late last night, and this morning I overslept a little. I didn't cause you any inconvenience, I hope?"

"You did," the commissaris said. "I'm not used to the streetcars anymore. They sell tickets in the cigar stores now, not on the cars. Without a ticket, I was caught twice and paid two fines. Twice a lady offered me her seat. I've been robbed and insulted."

"Good car," de Gier said. "I didn't see much on the way up, for Grijpstra likes to speed, but when I came back, the Inland Sea was beautiful; there was this slow swell, touched up by moonlight, and everywhere the bobbing birds. I got out three times to try and take it all in. I had the feeling of being between nowhere and nowhere. I no longer belonged, but I was still around. Do you feel what I was feeling?"

"To be nowhere?"

"Free," de Gier said. "Aren't we served *koffie*? In Friesland we were served *koffie* everywhere."

"*Koffie*?" the commissaris said.

"It just means coffee," de Gier said. "As I knew. I bought these books yesterday, before we set out, in a store specializing in foreign languages. Swahili, North Borneo-ese, even a Blackfoot Indian grammar. Blackfoot Indians use only verbs. They conjugate a table. Not bad, eh? Seeing that even tables do constantly change. But I happened to need Frisian, which they stocked. They stock just about anything in that store."

The commissaris telephoned and ordered coffee.

"Grijpstra is a lout behind the wheel," de Gier said. "He kept twisting and turning, but perhaps that's the right thing to do, for Friesland twists and turns too. The alleys in Leeuwarden all bit their own tails. We got lost a lot, and the local police found us and rode ahead, to take us to their headquarters. The Leeuwarden Police are housed in a cube, and some distance from the city, so that they can drive into their hunting ground in a straight line, but once they're in, they'll be going round and round again."

"Did you enjoy the Belgian endives, sir?" Cardozo asked.

"No," the commissaris said. "Then what happened, de Gier?"

"Douwe was no good," de Gier said. "His wife is a nice lady. Her name is Mem, meaning 'mother' in Frisian. She poured a good cup of *koffie*."

The coffee was brought in. De Gier accepted the tray and served the commissaris and Cardozo. "There you are. Did you make some progress, Cardozo?"

"Found Scherjoen's car, on Prince Henry Quay. Same brand as the commissaris's, but probably in better shape, for you two must have ruined the commissaris's Citroën already. Scherjoen's car has been towed in. A pistol was found in the driver's door pocket. Old-model Mauser. Not recently fired."

"Was Douwe rich?" the commissaris asked.

"Owned a country estate, which is now Mem's. There are no children." De Gier described the hawthorns, the evening lowing of a cow (a plaintive but beautiful stretched sound, suspended above a wide meadow), and the superior architecture of Frisian country buildings.

"Rich," the commissaris said. "And you liked his wife?"

"Her true name is Krista," de Gier said, "and she does have Christ's eyes, and a crown of thorns. Maybe she has lost the thorns now, because of Douwe's death."

"Details," the commissaris said. "Give us more."

"It's so *otherwise* out there," de Gier said. "Beautiful, detached; the colors, sir, the shades are so subtle. Remember the Jehovah's Witnesses, when they come to the door? Resurrection? Heaven on future earth? Heaven is there now. No crime, unfortunately—very little for the likes of us to do. The nobleman Lasius of Burmania acts as the chief constable of the capital—only acting, of course; maybe heaven is a stage too—what a wonderful man he is, truly civilized, correct in every situation. He wanted to know what Grijpstra might be doing there. Frisians don't go wrong, and if they do, they slide down the dike first, so if we look for misbehavior, we should watch them here. Not that we were unwelcome—that noble man Lasius of Burmania didn't give me that impression. Grijpstra was even given a house. For free. The house belongs to a Frisian adjutant who's on holiday at present."

"So you really know nothing," Cardozo said.

"Should I know more?" de Gier asked. "Grijpstra won't allow me to do any work. I'm on paid leave, I understand. There's no need for me. Okay, maybe to do some shopping. I'll be going back in a minute. It's handy, Grijpstra said, to have me around, perhaps. But there's nothing I'm supposed to do. That's why I observed all that exceptional beauty. If you're not involved in the activity, you sort of float, and while looking down much can be seen. You follow, Cardozo?"

"No," Cardozo said. "Ary and Fritz, sir?"

The commissaris collected his assembled facts. "Mere suspicions so far," the commissaris said, "but Jelle Troelstra is a reliable informant. Let's see what our electronic equipment, activated by the simple pressing of a few well-placed buttons, can do for us by way of confirmation." He picked up his phone. "Dear? Here are the names of two suspects, bank robbers. Please have them checked by the computer. The suspects are from the south. Will you do that for me? Please?"

"The south?" Cardozo asked. "Exiled Frisians?"

"The tip came from a Frisian," the commissaris said.

The phone rang. "Down?" the commissaris asked. "Thank you, dear." He replaced the phone.

"We do have some old files stored in the loft," Cardozo said, "due to be destroyed, but the shredder has been down. Shall I have a look?"

When Cardozo returned he was carrying dented file drawers and folded cards. He also produced some photos. "This is Ary, this is Fritz, both of them known to be violent and armed, but recently freed after serving long stretches."

They read the cards, de Gier and Cardozo standing at either side of the commissaris. "Bad boys," de Gier said, "but what are they to us? They'll be operating well beyond our limits. Douwe is fine; his corpse got into our hands here, and there's a hot trail to be followed. Ary and Fritz drank Frisian jenever at *chez* Troelstra. Their thoughts were bad, but we can't catch their thoughts."

"I'll have to pass it on," the commissaris said. "Pity. Why don't they commit their crimes in Amsterdam, like everybody else?"

"At a cattle market," de Gier said. "Just imagine." He read a little more. "Armed robbers." He shrugged. "Can't even catch them if they operated here. The new instructions state that in the case of armed robbery, an Arrest Team has to be alerted. The team will rush in with machine guns, and use sharpshooters peering through telescopes placed on cranes. They'll rumble about in armored vehicles. They'll be dressed in bulletproof vests. Their movements will be controlled from a mobile command post. Strategy. Tactics."

"Dear?" the commissaris asked through his phone. "Chief Constable Lasius of Burmania, Municipal Police, Leeuwarden. Please?"

"In the old days," the commissaris said, "we'd just follow a robber. We'd tap him on the shoulder. We'd address him in a polite way. Then we'd take him along."

"Was it really like that?" Cardozo asked. "But the robber would be carrying a pistol, surely. We can't do anything if we don't outnumber him twenty to one. With an Uzi submachine gun. Or an HK-33 SG/L rifle with infrared light. Or an MP-5 automatic pistol with shortened barrel. Or a battlecar-type Shorland, an armored UR-416, or at least the modern Sankey minitank. Scout cars placed around the corner, ready to start, all weaponry aimed, backed up by squads of the Military Police, special lads, Red Beret training, pushed slowly forward and backed up again by a SWAT team of the State Police. Sharpshooters on all rooftops."

The commissaris answered his phone. "Can't be reached? Get me the State Police, please. The commander, if possible. Yes, Leeuwarden again, I imagine that their headquarters will be in the capital too. If you please, my dear."

"You can't remember that far back, Cardozo," the commissaris said, "but in the past we were quite peaceful. The idea was not to disturb the peace even further. When we made an arrest, we never employed more than a few police; we believed in small numbers."

"Colonel Kopinie is out of his office?" the commissaris asked. "Do try the Military Police there, dear. If you please."

"I could perhaps take a look," de Gier said. "A cattle market is open to the public. You think that Ary and Fritz will case the location soon? Cattle markets are on Friday, right? So they'll hit the dealers the Friday after. I might be there, an interested spectator. In Friesland I can be a civilian again."

"Your police card is nationally valid," Cardozo said.

"Sure," de Gier said, "but you haven't been there yet. Friesland is so *otherwise*."

"You can grab anyone when you see a crime being committed," Cardozo said. "Just suppose that you happened to be strolling about in the market and Ary and Fritz robbed the dealers and I happened to be there too because, say, I was staying with you. You do have a house out there, there'll be a spare room."

"Not at all," de Gier said. "Grijpstra is the only one who'll be working. He doesn't need the disturbance that you'll bring along. Do something here, Simon, and don't get in the adjutant's way out there. If he sees you around, you'll be in real trouble."

Cardozo coughed and sneezed.

"No one there?" the commissaris asked his phone. "The Military Police commander is Major Singelsma? They'll all phone me back? Thank you, my dear."

"Now what's this with the sheep?" the commissaris asked. "Douwe dealt in sheep. Where did he sell them? Was he exporting them to Amsterdam?"

"You'd have to ask Grijpstra, sir." De Gier wrote down a number and handed it to the commissaris.

The number didn't answer. "I'm asking you now," the commissaris said to de Gier.

"I'm not in on this," de Gier said.

"Rinus," the commissaris said.

"Are you asking me in my function as an outside observer? Yes," de Gier said, "that'll be different, then. Grijpstra took care of the inquiry, but I was with him a lot and I happened to hear this and that. Dealing in sheep appears to be an unregistered and therefore tax-free and therefore illegal commerce. As all sheep look alike, their descriptions do not fit into the memory of a computer."

"Beg pardon," the commissaris said from behind his hand. "Had to laugh. *Computer*. Ha ha. Carry on, de Gier."

"Cows fit into a computer's memory because their spots are different. Sheep have no spots. Births of lambs are not registered. The nonexistent lamb turns into a nonexistent sheep and is sold and nobody knows anything. No sales tax, no income tax, nothing.

"Sheep are visible," Cardozo said.

"You register a few," de Gier said, "but they run about all the time. The Dingjum corporal explained the procedure to me. The average sheep has three lambs, but not in Friesland. Frisian lambs drown in moats a lot, or the fierce neighbor dogs maul them to death, or they die young of tuberculosis. You have a hundred lambs and you register maybe nine. The other ninety-one are hidden during checks."

"So Scherjoen bought the ninety-one sheep and sold them to the Middle East?"

"For cash," de Gier said. "Cash isn't registered either."

Cardozo blew the remnants of his influenza into his handkerchief and smiled at the sergeant. "That's where I caught on. There are ships moored in the Inner Harbor here. Scherjoen pushed a thousand unregistered sheep onto a ship. What's the price of a sheep?"

"Three hundred guilders."*

"That's a three-hundred thousand-guilder load. To be paid for in cash. Now the Moroccan, a buyer, doesn't pay. There are no invoices, no bills of lading, no proof of any sort. The Moroccan says he has paid already. Scherjoen loses his tem-

---

*One guilder is equal to about thirty cents in U.S. currency.

per. The Moroccan loses his temper too. He whips out a gun. Bang. No more Scherjoen asking for money. The Moroccan, a dangerous Arabian freedom fighter, isn't satisfied yet and burns Scherjoen's corpse. Oh, they're wicked in the Middle East. Beirut!"

The phone rang. "For you," the commissaris said.

"Jane?" de Gier asked. "The Volkswagen is repaired? You arranged it not for me, but because you serve the Service? You're such a wonderful woman, Jane. No? Well, I think you are." He observed the buzzing phone. He put it down.

"Something is bothering Jane," Cardozo said. "She's making everybody nervous. Some dissatisfied vibration oozes out of her and puts the colleagues on edge. Do you have plans with her or don't you?"

"I never have any plans," de Gier said. "Things just happen to me in spite of my defenses, or not, as in the case of Jane."

"I'll be looking for a Moroccan sheik," Cardozo said. "And once I have a photograph of Scherjoen, I could show it around along Prince Henry Quay. The woman in the health-food store recognized him as some sort of farmer, and others must have seen him too."

"You do that," de Gier said. "That'll keep you out of trouble."

"Will you get me a photo?" Cardozo asked. "Of Douwe? Please?"

"Ah," the commissaris said, "I keep forgetting to tell you, Sergeant. Tell Grijpstra that the chief constable here gave permission for you two to operate in Friesland, but you can't declare costs. The administration is tightening up. Since you have to eat anyway, you pay for your own meals, and any extras are at your own expense too."

"The photo," Cardozo said.

"Theoretically you couldn't even take the Volkswagen," the commissaris said, "but the vehicle was written off a long time ago and is no longer recognized by the administration, so take it along."

"That's understood, sir."

"I won't be declaring costs, either," the commissaris said. "I haven't declared anything for a while. Officers of my rank are considered to be a useless weight these days."

"But you will be around?"

"Of course," the commissaris said. "As a Frisian, I'm supporting the cause. I was born in Joure. A good opportunity to return to the land of my birth. What matters these days is to be able to combine circumstances in a propitious manner. I'm supposed to be home at night, so I can drive up and down the dike."

"Living well is the best revenge," de Gier said.

"You want to get even?"

"Me?" de Gier asked.

"You're not in this," Cardozo interrupted. "I am. I'll be doing something. I'll be doing something now. Don't forget the photo."

"I'll be going now," de Gier said.

"I'll be going later," the commissaris said, "once the Frisian authorities have contacted this office."

"A truly splendid country, sir," de Gier said. "I kept meeting you out there. You have something that I thought to be quite rare, but in your country it is offered from all sides."

"What something, Sergeant?"

"It's all so *oars*," de Gier said. "Beg pardon, that's Frisian, sir. So *otherwise*, I meant to say. How shall I express that exotic feeling?"

The commissaris pointed at the books under de Gier's arm. "You really managed to make sense of Frisian literature?"

"I did."

"Read me a little."

De Gier opened the novel and cleared his throat. "Are you ready?"

"Go ahead."

"Female thought, sir, thought by a certain Martha."

"Go ahead, Sergeant."

De Gier read in Frisian. "'I have to go to the bathroom now.'"

"Translate."

De Gier translated.

"A deep thought," the commissaris said. "And well expressed. Very different. Exceptional, are they?"

De Gier looked for a better quote.

"Never mind," the commissaris said. "Go join Grijpstra, he'll be needing the car. I'm quite sure he won't be needing *you*."

⫼⫼ 7 ⫼⫼

DE GIER RANG THE DOORBELL. A MAN OPENED THE DOOR. He wore a fisherman's jersey that followed his ample belly along a wide curve, and he had tied a bright red bandanna around his neck. A flat farmer's cap sat on his head.

"Is it you?" de Gier asked.

"It is," said Grijpstra. "How do you like me in Frisian?"

"Yes," de Gier said. "Are you living here?"

"You are too," Grijpstra said, "for you will be staying with me. Do try to be tidy, for it's most kind of Adjutant Oppenhuyzen to let us live here for free. He forgot Eddy. Mrs. Oppenhuyzen just telephoned about Eddy."

De Gier walked into a long corridor. "How police-like to forget your own son. Confirms my theory. Police-people do not function well within normal society. They therefore allow themselves to be cast out. Once they're cast out, they turn on society. The police are criminal in essence."

"Not his son," Grijpstra said. "His rat. The rat lives upstairs, I haven't seen him yet. Let's go look together. You'll have to take care of Eddy."

"A pet rat?" de Gier asked. "My hypothesis stands confirmed. Only the perverted will pet a rat. Cast out because of perversion, the policeman attacks the society in which he does not fit."

"Don't carry on so," Grijpstra said, dragging his feet on the staircase. "The adjutant was ill. Something wrong with his face. He kept grabbing at his cheeks. His wife was all worried. They suddenly had to move to their summer house, and they had to get everything together in a rush; surely the circumstances permitted forgetting a mere rat."

De Gier wandered in and out of rooms. "Too many roses on the wallpaper, and I don't care for the furniture either. Bought at sales throughout the centuries. Can we get rid of it? Stack it in the garage? Okay if I whitewash the walls? This jumble of colors should be an insult to your painter's perception. Where is this rat?"

"Here," Grijpstra said. "In the terrarium. By the way, he lives on a diet of Frisian cheese. Adjutant Oppenhuyzen has already phoned me twice. He left a pound of cheese. You think he got away?"

De Gier studied more wallpaper.

"In the sawdust?" Grijpstra asked, lifting the glass top of the terrarium and digging about with his finger. "Hey!" He jumped back.

A white pointed snout protruded from the sawdust. Red eyes peered out shyly. Long yellow protruding teeth extended beyond a receding bald chin. Ragged mustache hairs trembled. "And we've got to hold that?" Grijpstra asked nervously.

"Hi, Eddy," de Gier said.

"Got to hold him once in a while. Mrs. Oppenhuyzen's instructions. Put the top down." Grijpstra's voice broke into a squeak.

The rat rattled.

De Gier lifted Eddy from the terrarium, turned him over, and held his ear to Eddy's belly. "He must be hungry."

"Let go of that beast," Grijpstra said. "I don't want to engage in a relationship with a rattle-rat. I'll make a phone call. The Oppenhuyzens are in Engwierum. Has to be around here somewhere. Drop the rat and cover the terrarium. They'll have to pick him up."

"It's hunger that makes him rattle. Here, listen for yourself." De Gier held Eddy close to Grijpstra's ear. Grijpstra backed up against the wall. "Nice little animal," de Gier said, and buried his nose in Eddy's fur. "You come along with your Uncle Rinus."

Eddy hung over de Gier's flat hand. De Gier carried him downstairs, and together they looked into the refrigerator. Eddy waited on the table while de Gier sliced the cheese. "Here you are." Eddy ate. "You see?" de Gier asked. "Ravenous, the poor little sucker."

"You take care of the beast," Grijpstra said. "And of the plants. I've got a list here. All plants are numbered, and each plant has different watering times. The required quantities are listed in cubic centimeters, right here. You have to pour carefully, not slosh the water into the pots; there's a note to that effect. The plants marked with an *A* are fed crystals from this can, and the *B*'s are fed from the can over there."

"What?" de Gier asked.

"And here are cleaning instructions," Grijpstra said. "What cleaning product does what, and where the containers can be found. And here's some paper for the administration of our expenses. Make careful notes, for we can claim them afterward."

"We can't claim anything," de Gier said, "compliments of the commissaris. New regulations for out-of-town police officers on the job. It doesn't matter where we operate. No declarations."

"What?" Grijpstra asked.

De Gier stroked the rat.

"Leave the varmint alone," Grijpstra said. "Rats are loaded with disease. Ah, that's another thing, we've got to wash him too."

"Consider it done." De Gier turned on a faucet. The rat rattled excitedly. "You like that, do you?" De Gier mixed soap suds with hot water in a bowl. "Can you get in by yourself?" Eddy clambered into his bath. His head hung over the edge while de Gier kneaded the wet little body gently. The rat's rattle became louder.

"Now what?" Grijpstra asked. "He just ate a quarter-pound of cheese. Hungry again?"

"Limited program," de Gier said. "Probably expressing positive emotion now. Rats can't talk, you know." De Gier dried Eddy with a dishcloth and took him to the living room, where he jumped on the couch.

"Are you going to cook now?" Grijpstra asked. "And do some shopping first?"

"Will you be doing something too?"

Grijpstra prepared for a nap on the couch, after shooing Eddy away. The rat climbed a chair, wrapped his naked tail around his bare feet, and sighed contentedly. The sigh contained a vague shadow of a rattle.

"Rats are supposed to squeak," Grijpstra said.

"Maybe a cold?" de Gier asked. "Cardozo is suffering too. He found Scherjoen's car, a Citroën like the commissaris's, and there was an old-model Mauser in the door pocket, loaded but clean."

Grijpstra opened an eye. "Douwe didn't feel safe?"

"And drove an expensive car," de Gier said. "My conclusions are as limited as yours."

"Let's hear more."

"The car was parked halfway on the pavement. Locked."

"I often park halfway on the pavement," Grijpstra said.

"When you're in a hurry?"

"Nah," Grijpstra said. "When I feel like it. Lazy. Don't feel like parking the vehicle properly between others. Why bother? Nobody bothers in Amsterdam."

De Gier tickled Eddy's head.

"Do hurry up," Grijpstra said. "The stores are about to close."

De Gier came back with canned pea soup, bread, and butter.

Grijpstra opened the door. "I can't sleep with that rat."

They sat at the living room table. Eddy stood on a cushion placed on a chair, so that he could lean his head on the table.

"Can he go home now?" Grijpstra asked. "He's got a home. Take him upstairs."

"No," de Gier said. "Three is a party. Things are looking up again. I was about to get depressed. On the dike the exhaust fell off the car, and the traffic was clogged up again because of checkpoints stopping trucks suspected of transporting animals carrying the plague."

Grijpstra ladled out thick soup. "So what made the change?"

"Corporal Hilarius," de Gier said. "Remember her? With the hoarse voice and the golden hair under the orange helmet? She showed up again and guided me through the checkpoints and along to her father in the town of Tzum."

"Tzum," Grijpstra said. His knuckles beat out a rhythm on the tabletop. "Tzam. Tzom." The rhythm sped up, holding several patterns of a fairly complicated beat. De Gier sang and whistled in turn. Eddy's chin trembled as he rattled in the pauses.

"Tzum?" Grijpstra's hands stopped in middair.

"Her father runs a garage and was willing to exchange favors. The exhaust is back on the car again."

"What was your favor?"

"Admiration of his daughter. Some woman, that corporal. Did you hear her voice, added to a multitude of other charms?"

"That mechanized robot at a hundred and fifty miles an hour?"

"Okay," de Gier said, "she is that too, but she's mostly beautiful and female. She'll be taking me out later tonight, to a beer house—that's what they call cafés here. I'm sure she's well formed under all that leather." De Gier was quiet, impressed by the memory mixed with fantasy leading, perhaps, to future passion. "Hylkje," de Gier said, "that's her first name. To you, as a Frisian, the name is probably common, but to me the sound is exotic. Exciting too."

"And Jane?"

"She's exciting in Amsterdam, but I'm here."

"You aren't even faithful to your dreams."

"Faithful?" De Gier waved the word away. "Women aren't faithful either. An idea from the past. You're always running up from behind, Adjutant. You really think that the modern solitary female expects her casual male company to be faithful?"

The doorbell rang. Grijpstra struggled up and looked out the window. "A squad car outside. The corporal probably put in a complaint. What did you do to her? Never abuse a colleague."

De Gier opened the door. "Evening, sir."

"Rinus," the commissaris said. "How nice. Once again, together in a foreign country, but this time it's mine. I can show you around. I was born here, in the city of Joure."

"*It libben is hearlik, mynhear.*"

"What's that?"

"I spoke your language, sir. A sentence from the Frisian novel I'm reading. It says that life is wonderful here."

"Evening, sir," Grijpstra said. "Did you have a good journey? Please don't pay attention to de Gier. Perhaps you'll be good enough to take him with you when you return. Is it true that we can't declare expenses?"

"Where's your car?" de Gier asked, watching the squad car's taillights fade away at the end of the street.

"Lost my way a little," the commissaris said. "You already look like a local, Grijpstra. I got twisted out of my course in the alleys of the inner city here. One-way traffic, mostly. I did try to adhere to the rules, but the cars kept coming at me from all sides. Couldn't cope with the confusion. And when I parked, that was illegal too. The officers who told me that gave me a ride here."

"Do you remember where you parked?"

The commissaris felt through his pockets. "What did I do with the note? Some narrow street called Cellars or something? '*Above* the Cellars'? Street names are poetic here. I want to see the chief constable at headquarters later, and the officers drew me a little map. Kind of aim out of the city, reach a circular highway, quite complicated. It was all on that little piece of paper. Can't seem to be able to find it now. I wonder if I left it in their car?"

"De Gier will take you," Grijpstra said. "And we'll find your car. 'Cellars,' you said?"

"Or was it 'Well'?" the commissaris asked. "A little street called Around the Well? Would that be possible? And I crossed some Gardens too, but they were canals really, with narrow quays on the side, aquatic gardens perhaps? Water lilies? Flowering reeds? I think I noticed plants."

"We'll take care of everything," Grijpstra said. "Please come in, sir."

The commissaris looked about him. "Cozy. Too much wallpaper, perhaps? I say, Sergeant, there's a rat on that chair."

De Gier picked up the rat. "The name is Eddy, sir." He turned the rat over. "Cute, don't you think?"

The commissaris scratched Eddy's pale pink skin.

"Put him away," Grijpstra said. "He'll be rattling again."

Eddy twisted free, jumped down, and ran to the kitchen. De Gier followed. The commissaris came along. De Gier made coffee while Eddy slurped milk from a jug. "A dairy rat," de Gier said. "Fancies rare cheese too. I'd better wash that jug. So the local chief constable did contact you, sir?"

"And the colonel of the State Police and the major of the Military Police. General alarm, Sergeant. We'll be seeing some activity here. They'll bring in Arrest Teams from all over. Roadblocks manned by riot police, detectives from the capital dressed up as cattle dealers, and the chief constable himself in charge."

Grijpstra had joined them. "Big trouble, sir?"

"There'll even be psychologists to predetermine the subjects' behavior."

"What subjects?" Grijpstra asked.

The commissaris explained about the criminals Ary and Fritz.

"Two lone robbers?" Grijpstra asked. "But that's easy, one just grabs them. And then one takes them to the station."

"That's how it was done in the past," the commissaris said.

"Grab them by the collars," Grijpstra insisted. "Or no, not even that. If suspects are known, they can be picked up at their homes later, when they're drinking beer and watching TV."

"You ever heard about unemployment?" de Gier asked. "This little job can occupy a hundred police workers. All sorts of specially trained colleagues can be active and under the impression that they're functioning properly, which will add to their self-respect."

The commissaris looked over his coffee cup. "And Douwe Scherjoen?"

"I," Grijpstra said, "and Lieutenant Sudema of the State Police in the town of Dingjum have constructed a theory. It has to do with sheep, sir."

"And a buyer from Morocco?"

"You were thinking along the same lines?" Grijpstra asked sadly.

"No, no, Adjutant, I'm sorry I interrupted. Sheep, you said?"

"Unregistered sheep, sir. Scherjoen bought them, but he wasn't the only illegal buyer. Scherjoen, being nasty and far too successful, destroyed his competition's chances. He made use of unacceptable tricks. Scherjoen, in league with buyers from the Middle East, managed to monopolize the market. The other dealers would transport their sheep to Amsterdam and be ready to deliver and the Moroccans or Turks or Arabs or whatnot wouldn't buy all of a sudden. Then Scherjoen bought the sheep at a loss from his colleagues and cashed in from the buyers, paying them kickbacks."

"And Lieutenant Sudema thinks so too?"

"There are rumors, sir, to support the theory. I'll visit some suspects."

The commissaris nodded thoughtfully.

"You and I," Grijpstra said, "are both Frisians. We know how stubborn our compatriots can be. They'll accept their losses, but there'll be a certain line that should not be crossed. One or more of the impoverished fellow sheep dealers will have thought of a plan to stop Scherjoen's malpractice for good. Scherjoen liked to visit the Amsterdam Red Quarter. The other or others waited for Scherjoen. You and I know how patient Frisians can be."

"I don't know anything at all," de Gier said. "A pity I'm so ignorant of Frisian ways. If I knew just a little more, I might be able to help."

"Just a moment, Sergeant. So..." Grijpstra paused for dramatic effect. "So...a shot in the night and a burning dory."

"Have you listed possible suspects?"

"Lieutenant Sudema is making discreet inquiries, sir. I'll have some names later tonight."

"And Mrs. Scherjoen? As his wife, she inherits all of Douwe's possessions."

Grijpstra rubbed the bulging blue wool of his fisherman's jersey. "Mem Scherjoen was once a freedom fighter. During the war she was fairly heroic. She wasn't violent, however. Passed messages, transported arms, took care of fugitives that the Germans were after, and helped instructors dropped by the British. You and I know we shouldn't underestimate Frisian women. Lieutenant Sudema seems convinced, however, that she's too loving a soul..."

"That Mauser," the commissaris said. "I had a look at the weapon found in Scherjoen's car. Wicked looking, it seemed to me. Quite antique now, but in shape rather similar to our present automatic arms. Amazing construction, all the parts fit like a Chinese puzzle."

"But it hadn't been fired, sir, I hear."

"Loaded," the commissaris said. "Nine-millimeter, ten cartridges. Deadly. Yes."

"This has nothing to do with me," de Gier said, "but Mem Scherjoen? Such a dear elderly lady? Her own husband? And burn the fellow afterward?"

"Where was she that night?" the commissaris asked.

"Haven't asked her yet, sir. The lieutenant said he would find out."

"I once arrested a dear old lady," the commissaris said. "She had lived fifty years with a most miserable scoundrel. The miser lived in splendor, and the missus scrubbed the marble floors of his mansion. If she spent too much time under the shower, he would turn off the water. She throttled him one evening. They were both in their eighties."

"You dumped the old lady in a cell?" de Gier asked.

"I stretched the investigation a little," the commissaris said, "while she stayed at home. In the end she was diagnosed as irresponsibly senile. With her husband's money we were able to place her in a most comfortable home. Every Christmas she sent me choice chocolate pie and I would take it back to her so that we could eat it together."

The telephone rang. Grijpstra answered, listened solemnly, and replaced the receiver.

"Bad news, Adjutant?"

"Lieutenant Sudema, sir. Mrs. Scherjoen did spend that night in Amsterdam. She was staying with her sister, a Miss Terpstra. Returned the night after the murder."

"Lieutenant Sudema interrogated Mrs. Scherjoen?"

"His wife did, sir. Gyske Sudema. She's friendly with Mem Scherjoen. Mrs. Scherjoen was never allowed to leave her house, as Scherjoen wanted her to be waiting for him whenever he happened to come home, but she did manage to get away from time to time."

"Do I smell pea soup?" the commissaris asked.

De Gier filled a bowl. The commissaris ate, kept company by Eddy, whose snout lay flat on the kitchen table, between his pink paws. He rattled fondly.

"Asthmatic?" the commissaris asked.

De Gier picked up the rat and listened to the mysterious sounds. "I would think it's in his belly."

The commissaris listened too. "No, I think it's from his chest."

The doorbell rang. De Gier opened the door. "Hylkje, how nice to see you. Come in and join us."

"No time now, I'm only here to deliver the lieutenant's list of suspects." The corporal stamped her booted foot. "Bah, I'm running late. Two collisions here in the city. I'm State Police, but the civilians can't see the difference in uniform. And the Municipal Police are nowhere to be found again. I had to write the reports. Stupid civilians!"

A small girl ran toward the corporal. "Officer?"

"Yes?" Hylkje asked grimly.

"See that man there, he's watering against my father's car."

"Shouldn't he be?"

"He does that every evening, he makes me mad."

"Dear little girl," the corporal said sweetly. "Leave that poor man be."

The little girl pummeled the corporal's thigh. "Please, officer, please?"

"I'm tired," Hylkje said.

"One moment," de Gier said and ran off. He came back with the man, who was buttoning up his fly. The man was explaining his misdemeanor as the result of a small bladder.

"And you always pick that particular car?" de Gier asked. "Tell you what, sir. The corporal will take care of you for a moment. I'll be right back."

The commissaris came to the door and was introduced by Grijpstra. He shook Hylkje's hand. He also shook the suspect's hand.

De Gier joined them. "They're on their way."

A squad car drove into the street. "It's you?" the policemen asked the commissaris. "Would you like us to take you somewhere again, or was it you who was pissing?"

"Small bladder," the suspect explained.

"You can take me to your headquarters," the commissaris said, "but perhaps you should take care of this gentleman first."

"I'll take you," de Gier said, pointing at the Volkswagen.

"Is that your vehicle?" a policeman asked.

"Belongs to the Detective Department," Grijpstra said. "Amsterdam, used exclusively by the Murder Brigade."

"You sure it's not dead?" the policeman in charge of the squad car asked. "We saw it just now and phoned it through to our wrecker. It should be here any moment."

"Alive," Grijpstra said.

The police wrecker drove into the street.

"Hey!" Hylkje shouted. The suspect had run off. De Gier ran after him.

"I'll take you now, sir," Grijpstra said. "I don't like the way these colleagues are looking at my car."

De Gier brought the suspect back. One policeman pushed him into the squad car while the other spoke to the wrecker's driver, apologizing for the mistake.

"Take the lieutenant's list," Hylkje said, "before anything else happens. I need a shower and some sleep. I'll be back at eleven."

"Right," de Gier said.

"A rat!" Hylkje yelled, pointing at the threshold.

De Gier picked Eddy up and held him against his cheek. Eddy waved his paws at Hylkje. The corporal staggered back. She replaced her helmet, slid into the Guzzi's saddle, and pressed the starter. The motorcycle reared up briefly, came down, and shot off.

De Gier put Eddy down and pushed the rat gently across the threshold. He went inside, cleared the dining room and kitchen tables, and washed and dried the dishes.

Eddy was back on the couch, curled up on a cushion.

"Move up, please," de Gier said. "I want to read for a while."

The rat squirmed around.

"If I read aloud, will you stop rattling?"

Eddy, soothed by de Gier's voice, became quiet. De Gier read in Frisian, guessing at the meaning of the foreign words, which resembled English here and there, but the verbs were conjugated according to German grammar. The story he had selected was called "Optimal Functioning."

"He weighs heavily on my stomach," de Gier read. He closed the book. Eddy was asleep. De Gier slid his finger under the rat's tail, flicking it up. "Did you follow the general trend of the tale?"

Eddy rearranged his tail.

"She has just eaten her husband," de Gier said. "This author who calls herself Martha when she writes." Because Eddy wouldn't wake up, de Gier addressed the plants as he watered them, being careful not to slosh the water. While he poured and talked, he read Mrs. Oppenhuyzen's instructions. "Ten cc, primula, twelve cc, fuchsia." He poured from a measured watering can.

"The Frisian character," de Gier said. "Consciously pure, so the impurities are repressed. In order to function optimally, Martha has to eat her husband. A literary joke? Not at all. A revelation, rather. This is serious stuff, true art, well written. The author is telling me, the intelligent reader, that here in Friesland, where true goodness reigns, evil is active under pressure. So how is it released?"

De Gier returned the sleeping Eddy to the terrarium upstairs.

He went back to the couch and immersed his mind further in the Frisian female aspect. Woman eats her man. De Gier penetrated into the next short story, where Martha beats her man to death. In the next tale she drowns him in a bath of black paint that, once he's quite dead, takes on a brilliant green color.

The book dropped away. De Gier dropped away with it. He changed into a spider. So did Martha, but she was three times his size. She rang a bell at him while she ate him slowly. He woke up with a shriek and was no longer being eaten, but the ringing persisted. De Gier rolled off the couch and reached for the telephone.

"Hello?"

"We dropped down a dike," Grijpstra said. "Save us, Sergeant."

"Where are you?"

"Between the towns of Tzum," Grijpstra said, "and Tzummarum. In a village, but it's closed. In a phone booth without a phone book. Do something, Sergeant."

"You'll be all right," de Gier said, "but do tell me how you got there."

///// 8 /////

"Do you two really have to content yourselves
with this little rustbucket?" the commissaris had asked, while
bouncing about in his seat. "I'm against total equality, but
maybe some distances between ranks are a little stretched.
Now look at me, with my super Citroën. Can't you two
wangle a new car out of the administration? If you'd only
try, you'd have a brand-new vehicle within a month. I'll
countersign the application with pleasure. It'll make me feel
less guilty."

"Yes sir," Grijpstra said. "I'll take up your request with
de Gier. I myself don't care much one way or another, but
you know how willful the sergeant can be. Old love. De Gier
can be persistent." The Volkswagen jangled into a long street
lined with factories, and wheezed past a railway station.
"Didn't you say we would have to find a circular road?"
Grijpstra asked. "Yesterday I kept finding it, but now I seem
to be missing it altogether."

"Some sort of dike?" the commissaris asked. "Built around
the city? All roads leading out of town are supposed to connect to this circular road. That's what the local officers were
saying. If we kept following the Ringway, we would see the
headquarters of the Municipal Police, the State Police, and

the Fire Brigade, three sizable six-story cubes. Very clever, all services within each other's reach."

"The signs are pointing to Germany now," Grijpstra said. "Pity I can't use our radio. It's still on the Amsterdam channel. Wouldn't work here anyway, the provinces have changed to more modern equipment."

"Keep driving," the commissaris said. "There'll be other signs that should guide us back to Leeuwarden."

The signs kept pointing east. Grijpstra made the Volkswagen cross the center division. "That's illegal, sir," the adjutant said. "I hope we were seen so that they can switch on their sirens and chase us and then we can listen to what they have to say and ask for directions when they're out of breath."

"Quite," the commissaris said.

"Now we're headed for Amsterdam," Grijpstra said, pointing at a sign. "That's much better. We're going south. In Germany we would be lost."

"Keep following these rural lanes," the commissaris said. "They may twist and turn a bit, but they should take us back to Leeuwarden."

Together they enjoyed the changing vistas of meadows lined by woods.

"Dingjum?" Grijpstra asked, half an hour later. "I've been here before. This is where Mem Scherjoen lives, and over there's the State Police station where Lieutenant Sudema is the chief."

"Why don't you stop?" the commissaris asked. "It's time for coffee. The lieutenant can give us directions on how to get back to Leeuwarden."

The lieutenant had gone home, but the corporal who had replaced him poured coffee. "Are you in charge of this murder case, sir?"

"I am."

"Maybe," the corporal said, "you should take a few minutes to visit the lieutenant. I'm sure he would like to keep informed of your progress. He lives close by. Your adjutant knows where."

"Nice walk," Grijpstra said.

The commissaris phoned his wife.

"Where are you?" she asked. "I was expecting you. Couldn't you let me know you were planning to work late? You shouldn't be working, your leg is in bad shape. I could run you a hot bath."

"I do love you," the commissaris said, "and I would like to get back to you, but you've no idea how vast this country is. We keep driving forever. I wish you were here, you have a feeling for shortcuts."

"And a feeling for you."

"Yes," the commissaris said. "And don't worry, dear."

"Don't overstrain yourself."

"Grijpstra is taking care of me," the commissaris said. "De Gier is around too. As he isn't Frisian, he won't be of much use to us here; he can't identify with the locals. Grijpstra and I fit within the mental climate. You know I was born here, in Joure. I thought I had forgotten, but my origins have bubbled up again. We always forget how important first impressions are. They shape our characters, inspire us all our lives."

"Dear Jan," his wife said. "Do what you have to do and then come back quickly."

A little later, strolling between majestic beeches towering above fields of corn where songbirds chanted divine compositions, the commissaris and Grijpstra discussed their shared roots. A most beneficial beginning, they agreed, that had influenced both their lives. Corruption that occurs later can do little to spoil a truly blissful start. While Grijpstra searched for proper expressions that would illustrate his happy feelings, the commissaris talked about rural peace, forgotten by city slickers, so that they become irritated by their own and each other's spiritual filth, but here—his arm followed a leaping jackrabbit between neat rows of cabbage and waved at a low little cloud, glowing in late light—"here in the natural harmony of untrammeled nature . . ."

"Evil will have a hard time here," Grijpstra said.

"Exactly, Adjutant. No wonder a spoiled soul like Scherjoen had to commit his misdeeds on the low side of the dike, and that he had to come to a horrible end in our parts, where the blessings of his homeland could no longer defend his miserable existence."

The commissaris shook his head, to rid himself of Amsterdam associations. "*Ach, how hearlik is here ut libben.*"

"You're speaking Frisian, sir?"

"De Gier found that expression. It means 'life is wonderful.'"

"Bah . . . de Gier," Grijpstra shook his head too. "What does de Gier know? He's got a gift for languages, but it's all on the surface. How can he feel what truly goes on in our land? There's Lieutenant Sudema's house. Under the chestnut trees. A most pleasant little dwelling."

Gyske Sudema stood in her front garden, under waving branches that held clusters of white flowers. The commissaris enjoyed the sight. Gyske impressed him as a very attractive woman, tall and slender, her long blond hair lifted by the breeze, her body tight in gleaming leather trousers and a clinging white blouse. Coming closer, the commissaris regretted to see that she was wearing a man's jacket across her shoulders, of too large a size, and hanging down on one side.

"Evening, Mrs. Sudema."

Grijpstra introduced him. Gyske's supple hand felt moist. Her long eyelashes twitched. "Not a good time for a visit," Gyske said. "I'm sorry, yes. Problems tonight. No, this is hardly the moment."

"Your husband isn't home?"

"Visiting," Gyske said. "Sjurd is making a friendly call. He swallowed all my tranquilizers and drank some jenever. He's crying on the neighbor lady's shoulder now. She's alone too, for her man is a sailor. It's all right with me, they can do what they like."

"Marriage problems?" Grijpstra asked. "How could that be? Yesterday you and the lieutenant seemed so happy."

"Happened just now," Gyske said. "Bit of a problem. The whole thing blew up."

Grijpstra gasped. "But he just sent me some information via Corporal Hilarius."

"He had to look for comfort," Gyske said. "An hour ago, first time. Never visited the neighbor on his own before, my Sjurd, such a clumsy oaf." Gyske's laugh was shrill. She patted the side pocket of her jacket. "I took his pistol. He can't shoot himself now. He wanted to, but that's all crazy."

"Could I have the weapon?" The commissaris extended a small hand. Gyske passed him the pistol. The commissaris handed it to Grijpstra. Grijpstra pulled the clip, ejected the chambered cartridge into his hand, and dropped the various parts into his pocket.

"Why don't you tell me what happened?" the commissaris said. "Once a problem is shared, it can be solved. Let's hear about the mishap, dear lady."

"All right," Gyske said. "I started it, I know that very well, but I'm damned if I'll feel guilty. It wasn't sinful at all. Sjurd is from the past. I'm not. I read magazine articles and the psychological column in the paper. I live with the times. I know what things are like today. When I do it, I do it."

"With whom, dear lady?"

Gyske lifted one shoulder. "With a man, of course."

"Let's go in," the commissaris said. "Or are your children in the house?"

"Gone out," Gyske said, "to play with friends. So that they don't have to work in Sjurd's greenhouse tonight. They don't want to do that, they're too little anyway. Sjurd's idea of duty is too heavy. Slave away, day after day, that's a bad example."

"I like your furniture," the commissaris said when they had gone inside. "Real antiques, I'm sure."

"From the past," Gyske said. "Like my husband. Passed down through the generations. Clammy, moldy, sealed off from fresh air. I'm a modern woman. Would you like a beer?"

"I still have to drive," Grijpstra said, "and the commissaris has to see the Leeuwarden chief constable. We'd better stay sober."

Gyske plucked at her jacket. "It's Sjurd's, it doesn't fit. I'll take it off now. I only put it on to have something to carry the pistol in. Sjurd wanted to shoot Anne."

"The neighbor lady?"

"No," Gyske said. "Anne is a man. You're from Holland, are you? Our names are different here. Anne is the man I had been doing it with. He lives close by too. Everybody lives close by." She began to cry. Grijpstra supplied a handkerchief, the commissaris gentle words. "Now, now, Mrs. Sudema."

Gyske stopped crying. "Anne's the Christian therapist here, qualified, with proper papers. He does social work for the municipality and the church. He's Dutch Reformed, too, same denomination as Sjurd and I. He was supposed to help me. I wasn't sleeping well at all, and cramps down below, and crying all the time. Sjurd got the parson to pray with me, but that made it worse, and then the pastor sent his therapeutical man."

"Who went to bed with you?" the commissaris asked.

Gyske shook her wealth of golden hair. "I went to bed with Anne. It was *my* decision. And we didn't use the bed; the bed is Sjurd's, from his grandparents, I won't use that bed for that. I did it over there."

Surprised, Grijpstra looked at the cupboard door.

"Yes," Gyske said. "On a shelf. Wide enough. It's okay for sitting on and leaning back. Sjurd got upset too, when he heard."

"You went into details when you talked to your husband?" the commissaris asked.

"Isn't that what Sjurd wanted? Didn't I have to make a complete confession? And what did it all amount to, anyway? Hadn't it come to an end a long time ago? I knew it wouldn't last. I wasn't doing it anymore. But Sjurd had to know everything, that's what he kept saying. I had to tell all, and then it would be all right forever. Anne no longer came to visit because I no longer cared for treatment. He was in love with me, Anne said, but later he changed his tale. He let me do it because his wife was a lesbian. Some reason, right? What sort of reason could that be? I told him never to come again. That's a month ago now."

"And Sjurd suspected?" the commissaris asked.

"He sensed it. He kept nosing about. It made me so nervous. If I came clean it would be good between us again, Sjurd told me ten times a day. We could make a fresh start."

Grijpstra covered his eyes with his hand.

"Right," Gyske said. "I'm a silly goose. But you men never give in, do you now? So I told him this evening that Anne and I . . . in the cupboard and all . . . and Sjurd ran off, beside himself with fury. To Anne's house. He broke Anne's glasses. Anne's wife stood next to the poor man. Me too, I had run after Sjurd, and then Sjurd hit Anne in the mouth, Anne's lips were bleeding, and he hit him once more, and again. Good thing I was there, I didn't trust it at all, Sjurd pretending he was taking it all so calmly and then suddenly running off. 'I'll take care of this.' Ha, I know Sjurd. And Anne's wife, the lesbian—she isn't one, you know—she thought she was, so she spent a weekend on the island with that other woman, but she wasn't after all. The other woman was, yes, sure, but not Anne's wife. So when Sjurd kept trying to smash Anne's face, Anne got away, in his car, at full speed, through his own fence, not the gate, he couldn't find the gate, and Sjurd rushed home to swallow all my pills, and then to the pub." Gyske bit a fingernail. "He was back again, to fetch his pistol, but I had it and wouldn't give it to him, and then he went to see the neighbor lady. She isn't happy either, her husband is first mate on a supertanker. He's never home."

"Good evening," Lieutenant Sudema said, wobbling through the door, trying to stay upright.

"My chief from Amsterdam," Grijpstra said. "Lieutenant Sudema of the State Police."

"How do you do?" the commissaris asked.

"Not so well, sir. I've been a little stupid, I think, for some time now, and it hasn't gotten any better. I was born stupid, that's always a bad start. Hello, Gyske. Evening, Adjutant."

"Are you drunk, Sjurd?"

"Yes," the lieutenant said, "and stupid too. And I was wrong, I think." He staggered to a chair. "But Anne was wrong too. He can't come back to Dingjum. Won't have it, you know. That randy bugger will have to find himself another country. Let him settle down in the Netherlands somewhere. He'll have to remove himself completely. We can't have that here, something like that will have to go. And the money I paid him for his professional services. Gyske, I want that money back."

"To the Netherlands?" the commissaris asked. "Isn't Friesland part of the country?"

"No," Lieutenant Sudema said. "He can go to Amsterdam for all I care. Anywhere in the hell below the dike. Not here. The smudge has to be rubbed off."

"And the other cheek?" Gyske asked. "Shouldn't we turn the other cheek? Aren't you Christian, Sjurd?"

"You've got two cheeks," Sjurd said, "but only one . . ." He stopped and thought, and concluded, "Only one." He thought again. "But what I was saying about you"—he had trouble not sliding off his chair—"that isn't true, Gyske. I've been truly stupid. You're right. I'm sorry. It'll be different from now on."

He managed to get up and steered an unsteady course for the cupboard. He clawed the handle. He skated back and pulled the cupboard door open. "Here is where it all happened, here on the shelf, in the name of the Lord. An insult to Our Lord, Gyske, by an authority of the church." He kicked the shelf, tore out the broken boards, and cracked them on his knee. "I will burn these outside. I'll take the entire cupboard out, but not now, right now I'm a little tired."

"Why don't you lie down?" Gyske asked.

"In a minute," Lieutenant Sudema said. "But the gentlemen should come along with me for a moment. I have a present for the gentlemen."

Six crates of tomatoes had been placed outside the greenhouse. "My occupation outside of work hours," Lieutenant Sudema said sadly. "More work. To sweat to please the Lord. I was wrong there too. They all got ripe at the same time. You do like tomatoes, I hope?"

"Delicious," the commissaris said.

"I'll fetch the car," Grijpstra said.

Gyske got hold of her husband. "You have to rest now, Sjurd." She pushed him into the house and came back alone, mumbling to herself. She passed the commissaris. "You're leaving us?" the commissaris asked.

"I think I'll visit Mem Scherjoen for a moment."

"A good idea," the commissaris said. "In times of stress, one needs a friend."

"Mem understands," Gyske said. She turned. "Mem's pain is all done now. But Sjurd can stay alive, I would like that better."

"Mem prefers Douwe dead?"

"Mem understands, that means she can accept. Do you have a cigarette?"

"Only small cigars."

Gyske took the cigar. The commissaris flicked a light. Gyske inhaled hungrily. "Mem even accepted the dead kittens. She used to have a limping cat that showed up one night. Douwe didn't want her to feed the cat, but Mem did it anyway, behind the barn. When Douwe was away, Mem would talk to the cat. The cat had kittens, funny babies, that frolicked and gamboled all over the yard, but then they all began to die one afternoon. They didn't know they were dying, they still tried to play. Douwe had poisoned their milk, of course. He had to laugh, because Mem didn't know what was wrong with the kittens. Mem was going crazy."

"There's a turtle," the commissaris said, "that lives in my rear garden. He's my good friend, I like to share his silence. If someone hurt my turtle, I would probably be quite upset."

"I wanted revenge," Gyske said, "because Sjurd believes in good, and that's too boring. He would say that I should put my bottom in a bucket of cold water, that would soothe the urge, so I made a grab for Anne. That bald little Anne, with his few hairs plastered over his skull, and his wrinkled neck, and his spectacles without rims, only because he happened to be around, with his three-piece suit and with his watch chain across his stupid belly and with his arrogant accent. I took revenge. I committed a sin. Mem doesn't sin."

"I see," the commissaris said. "I wish you strength. Your husband seems rather an excellent fellow."

"I'm madly in love with Sjurd," Gyske said, "but I can't go on like this. It'll have to change. There's your car backing up, I'll help you lifting in the crates."

"Enough of this," the commissaris said in the Volkswagen. "Take me to Municipal Police headquarters in Leeuwarden, Adjutant. Select the shortest route. We've wasted time."

"You think this is the right way?" Grijpstra asked.

"What are you mumbling, sir?" Grijpstra asked a few minutes later.

"I'm sinful," the commissaris said. "It's rather weak to manipulate a lady who's having a mental breakdown. Indeed! And did I learn anything?" He banged his fist on the dashboard. "Nothing, Adjutant. But what do you expect? What can anyone expect from someone like me? Bald, small, with one and a half hairs on my naked skull, with spectacles without rims, a suit complete with waistcoat. Pathetic, Adjutant, a clown from long ago, expressing his ignorance in old-fashioned language, rattling a watch chain on his belly."

Grijpstra glanced at the commissaris. "Your neck is not too wrinkled. On the contrary, it's still quite smooth."

Looking ahead again, he read a sign aloud: "Tzum."

The commissaris pondered. "That Gyske," he murmured. "She wasn't too fond of Douwe Scherjoen."

"Tzummarum," Grijpstra said, reading another sign. "*Marum* means 'sea.' The Romans must have been here."

"We're lost again," the commissaris said. "We shouldn't be close to the sea. The Romans came to collect taxes too. Another bunch of foreigners injecting their evil into my pure soul. Leeuwarden is more inland. Better turn the car, but be careful, this dike is rather narrow."

||||| 9 /////

"I WON'T HAVE IT," MRS. CARDOZO SAID. "YOU'RE NOT TO clean your pistol on my kitchen table. The oil gets into the wood. That's expensive oak, I'll have you know, I polish the top daily."

"Please, Mother," Cardozo said. "Don't bother me now. You've no idea how tricky...look, see what you made me do? You know what I'm doing? I make the light reflect from my thumbnail, like this, and then I look through the barrel. I'm seeing spirals now, gleaming in blue steel. I can see that when the barrel is clean. When it isn't, I see some nasty grit."

"It'll go off. Stop that, Simon. There shouldn't be instruments of murder in the house."

"I've got it out," Cardozo said. "A detached barrel can't possibly fire. You're living in unreasonable fear. Like with the lamp the other day. I had pulled the cord out of the wall and you wouldn't let me fix it."

"Because there might still have been electricity in that lamp."

"Oh, Mother."

"And who lives under stress here?" Mrs. Cardozo said. "Do you ever hear me complain? Would you ever hear me complain if you stopped complaining yourself for a minute? Your whining wears me down. Chuck your job if you don't like it. You can help your Uncle Ezra in the market, he earns more in a day than you do in a month. Uncle Ezra has no kids, you can take over his stall when he retires to Mallorca. He wants you to have his business, you only have to learn for a year. Ezra said that to me the other day. 'Manya,' he said, 'your Simon isn't serious yet. He can pick up some seriousness from me, why don't you tell that to your Simon?'"

"Oh, Mother."

"And then maybe you can learn how to dress," Mrs. Cardozo said. "And have a haircut for a change. Do you have to show yourself as a ragamuffin?"

Cardozo reassembled his pistol and slipped it into its holster. He buttoned up his rumpled jacket. "Mother, I fight evil. I don't like the way Uncle Ezra evades taxes."

"Your Uncle Ezra is a serious man."

"He's a silly man," Cardozo said. "He refuses to develop. He's a capitalist during the day and a hedonist in his free time. Greed and luxury will get him nowhere."

"Oh, Simon."

"Egocentric," Cardozo said. "*I* work for others. So that others may have a chance to develop and grow too. It isn't easy and I may occasionally be heard to complain. That's a weak trait in my character, and I'm sorry."

Cardozo dialed the telephone. "Not outside the city," Mrs. Cardozo said. "Your father doesn't like that. The bill is too high already."

"Sergeant?" Cardozo said. "It's me."

"You were dialing too long," Mrs. Cardozo said. "You're outside the city. Keep it short, Simon, or your father will be at me again."

"Do you have Douwe Scherjoen's photo?" Cardozo asked.

"Ask Grijpstra," de Gier said. "The commissaris went off with Grijpstra, but something must have gone wrong. They're presently being saved by the State Police, between Tzum and Tzummarum."

"Is that close to Dingjum?"

"It's in Friesland," de Gier said. "I'm not Frisian. I'm not in on this. I cook pea soup from a can and take care of a rat—and of a Frisian lady who'll be fetching me in a moment."

"I've got to have that photo," Cardozo said, "if I am to do my work. Shall I come and get it myself?"

"How?" de Gier asked. "Grijpstra has the car. The commissaris has lost his car, in a well between gardens. You can't declare expenses because you'd be moving outside your area."

"A train ticket will cost some money," Cardozo said.

"You're an idealist, aren't you?"

"Aren't you one too?"

"A nihilist," de Gier said. "Nihilists don't give a shit about anything—at that depth one has to be advanced. You aren't anywhere near there yet. Look here, why don't you cycle to Friesland tomorrow? I've just watched the news, the weather should be fine. It's only forty miles or so. Make it a holiday, watch the birds from the dike. Ever seen a cormorant land? They splash down and flop up. A great sight."

"You're really not in on this?" Cardozo asked.

"No," de Gier said. He replaced the phone. The sergeant wandered past the flowery wallpaper, the imitation Gothic dining room table, the copy of a Louis XVI recliner, and then past a clothes chest modeled on an antique Eastern Dutch design. The novel by the Frisian woman author was on the table. On a shelf, Chinese knickknacks had been arranged: porcelain rice bowls, plastic soup spoons, stacked together. On another shelf, a foot-long model of a Chinese junk sailed toward a smiling fat god, with happily grinning toddlers climbing up his belly and shoulders. De Gier remembered the calendar in the neatly painted bathroom, with a dozen color photographs of places to see in Singapore.

A holiday in Singapore? Why not? An elderly adjutant of the Leeuwarden Municipal Police who, once in his life, takes his wife to the other side of the earth. Probably a special offer by the local travel agency, there and back for a couple of thousand, hotel included. By now the mortgage would be paid, the children married. "Dear, we'll be off!"

"Where to?" Mrs. Oppenhuyzen asks, not too sure whether she should be pleased.

The adjutant's eyes twinkle. "To Singapore!"

She would rather have spent another holiday on one of the islands just off the Frisian coast, but if he really wants to surprise her, okay. She smiles. "Great!"

A subject that can be discussed on many an occasion, during birthday parties or while visiting neighbors. "You went to the Italian coast? That's nice. Yes, we were out of the country too. Where? Oh, we hopped over to Singapore." Detailed descriptions of assorted adventures. "You know, when we were in Singapore last month..."

"When I was in Friesland..." De Gier picked up the novel and flopped down on the couch. Then he was up again to look for the dictionary. She brushed her *tosks*? Is that what they call teeth? And *mûle* would be 'mouth.' What a primitive way to describe a woman's intimate bathroom occupation. He tried to lose the image of a ghoulish shape poking between her fangs. It would be better to read on, and try to fit what he would later understand into the material he was now digesting. He plodded on, guessing, gleaning meaning from words that looked like Dutch or English or German, and gradually obtained glimpses of the heroine's insights and beliefs, her hatred of men and her attraction to those very same men; some of them seemed handsome to her, and she minded them less than others, but she still abhorred their presence until one of them, a laborer working with a dragline, picked her up, first with his machine, by accident, then in his arms on purpose. Close to his chest, she gave in, but he didn't notice her orgasm, he was only carrying her to a safe place.

Tragic, de Gier thought, and read on, slipping more easily into the next tale. Martha was married now, for some twenty years, to the same fathead, every new day another gray space. Fathead wanted nothing of her, right through the twenty years. Martha could do anything she liked, there was plenty of money, as long as Fathead didn't have to join in whatever activity she chose for herself. So now what does she do? She goes to Belgium, where firearms can be bought fairly easily, comes back with a pistol, blows a hole in Fathead, and devours him slowly.

De Gier frowned. He remembered struggling with the same tale earlier that day, when the words were still unclear. Now he grasped all the horror without having to grope for dubious meaning. The lady ate her murdered spouse because she didn't know what to do with the one hundred and seventy-five pounds he had left. Frisian women are practical; for ages they have lived off the land. They haven't forgotten tricks picked up in the past. Martha had bought just the right size freezer to fit Fathead's bulk. And she boiled him in her pressure cooker, in cuts of *twae pûn*—two pounds, of course—enough to serve breakfast, lunch, or dinner. *Fathead weighed heavy in her stomach.* The last sentence of the tale.

De Gier ruminated. Mem Scherjoen? Gyske Sudema? Two intimate friends, two Frisian ladies, tough, practical, and frustrated. On the phone, Grijpstra had been explaining the suspects' presence just now, not so much as a detective informing his colleague of developments in his quest, but rather in his role of complaining friend—how everything, once again, had turned for the worst and how he could in no way be blamed for any mishaps. First, he'd lost his way; second, he'd got stuck in marital problems; third, he'd slipped off a dike. Grijpstra, through no fault of his own, caught in a web spun by fateful circumstances. Does nothing ever go right?

Think a little, de Gier thought, catch the hidden thread. And make use of helpful hints supplied by literature manufactured in this very country, showing images in a foreign language that, with a little trouble can be grasped. Literature exaggerates. Mem never ate Douwe. Reality exaggerates too, but with less use of symbolism.

De Gier, barely awake on the couch, surrendered to hellish scenes. He saw local witches, degenerated from abuse and neglect, feeding ferocious flames of revenge emerging from the darkness of each other's souls. Their fury takes on different forms: one changes her home into a trap and lures a hapless male into her cupboard, where she humiliates her prey on a shelf; the other ventures out into the damnation of the Amsterdam night, and Douwe crumbles and floats away in a burning dory.

Both scenes were equally terrifying. De Gier preferred to wake up, to drag his body off the soft couch to a hard chair at the table, where he returned to the study of literature. What conclusions could the female author offer? A sentence stuck out. *The male can never be a true source of pleasure*.

Well now, that would hardly be a good reason to dust off an antique German pistol left over from the war. Just because there was no pleasure in the beast? He read on. A dialogue emerged between two women—between Mem and Gyske?

Gyske: "Tell me, why did you get married?"

Mem: "It was just a vague hopeful feeling."

Vague. Too vague. So Mem had married because she thought there was some slight hope in Douwe's company. Hope for the better, of course. And the opposite came up. Even the Amsterdam dentist had seen the devil in Douwe. How devilish had the poor bugger been? Had Douwe, evilly and by premeditation, sucked Mem of her strength? Had he bedeviled her daily? Had she slowly begun to believe in a possible revolt? Had she used the courage that had served her so well in her struggle with the German army? Was her motivation clear now? Had opportunity been available? Mem knew Amsterdam, where she often stayed with her sister.

How would Grijpstra plan his attack? By himself, he wouldn't have a chance, of course, but the commissaris was sly, subtle, a more dangerous sleuth than even the sergeant himself. Once the commissaris got hold of this case...

De Gier turned pages, eager to discover another phrase that might fill a gap. What else was the literary woman thinking? *In no way will I ever be satisfied . . . here I am, left to my own resources . . . how boring . . . I could climb the walls . . . alone . . .*

Clear enough. Mem, unsatisfied, hollow in her soul, locked in a solitude created by her willful and often absent husband, was ready to jump through her restraining walls. Egged on by the equally unhappy Gyske to find a solution, no matter how painful. But was Mem wrong?

Where did the finger of justice point? de Gier thought theoretically, for he himself couldn't care less. If order had been disturbed, it wasn't *his* order. He was quite content to heat pea soup from cans and bathe a rat.

He strolled through the room, circled the Louis XVI chair, and counted a row of roses on the wallpaper.

Was order disturbed? Shouldn't someone like Douwe be deftly removed? Hadn't Mem been kind enough to do society a favor? The commissaris, once on her trail, would corner her and interrogate the woman politely. Then what? Lead her on to an institute for the elderly insane? Mem wasn't quite that old.

De Gier picked up a scrap of paper left by Grijpstra on the other side of the table. He read the names of the sheep exporters who had been stripped of their profits by Douwe. He read the names of the men and their towns:

> Pry Wydema, Mummerwoods
> Tyark Tamminga, Blya
> Yelte Pryk, Acklum

Weird names—he wondered if there was a proper pronunciation. So far the names meant little. What if the unused Mauser had been used after all, and later cleaned and reloaded, slipped back into the door pocket of Douwe's Citroën? Too much effort in too little time? The shot might have attracted attention. The caliber was wrong too. A nine-millimeter bullet might have smashed Douwe's skull. Could Mem, like the freedom fighter in the book, have risked a trip to Belgium to buy a more suitable weapon that would make less noise?

He could leave it at that for now. Since when had minding someone else's job been profitable to him?

The doorbell rang. The sergeant, deep in thought, opened the door. "Yes? Good evening, miss."

"Hi," Miss said brightly.

"Hi," de Gier said. He checked his watch. Eleven, a little late for a visit. "Miss," the sergeant said, "Adjutant and Mrs. Oppenhuyzen are on holiday in their summer house in Engwierum, at the coast I believe. I'm looking after the house in their absence. De Gier is my name."

"Hi."

De Gier scratched his buttocks, first the left, then the right. "You don't understand? You speak only Frisian?" He paused. "I can read some now, but I don't speak it yet. Can you read Dutch? Shall I write it down for you? Wait, I'll speak slowly. Listen, miss. The adjutant, right? Adjutant Oppenhuyzen? With his, uh, *wyfe*? Gone away?" He waved widely.

"It's me," the young woman said. "Hylkje. Hylkje Hilarius? Corporal? Motorcycle brigade? Now dressed in civilian clothes? Come to fetch you for a beer? You're still following so far?"

"Right," de Gier said gratefully. "Skinned. Stripped out of your leather. You're even more attractive than I had dared hope. How delightful life can be if, for once, disappointment is taken away for a moment. Do come in."

"Five minutes," Hylkje said. She curled up in the Louis XVI chair, her long denim-clad legs twined loosely, her breasts tightly outlined in a velvet T-shirt, her perfect teeth displayed in a warm smile between stiff blond ponytails, innocently standing away from her cheekbones daubed with rouge, her sparkling blue eyes shadowed cleverly to maximum provocative effect.

"Where is that rat?" Hylkje asked.

De Gier ran upstairs and came back with Eddy. "You can hold on to him. I'll fetch his cheese."

Hylkje withdrew into the embrace of the chair, but Eddy stood against her shirt, his pointed pink nose trembling between her breasts.

"Bah," Hylkje squeaked.

"Harmless little chap," de Gier said. "Smells nice too. Just washed him with lemon-scented dishwash detergent. Here, Eddy, have some cheese."

Hylkje held the morsel between her fingertips. Eddy snatched at it with darting little paws. His yellow teeth sank into the cheese.

"Now who would ever keep a rat?" Hylkje asked. "I've got a rabbit. Durk looks better, and feels nice and fluffy. Makes me itch a little at times, but otherwise he's the sweetest thing."

"I've got a cat," de Grier said.

Hylkje grabbed hold of Eddy and gave him back. De Gier took the rat upstairs. He came back in two bounds. Hylkje observed the sergeant's movements with approval. "You wanted to upset me, right? Thought I would scream the ceiling down? Frighten the little woman? Missed out again?"

"Men are weaker," de Gier said. "I've known it for some time. I keep trying, but women always floor me. Doesn't take them long either. Now that I know it doesn't make me feel so bad."

"What else do you have except a cat? A wyf? Bern?"

"Don't know all the words yet," de Gier said. "Haven't met any bern yet in the local literature. Some Frisian animal that hasn't yet crossed the dike?"

"Frisian children."

"Never had any," de Gier said, "of any source. I would really rather have nothing at all, but that's hard to get. There are the necessities. Got to live somewhere, and once you have an apartment, there's furniture that flies in, and plants on the balcony, and the cat sneaking about. There are always the complications. I've got neighbors, too, to look after the cat when I'm away."

"You never have visitors?"

"Grijpstra drops in. Not too often. Too bulky. The apartment is small."

"The adjutant is your friend?" Hylkje stared at the sergeant's chest.

"Yes." De Gier analyzed Hylkje's steady gaze. "Oh, you mean it that way? No, no, are you crazy?"

Hylkje jumped off the low seat and walked around de Gier. "You sure, now? I hate to start off wrong. Last week I was shopping in the Gardens here, and there was this man, as handsome as you are, dressed well too, the very same type, a most attractive male. I smiled a bit and he didn't even see me, and then there were suddenly two of them. The other had been looking at a window display."

"There's only one of me."

"Not an uncommon variety," Hylkje said. "They pop up on the screen and on magazine covers. Wide shoulders and full mustaches. Strong bones covered with firm flesh."

"I'm a normal male," de Gier said, "at your service."

"It'd be easier if you were married," Hylkje said. "You came up the dike, you're around for a few days, and then you're gone again, forever. No problems, if you can see what I mean. Durk and I have a good life, but a change . . . at times . . . variety . . . a dream . . ."

"Aren't you going a little far?" de Gier asked. "I'm sorry I was silly enough to try and frighten you with Eddy. You've evened things out now, don't overdo it. I'm normal. I adore and cherish women."

"Unattached males are often hard to handle," Hylkje said. "They make for heavy going. If they're married, there's something to pull them back and I'll be rid of them again."

"Who's being hard to handle here?" de Gier asked. "Did I throw myself at you? I thought we were going out for a beer?"

"Asshole," Hylkje said, smiling politely.

De Gier grinned. He gave her his arm. They walked to the door together. He pulled his arm back and opened the door.

"Are you usually so well mannered?" Hylkje asked. "Or is this an act for the occasion?"

"No," de Gier said. "I was taught to be civil, by my mother. If I wasn't, I was hit. Conditioned behavior. Pavlov's dog. Ring the bell and the animal slavers."

"Is your mother still alive?"

"I take flowers to her grave," de Gier said, "every other Sunday. We hated each other, when we didn't share some love. I have her engagement photo above my bed. My father is in it too. He wears a bowler hat."

Hylkje's car was a Deux Chevaux, high on its wheels and colored bright orange. She maneuvered it cleverly through winding alleys. A passing church tower pointed the hands of its clock straight up. "Isn't it getting late?" de Gier asked. "Surely provincial pubs close early?"

"Our beer house goes on until one, and later, for the likes of us."

"The police?"

"And the other powers," Hylkje said, "as you will see."

"And the ordinary folks? Common pleasure is cut off by midnight?"

Hylkje pointed at a square house straddling two canals. "A sex club, open until four. Soft drugs are sold downstairs, and hard drugs in the loft."

"With police protection?"

"The Municipal Police ignore the house somewhat. It's known as 'channeling the tension.' When they close everything down, they don't know where it goes. It's also a hangout for colonial types and citizens from the province next door. The foreign element, their private niche."

The little car reached a square surrounded by impressive buildings. Hylkje defined their plastered gables. "Provincial Government, the mayor's office, the Queen's representation.

All the powers that lead us, and the pub in between, for when the pressure depresses."

De Gier stopped to look at the stately stone shapes. High windows stared back, arrogantly sedate. Flowing walls ended in slowly rising gable tops holding up a golden lion stepping out of a sky-blue plaster frame. Downstairs, wide pavements led, step by slow step, to very large doors painted in lush greens offset by copper ornaments. From the square rose huge trees with overhanging branches, rustling their loads of leaves.

"Nice and quiet," de Gier asked. "The law lives here?"

"We don't care for being told what to do," Hylkje said. "We have better ideas ourselves; the law knows that and hardly interferes. The result is peace, not the clamor you're used to in the nether parts."

"Do you ever visit the other end of the dike?"

"I've been there. I was a cop in Amsterdam for a year. Some police like to swagger down there, and it invites reaction. Some motorcyclists rode me down one night. Hurt my leg, couldn't wear a dress for years. Scar tissue—the cylinder of my own bike burned my shin. They pushed me over from the side and were off again."

"Revenge burns in your gentle soul?"

"A little less every day. A beer, Sergeant?"

The pub spread out under low, heavy beams. Hylkje was greeted by an aged bartender, hopping about spryly behind the weathered shelves and counters in the back. The glasses were foaming already, waiting to be beheaded by the wooden skimmer in the old man's bony hand.

"Working for the same boss?" the bartender asked, pointing his scraggly beard and gleaming sharp nose at de Gier.

"He's ours," Hylkje said. "But from down below. Maybe you can trust him, Doris."

"Rinus," de Gier said. "All yours, forever after."

"Don't stay long," Doris cackled. "Keep the bad elements down on your end. We've got it good here, and it may still last for a while." The wrinkles around his eyes folded in and out. The dark beady eyes glinted. "Meanwhile, enjoy what we can offer. Have her and strong beer."

"He's here to work," Hylkje said.

"I can recommend her," Doris said loudly.

"That's enough," Hylkje said, "or we'll go to another pub."

"Still have your cold?" Doris asked.

"It's my voice," Hylkje said. "If you weren't so decrepit and a little more male, you might find the low pitch exciting. Do your job, Doris, there are customers waiting."

Doris was off, carrying a tray, shouting insults at clients in the rear. "I quite like your voice," de Gier said.

"You too? It isn't nice to criticize the voice of your hostess. People used to say I lowed."

"Like a cow."

"A what?"

"Don't keep taking what I say the wrong way," de Gier said. "Here in Friesland, the sound is romantic. Yesterday, in Dingjum, I heard how lovely the sound can be. We landed in a meadow, and once the chopper was gone, the silence was audible and the cow chanted through it, softly. She sang, the way you do when you talk."

"A cow," Hylkje said, "swinging her udders. I don't do that. A cow chews, burps, and chews again—I don't do that either. A cow digests everything five times. A cow is gross. A cow has diarrhea."

"I didn't get a good look at her," de Gier said. "She was behind us and we had to go ahead, but she was, of course, a small good-tempered beast, on slender legs, with a dainty body and tender eyes."

"You should watch your approach," Hylkje said. "You won't get far with me this way."

De Gier asked for more beer.

"Closing time," Doris shouted. "Away with you. I don't care for your company. Out. Maybe I'll fill you up tomorrow again. There's the door. Go on. The police are due any second now."

He passed Hylkje and de Gier their beers. "You're doing okay, son. Keep pushing now, you hear? Or are you planning to be around for a while and hoping for something better?"

The police entered, but there was only one of them. He moved next to Hylkje. "Meet my friend," Hylkje said. "This is Officer First-Class Eldor Janssen. Sergeant de Gier. Colleagues and subjects of the same queen."

Customers squeezed out through the door, harassed by Doris's shouts and waving fists. The constable had finished his coffee and moved along. Here and there a customer still slumped behind a table. Doris closed the curtains. "Right, now what will it be?" He filled the slurred orders. The door opened. "All closed up," Doris shouted. "Out, or I'll call the cops."

The trespassing customer aimed for the bar. "So open up again. I work for the boss. Hi, Hylkje." Lieutenant Sudema covered one eye with an unsteady hand. "Hi, you too."

De Gier straightened. "Evening, sir."

Doris locked the door and supported the lieutenant simultaneously, for Sudema was losing ground. "Whoa!" Then he was back on his feet, flapping both hands. Doris withdrew behind the counter. The lieutenant slipped again, swinging his arms in desperation. Hylkje pushed, de Gier pulled, and the lieutenant found a stool.

"Now what?" Hylkje asked. "Got yourself sozzled?"

"Completely and helplessly intoxicated," the lieutenant said. "Been everywhere already. Mixed the local brew with all available imports. I'm still not quite where I'd like to be. Does anyone know why?" He held on to the bartop while Doris poured beer. Lieutenant Sudema raised his glass. "Your very good health. Nobody knows why? Because tomorrow I have to take my kitchen cupboard down. My wife fucks in there. Not with me, you know. I sleep in my father's antique bed." The lieutenant closed both eyes and drank to his father's image, mumbling devoutly. "There you go, old boy. Thanks indeed. I don't want this life at all. A lot of hard work and I'm busy already. Insufficient staff and a station deluged with complaints and charges. Tons of tomatoes in the greenhouse. Will it ever end? When I destroy that cupboard, the wall will fall out of the house. I'll have to place posts." He opened an eye and tried to wipe the foam off his mouth. "One more." He looked about in triumph. "For everyone."

Doris filled glasses and delivered. The officials shouted toasts.

"Why does your wife copulate in a cupboard?" Hylkje asked.

"So that she may debauch herself in secret." One of the lieutenant's eyes focused on de Gier, the other wandered. "You have a wife?"

"No," de Gier said.

"Help yourself to Hylkje," Lieutenant Sudema said. "She's all yours." He lurched toward Hylkje, kept back by de Gier's suddenly extended arm. "You like cupboards too?"

"I don't mind where I do it," Hylkje said.

"Didn't even know it could be done," Lieutenant Sudema said. "Stupid, eh?" He nodded upward while he sucked more foam. "Couldn't you tell me, Sir? Why don't You ever fill in gaps?"

"He guides us into suffering," Doris said softly.

"Doris," Hylkje said softly.

"Doesn't He?" Doris unfolded both his beady eyes. "And don't only drunks know what He is up to?" He snarled. "Enough of this, I'll sweep you out." The broom swishing in Doris's hands drove protesting customers to the door.

"I'll do some fancy driving now," Lieutenant Sudema said cheerfully. "To the neighbor lady. She has a cupboard too."

"He can't drive," Hylkje said to de Gier.

"Amazing," de Gier said. "Yesterday I was at his house. I thought he was everything that I should have been. My mother's dream for my future that kept missing me. An upstanding gentleman, sane in body and mind, completed by just the right sort of spouse. When I saw them together

I was almost ready to change my ideas. And now look at this."

The lieutenant had fallen off his stool and knelt toward the counter. He talked. Doris hung over the bartop. "A devout social worker qualified in psychiatry?" Doris asked.

"In the cupboard," Lieutenant Sudema said. "They shared their togetherness in there, and their joy, and inner longings."

"On a shelf?" Doris asked.

"I'm not going to drive all the way to Dingjum now," Hylkje said. "I'm working early tomorrow."

"Dump him in a motel."

"In his condition? They'll never accept him," Hylkje decided. She knelt next to the lieutenant. "Darling?"

"Beloved?" Lieutenant Sudema asked.

"Doris is closing up. Are you coming with me?"

The lieutenant sneered. "You stock no liquor."

"But I do, I do. A choice. Anything you care to name."

"I'm going all the way, do you have communist vodka?"

"With the label that falls off?"

"That and no other."

"I have it," Hylkje said. "The worst kind. All yours."

"The foulest," Lieutenant Sudema said. "The wickedest. The shortest path to hell. You sure you have that now?"

"A cupboardful," Hylkje said, narrowing her eyes.

"But that's where they did it." The lieutenant began to cry.

"No, not in a cupboard, on a shelf under my sink. Come along, my dearest."

De Gier pulled the lieutenant up. "You don't have to join us," Lieutenant Sudema said.

"Never. I'm just taking you there. I'll say good-bye at the door. She loves you. I swear."

"He'll rape you," de Gier whispered into Hylkje's ear.

"Promise?" Hylkje asked.

"I don't really mind you," Lieutenant Sudema said to de Gier. "I'll make sure you get more tomatoes. Come fetch them tomorrow." He grabbed hold of de Gier's arm. "And then you should plan a trip to the island of Ameland. Just the place for you. Speak to the Military Police and ask for my nephew. Same name. Hey-ho!" He didn't have to find his legs again, for de Gier's hold was firm.

"Nephew?" de Gier asked.

"Private Sudema. The copper deal. The AWOL fellow. Hey-ho!"

Lieutenant Sudema was lowered into the back seat of Hylkje's car.

"In exchange for sole," the lieutenant said. "Don't forget now. Bring the sole back. The Water Police or whoever is around, no need for the ferry. You got all that now?"

Halfway up the stairs to Hylkje's apartment, the lieutenant fell asleep. When he woke up on her bed, he wasn't feeling too well. He wondered if there might be a bucket around. De Gier greeted a passing rabbit. He picked it up. "Don't," Hylkje said. "That rabbit is loaded."

Small hard pellets ricocheted off the floor and twanged against the lieutenant's bucket. "Messy," de Gier said, "both of them. Yach!" He swept up the pellets while Hylkje mopped the floor.

"Never shake Durk," Hylkje said. "He manufactures them so fast, and his tube is always full. If you touch him they'll shake free."

Lieutenant Sudema sat on the bed. "Coming, darling?" He dropped backward and stretched, rumbling into a snore. "You undress him," Hylkje said. "I don't know about suspenders and such."

De Gier tucked the stripped lieutenant in.

"I'll take the couch," Hylkje said. "Consider yourself thanked."

"Am I welcome some other time?" de Gier asked, putting the broom away in the cupboard where Hylkje arranged her mop. Hylkje pushed him away.

"No kiss?"

"Whatever for?" Hylkje asked. "Why did I get into this mess? Let's try again, call me tomorrow."

≣≣≣ 10 ⁄⁄⁄⁄

"ARE YOU GIVING IT TO ME OR NOT?" CARDOZO ASKED.

"Never," his brother said. "Buy your own bicycle. Everybody has a bicycle except our Symie. So what does Symie have? A bound edition of the collected adventures of Tintin, the child detective. Sell that bundled nonsense and take the train tomorrow. At the comic-book store they'll give you the price of the ticket."

"Mother?" Cardozo asked.

"Samuel!" Mrs. Cardozo said loudly.

"He wrecked my boat, complete with outboard," Samuel said, "also to restore public order, and now the bicycle will go, to be demolished on the dike. Never. Not again."

"If we all only think of ourselves . . ." Mrs. Cardozo said.

"He only thinks of himself," Cardozo said. He walked along the rampart of the Old Fortress, in the direction of the Inner Harbor. A detective is irrevocably attracted to where the crime was accomplished. Now where would that be, exactly? Scherjoen could have been shot through the head in any location, and dragged afterward to the slow-moving water of the Inner Harbor. Had there been a mere unfortunate coincidence of negative powers resulting in impromptu manslaughter? Or had the intention been there all the time and had the guilty party simply waited for an opportune moment? Cardozo stopped, weighing and comparing definitions, under the Montelbaen Tower, which pointed at low clouds with its elegant peak, between tall, slender mansions that, leaning forward in an interested manner, observed the contemplator. Murder, to a detective working on Amsterdam's most serious crimes, might be the ideal solution, but the verdict hardly mattered at this time. Who had been manipulated by self-willed fate? This was the way it went: Scherjoen was forever grabbing the competition's loot, and his victims had decided to minimize future adversity. When and where had they acted? At a time and place that suited them best. Armed, they had lurked on Scherjoen's path.

Now here we have Scherjoen, weakened by alcohol and unsteadily pointed in the direction of his Citroën, parked halfway on the pavement. The avengers touch elbows. It's late, the street is theirs. A shot rings out on the deserted quayside. Scherjoen stumbles and falls. Is that it? No, Douwe has to be done away with altogether. No corpse, no pursuit. Whatever disappears completely has never been. Who will miss Douwe? Only Douwe's wife, but Mem had no idea where Douwe could have gone. Where, then, would Douwe's body be looked for? And when? The later the better.

Clever rural types from the far north. What are they doing now? They leer innocently from under their flat caps. They pick up Scherjoen from two sides and walk on. Three rural types from a distant province, the one in the middle heavily under the weather.

Where is a body best disposed of in Amsterdam? In the water. The harbor's current will most likely push it out to sea. But wait, there's a dory over there. A much better plan indeed. Gasoline is poured on the remains, and a match is scratched to life.

But where, Cardozo thought, did the gasoline come from? A gun fits into a pocket, but the pedestrian cannot easily lug a gasoline can. Did they have one ready in a car? Did the empty can then go back into the vehicle?

Cardozo looked at the smooth movement of the Inner Harbor's surface. The swell broke up in whitecapped waves. He walked along the water's edge, found an old broomstick, and moved it slowly through floating debris.

"Got him!"

The detective, jumped from both sides, waved helplessly with his stick.

"In the name of the law," two rough voices growled. "What's this here? You're behaving in a suspicious manner. What are you digging in the filth for?"

"Hi, Karate. Hi, Ketchup."

"The Frisian corpse?" The uniformed officers helped in the search, Karate with a branch, Ketchup with a broken fishing rod found on the spot.

"Can I guess?" Karate asked. "You've got the corpse. A gun doesn't float. A gas can, maybe?"

"I know the report on the Frisian corpse by heart," Ketchup said. "I read everything that's around. Nothing else to do anyway. We can't bring in muggers for a while, all the cells are filled, in the city and all municipalities of this province. At the station we read, and out here we pass the time."

"Like now," Karate said

"No can in sight," Ketchup said. "Here, a piece of mattress. Here, a cleaning product jar."

"You really do not work now?" Cardozo asked.

"There are always the Chinese," Karate said brightly.

"You've got cells for them, then?"

"There's the large cage at Headquarters," Ketchup said. "Every time it fills up, the Military Police fly a load to the Far East. Chinese without proper papers, we can catch some if we insist, provided we take them straight to the cage and don't bother our own station."

"It's fun," Karate said, "because they keep coming back so that our work may never end. Our sergeant likes us to keep active. Take Ping Hop, I've had him three times already. I even remember his face. 'Hi, Ping,' I say. Does that fellow put in a lot of flying hours! There..."

"... and back," sang Ketchup.

"How about a break?" Karate said. "Dinnertime. We can have it close by. Fried noodles and shrimp?"

Wo Hop was about to close, but because the police came in and inquired about the present address of his nephew Ping Hop, he would be still open for a short while. "No know," Wo Hop said kindly.

"This Wo Hop has papers?" Cardozo asked.

"He has a restaurant," Karate said. "Good grub and reasonable prices. We do have to eat."

"Papers?" Cardozo asked.

"Papers, who cares?" Karate and Ketchup were reading the menu.

A gent came in, with a red round face above a well-worn but clean tweed suit. "Evening," the gent said.

"Adjutant," Karate and Ketchup said.

"He's learning the language," said Karate. "Doing pretty well. You can hardly hear his Frisian accent."

"What," Cardozo asked, "would a Frisian police officer be doing in our city?"

"Adjutant Oppenhuyzen, Alien Department, trying to block the route to the north," Karate said. "He doesn't want them there, he wants to keep them here."

"You tolerate Frisian interference?"

Wo Hop brought bowls heaped with fried noodles, and a glass of cognac for Cardozo. Cardozo refused. "On the house," Wo Hop said.

"We tolerate just about anything," Karate said. "We can't be helpful to the illegal Chinese, for if we are, the newspapers will accuse us of taking bribes. We still assume that some of the Chinese visitors are okay people. Not too clever, maybe, for they don't understand Dutch red tape. It would be nice if someone could help them fill in their forms. If the Frisian adjutant wants to help, we'll wish him well."

"And he doesn't take bribes?"

Ketchup and Karate ate.

"Hello?" asked Cardozo.

"You don't know what goes on here," Ketchup said. "When we overhunt the Chinese, they slide up the dike and hang out in Friesland. We recognize two types of suspects, from Singapore and from Hong Kong. They also hunt each other. Let's call it sport. They practice a little karate, some sharpshooting, stick-swinging, artistry with rope. Adjutant Oppenhuyzen is against all sport. He wants them to train here, where there's so much sport already."

"Take last year," Karate said. "Ten dead Chinese in the city. Who notices ten corpses in a town the size of Amsterdam? The reports have been filed away a long time ago."

In the back of the restaurant, nervous young Chinese men had been arguing loudly. The presence of the burly adjutant seemed to restore their ruffled tempers. "Laid back, isn't he?" Cardozo asked. "Same type as our very own Grijpstra. Would the rank of adjutant be a common denominator?"

"Hysterics, both of them," Ketchup said. "But they're older than we are, and more used to the affliction."

Wo Hop brought the bill. The cognac wasn't added in. Cardozo checked the price in the menu and put down more money. "It all starts with accepting cognac . . ."

"Right," Karate said. "He doesn't bring us any. We always refuse, but he doesn't know you yet. You could accept, of course, but the next thing will be that you're picking up parcels."

"Parcels?" Cardozo asked.

Karate related how a nameless colleague had been following a nameless Chinese. The Chinese carried a parcel. As he found it hard to carry a parcel and be followed at the same time, the nameless Chinese dropped the parcel. The nameless colleague picked it up.

Cardozo watched Adjutant Oppenhuyzen. The adjutant smoothed Chinese questions away, mostly with gestures that were received with grateful guffaws.

"Well?" Karate asked.

"Ask what was in the parcel," Ketchup said. "Go on, be a good fellow."

"Heroin," Cardozo said.

"And now you should ask," Karate said, "what happened to the parcel."

"The Chinese got it back," Cardozo said. "The nameless colleague got money. He still had some holidays due to him that he could add to his sick days, and he went to a Spanish island."

"And he's still out in the sun," Karate said. "The lucky devil. Our sergeant would never let us get away with such a harmless exchange. Narrow-minded, don't you think?"

"You don't want me to be practical now," Cardozo said, "but suppose you're shortsighted enough not to see that the nameless colleague will end up nowhere, then why should I tell you?"

"Nowhere in the sun? Served by naked maidens? Surfing between naps?"

"I went to that Spanish island," Cardozo said, "and shit for two weeks. Tainted mussels. I'm better off up here. Playing my favorite game."

"Looking for a gas can," Ketchup said. "Let's say you find it. What will it tell you? Esso or Shell? You're nowhere *here*, and in the wrong climate. The summer is half rained away. We'll never see the sun."

"Colleague?"

Cardozo looked up. Adjutant Oppenhuyzen smiled down kindly. He introduced himself and grabbed a chair. The Chinese in the back were also smiling, having rediscovered the joy of detachment. "Good boys," the adjutant said, "but they keep losing their damned papers. I help them a little with their everlasting forms. You can imagine what it's like. They have spent years in the country, making their bowl of rice by working their asses off manufacturing fried chili paste or shrimp crackers, but as they don't know the language and customs, they're always running afoul of our potato-picking authorities. Don't arrest any of them now, you hear? I can vouch for their integrity."

"That's understood, Adjutant," Karate said. "If, by mistake, I happen to get one in cuffs, it's because he looks like another."

"And in the event," Ketchup said, "that I, through sheer silliness—because I can't remember their names, let's say—happen to catch one, it'll be an error that I'll blame on myself. We'll back you up."

The adjutant wanted to know if he could buy them a glass of this or that.

"We were just on our way out," Cardozo said.

"The adjutant is absolutely right," Karate said outside, "but I have this bad habit. I just love catching drug dealers without proper papers. I think I'll catch some now. Why don't you assist us, Cardozo?"

Cardozo glanced at his watch.

"Don't leave us when we need you, Symie. We helped you look for the can. You're just what we want. You're looking more civilian than ever. If I didn't know you, and the sergeant wanted suspects again, I would run you in on a charge of vagrancy. We are hindered by our uniforms, and it's hard to get the patrol car through these alleys. Give us a hand. Won't take an hour."

"Doing what?" Cardozo asked.

"We give you a portophone from the car, and you walk about in the quarter. Slip into the narrowest passages and look a little at what you see. There are two secret societies about that tend to get on each other's nerves—Hong Kong versus Singapore, it seems. They're always on the verge of becoming violent, and when that happens, we like to be in there too. Right now they're more short-tempered than ever, because we've been kicking their members out of the country and arresting recent arrivals, so their supply lines are all mixed up. They both want all the drugs that are left. If you do notice something, breathe into the portophone and we'll be with you in half a minute."

"That's understood," Cardozo said.

What lovely ladies, Cardozo thought, shuffling about in the hushed pink light of the prostitution quarter. No Chinese

anywhere—a pity, maybe. He did see Adjutant Oppenhuyzen, who, peaceful and content, lumbered out of a red door
while the lady he'd enjoyed only a few minutes ago tore open
her curtains and arranged herself diligently on the cushions
of her wide windowsill. The adjutant winked and was about
to comment cheerfully on his recent excitement, but Cardozo
turned away. Policemen have the urge too, he was aware of
that fact, and if the adjutant happened to be in Amsterdam
and was tricked into a slight deviation from the path, between
attending to his duties, well... Not well at all, Cardozo
thought. I'm not doing it, so why should he? The hell with
the bastard.

I won't even look at them, Cardozo thought. I don't have
the money anyway. I'm also hindered by having to carry a
pistol and a portophone.

He did look a little. No! There She was, not too visible
in the rear of a cozy little room, lit from below, in a red glow
that warmed her slender shins and billowing thighs. And She
returned his stare from one inviting eye; the other was hidden
by combed-down thick hair. She wanted him. Her longing
made her tremble.

Just another show. Cardozo walked on.

When She offered herself again, She was Thai, from the
golden country far beyond his reach. The ocher-tinted skin
of the small, lithe body that writhed toward him was covered
only in one spot, by a small square orange silk attached to
a cord, moving all the time, covering nothing, really. Will
you join me, Cardozo?

And now She was dark, dancing to a rhythm that penetrated through the glass, stretching her long arms, begging
him—him, the lover named Cardozo.

An Egyptian slid past in profile, moving out of tapestry,
a temple maiden who had cut her white cotton dress so that
the priest could ceremonially possess Her. The priest's name
was Cardozo.

An icy German ordered him in, dressed in jackboots and
an army hat, the whip ready in her small but strong hand.

She accepted applications from slaves to work themselves to death in her camp, so that the last feelings of guilt might be dissolved in pain. At this moment She was interested in Simon Cardozo.

Good day to you, Cardozo thought.

Where could the Chinese be?

He found a crescent connecting two lesser alleys, where a surrealist had plied his trade. A toilet bowl, mortared into a crumbling wall, housed a sturdy and healthy goldfish. A baby doll with pointed teeth and long eyelashes, with live worms crawling out of dear little nostrils, was being smothered slowly by ivy. In a burned-out shop window a sign was displayed with a neatly lettered text. *Balthazar does not bark, but bites when provoked.*

The surrealist himself was available, a trim elderly man in an impeccable three-piece suit, who addressed the passersby. "Please, dear people, can you tell me where the Bardo Tödol is? I've been silly enough to lose my way. I'm dead, you see. Should I turn right or left here? Could you direct me, if you please?"

"Any Chinese around here?" Cardozo asked.

"Oh yes," the surrealist said. "Next alley. A barber's salon, go right at the fork, can't miss."

The indicated passage was overgrown with smelly weeds rustling with vermin. A sign in Chinese dangled from a rusty bar. Under the sign a rotten door was hung in a partly broken frame. The cracked window in the door was covered by a dirty cloth. Rough voices shouted inside. The cloth was torn and Cardozo could peek.

The portophone jumped into his clawing fingers. "Karate? Ketchup?"

That there was no immediate answer could only mean that the colleagues had been properly trained. They heard him but didn't acknowledge so that their suddenly ringing voices would not disturb the already delicate situation. Cardozo whispered his position and became active at once. Kicking in the door and jumping ahead, he found himself in

a low whitewashed room. Cardozo's pistol pointed at four
Chinese in turn. Two sat, two stood. The Chinese tied down
in barber's chairs couldn't turn around, but the two who
were standing did, following Cardozo's crisp order. They
clasped their hands to their necks when he barked at them
again.

"Hello?" Cardozo said. "Ketchup? Karate? Come quickly.
I've got them."

The portophone crackled emptily.

One of the sitting Chinese was Wo Hop. "Untie me?" Hop
asked.

"Me help you?"

"That'll be all right," Cardozo said. "Karate? Ketchup?"

He grabbed a stool with his foot and moved it closer. He
sat down. There was a clock on the wall. The minute hand
moved once in a long while, creaking loudly. "Hello?" Cardozo asked after every creak.

"Hello? Hello? Hello?"

Cardozo got a little tired. The pistol's weight increased.
Flies moved about sleepily. The Chinese facing the wall moved
now and then. "Keep still," Cardozo shouted. "Hello? Hello?
Hello?"

His arm began to hurt.

"Friends no come?" Wo Hop asked. "Untie me now?"

"Hello?"

"Symie?" Karate asked. "You there? Over."

Cardozo cleared his throat.

"Nothing doing, right, Symie? We're signing off and will
return to the station. Join us there. We're off now. Buy you
a drink?"

"HELLO!" Cardozo yelled.

"You're there," Karate said. "See you in a minute. Over
and out."

"COME HERE!" Cardozo yelled.

The portophone creaked.

"YOU HEAR ME?"

"Quiet," Karate said. "Mind my eardrums. Where are you?"

"Here." Cardozo gave his position. "Hurry up. Bring any assistance you can find. Every cop in the station. Do hurry. Emergency."

"Understood," Karate said.

Cheerful sirens tore the air near the Inner Harbor. Jolly running footsteps cut the silence in the passage outside.

"Hurrah!" Karate shouted.

"Victory at last!" Ketchup shouted. "Four fried noodles. Two double fortune cookies. Step right up. Take your pick."

The assistance, eight officers in uniform and four in jeans and leather jackets, untied the prisoners and handcuffed all four suspects. A minibus transported the catch to the station. An inspector, raised from his bed, patted Cardozo's shoulder. "Two counts of deprivation of liberty, two counts of illegal firearms, one plastic bag containing a hundred grams of high-grade heroin. Nobody seems to have the proper papers. Good work, detective."

"Sir?" an officer in a leather jacket said.

"Let's have it, old chap."

"I'm Drugs, sir. Something about this heroin."

"Not the real thing? Don't disappoint me."

"Good quality, but not Chinese."

"And how do we know?"

"Packing, sir."

"And what do we notice when we study the packing?"

"Chinese heroin, sir, is never supplied in this type of thick yellow plastic wrap."

"No disturbing details now," the inspector said. "Tomorrow, maybe. I'll be reading the reports. Have a good night, the lot of you." The inspector went home.

"Turkish heroin," the expert explained. "Coarse grains, see?"

Cardozo was invited to type out his report. Wo Hop was sent home. There was no need to detain his mate, either. The two other Chinese were lodged in a small cell.

Karate and Ketchup changed clothes. "A drink, Cardozo?"

Why not? In Jelle Troelstra's bar, a stone's throw away. "I can't stay long," Cardozo said in the street, "for tomorrow I bicycle to Friesland."

Wo Hop's mate was trailing them, but neither Karate nor Ketchup nor Cardozo paid attention, for they were now off duty. "Bicycle?" Karate asked.

"I'll go up the dike," Cardozo said.

"Why?"

"I don't really care to discuss that now," Cardozo said. "It's late and I'm tired."

"You'll *bike* up there?" Ketchup asked. "That dike is thirty kilometers long. All the way to Friesland? It'll take you a day. Whatever for? You want to lose weight?"

"I'll be leaving at 6:00 A.M." Cardozo said.

Troelstra was closed, but he opened up.

Wo Hop's mate waited outside.

Cardozo explained, once settled behind a small glass of jenever, that he needed Douwe Scherjoen's's portrait because the photographs of the corpse were useless; they showed only bits of skull and a semi-burned spine.

"But *bicycle*?" Karate and Ketchup shouted. Jelle saw no reason to get upset. He remembered times when almost no one owned a car, and a trip along the dike could be quite an adventure. A bicycle is slow enough to afford the rider a view. And, besides, the trip was supposed to be useful. Yes, sure, they too were prepared to exert themselves when on duty, Karate and Ketchup said—certainly, no question about it—but to be exploited was something else again. If the State would not pay for elementary expenses, criminals could go free. Criminals were driving about in silver cars. The commissaris had just been issued a silver car too, Cardozo admitted. Yes, for the higher-ups no cost was too little either, Ketchup and Karate said, while common folk could be abused, their comforts ignored, their well-being unconsidered.

"Can't we rise above the common folk?" Karate asked. "This eternal complaining, does it get us anywhere? Suppose we surpassed ourselves, made use of all that's given to us, conquered our weaknesses, would there be no reward?"

"Sell our souls for silver Citroëns?" Ketchup asked. "I wouldn't mind doing that. Citroëns are good cars."

Cardozo sipped his drink, frowning and growling that mere materialism never got anyone anywhere. The trick was to step aside and still do your very best. Who cares for results?

Had he thought of that himself? Ketchup and Karate wanted to know. Sergeant de Gier had been known to come up with bullshit like that. Now look at the sergeant—wasn't he just another sucker, by accident provided with impermanent good looks and the ability occasionally to win a fight? Where had that got him? The saintly sinner, adored by Cardozo?

Troelstra kept filling up their glasses. "Would you know a certain Adjutant Oppenhuyzen?" Cardozo asked. "Aren't you Frisian too?"

Troelstra nodded benignly. "Not a bad fellow, comes in for a beer every now and then."

"He *is* a bad fellow," Cardozo said. "Pushed over by evil. Trying to squeeze personal good out of a bad situation."

Shouldn't accuse so easily, Karate and Ketchup said. Never guess the worst about the character of a colleague.

Cardozo stated that he would guess what he liked, and voice his theories without making exceptions for possible traitors. Colleagues? Ha! Weren't there colleagues who weren't on the portophone when they should be? Weren't there colleagues who had left him in danger, who had made him hold a heavy pistol for an hour or so, while he was surrounded by gangsters?

They were sorry, Ketchup and Karate said, but they had been busy; drunk and belligerent German tourists had to be wrestled to the ground, and before you know where you are, an hour is gone.

And why, Cardozo wanted to know, was Turkish heroin found on Chinese dealers?

Ketchup and Karate said that they really had to be leaving now, and that any situation is built up out of a large number of unknowable details. You can never get to the bottom of anything. They elbowed Cardozo. "But isn't it fun?"

"Not right now," Cardozo said.

He walked home, fuming jenever vapors.

Close to his home, a suspect mounted a bicycle. Cardozo, breaking into a sudden trot, managed to grab hold of the suspect's sleeve. "Where are you off to? That bike should be in the corridor by now."

"Since when," asked the Hider of Bicycles, "can't I be riding my very own bike?"

"Bring it into the house," Cardozo said. "At once. Give me the key to the lock."

The suspect dismounted. He struck while he turned. Wo Hop's mate watched from a doorway. It had been a long night for him—caught and bound, liberated and arrested, temporarily released and still up and about, in the early hours.

The suspect's fist was caught by Cardozo, who had passed only a few days ago, the examinations of the Unarmed Combat class. Cardozo twisted and pulled the suspect's fist across his shoulder, and turned. The suspect was forced to follow the compelling movements, and lost his footing, fell, got up again, and attacked with a kick. His foot was hooked away by Cardozo's ankle. The suspect again fell.

"Ouch," the suspect said. "You don't fight fair."

"You shouldn't be fighting me," Cardozo said. "Would your name happen to be Cain? Am I, perchance, called Abel?"

"You're so right," Cain said. "Will we never learn? The Age of Aquarius is already upon us, and it'll be raining in a minute. From now on we'll practice true brotherly love and fight only to defend ourselves against the enemy from outside."

Arms linked, Samuel and Simon walked home; Samuel pushed the bicycle along. Simon helped him to carry the bicycle up the stairs. He was given the key. A thunderclap confirmed their mutual decision to cherish their mutual benefit, forever after.

Wo Hop's mate returned to his cheap lodging in the Red Quarter, but first he checked with the boss of his triad, the venerable Wo Hop.

"So Mophead fought with another Mophead?" Wo Hop asked. "Amazing. And the first Mophead will be cycling to Friesland tomorrow, by way of the dike? Suprising."

"And your decision?" Wo Hop's mate asked humbly.

Wo Hop closed his eyes and mumbled, no longer in fluent Cantonese, but in the ancient language of forgotten lore. He lit incense sticks, bowed, threw coins, and was instructed by the book from the past.

"You," Wo Hop said, "and the two others of your selection will be bicycling on the dike too, tomorrow at six, which is in just a few hours, tomorrow being today and all time being illusion."

The mate found the two others and passed the order. The maid of the lodging house brought in tea, and her ears. A little later she telephoned another cheap lodging house, on the other end of the dike.

Cardozo slept peacefully. Six Chinese grumbled in their shallow slumbers, exhausted after having stolen six bicycles, three near the Central Railway Station in Amsterdam and three near the railway station of Bolsward, a Frisian town.

LEEUWARDEN, THE FRISIAN CAPITAL, WAS AMSTERDAM IN miniature and perfect in detail, as the architects of the Golden Age, over three hundred years ago, had planned their creation. That I'm allowed to partake of that well-meaning and artistic dream, de Gier thought as he strolled along empty quaysides and silent gables, reaching for the expanse of the night, which sparkled with clean stars. No people, but who needs them? Humanity never fails to disturb abstract beauty. The Frisians created this work of art and now they rest, allowing me to admire the beauty of their realization. Tomorrow they'll be about again, each house releasing a fresh female worker who'll immediately drop to her knees and scrub pavement and gable. No crumpled cigarette packs, no dog droppings, not even in the gutter. Too clean, maybe? De Gier felt uncomfortable. Once contrasts are pushed aside, once everything becomes the way it should be, what do you do? And why was he here? Why didn't he find the shortest way to his temporary quarters and extinguish himself in bed? Where would his Spanish Lane be? Could he ask anybody? Was anybody left? At two in the morning?

A gent in a deeply dented, broad-brimmed felt hat emerged

from an alley and walked ahead of the sergeant. The gent slowed his pace. He looked around. *"Jûn."*

It sounded like a greeting. De Gier said *"Jûn"* too.

The gent looked expectant. De Gier explained himself. Out for a walk.

The gent spoke at length. It seemed he was describing undressed women. "Sure," de Gier said. Why not? There are women, and they do undress. Their image is a powerful motivation for lone gents walking through the night. Maybe the gent had been saying that.

The gent got hold of de Gier's arm and they were now walking together. "Mata Hari," the gent said, and giggled and tittered. He pointed at a bronze statue in charge of a little bridge spanning a miniature canal. They stopped to admire the metal female form. Mata Hari was undressed. The gent again spoke at length, and the sergeant, catching a word here and there, remembered that Miss Hari had once, several wars ago, danced her way into Paris and into the hearts of Prussian spies and that her hosts, French noblemen and officers of rank, became jealous and did away with her.

"Whore!" the gent shouted. De Gier caught more words. Miss Hari's statue was alone now, immobile, a reminder, but once upon a better time this bridge and all the alleys around had been populated by live prostitutes. The gent pointed here and there and suddenly stiffened his arm. The arm, horizontal now, pushed and pulled rhythmically while the gent whistled. De Gier grasped that the movement was symbolic of an activity the gent used to delight in, in earlier days, and lower in his body.

"So that's all over now?"

De Gier didn't quite follow, but according to the gent, the general sexual decline was somehow connected with the cattle market and the development of modern machines. Many years ago, when there were no spacious trucks, the farmers would walk their animals to market. They were stabled somewhere and sold the next day. The night in between was filled with push-of-the-arm-whistle, pull-of-the-arm-whistle.

He would never have guessed, de Gier said politely.

But now, the gent was saying, the big trucks—*vrrrum, vrrrum*—they throw open their rear doors—*whop*—the cows charge into the street—*kuttubum, kuttubum*—where they are chased into the market hall and sold.

"Why would that prevent their owners' later pleasure?"

The gent wobbled his eyebrows. De Gier pushed and pulled his arm, whistling shrilly.

Again, de Gier wasn't quite following the gent's explanation, but the fact that the pleasure had gone would have to do with modern business routine. Cows sold, cash collected, in the middle of the day, rather spoils pleasurable possibilities. Did he mean *that* again? Sure, push-whistle-pull-whistle. Even so, there might still be a way. He grabbed de Gier's arm again and pushed him along. "Where?" de Gier asked.

"*Hjir*," the gent said, and was gone.

De Gier recognized the square building straddling two canals that Hylkje had pointed out before. A sex club? Members only? He read the sign above the door. *Mata Hari*. He rang the bell. The doors swung open, and Ali Baba bowed deeply. The doorman was dressed in billowing silk trousers, a brocade waistcoat, a shirt embroidered with flowering palms; he stood on curly-toed slippers, a curved sword stuck into his broad belt. A large turban crowned the beard that almost reached around his made-up eyes. His belly rose majestically toward his chin.

"Hi, Ali Baba," de Gier whispered, impressed.

"You were brought here?" Ali asked, first in Frisian, then in Dutch.

"Try Arabic," de Gier said. "You must be trilingual. An Arab in Friesland. What brought you here?"

"I speak German too," Ali said. "And the other languages of the tourists. Did the runner bring you here? Our advertiser?"

"Gent in a felt hat?" de Gier asked, pushing and pulling and whistling.

"That's him," Ali said. "Brings in the customers, but he shouldn't tonight. Couldn't reach him in time. We're closing early. Hardly any customers showed up. Would you be desiring a full show? There's only one artiste left, Trutske Goatema, not quite the first choice, but if you insist. Do you favor fat women?"

"Joe!" de Gier shouted.

Ali's sliding slippers brought him forward. "What do you know! Would it be *you*, the Amsterdam sergeant?"

"Good memory," de Gier said, "which we share. Black Joe, isn't that right? I don't recall your surname."

"Do come in," Black Joe said. "What a surprise. Is Amsterdam still doing as well as I remember? What are you after? A little pleasure on the side?"

"Not sure," de Gier said. "Forget the fat lady."

"An angel at heart," Joe said. "The good lookers were all crafted by the devil. I sent them home already, couldn't stand them tonight. I'll be gone myself next week. The joint is too much for me; let the owners find out what it's like to be Ali Baba." Joe flipped off his turban and showed de Gier the way to the bar. "A beer for the guest of honor?"

"So good to see you," Black Joe said. "Your health, Sergeant. I've thought of you often. You did that nicely, a classy trick. No, I won't forget that. I always underestimated the likes of you. That was quite subtle."

"Musn't exaggerate," de Gier said, halfway through his beer.

"Don't be modest now," Joe said. "Credit where credit is due. A difference of six months' jail for me." Trutske stepped out from the back door of the bar, illuminated by pink neon tubes speckled by uncounted generations of Frisian flies and hanging from warped ceiling tiles. "Client?" She eyed de Gier greedily.

"Friend," Black Joe said. "From the merry past. You're off now, dear, have a good rest."

"Listen," Trutske said. "I could do my number, a shortened version, but I'll do it good."

"That'll be fine," de Gier said. "Thanks anyway. Don't bother, really."

Trutske waddled off.

"What would she have done?" de Gier asked, twitching as the front door slammed.

"Frustrated self-love," Black Joe said. "Specialty of the house. She's an expert at evoking self-centered passion. Groans, wriggles all over, uses all the furniture of the stage, the walls tremble, the clients go wild, pink flesh up to the ceiling, screams of lustful agony, that sort of show, mostly."

"All that in Frisian?"

"Crazy language," Black Joe said. "I'll never master it, although it's easy to pick up. I have a Frisian girlfriend. We're to be married soon. I bought myself a house in a rustic village nearby. I'll be fixing bicycles there. No, I'm not kidding. This side of life is driving me whoppo. You don't believe me? But it's true. I'm qualified. I went back to school during the day. I got the tools, a barn, I'm all set up. Everything you want."

"Everything *you* want," de Gier said modestly.

"No," Black Joe said. "That's what *you* wanted me to do. Beer?"

"Your health," de Gier said.

Black Joe dropped his voice to a confidential whisper. "You remember how you got me to turn myself in?"

"Wasn't that your own idea?"

"Never," Joe said. "You led me to the station. If you hadn't, I would have been watching bars for half a year longer. The judge changed his mind when he heard I'd gone to the station by myself. He didn't like that scene in the Red Quarter. Ha!" Joe bellowed. "Another lush who wanted to fight the doorman of a reputable brothel. One little push of this..." His hairy fist trembled in front of de Gier's nose. "Just one little touch and there the lush goes. Ended up all in a broken heap."

De Gier nodded. "Ran backward across the street and mashed himself against a wall. You can be thankful that he was still alive. You should be aware of your strength, a little."

"And then you showed up," Black Joe said. "The very next day. I had retired to that posh terrace across from Central Station, the last place where you'd be looking for me, but you found me anyway and I was going to push you too. You didn't want that. You asked me to buy you coffee."

"I never fight in the mornings," de Gier said.

"Ha!" shouted Joe. "That's what you said then. And that I should turn myself in. Tell them I was sorry. Inquire about the lush's condition. Express my hopes that he'd soon feel better. Smile and stutter. Scratch my beard."

"Always the best way," de Gier said.

"Much better," Joe shouted. "That lawyer was ready to kiss me. He talked good, too. The judge had tears in his eyes. Just one month and some time suspended."

"You don't push clients anymore?"

"None of that now," Joe said. "None of anything, soon. One more week and I'll be taking bikes apart. I've been planning for a while, but I still had to do this for the money."

"Why here?"

All part of the new way, Joe told him. Not the good way, he wasn't going to go as far as that. It wasn't that he had been bad before. He wasn't sorry, if that was what the sergeant meant. Not a choice, either; you do something for a while and then you come to the end of it. If you don't accept the end and go on, the routine becomes boring. If you don't feel good about it anymore, you got to quit.

De Gier listened and meanwhile studied a painting on the bar's wall. A chubby lady had spread herself out on the canvas, under a hairdo that reminded him of antique maids. Her rounded belly line turned in and popped up on her other side again, as cute raised buttocks.

"That's Mata Hari," Black Joe said. "Genuine, done in Paris. And I'm Ali Baba, as you saw just now. That's okay for a while. If you die young, you can keep it up all your life, but if you survive, you begin to see through it. Take Mata Hari, for instance. You know her real name?"

De Gier's ignorance surprised Black Joe.

"Margaretha G. Zelle," Joe said. "Born in this city in 1876, around the corner from here, on the Gardens—you must have passed the house. Beer?"

De Gier declined. Joe emptied a can into his beard. "Right. Thirty-one years old, she got shot by soldiers in parade uniforms. She wore a fur coat and nothing else, opened it just at the fatal moment. Very romantic. Like her life out there. Did some fancy musical stripping on expensive stages. Got herself pawed by the powers on both sides. Never knew or passed too many secrets, but got shot anyway, for *Commande* was *Commande*." Joe sighed. "Silly. Right?"

"Didn't she have a good time?" de Gier asked.

"For as long as it lasted." Joe sighed more deeply. "You know how long it lasts?"

"Let's see," de Gier said. "Some constructive fantasizing and positive thinking, it could last a good while."

"I'm forty-one," Joe said. "I've seen it all a hundred times. My dad was a bicycle repairman too; I thought that was real stupid at the time." Joe stared at a horizon receding toward the infinite. "I used to drive a Ferrari. You ever drive a Ferrari?"

"No," de Gier said.

"You ever live in Casablanca, overlooking the Casbah? In Tunis? In Morocco?" Joe sang in Arabic. "You know what I just sang?"

"No," de Gier said.

"I don't either," Joe said, "but that's what they would sing outside my window. 'Jacques Ferrouche,' I called myself. I rode a racing camel. I sailed a yacht on the Mediterranean with braid on my cap and a girl who was built like this." Joe indicated the dimensions. "And it still wasn't enough, I still wanted to go somewhere to do something, but then I had to go. And now I want to repair bikes and take the dog for a walk. You think that'll be okay?"

"I think so," de Gier said.

"You got a dog?"

"A cat," de Gier said. "Nothing special. Ugly, too."

Beer foamed out of Joe's beard. "Nothing special!" His fists hit the counter.

"That's funny?" de Gier asked.

"Nothing special can be fun," Joe said. "You know that? Take my girlfriend, she teaches embroidery at school. You should see what she gets together at home. Regular landscapes, but if you look they go on forever. There's a difference, but I can't place it. You wanted me to be there, you told me to try something else, nothing special. You remember that you said that?"

"Joe," de Gier said, "would anyone be selling heroin here?"

"Didn't you want me to do nothing special?"

"Heroin," de Gier said. "Is it dealt here?"

"Two assholes," Joe said. "They come in once in a while. Junkies. Half a gram or so. Crumbles."

"And where do they buy the crumbles?"

"From the Chinese."

"The Frisian Chinese?"

"Never," Joe said. "The Amsterdam Chinese. Amsterdam is close enough. The dike goes down. Put one foot on the dike and you slide easily enough. Takes a long time to get back here sometimes. Have you noticed?"

"Not yet," de Gier said.

"I have," Joe said. "Homesickness, maybe? Or the power of seduction? That sometimes bothers me."

"Does the name Douwe Scherjoen mean anything?"

"Saw it in the paper," Joe said. "Dead in Amsterdam's Inner Harbor, and none too soon." Joe smiled.

"No-good shithead?"

"Absolutely," Joe said. "Good friend of mine worked for Douwe for a bit. Had to collect the payments. Douwe was a shark."

"Tell me," de Gier said.

"You didn't know that? Scherjoen would advertise in the

paper here. '*Need money? You'll have it today*.' Used to keep an office here in town, my friend worked there. You could borrow up to three thousand, at thirty percent. The interest was deducted straightaway, and then you paid three hundred a month for ten months. My friend picked up the payments. He was supposed to lean on the victims if they were a little slow."

"Didn't work out well?"

"No," Joe said. "Frisians don't like to be leaned on so much. My friend fell into a canal and was in the hospital for a while, and Douwe wouldn't pay for the stitches."

"So it came to an end?"

"Douwe closed up."

"I have a home here," de Gier said, "but it's hard to find. I'd better go look for it."

Joe drove him home, in an old-model Mercedes. "You see how neat I've become?"

"Where do I see it?" de Gier asked.

"Check the mileage."

De Gier read the numbers. "Four hundred eighty thousand?"

"Old taxi," Joe said. "Found it at an auction for six months of my savings. In the old days I would earn the price of a junker in a week. Here's your street. Any particular number?"

"Here," de Gier said.

"I've been here before," Joe said. "A colleague? He's putting you up for free?"

"The police arranged it. Don't know the man."

"I do," Joe said. "Collected a Mata Hari bill here once. He'd left it on the bar. A while back. Cheng was our barman then, and your colleague would have a cognac with us every now and then."

"While visiting Cheng?"

"That's it."

"And the adjutant didn't have to pay?"

"Maybe five or six cognacs," Joe said. "We didn't mind

so much, for Cheng never had any proper papers, but one night our boss came in and he didn't like Cheng, or maybe he was just teasing him. Saying Mao never knew nothing either. So Cheng threw a bottle at the boss, and then he was all done. Your colleague had been around that night and left his bill again, so the boss thought he should pay."

"Could you describe my colleague?"

"Feels cheeks a lot," Joe said.

"The ladies' cheeks?"

"His own," Joe said.

"You're still up?" de Gier asked.

"That rat," Grijpstra said, "rattled about in his terrarium so I got him out and now he's around somewhere."

"Over there," de Gier said. "Why don't you pick him up?"

"You pick him up. He tickles with his little hands."

"Eddy?" De Gier squatted next to the rat. He put his hand out. Eddy rolled into the hand. The rat picked up his tail and wove it between his legs. The long snout rested tragically against de Gier's thumb.

"That rattling drives me crazy," Grijpstra said.

"Animals make all sorts of weird noises."

"Rats don't rattle," Grijpstra said angrily.

"This one does. You're oversensitive. Get any work done tonight?"

"I thought," Grijpstra said. "Tomorrow I'll be getting hold of Pyr, Tyark, and Yelte."

"I'll be on the island of Ameland," de Gier said. "On food-searching business."

"Out of it for a day?"

De Gier shrugged. "I thought you wanted me out of this altogether."

"Correct," Grijpstra said. "Try and keep it that way. You're too outlandish here, you'll be upsetting suspects."

De Gier climbed the stairs, cradling Eddy in his hands, murmuring endearments.

‖‖‖ 12 ‖‖‖

I'M A MINORITY, THE COMMISSARIS THOUGHT, LOOKING down the long conference table headed by the lofty figure of Chief Constable Lasius of Burmania, flanked by the equally tall Colonel Kopinie of the State Police and the even taller Lieutenant Colonel Singelsma of the Military Police. He ignored the other participants, but they were tall too, upright and all in complete agreement. It isn't that their combined forces are *against* me, the commissaris thought. Maybe it looks that way, but that can't be the case at all.

"Hello?" the commissaris said.

The conversation flowed on, in Frisian.

The commissaris told himself that he should keep quiet, not because the majority were against him, but because he had made a habit of keeping quiet. "The commissaris," those who knew him always said, "is a quiet man."

"Coffee?" asked the secretary. "Care for coffee, sir?"

He got up and followed her unobtrusively. But I would like to be obtrusive, the commissaris thought. I would like to shout 'Murder' and 'Fire,' for that's what interests me these days. The secretary was tall too, a majestic figure in a tight tweed suit; she wore high heels to accentuate her height, and had steely blue eyes set off by her long, soft, white-blond hair.

"Thank you," the commissaris said, holding up his cup. "Ma'am? What's Frisian for 'murder'?"

She thought.

"You're familiar with the term?"

"We don't have much of that here," the secretary said. "Ah, it's come back to me. The word is *moard*."

"And 'fire'?"

"*Brân.*"

"I'll be shouting that in a minute," the commissaris said. "When I've finished my coffee."

She laughed down on him, but that wasn't polite. She bent her legs. "Murder," the secretary said, "isn't a contemporary word. I am very contemporary. I'm only in my twenties. We used to have a lot of murder in these parts. It was always committed by forces from outside. We're rich here, and the outside people were after our wealth. They sent mercenaries, to commit murder and arson. The outside greed was a plague on the land. Friesland has some horrifying history that I was taught at school. WIll it begin all over again now? With the visit of Bald Ary and Fritz with the Tuft?"

The commissaris replaced his cup. He turned about. He took a deep breath. "*Moard!*" the commissaris shouted. "And *brân!*"

The gathering looked up.

"Could we discuss those subjects for a minute?" the commissaris asked.

"In respect to what?" the chief constable asked.

"Murder and fire, to which Douwe Scherjoen was subjected. The purpose of my visit here. Who's in charge of the local detectives?"

"That's me," a tall man said.

"And what do you know that can be beneficial to my inquiry?"

"Nothing," the tall man said, and introduced himself.

"Chief Inspector Sipma. Nothing at all. I state my information simply, as is the custom in this province. My computer is connected to yours at Amsterdam Headquarters, and the machine malfunctions. When I switch it on, I see only a small green square, trembling a little. The trembling is caused at your end, I'm told. Douwe's remains are kept at your end. The crime was committed in your city. Both cause and effect are well outside my files. *Float* well outside my files." There was polite laughter all around the table.

"A joke?" the commissaris asked.

"An architect from The Hague," Chief Constable Lasius said. The laughter increased in strength.

"Another joke?" the commissaris asked.

"Our files," Chief Inspector Sipma said, "were hosed down by the fire brigade; the boxes are still afloat in our basement. The firemen came to douse the flames, which had been lit by a suicidal prisoner as a protest against outside influence."

"Quite," another tall man said, and introduced himself. "Commissaris Colmjon. We should never have surrendered, but what can we do if the threatening masses keep running us down? We had to subject ourselves to authorities from below the dike. They sent us an architect from The Hague—The Hague, of all places, that cemetery filled with floating ghosts—and he designs a cube that's supposed to house us. Well away from the city, of course. We're Municipal Police, but we're no longer in the city. A fact that was lost on the foreigner who only learned how to draw ninety-degree angles at school. Police above, suspects below, all boxed in by squares. Contact between the law and the lawless is never smooth, but once we pour it in mathematical cement, the misery increases. So where does this lead? To a burning mattress in a dungeon. The fire brigade puts it out. Then where do we go?"

"Downstairs," Chief Inspector Sipma said. "To see our files floating in the basement."

"Foreigners," Chief Constable Lasius snarled, "who interfere."

"Who destroy," Colonel Kopinie said.

"Who encumber," Lieutenant Colonel Singelsma said.

"Who endanger," Commissaris Colmjon said.

"Moard," said the commissaris.

"At your end," the colonel said. "In Amsterdam. If Douwe had stayed in Dingjum, on his estate, in his country mansion, the pride of the region, his mind would still be sound, in a healthy body. Foreign greed sucked him away from here, from under the poplars where blue herons nest, from his greenhouses and his crop of grapes, from his pond filled with goldfish and covered with ducks. All the Frisian glory was Douwe's to enjoy. So what does the asshole do? He allows himself to be sucked into Amsterdam, where his peace of mind is interfered with."

"Destroyed."

"Encumbered."

"Hopelessly endangered."

"And so it goes on," Colonel Kopinie said. "My Lieutenant Sudema is going down too. A nervous breakdown. Sick leave and all. Can we never defend ourselves from the wickedness from without?"

"You'll have to live with the rest of the world," the commissaris said. "I did, and I'm from here."

"From here?" sang the chorus.

"I was born in the city of Joure."

The statement impressed the majority, but not for long, for what about Ary and Fritz now? They were due tomorrow, when they would scout the cattle market. How could the attack be withstood?

"And my *moard*?" the commissaris asked.

Nothing to do with them, they kept telling him.

"Remember the Japanese student?" Commissaris Colmjon asked. "Found in a chest, chopped up, bobbing in one of your Amsterdam canals? Remember what you did? You went to Japan."

"Spending some funds," Chief Inspector Sipma said. "That could be done in the past, when there were still funds."

"And the murder had been committed by French students," Lieutenant Colonel Sipma said. "The Japanese was curious about heroin and was given an overdose. Foreign filth again, concentrated in your city. So what can you be looking for here?"

"Simple case," Colonel Kopinie said. "Douwe's murder is another repeat. When we wander about outside, we invite the worst of troubles."

"We'll deal with Ary and Fritz first," Chief Constable Lasius said, "and then you'll have your turn."

The meeting continued. A large number of subjects were brought up: the commando post in the market, the machinery that would be required, how to dress the detectives, coordination with the Arrest Team that had been ordered from the Military Police, where to house the officers, and the central kitchen and bar.

"Can I phone for a cab?" the commissaris asked.

Why did he need a car? What had happened to his own? The commissaris had lost his car? Between the Well and the Gardens?

"Poor fellow," the chief constable said. "We'll find it for you. This meeting is over." The commissaris was guided along plasticized corridors to a gleaming metal elevator.

"What do you think of the building?" the chief constable asked.

"Modern?" the commissaris offered.

The elevator hummed efficiently, the door hummed open. More corridors stretched away. A ghoulish scream tore itself from below and hung above the company, in a hall lined with artificial marble.

"Douwe, screaming for revenge?" the commissaris asked.

"A prisoner," Chief Inspector Sipma said. "They all become hopelessly neurotic after a while. The cells look like this hall, but they're considerably smaller."

"And will my suspect be locked in there too?" the commissaris asked in a frightened whisper.

"Suspect of what?"

"My murder?" the commissaris asked.

"You won't find him here."

"I hope not," the commissaris said.

"You won't."

"I may."

"Stubborn, aren't you?" the chief constable said. "A Frisian trait. Shall we go look for your car now?"

"I'm stubborn," Grijpstra thought the next morning, after he had dropped de Gier at the Military Police barracks, where the sergeant was met by Private Sudema, nephew of Lieutenant Sudema of the State Police. A nice break for the sergeant, Grijpstra thought kindly. Enjoyment of nature. I'll be stubbornly at work. I'm not a foreigner, like silly de Gier. I can see what goes on here from the inside out.

Grijpstra, in his Frisian jersey and his Frisian cap, lost his way between the villages where his suspects lived. He flagged down a State Police Land Rover and was escorted, but lost his way again. I'll never give in, Grijpstra thought, I'll untie the Frisian knot.

Pyr Wydema, Tyark Tamminga, and Yelte Prik, exporters of sheep, grown into their gleaming, smelly jackets, with their caps pulled over their leering eyes, denied all charges in all languages available to them. They denied them in High and Low Frisian, in the dialect of Leeuwarden, and even in Dutch. "My parents were born in the Frisian port of Harlingen," Grijpstra kept saying.

The suspects wanted to know if they could be arrested at this stage of the inquiry. They could not. They ordered the adjutant to leave. They brought out No Trespassing signs and untied their dogs. Their wives interfered and confiscated their shotguns and poured coffee for Grijpstra, who sat exhausted under the gnarled old trees, cooled by a breeze from the sea, surrounded by dainty church towers penetrating the peaceful greenery all around. Grijpstra sighed when he saw the brown sails of fishing boats on the lakes.

He listened to the rustling of corn at the end of fertile meadows. How pleasant the landscape, how hard his task.

"Off with him," Pyr, Tyark, and Yelte shouted at their wives. "There's work to do. The cattle market is tomorrow. Will he never be gone?"

The Volkswagen circled small dikes and was lost again. The calm expanse of the sea was on Grijpstra's left. Wasn't he supposed to go south? He turned the car again, aiming for the capital and missing Leeuwarden once more.

"Where are you headed now?" a State Police sergeant asked from the window of his Land Rover.

"Leeuwarden," Grijpstra shouted furiously.

"A break for coffee?" the sergeant suggested. In the pub, other colleagues mentioned the presence of another lost soul, a commissaris from Amsterdam in a silver Citroën. "We kept setting him right and he keeps coming back at us again."

"What might you be doing here?" the sergeant asked.

Grijpstra explained the nature of his visit, mentioning his three suspects.

"Pyr?" the sergeant asked. "Tyark? Yelte? How could they ever be suspected? Surely you know better. Didn't you say your parents came from Harlingen? Ah, I see," the sergeant slapped his brow. "You're on official leave of absence."

"I am?" Grijpstra asked.

"Stress," the sergeant said. "I read the *Police Gazette*. A common affliction in Amsterdam. Your superiors must be trying new cures. Sending you off on odd errands to more restful locations."

"Is that right?" Grijpstra asked furiously.

The sergeant patted the adjutant's arm.

"Just stay around. After a while you'll feel much better."

IIIII 13 IIIII

CARDOZO CYCLED. IT WAS THE RIGHT DAY FOR SPORTING activity, with a sunny sky and hardly any wind—a day for a bike ride, but biking from Amsterdam to Dingjum was lunacy, he granted that much. He defined his behavior as childish, caused by his own hotheaded insistence on getting ahead, and he even considered his own appearance childish, dressed as he was in shorts and a touristy shirt, and especially because of his equipment—a tin lunch box strapped to the luggage carrier in the rear, containing cheese sandwiches and an apple. Moreover, he was breaking a promise. To break promises one made to others could be excused, but when the promise was made to oneself, some respect was due. All those years he had biked to school, always with the wind pushing him back, beaten by rain, with a painful crotch, pulled to and fro by cowardly obedience to teacher and parent, he had looked forward to the day when he would be free of the heavy bike. When school was over, he'd thrown the bicycle into the canal, and after that he had used only engine-driven transport, like real people use. So what was he doing here now, on Samuel's dated contraption?

Next to him, cars raced along, and on the other side the green dike flowed slowly up, topped by high grass where

145

seagulls stalked about. On the Inland Sea, a fishing boat bobbed slowly. Against shreds of fog the sails of a flat-bottomed pleasure yacht emerged from the pure blue swell. In the yacht, holiday makers would be lounging about. I'm not living properly, Cardozo thought, pedaling with force. If I were as intelligent as I thought I was, I would be doing something pleasurably clever now.

Did a hunch get me here? Cardozo thought. Do my hunches ever work? Why did I forget about practical cooperation? Am I not part of a team? He could have telephoned the commissaris. "Sir, I'll be bicycling to Dingjum today." "Don't do that," the commissaris would have answered. Wouldn't that remark have saved him insane trouble? And shouldn't he be covered? Some risk is involved in the work of a police detective. Wasn't he hunting a dangerous fiend who thought nothing of putting a bullet through a fellow being's head and setting fire to his remains? Suppose the psychopathic demon knew that Cardozo was now cycling up the dike?

One of the handlebars on Samuel's bike carried a rear view mirror. In the mirror, three Chinese could be seen. The Chinese cycled in line. The nearest Chinese looked unhappy. The nearest Chinese's pedal ground past the chain case with an irritating, repetitious, squeaky moan; unmusical, proba-bly also to Far Eastern ears. The farthest Chinese cyclist was Wo Hop's mate, unrecognizable at that distance. Wo Hop's mate was tired. The various stages in his recent career had convinced him that he was indeed a Rotten Egg. How could he ever have allowed himself to be riding a low-quality bike to an ever-extending nowhere?

Isn't it about time, Cardozo thought, that I got off my bicycle to eat an apple? While he contemplated the pos-sibility, three more Chinese cyclists appeared, coming toward him. A coincidence, Cardozo thought. To be followed by three bicycling Chinese, to be confronted by three bicycling Chinese—anything is bound to happen if life lasts long enough. The occurrence could even be turned about. It should be possible for a Chinese to cycle on a Chinese dike and be

followed by three Dutchmen on bikes and approached by
three more Dutchmen. But if I were that Chinese, Cardozo
thought, I would get off my bike, peel an apple in some quiet
spot, watch all those Dutchmen until the horizons swallowed
them up, and hope never to see any of them again.

Cardozo slowed and jumped off his bike. The Chinese
followed his example. The Chinese produced pistols. Cardozo clawed his way deep into the grass.

The Chinese opened fire. Cardozo rolled into a shallow
ditch left by a careless bulldozer driver, filled with flowering
weeds. Nettles stung him, reed stalks scratched his ears,
disturbed ants sank their jaws into his flesh, and a bullet cut
off a leaf. The Chinese kept shooting, aiming at each other
now. They weren't bad marksmen. Not every shot was successful, and two Chinese remained, crawling toward each
other. They kept firing as they crawled.

Ten Arrest Team members, military policemen, kenneled
and trained in the south of the country, dressed in combat
fatigues, were driving along the dike in five cars. They had
been issued orders to exterminate or, if possible, to arrest
two dangerous criminals, Bald Ary and Fritz with the Tuft,
in the cattle market of Leeuwarden, in another week's time.
Because the extermination or arrest of two dangerous criminals who would be well armed and most likely in possession
of a fast car would require coordination on the road, the
Arrest Team was now on exercise. The five cars were connected by radio. The commander was in the first vehicle.
He saw and heard the Chinese cyclists shooting at each
other.

"All cars stop and park, over."

"Weapons ready to fire, over."

"Prepare attack direction Friesland, over."

"Leave cars, follow me, attack. Over and out."

P-5 machine pistols with shortened barrels crackled, and
fully automatic Uzi carbine/machine-gun combinations fired
away. The men crawled, got up, broke into short runs,
dropped down again. The Chinese pistols boomed individual

heavy dots in the pattern of lines that the Attack Team's superior weapons were drawing. *Turram. Voom. Tack-tack-tack.* There were other heavy sounds caused by cars hitting each other and tires shrieking on the dike's tarmac. Surprised highway traffic, which had been moving along at easy speeds, clumped together, accompanied by the ragged blowing of horns.

The Arrest Team members reported to their chief. "They're all dead, sir, will that be all right?"

"Very nice," the commander bellowed. "You and you, guard corpses, the others, see what you can do about rearranging the traffic. Hello? Not you. Get back to your car and radio for ambulances."

A silver Citroën parked on the shoulder. "Drive on," a military policeman barked. He strengthened his order with a sweep of his weapon. A small gentleman left the Citroën.

"Back to your car and remove yourself, sir."

"Police," the little gentleman said. "What's going on here?"

"Chinese, sir. Six of them. All taken care of."

"Your chief?"

The military policeman pointed.

"Get the hell out of here," the commander shouted.

"Police," the commissaris said. "You didn't happen to hit a tousle-headed compatriot, I trust?"

The commander didn't think so. They went over together to look. The commander suddenly felt sick, and the commissaris didn't feel well either. One corpse showed a partly blown-away head; another had lost half an arm, and blood was pumping out of the stump; Wo Hop's mate observed the commander and the commissaris from one staring eye and one hole.

"Captain," a military policeman shouted. "Over there."

Two pink hands waved from a tuft of weeds.

"Arrest him."

Cardozo was arrested from six sides simultaneously.

"He's mine," the commissaris said. "I want him, Captain."

Cardozo was handed over.

"What happened?" Cardozo asked, laughing.

"Poor boy," the commissaris said. "Come with me, Simon, we'll sit down over there."

"An apple," sobbed Cardozo. "I was just going to peel it."

"Yes, dear boy."

"And they were all killing each other, all of a sudden."

"Care for a cigar?" the commissaris asked. Cardozo preferred to roll his own cigarette, but his hands were shaking uncontrollably. The commissaris lit a cigar and stuck it between Cardozo's lips.

"There are too many Chinese," Cardozo stuttered. "I had them in the Red Quarter too. Last night. Wo Hop and his mate, tied up. I released them, and two others too, and now this lot again."

"The same Chinese?" the commissaris asked.

"Lots of them, sir."

"Are you doing better now?"

"Because I wanted to eat an apple."

"It won't be an appetizing sight," the commissaris said, "but maybe you should take a look."

Ambulances climbed the dike crying plaintively with their sirens. A motorcycle cop rode slowly along the path reserved for cyclists. "Hey!" Cardozo shouted. "Watch it! Officer, that ambulance has flattened Samuel's bike. Oh, no. Officer, *do* something. I've got to bring that bike back, it belongs to my brother."

The cop took off his helmet. "Hello, Hylkje," the commissaris said. He introduced Cardozo.

"Will you be writing a report?" Cardozo asked. "I'll need it for the insurance."

Hylkje staggered off.

"Too many dead Chinese," the commissaris said. "Do you recognize any, Cardozo?"

"Here," Cardozo said. "Wo Hop's mate. This man who's missing an eye." Cardozo staggered off too.

Cardozo turned, grabbing hold of a fencepost. "What are the commandos doing here, sir? Paratroopers? Is there a war? I haven't been reading the paper for a few days."

The commander of the Arrest Team reported to the commissaris. "Do you know what was going on here, sir? We were on our way to Leeuwarden, when we came upon these cyclists gunning each other down."

"I'm going to Leeuwarden too," the commissaris said. "I'll construct a theory on my way up. You'll be hearing from me."

"Chinese, all of them," the commander said.

"I was just going to eat an apple," Cardozo said. "I jumped off my bike. And suddenly, from nowhere, slaughter all over."

"You're on our side, right?" the commander asked. "And your chief was looking for you? He seemed to know that something was amiss."

"I'll reconstruct an acceptable situation," the commissaris said. "You'll be the first to know. You'll be securing the cattle market against predicted trouble?"

"You know about that too?"

"I heard rumors."

The commander took his helmet off and put it on again. "The Chinese are cattle dealers?"

"I hardly think so," the commissaris said.

A State Police Land Rover climbed the dike. A sergeant and a corporal got out. "What is going on here?"

"I was going to eat an apple," Cardozo said. "But I had to peel it first."

"Cycling Chinese," the commander said.

Hylkje came closer, holding a ballpoint pen and a notepad. "Who owned the bicycle that has just been totaled?"

"Any witnesses?" the state cops asked. "Why is everybody dead? Is the army involved?"

"Can we pick up the corpses now?" an ambulance attendant asked.

"I'll come up with a suitable hypothesis," the commissaris said.

"Did we manage to hit anyone?" the commander asked. "Hey. You and you. Did you get anyone?"

"This is where I jumped off my bike," Cardozo said. "They were all coming at me. Three from the rear and three from ahead."

"Not the army," the commander said, "although technically we might be, of course. An Arrest Team, trained in the south. I'm in charge."

"I got one, Captain, the man over there. I was spraying low, and as he fell I must have hit him in the head," a military policeman said.

"We're not authorized to pronounce them dead," the ambulance attendant said, "but they are, they're ripped to pieces."

"I'm going to call everybody in here," the State Police sergeant said. "Anyone I can think of. This is not for me. I can't even look at this mess. What could have done it?"

"I'll pass my solution to your Colonel Kopinie," the commissaris said, "and he'll pass it on to you."

"A battle," the State Police corporal was yelling into his microphone. "Maybe an attempted invasion. Come here, I say. The Chinese are losing."

"Come along, Cardozo," the commissaris said. "This is no place for us."

"I'll guide the way," Hylkje said. "There's cattle plague around again, and the north exit of the dike is clogged because of checks. I'll get you through them."

"I'm going to Dingjum," the commissaris said. "Put your bike in my car."

"Are you in a hurry?" Hylkje asked.

"Yes," the commissaris said. "No time to lose."

"Siren?"

"If you please."

"Two hundred kilometers an hour," the commissaris said. "Hylkje certainly knows her job."

"Are you sure we're in a hurry?" Cardozo asked.

"I think better at high speeds," the commissaris said. "Tell me now, what were you doing with the Chinese suspects last night?"

Cardozo reported.

"Of course," the commissaris said.

"Is it clear to you now, sir?"

"Surely," the commissaris said, "but my explanation might be farfetched, and the theory cannot be confirmed, as both parties have left the situation. But that's the way it all fits."

"What way?" Cardozo asked.

"Just one little question," the commissaris said. "Do you recall having stated in public that you would be cycling along this dike starting early this morning? Think carefully, Cardozo."

Cardozo thought carefully.

"Yes," Cardozo said. "On the way, between the station in the Red Quarter and Troelstra's bar, I did make such a statement. Karate and Ketchup refused to believe me. Then I said it again and they repeated what I said, loudly. *By bicycle. Six A.M. To Friesland. Along the dike.*"

"Aha," the commissaris said.

"It's really all clear to you now, sir?"

"Two hundred and five kilometers per hour," the commissaris said. "A most helpful speed. Pity. We're slowing down already. There's the end of the dike."

Hylkje chose the emergency lane. The Citroën followed. "This is the way it came about, Cardozo," the commissaris said. "Heroin dealing in Amsterdam is at present controlled by two Triads, secret Chinese societies that have been active here for years. Each Triad wants a monopoly, so friction results. The Hong Kong-based society fights the Singapore society here, in our city." The commissaris raised a slender finger. "Always the same thing. Conflicting interests. They could join and share, but that's too much to expect, when we consider human greed. So now what do we get?"

"Dead Chinese?"

"Ah," the commissaris said. "This part of the trip may be even better. Narrow country roads, Cardozo—we'll see what this exclusive car can do. We'll be glued to that motorcycle no matter what the corporal has us do. Just pay attention."

"Yes," Cardozo said. "Easy now, sir. Blind corners. Easy now."

Hylkje turned sharply, and the Citroën equaled her performance. "A hundred kilometers an hour," the commissaris said. "That's an easy speed, but in view of the road condition it's still an appreciable figure."

"So what would the Triad members want of me, sir?"

"Postulating," the commissaris said, "that this Adjutant Oppenhuyzen, who you found in Hop's restaurant contacting young Chinese toughs—assuming that this colleague, let's say, entertained intimate communication with the opposing party, we might possibly conclude"—the commissaris raised a finger again—"that the enemy, seeing you with the adjutant, surmised that you were in their business too. Moreover, they saw you having dinner with two uniformed constables. So they now know you're a police officer too. Look at it through their eyes, Cardozo, what do you see?"

The Citroën leaned into the next tight curve.

"Couldn't we park somewhere?" Cardozo asked. "It's hard to concentrate when I try to imagine what may happen any minute now."

"Close your eyes," the commissaris said. "Darkness helps at times. After you had dinner with the Red District constables, you were seen again, liberating two members of one Triad from the sadistic claws of the other. Where does that place you now?"

"On Hop's side?" Cardozo asked. "But I arrested both sides."

"And you let one side go later," the commissaris said. "Become a Chinese gangster for a moment, Cardozo. What is your aim? You're trying to increase your own happiness and possessions. Always the same motivation. Strengthening of one's own position. What's your next step?"

"I was going home."

"No, no," the commissaris said. "Switch your position.

You're *them* now. See through their eyes. You'd be after a considerable sum of money. How would you plan to get that? What do cops have that the other side wants? Heroin, of course. We confiscate the drug and sell it back to the suppliers."

A straight line of road loomed up. Trees swishing by changed into a hedge of solid green, which broke for a moment and showed black and white dots—cows. Ahead of the Citroën, the large white motorcycle picked up speed. The siren sang her song.

"No!" Cardozo yelled, as a railway crossing humped up ahead. Motorcycle and car took the bulge spectacularly.

"Yes," the commissaris said. "The Chinese like to complicate simplicity. Ever interrogated a Chinese? They even change their names every two minutes. They expect the enemy, us, to like complications too. In order to get wise to what you would be planning, they dogged your steps. You were heard to say that you'd be bicycling to Friesland. Who would you want to visit out there?"

"Frisians?"

"More Chinese," the commissaris said. "Chinese finding refuge there because we hunt them out of Amsterdam. And what would you be taking to more Chinese?"

"Really?" Cardozo asked. "They thought my tin lunch box was filled with dope?"

"They did."

"Now where were the Chinese who were cycling toward me coming from, sir?"

"From Triad headquarters in Friesland."

"Please," Cardozo said. "You're driving too fast, sir, do please slow down."

"Had to pass that slowpoke," the commissaris said. "If I hadn't, Hylkje would have lost us. Now do you understand?"

"No."

"Betrayal?" the commissaris suggested. "There's always betrayal. Evil can't help betraying itself, we see that so often."

"The refugees in Friesland had been informed by a spy

in the Amsterdam Triad that I would be taking them supplies? And that I would be followed? But there were only cheese sandwiches in my lunch box. And the apple that I was about to peel."

"Evil is suspicious—paranoid, in fact," the commissaris said. "If it weren't, it wouldn't destroy itself, but keep growing and eventually take over. I've always wondered about that theoretical possibility," the commissaris said softly. "If evil took over completely, what would happen to our struggle? If it swallowed the last vestige of good, would it become good itself?"

Hylkje switched off her siren and applied her brakes.

"Dingjum," the commissaris said. "And that dear little house where Lieutenant Sudema lives, in the company of his lovely wife, Gyske. Such a delightful woman."

Gyske welcomed them at her gate. Hylkje placed her helmet on the saddle of the Guzzi. "It's you again?" Gyske asked. "I owe you thanks for bringing Sjurd home this morning. He's still asleep, thank God. When he wakes up he'll be tearing down the wall, after he rips out the cupboard."

"Pity," Hylkje said. "Such a nice wall. He'll kill the ivy and climbing roses. Can't he forgive the cupboard?"

"The cupboard of my sin," Gyske said sadly.

"Didn't you have a good time in there?" Hylkje asked. "Wasn't your lover a therapist? If it was part of the treatment, it should have been fun."

"It wasn't," Hylkje said disgustedly.

"Would you happen to know," the commissaris asked, "how we can get to Mrs. Scherjoen's home? I've been there before, but I can't remember the way."

Gyske pointed. "That way, hard to miss."

"Will I see you both tonight?" Hylkje asked. "Rinus invited me to dinner. He's picking up some fresh sole in Ameland."

"More trouble?" Cardozo asked. "Mrs. Sudema didn't look too happy."

The commissaris and Cardozo were walking. "A marriage crisis," the commissaris explained. "Sjurd Sudema did not properly love his beautiful wife, and then she picked on a certain Anne."

"A lesbian affair?" Cardozo asked. "Do they have that here too? It's quite popular nowadays, understandably so. If I were a woman, I would go after women too."

The commissaris was quietly thoughtful.

"You disapprove of normal abnormalities, sir?"

"I watched it once," the commissaris said. "In Paris, an age ago. Most interesting. But that Anne is a man."

"Homosexual?" Cardozo asked, shocked. "No wonder that lieutenant is about to demolish his house. A homosexual raping his wife, in his very own cupboard."

"No, no," the commissaris said. "And the fellow supposedly looks like me. Are you trying to upset me, Cardozo?"

"*I'm* upset," Cardozo said. "I still can't understand why the Chinese cycling behind me would invite the Chinese cycling toward me to have themselves shot."

"Themselves?"

"The behind-me Chinese, sir."

"Oh, *those* Chinese," the commissaris said. "Because, no, that was different, someone else again, *another* Chinese, must have heard the behind-you Chinese plan their trip on the dike, and passed that information to the toward-you Chinese."

"Right," Cardozo said doubtfully.

"Are you pretending to be that stupid," the commissaris said, "or are you trying to prove that I've underestimated you for the last few years? The Chinese have nothing to do with us. You shouldn't have been on the dike. If I hadn't thought of phoning your mother, I wouldn't even have known that you were trying to peel apples on the dike. That conceited attitude of yours, Cardozo, I don't know whether I like it."

"I'm doing everything wrong," Cardozo said. "Uncle Ezra wants me to take over his market stall, but I don't feel like doing that either. I don't feel like doing anything at all."

"Feelings will change," the commissaris said. "Where is this Scherjoen house? Didn't Gyske say we couldn't miss it?"

"It's beautiful out here," Cardozo said. "The soft, lush shades of summer, the flowering bushes."

"This would be quite a simple case," the commissaris said, "if Mrs. Scherjoen would confess."

"No houses here," Cardozo said. "The emptiness of the past. I feel rather empty myself, I'm quite hollow inside, even my cold is gone. Maybe I'm about to disappear."

"Mem is Frisian," the commissaris said. "Perhaps she thinks that what she did is justified. The way society views the law doesn't equate with the individual's attitude. Take Mem Scherjoen, for instance. We see her as a dear rustic old lady and she probably is, but just how far can such a sweet soul be pushed?"

"I see where you're going," Cardozo said, "but you want to push her into murder? If it were simple manslaughter, violence of the moment—but this was thought out, and executed without mercy."

"Listen here, Cardozo. Continuous abuse, twenty, thirty years of torture..." He looked around him. "I think we should go back, this path is a dead end."

They walked back. "It has taken me a while," the commissaris said, "to see clearly how potentially dangerous marriage can be. Applied boredom, nonsensical pursuits, may wear down the sharp points, but if the togetherness started with passionate love, passionate hatred may easily result. And you're right too, Douwe's end was obviously premeditated. No emotion that suddenly flared up, no unprepared attack that may make the killer feel sorry later. Whoever commits murder in cold blood will be able to forestall our investigation in some sly and clever manner. No, a simple confession is probably out of the question."

"We're back at the Sudemas' house," Cardozo said. "Shall I ask for more precise directions?"

"Don't trouble those poor people now," the commissaris

158 JANWILLEM VAN DE WETERING

said. "We'll take the car. It can't be far. Just down that road, Mrs. Sudema said."

"The proof," the commissaris said in the car. "That might be another hassle. What happened to the weapon? The Inner Harbor is a mess, our divers won't easily find it in there. Witnesses? I don't think there were any. If Mem persists in protesting her innocence, we can't even trick her. She's Frisian, Cardozo, you have no idea how self-willed we Frisians can be. I was born in Joure."

"So you won't give up."

"Never."

"And Mem Scherjoen won't give in."

"Never."

"I heard a Frisian joke once," Cardozo said. "Two Frisian coachmen travel from opposite directions toward a bridge that's only wide enough for one carriage. On the bridge they stop, facing each other. One coachman unfolds a newspaper and begins to read. After an hour the other coachman asks if he can have half the paper. The first coachman gives him half his paper. The second coachman begins to read too."

"Yes?" the commissaris asked.

"How do you mean?"

"So what happens then?"

"They're now both reading the paper," Cardozo said. "Nothing more happens."

"How did we manage to reach the freeway?" the commissaris asked. "And why do all those signs point away from Dingjum?"

A State Police Land Rover stopped behind the Citroën.

"Now where do you chaps come from?" the commissaris asked.

"Where would you like to go?" the sergeant asked. "Just tell us and we'll drive ahead. We just heard about you over our radio."

"Heard what?"

"A silver Citroën and a disabled but mobile Volkswagen.

Call for assistance to colleagues from abroad who are constantly getting lost."

"I suppose," the commissaris said, "your headquarters considers us to be retarded."

"Not used to the ways of a country foreign to your own," the sergeant said. "Doesn't that sound better?"

"The mansion of Mr. and Mrs. Scherjoen, Dingjum," Cardozo said.

The Land Rover drove off.

"Some learn a little slower than others," the sergeant said to the corporal riding with him.

"These may never learn," the corporal said.

⑊⑊⑊ 14 ⑊⑊⑊

DE GIER, DROPPED OFF THAT MORNING, WITH HIS CASES of tomatoes, at the Military Police barracks, shook Private Sudema's hand.

"I telephoned just now," de Gier said. "Here's a present. Tomatoes, ripe and fresh, a gift from your uncle."

Private Sudema was taller than his uncle, and broader in the shoulders. His blue eyes sparkled in the sun. "Morning, Sergeant."

"Shall I help you carry this load in?"

"Not necessary," Private Sudema said. Other policemen marched about in the yard, giants topped by gleaming hats above white braid draped across their muscular shoulders and torsos, musclemen in black tailored jackets with folded-back lapels, showing off starched white shirts and collars and faultlessly arranged blue scarves.

"Assistance!" bellowed Private Sudema.

A still younger man turned sharply, marched up, stopped smartly, and stood to attention. "These cases," Private Sudema barked, "have to be taken to the kitchen."

The other policeman bent his knees, stacked all four cases, picked up the lowest, and stretched his legs. He marched away at speed. "One, two," shouted Private Sudema.

"You're both privates?" de Gier asked.

"I'm first-class," Private Sudema said, pointing at the thin white chevron on his sleeve. "Rank. We're in the military here."

They walked to the main building. "You wish to visit the island of Ameland?" Private Sudema asked. "In connection with the murder of Scherjoen? You wish to interview the deserter? We'll arrest him today."

"That would be nice," de Gier said. "Just following up on information received. I'm a detective. I like to detect."

"Would you mind repeating your purpose to our adjutant, please?"

The adjutant waited behind a polished mahogany table.

"Sergeant de Gier," Private Sudema said, "who telephoned earlier on. Municipal Police, Amsterdam, detective. Request for assistance re murder Scherjoen. The sergeant brought us four cases of tomatoes, with the compliments of my uncle."

"The deserter," the adjutant said. "A connection? Please sit down, Sergeant. Were you tipped off? I don't quite get it. Of course, I don't have to get it. But if I did get it..."

"We sometimes hear something," de Gier said. "Last night I happened to be in Leeuwarden. An irresponsible drunk mentioned your deserter. Nonsense, maybe, but then we never know. We like to follow up. I'm here anyway, so I thought I might check."

"Is our deserter suspected of having killed Scherjoen?"

"No," de Gier said. "But there might be a divergence of lines that once met. Separate causes that shared the same effect. One never knows."

"Coffee?" the adjutant asked. "Sudema?"

Sudema stood a little more at attention.

"Could I have the file on the deserter?"

Sudema marched to a cabinet and yanked open a drawer. He pulled a carton file, brought it over, and handed it to the adjutant.

The adjutant consulted the file. "Deserter. Air Force. Airbase Leeuwarden. Gone three weeks. Plays football. Champion runner. Hm. Yes. Likes to sail. Almost arrested on three occasions. In Rotterdam. On a highway in the far south and in Dingjum. Hm. Right. Didn't Scherjoen reside in Dingjum?" He looked at Sudema. "Your uncle, now. Isn't he the lieutenant in charge of the State Police station over there?"

"Lieutenant Sudema sent you the tomatoes," de Gier said.

"Private Sudema," the adjutant said softly. "Does your uncle drink?"

"He doesn't *not* drink, but one can't say he drinks." Private Sudema looked straight ahead. "Uncle Sjurd knows his limits."

"Where's that coffee?" the adjutant asked loudly.

Private Sudema marched off. He marched back again. "They're coming, Adjutant."

They came. Eight privates.

The private who had carried the tomatoes poured the coffee. The coffee had been waiting on the mahogany table, in a silver pot between a silver milk jug and a silver sugar bowl. The adjutant was given the first cup, de Gier the second; the others received their coffee in order of rank.

"There you are. Thank you."

"Why are all of you so tall?" de Gier asked.

"Fertile Frisian soil," the adjutant said. "Pure air. I won't say that we are a super race, but we came out better. Handsome people, handsome cows."

"Handsome sheep too?" de Gier asked.

"Yes," the adjutant said. "When sheep originate here, they come out better." His gaze shot down the length of the table. "Has everyone been served?"

"Yes, Adjutant," Private Sudema snapped.

The adjutant stirred. Everybody stirred. The adjutant took a sip. Everybody sipped.

"Scherjoen bought and sold sheep," de Gier said. "Any sheep in Ameland?"

"Yes," the adjutant said. "Ameland is a Frisian isle, so

Ameland sheep are Frisian too. A murder motivated by sheep?"

"I've never been to Ameland," de Gier said.

"You'll know better," the adjutant said. "I'm only a simple guardian of frontiers, a hunter of deserters, and a protector of royalty, that's all."

"I don't know anything better," de Gier said. "I know nothing at all. I keep busy in case my superiors might be watching. And it would be nice to spend a day on one of your beautiful islands."

"Good," the adjutant said. "We all do what we have to do. Sudema."

Private Sudema replaced his cup.

"You'll be going to Ameland today."

"Yes, Adjutant."

"Or do you have something better to do?"

"Not today, Adjutant."

"Fine. The deserter is at home, we have received a report. He doesn't show himself much, but he does happen to be at home. He's been betrayed. The deserter was born in the village in the north and the informer is from the village in the south. The northerners and the southerners do not live in harmony."

"Adjutant?" said the private who had carried the tomatoes.

"Yes, my boy."

"He wasn't betrayed," the private said. "I was on the island and had a drink in the pub, and the southerners were there and had been drinking too. Southerners have a habit of raising their voices. I happened to hear that the deserter would be at his home in the north."

"You were in uniform?"

"No, Adjutant."

"But everybody knows you on the island. You're from the south, aren't you, my boy?"

"I am."

"We'll call it a coincidence," the adjutant said.

"Adjutant?"

"Now what, my boy?"

The private was quiet.

"Whatever you like. Old wives' tales. Foam on a wave. The swirl of a tea leaf. Are you busy today, my boy?"

"Yes, Adjutant, I have to fetch my motorcycle."

"You have motorcycles here?" de Gier asked. "What brand? I used to be a motorcycle cop. I rode a BMW."

"My private motorcycle," the private said. "A brand-new thousand-cc Kawasaki. The dealership is closed after our hours, so I have to pick it up during the day."

"How about you?" the adjutant asked another private. The private had to visit the doctor. The next in line had to see the dentist. The next three had to attend a party, to celebrate the transfer and simultaneous promotion of a colleague. The last two privates were available for duty.

"So you two stay here," the adjutant said, "for otherwise there'll be no one in the barracks. Sudema, you'll go alone, but keep things quiet. Two years ago we had some trouble on the island. A Marine, remember?"

"A deserter?" de Gier asked.

"Subject was on holiday," the adjutant said. "Ripped a tent while camping—his own, but we don't like boisterous behavior in a military man. Sudema, you go to the subject's house, ring the bell, and ask him to accompany you. If he's unwilling, we'll see what we'll do. Report to me first. Is that understood?"

"Yes, Adjutant."

"Call our vessel. The vessel is available? Did the skipper get over his cold?"

"The ferry?" de Gier asked.

"Our own vessel," the adjutant said. "Or, rather, lent to us, for it belongs to the Army. The Wet Engineers, to be precise. The skipper is an Army sergeant. Our name has been painted on the ship, so people may think it's ours, but that isn't really the case. The sergeant is borrowed from the

Engineers, but the crew are footsoldiers. We're not really in charge, but we make use of the craft."

"Hello?" Private Sudema asked through the radio. "Barracks here. Over."

The radio coughed.

"Are you all right again, skipper?" Private Sudema asked.

"Right, right. A bit better, let's say."

"Can you take two men to Ameland?" Private Sudema asked.

"Why not? It's a nice day."

"We'll be there soon. Over and out."

"Fetch the bus," the adjutant barked. "You. Before you fetch your motorcycle."

The private drove the bus into the yard. The adjutant inspected the vehicle. The ashtray contained two butts. The private excused himself, took the ashtray inside the building, and came running back. He pushed the ashtray back into the dashboard.

"Where did Sudema go?"

The adjutant went back into the building. De Gier followed.

"Can't find cartridges," Private Sudema said.

The adjutant and Sudema opened and closed cupboards.

"I emptied my last clip on the shooting range," Private Sudema said. "There should be a box here."

The adjutant looked in a file. "Ordered a thousand rounds three weeks ago. They usually take a month. Next week, maybe?"

"I have an extra clip," de Gier said. "Same caliber. You use twenty-two Magnum too."

"No," the adjutant said. "Thanks all the same. You have Municipal Police cartridges, and if Sudema lost them, we'd have a week of paperwork. I'm short on clerks too."

"Don't really need them," Private Sudema said.

"Exactly," the adjutant said. "Just imagine that, God help us, you wounded a subject. Do you have any idea what a room in the hospital would cost us per day?"

"But we never shoot anyone," Sudema said.

"It could happen," the adjutant said, "if we had something to shoot with. It's simple enough. All you have to do is pull a trigger. What happens afterward may be beyond all hope."

Sudema closed his eyes, considering possibilities.

"It happened to me once," the adjutant said. "Long ago, but still . . . In Korea. I'll never forget. We had eight hundred men out there, and ten military policemen. We mostly directed traffic. I was in charge of a crossing. I was short-tempered then. Nobody ignored my orders. We were near the front line, and a carload of Koreans came at me. I motioned to them to stop. The stop sign is international, everybody is supposed to know it, but that vehicle kept coming. Some sort of jeep, of Russian manufacture, and the soldiers in it were from the north. By chance—there's always chance, you know—an American soldier stood next to me and was carrying a bazooka, complete with a rocket in the tube, but he wasn't doing anything, for I was in charge of the position. I took that bazooka and fired it at the jeep."

"A hit?" de Gier asked.

"Not much distance, and a big rocket. Hard to miss, Sergeant. It happened that I'd been trying out a bazooka the day before, so I knew what to do."

"North Koreans were the enemy?" de Gier asked.

"Let's go," Private Sudema said.

The bus drove off, the young private at the wheel. "The adjutant is still as short-tempered as ever," Sudema said, "but that time he got a medal."

The trip didn't take long. The ship was waiting in the port of Harlingen. It seemed in excellent order, sixty feet long, painted blue and white, a clean new flag on the after deck.

"Nice," de Gier said.

The skipper welcomed his passengers. "You like my boat? I do too, but she's obsolete, I'm told. There'll be a new vessel next month. Cost as much as a jet fighter, and this one will be sold for scrap."

"A sturdy craft," de Gier said.

The skipper caressed the railing. "She'll take you to the end of the oceans, provided you stick to the channels. She's really too deep for here." The boat, with the help of two soldiers, detached herself from the quay. The skipper showed off the engine room. "Nothing ever breaks down," he said. "Pity, really, I do like repairs. Every two weeks the boys and I take everything apart and fit it back together again, but the material is outdated, couldn't break it if we tried."

"Look here," the skipper said. "Every part is made out of copper. Nice to polish. We do that a lot."

"Stolen copper?" de Gier asked.

"What's that?" the skipper asked. "Are you here because of theft? You're a detective, aren't you? I won't have thieves on board, ever. Couldn't stand it. What's this copper that was stolen?"

"Not on your boat," de Gier said. "I heard that copper was stolen on the island—maybe a rumor. You mentioned copper, and I thought of what I heard."

"On Ameland they like to steal," the skipper said. "Have you heard their song?" He sang to the beat of his wrench, tapping on a tube:

> *"Three good men from this isle*
> *Without forethought or guile*
> *Lifted three beams from a house*
> *As quiet as a mouse*
> *The house fell apart*
> *Now wasn't that smart?"*

De Gier and Sudema applauded, for the skipper had a good voice. They climbed to the bridge, where a soldier handled the wheel. Sudema lit a pipe. The skipper began to cough. "Does the smoke bother you?" Private Sudema asked.

"The old chest, you know. Should be in bed, but it's a bit boring at home. Better to be here."

Sudema looked for an ashtray. "Knock it outside," the skipper said. "Portside."

"Where?"

"Left. That side. Where the wind isn't coming from."

De Gier observed the sea that stretched away beyond the merry bow wave, deep blue to the horizon. The flag behind him snapped in the breeze. Seagulls planed effortlessly above the thumping ship as it began to ease itself into the waves. "Lots of thieves in Ameland?" de Gier asked.

"All residents of islands are thieves," the skipper said. "I'm from an island myself. The sea brings gifts and you pick them up, and before you know it you're picking up everything in sight. A good habit, in a way, as long as you can keep mum about it. The people of Ameland like to talk too much. They even show their thievery in their flag. You know the Ameland flag? Three beams on a blue field, and the moon in it too. Because they like to steal at night. They put in a crown as well, to make things all right again."

"What did they want with the three beams?"

"Sell them to a builder," the skipper said. "On the mainland. All landlubbers are fences. They leave the adventurous part to us."

Sudema came back to the bridge. "Can I smoke down there?"

"As long as you keep portside," the skipper said. "That's left."

De Gier followed Private Sudema.

"Your uncle mentioned copper," de Gier said. "Would the deserter have been lifting copper? There must be a connection to Scherjoen. Did Scherjoen like copper?"

"Uncle Sjurd was really drunk?" Sudema asked.

"Sorry," de Gier said. "I shouldn't have said I got the tip from a drunk."

"Uncle Sjurd can be as drunk as he likes," Sudema said. "But he helps to run the church, and I've always seen him slam the cork after he's had two drinks."

"Not this time," de Gier said. "Let him be drunk for once, and tell me about the copper."

Sudema watched the sea. De Gier watched the sea too.

"Aunt Gyske," Sudema said dreamily. "You met her, did you?"

"Yes."

"If I ever get married," Private Sudema said, "she'll have to look like Aunt Gyske."

"She came out better," de Gier said, "because of your pure Frisian soil. Tell me about this copper."

Sudema sighed. "The copper was used to manufacture cartridge casing for the guns of the Air Force. The jets drop them above the islands, when they exercise on their range. Copper is expensive and the Air Force wants it back, so the Air Force soldiers pick them up, in their own time, at a quarter a casing. Because we patrol around here, we take the soldiers along, or they can hitch a ride with the Water Police or the Navy. Water Inspection will take them too. The Air Force lets us ride their planes at times, if we can think of an excuse. It helps to relieve stress."

"Do the pickers-up of Air Force cartridge casings make a lot of dough?"

"It all adds up," Private Sudema said. "But it takes a while before they get it, because we're all military and nothing ever comes at once. The casings are stored in shacks, and the shacks are emptied only once in so many months. Then they get their pay. The Air Force sends a vessel for the casings."

"An Air Force vessel?" de Gier asked.

"No, Marines. They ride their armored vehicles on the islands' beaches, and one of their ferries will be lent to the Air Force, but the ferry is really Army."

"The Wet Engineers?"

"The Dry Engineers," Private Sudema said. "The ferries are built to transport tanks, and tanks are dry, but the Dry Engineers don't have boats, so they borrow them from the Wet Engineers and run them temporarily—but that can take forever—for the Air Force."

"The ferry picks up the cartridge casings?"

"If things go right. Last time things went wrong." Private Sudema made his pipe gurgle. "All the shacks were empty."

The vessel cut through mirror-images of clouds. The sign reading ROYAL MILITARY POLICE reflected a thick ray of bright sunlight and became a blue and white symbol of joyful energy above the gray engine room's powerful hum. Fishing vessels heading for the mainland greeted authority by blowing their horns briefly. Sudema saluted stiffly to acknowledge their respect. The ship followed the channel indicated by buoys and by branches, most of them still with their leaves, stuck into the water at the edge of mudbanks. "A service tendered by Water Inspection," Sudema said, "or rather by Forestry. They have their own boat too, but registered in the name of Water Inspection." Sudema's pipe erupted in sparks. "No, let's see now, maybe the Pilot Service plants those branches, in a boat that belongs to the Port."

De Gier's cigarette smoke went down the wrong way. He coughed and frantically waved his arms. "You should change to a pipe," Private Sudema said. "Pipe tobacco calms the mind." He blew a smoke ring that was torn up by the wind.

A seal appeared and watched de Gier curiously from inno-cent round eyes, sunk in his round head. "Morning," de Gier said. The seal looked away shyly. The round head changed into a pointed snout as it sank backwards into the waves.

"That deserter," Sudema said. "He sails a nice boat. Made it himself, I believe, a copy of an antique flat-bottomed sloop. Must have nosed past the islands one dark night and darted in and out before disappearing with the loot."

A patrol boat of the Water Police came by, sinister and low in the water, with a sharp prow like a warship and painted light gray, with large white numbers.

"Well armed, I suppose?" de Gier asked.

"Not as far as I know," Sudema said. "A carbine, maybe. We own a few too, but they stay in the barracks."

A larger vessel came by, of the same gray color, again with square white numbers.

"Navy," Sudema said. A cannon without a barrel stood on the foredeck of the boat.

"Does that work?" de Gier asked.

"Used to," Sudema said. "But they lost the barrel years ago. I sometimes ask the sailors about it, but they prefer not to discuss the matter. The barrel cracked during an exercise. They're trying to replace it, but so far nothing seems to fit very well."

The warship crossed the wakes of Water Police and Military Police vessels.

"Quite a show of strength," de Gier said. "To what purpose, do you think? Any smuggling here?"

"Only on weekends," Sudema said, "but we aren't around then. The harbormaster of Ameland reported a suspicious boat some weekends ago, when he was out here fishing. He phoned, and one of us happened to be in the barracks and he might have wanted to go out, but he couldn't raise the skipper. Wouldn't have been any good anyway. Smugglers use flat-bottomed craft so that they can operate outside the channel."

"So you did nothing?"

"We did something," Sudema said. "Our man phoned the alarm stations and an Air Force helicopter went out to take a look. Couldn't see anything. By then the fog had come in."

De Gier rubbed his eyes. "Yes," Sudema said, "I noticed it just now. You have a nervous tremor in both eyelids. Should watch that, you know. When I had that, it was diagnosed as stress; a week's leave and it got much better."

"Stress?" de Gier asked. "You were working too hard?"

"That too," Sudema said. "Long hours, but I think it was my engagement. Aunt Gyske had her birthday, and Jymke and I were invited to the party. Uncle Sjurd kept going to his tomatoes in the greenhouse, and Aunt Gyske kept dancing with me. She had this record, slow blues, and the stereo was switched to automatic so the tune kept coming back at us. Jymke got bored and went home, but I didn't notice."

"End of the engagement?"

"I did take her some tulips," Sudema said, "from Aunt Gyske's garden, but she didn't want them, it seemed. Wouldn't come to the door."

Ameland showed as a thin yellow line, dotted with green. De Gier practiced deep breathing on the after deck. A soldier came to fetch him to have coffee in the skipper's cabin. The other soldier was in charge of the bridge. The skipper and Sudema were waiting at the table.

"An exciting life," the skipper said. "I'm due to retire next year, but they won't get me to stay at home. I'm building my own boat on weekends. I'll just keep going."

"Here?" de Gier asked.

"Where else?" The skipper pounded the table. "This is where I belong. I'll be here until doomsday."

The harbormaster welcomed the ship, telling the skipper that he came in too fast again.

"Can't go any slower," the skipper said. "If I did, I'd be in reverse."

"That bow wave of yours is ruining my dock."

"Next time I'll come straight through it."

"I'll report you to your boss."

"Why don't you?" the skipper asked. "You'd do me a favor. I don't think I have a boss, but if I have, I would like to meet him."

"We brought some very nice fresh tomatoes," Private Sudema said kindly.

The soldiers carried two cases of tomatoes ashore and walked back lugging a crate filled with sole.

"Your own catch?" de Gier asked.

"No time for that," the harbormaster said. "You have no idea how busy they keep me here. The fishermen bring in the sole. Undersized, but each fishing boat can bring in two crates, by permission of the Fishing Inspection."

"Are they around here too?"

"Not in their own boat," Sudema said. "They're using a NATO vessel now, temporarily registered with our Navy."

Two State Police officers drove down the jetty and parked their Land Rover near the harbormaster's office. The harbormaster invited them in for coffee. There was time for conversation, on the subject of tennis. The State Police officers played a lot of tennis on weekdays, they said, for they were off duty over the weekends.

"Do you close down your station during weekends?" de Gier asked.

"Yes," said the officer in charge, "but we could still be reached by phone through headquarters ashore. Headquarters could then call us at our homes, and if there was some urgency, let's say, we would probably be able to go see what might be going on."

"As long as it doesn't happen too often," the subordinate officer said. "Listen, we've got some forty square miles here, and there are only seven of us. There's a lot of overtime already. All sorts of things to do."

"I hear you allow nudism on the beaches," de Gier said.

"Yes," said the officer in charge. "We used to look at them a lot when nudism was still new—some nice ladies around—but you get used to what they have on show. I prefer birdwatching now. More variety. I check them in my birdbook, and as soon as I identify them I cross them off."

The harbormaster excused himself. A boat approached the jetty.

"Shall we go?" the officer in charge asked.

The trip didn't take long, although there were two interruptions. A cyclist had strayed from the path reserved for cyclists and had to be spoken to, and a man who was cleaning his ashtray above a garbage can provided by the authorities, but who had dropped two butts on the way, was criticized politely. Both lawbreakers apologized profusely.

"Got to pay attention to everything here," the subordinate officer said, once they had reached their station. "Coffee, Sergeant?"

"No thanks," de Gier said. "I'm suffering from a little stress. Coffee makes it worse."

"Should try some fishing," the officer in charge said. "We have been told to fish in lieu of expensive therapy. Fishing for eel is most recommended. We put out our trap and pull it in after six hours. Meanwhile we wait." De Gier was shown the eel traps that were drying on lines in the yard. A motorcycle leaned against a wall. "Dirt bike," the subordinate officer said. "I enjoyed it for a while, but it's for sale now. Good rough tires. Will take you across any dune, but the movement is too hectic, gives you a pain in the kidneys."

"The sergeant used to serve with the Amsterdam motorcycle brigade," Private Sudema said.

"Be my guest," the officer said. "Take her out, once you've made your arrest. The deserter is home, I caught a glimpse of him this morning."

"Couldn't you have grabbed him?" de Gier asked.

"I?" the officer asked. "A State Police official? Bother a military subject?"

Private Sudema coughed behind his hand.

"I'm sorry," de Gier said.

"We do try to help our colleagues at times," the officer said, "but we don't mind their business, that's something else again."

The house that Sudema pointed out was surrounded by rosebushes. "I'll ring the bell," Sudema said. "He might not want to come out, in which case he'll probably leave by the door in the rear."

"Should I hang around in the back?" de Gier asked.

"Why not?" Sudema said. "Wish him the time of day. He's supposed to be a pleasant fellow. Easy to talk to, I'm told."

De Gier squatted behind the fence and peered through the roses. In the garden, a cat had stretched itself out to enjoy the sun. Crows conversed slowly on the roof. A peewit tumbled about in the sky. Ducks flapped their wings on their way to the sea. A young man came out of the kitchen door and picked up a rake. He raked the path to the barn, left the rake against a doorpost, and went inside. In the barn a motorcycle started up. De Gier jumped up and waved. "Hello?"

The young man on the motorcycle raced through the open gate.

Sudema strolled around the house. "That was our friend."

"Too fast for me," de Gier said.

"Gone now," Sudema said. "Pity, in a way. Well, there's always another time."

"Got to talk to the subject," de Gier said. He ran back to the station. The officer couldn't immediately find the key to the motorcycle. De Gier jogged around the yard. "Here," the officer said. "In the tray for pencils and ballpoints. We're too disorganized. It's driving me bonkers."

De Gier kicked the starter and manipulated the gears with his foot. The bike climbed a dune with ease, jumped, bounced down, and was off again. De Gier increased speed on the beach. The wheels hissed across the moist sand left by the ebbing tide. De Gier switched the engine off and applied the brake. He listened.

A growl, far away, ahead.

He kicked the engine back to life. The speedometer heeled over. An island, de Gier thought, has an end.

The dot ahead had reached the end and would have to come back. De Gier maneuvered. The motorcycles turned around each other, in decreasing circles.

Cat and mouse.

If you like, Mouse, de Gier thought. Tell you what. I'll give you a break. Go on, escape.

The mouse sped away, but the cat cut him off, speeding through a mean short curve. The mouse fell over and no longer moved.

"Hurt yourself?" de Gier asked.

"Pulled a muscle," the deserter said. He jumped to his feet. The deserter was a slender boy with whitish-blond hair, muscled legs, and long, mobile arms. He hopped up and down, waving his fists. "Are you ready?"

De Gier brushed sand from his mustache. "Not really. I'd

rather have a cool drink. Hot day today. You know the way around here, don't you? A good café with a view?"

"You a military cop?"

"De Gier, Municipal Police, Amsterdam. I'm not after you. I only have a few questions."

"The officer who rang the bell was a military cop."

"I won't tell him," de Gier said, and smiled.

The young man kept hopping up and down. "Can't trust policemen."

De Gier raised a hand. He pressed it to his chest. "You can trust me. I'm a tourist, a foreigner, visiting your lovely land."

"You're putting me on," the deserter said.

"May I never eat fried sole again," de Gier said, "if my word can't be trusted."

The young man righted his motorcycle. "Follow me."

On the café's terrace, peacefully staring at the barely moving sea, across sand castles built by German tourists, disturbed only by children grabbing french fries from each other's paper bags, distracted only by a fairly young mother and her almost-full grown daughter who had taken off their blouses to rub suntan oil on their breasts, the deserter complained. Life in the Air Force did not agree with him. He explained the routine: getting up before sunrise to start another day, during which there would be little to do except pull an airplane to a specified spot. Once there, it had to be taken elsewhere. Back again, maybe a couple of times. The airplane never flew; it was parked. Malfunctioning, perhaps? Could be, nobody knew. Maybe the airplane didn't work. Let's pull it back. The plane is in the way. You, would you mind placing it over there? Who put this plane here? Please, private, take it away. This is the wrong plane. It should take off from the other strip. The pilot is waiting. There's no pilot waiting? Let's find a pilot. No, not you, you're the one who pulls the plane.

"Please," de Gier said.

"That's the way it goes," the deserter said. "I've got a

lot to do, but they drafted me anyway. I have to finish my new boat so that I can rent it out and make some cash to fix up my other boat. I've got to go to Fiji."

"Why Fiji?"

The deserter had read about Fiji. His father had been away too, but not that far away. "They got bones through their noses out there, and when the ladies want you to love them, they take off their blouses. Got to be careful, though. Sometimes they take off their blouses because they want to dive for crayfish. But they take off their blouses in a different way then. You got to study their ways and then you'll be all right."

"They take off their blouses here too," de Gier said.

The deserter looked at the fairly young mother and her almost-full-grown daughter. Mother and daughter smiled at him.

"They don't have bones through their noses," the deserter said. "And they don't do any diving. I really have to go to Fiji."

The deserter put his glass down. De Gier ordered refills. "Your solution is simple."

"Not now. I'm about to be arrested. So far I've outrun them, but they keep coming back."

"Quite," de Gier said. "Don't get caught. That's the easy way and also the least pleasant. Why don't you go the clever way? Take your boat and sail for the mainland. Go to the airbase. Climb the fence. Go straight to the commander's office, knock on the door, and present yourself."

"You think I'm retarded?"

"Not at all," de Gier said. "You're tough and you're intelligent. Explain to the commander that you don't want to be in the Air Force anymore."

"They'll put handcuffs on me."

"Never," de Gier said. "You'll be sent home."

"Why?"

"Because you don't want to join them. They don't like

that. Most military people are group-oriented. The individual frightens them."

"They think I'm crazy."

"You are," de Gier said. "One of the happy few. *I'm* crazy, but I'm very discreet. You should be discreet too. Tell them their life doesn't suit you, that you can't figure out why. Say you're sorry. Then go back to your island, finish your boat, and sail for Fiji."

The deserter thought. "You sure you're crazy too?"

"Ssh. Don't tell."

"You want to go to Fiji too?"

"I'm bound for Papua New Guinea," de Gier said. "That's about as far as you're going. I've been taking my time. My urge grew slowly. You're lucky. It's better to go when you're young."

The deserter grinned.

"Now tell me," de Gier said, "about the copper."

"You're after me for that?"

"I'm not after you at all," de Gier said. "Please put that out of your head. An intelligent man shouldn't have to repeat himself. Go on, what about this copper? Is that why you were in Dingjum? That time you escaped again?"

"Yes," the deserter said. "But I didn't sell it to the fence. I'll bring it all back if you like. It seemed like a good thing, in the middle of the night, three shacks filled with expensive copper, gathered by those silly soldiers, but once I had it the fun was gone."

"You planned to sell it to Douwe Scherjoen?"

"Nasty little man," the deserter said. "He thought he had me. The copper was just the beginning. He had other plans and I didn't like them at all."

De Gier sipped his soda.

"You know what he was up to?" the deserter asked.

De Gier rolled a cigarette.

"I don't go for that sort of thing," the deserter said.

"But you don't mind stealing copper?"

"That was fun." The deserter laughed. "And part of Scherjoen's plan was fun too. Meet some rusty tramp under the eyes of all the patrol boats and pick up some cargo. You've no idea what snoops around here. Water Police, Military Police, Navy, Water Inspection..."

"I've been told."

"But I didn't like the cargo."

"You refused?"

"Of course," the deserter said. "They give that stuff to schoolkids for free, and once they're hooked, they make them wallow in the filth of Amsterdam. Why should I have anything to do with that? Not me, never."

"What did Scherjoen say the cargo would be?"

"He didn't."

"What sort of vessel will bring it in?"

The deserter shrugged.

"When is the tramp due?"

"Soon, but I refused straight off. Wouldn't have anything more to do with Scherjoen. I never gave him the copper. I'll take it back to the shacks if you like."

"That's a good idea," de Gier said.

They rode off together. De Gier returned the dirt bike to the police station. "You'd never catch him," the officer in charge said. "He knows the island inside out. Did you get to see him?"

"I heard him," de Gier said. "Never got close. Well, I tried."

The skipper telephoned. It wasn't that he was in a hurry, but it was getting late and he thought he might be going back to the mainland.

"Been catching any eels lately?" Private Sudema asked.

The subordinate officer brought two fat eels and wrapped them separately. "We smoked them for you, too."

Sudema and de Gier thanked their hosts.

The Military Police vessel was ready to leave to make space for the State Police patrol boat. The Navy ship was expected any moment too. Two helicopters roared across the jetty.

"CIA," the harbormaster said, "cooperating with our Security Service. There's an East German fishing boat offshore, loaded with electronics, to snoop on the NATO exercises that are going on again. The helicopters will be Army, I guess, but they could be Navy too. Air Force pilots, probably."

"And what will they do to the spy ship?"

"Maybe fly around it?" the harbormaster asked.

"Should be our job," Private Sudema said, "but we haven't got the right ship. The Kraut will be in shallow water, outside the channel."

Jet fighters drew cloudy lines in the sky.

"And what would they be doing?" de Gier asked.

"Making hours," Sudema said. "The Air Force is always making hours. They have a different system from ours."

The soldiers brought folding chairs, and de Gier and Sudema settled on the after deck. Sudema lit a pipe. The soldiers brought tea and a dish of fresh-baked cookies on a tray. Seals frolicked in the vessel's wake.

"Seals have the good life," Sudema said. "Nothing to do but enjoy themselves. Makes a man envy dumb animals. Just look at them."

De Gier thought he saw the biggest seal wink.

"You're too right," de Gier said. "All we ever do is work."

〰 15 〰

THE COMMISSARIS'S CITROËN SLID PAST THE VERANDA OF
Scherjoen's last known address. The Land Rover that had
been leading the way parked, and the sergeant and his mate
got out. The commissaris shook their hands. "They sort of
smirked," the commissaris said, climbing the steps. "Did you
notice? I don't really like that. Guides who pretend to know
everything better, and this is my own land."

"How old were you when you left Joure?" Cardozo asked.

"I remember subconsciously," the commissaris said, "but
I do remember. The landscape, the atmosphere, the way in
which the locals think, even the language sounds familiar."

"I went to Israel last year," Cardozo said.

"Did you remember, too?"

"No," Cardozo said. He rang the bell. "Only the street
market in Jerusalem, perhaps, but that was Arabic. I'm not
an Arab. Even so, the stall owners reminded me of my Uncle
Ezra."

They waited.

"Like in a dream," the commissaris said. "Last night I
had a significant dream. I was a little boy and running after
my mother. The house was enormous. Corridors every-

181

where, and doors, lots of doors. She kept closing them in my face, and I could hardly reach the handle."

"I really don't see much difference here in Friesland," Cardozo said. "Looks like the rest of the country. The language is funny, maybe. Samuel and I used to play 'funny language' when we were small. We would change all the words a bit and then pretend we understood each other. I think they do the same here. I don't think there's anybody home."

They walked around the stately mansion, admired the large bunches of grapes growing under the eaves, and sidestepped the attack of a multicolored rooster. Blue herons looked down from their nests in the poplars. The commissaris found an herb garden dominated by rocks overgrown with silver thyme. They heard tires grinding the gravel of the driveway. Cardozo ran off and came back with a bald fat man. The man's cheeks trembled while he bowed to the commissaris. His gaze, through thick glasses rimmed by tortoiseshell, looked forbidding.

"This gentleman works for the Tax Department," Cardozo said.

"Verhulst," the man boomed. "I'm after the same suspect. Are you the chief of detectives?"

The commissaris showed his card. "Shall we sit down?" Verhulst asked. There were some garden chairs. Verhulst cleaned them by flapping his handkerchief over them. Cardozo walked under the poplars.

"You'll be after money, mostly," the commissaris said.

"A hard task, sir." Verhulst folded his red hands on his waistcoat. "We're not as powerful as the police. The public detests us. You hunt, we patiently fish, but I do think I have a bite."

"You do?" the commissaris asked politely.

Verhulst pointed at the mansion. "Behold. Where did the money come from that bought this costly property?"

"Surely Scherjoen disclosed his income?"

Verhulst laughed loudly.

"He didn't?" the commissaris said. "It seems your job is easy. Confiscate the house and lands. Scherjoen's new car is at present parked in our lot. You can take his vehicle too."

Verhulst admired his well-polished boots. "Mortgage on the property and the car is leased."

The commissaris smiled.

"You're amused?" Verhulst asked. "The State is embezzled, sir. Scherjoen earned a daily fortune, by illegal means, in cash transactions. He collected exorbitant interest on unregistered loans. He fenced stolen goods. But on his tax forms, income was balanced by write-offs. Here"—Verhulst waved his hands—"at least two million was embezzled. Where did it go?"

"He hid it?" the commissaris asked.

"I count on your cooperation," Verhulst said heavily. "I suggest that you order a search of the house. I can do that too, but the locals are reputedly fierce, and I don't want to be attacked with pitchforks and scythes. Mrs. Scherjoen is a widow, always a delicate situation. If you step in, the Frisian attitude will be more accepting."

"You know," the commissaris said, "I detest being overtaxed."

"Who doesn't, sir?"

"The system your department is using these days," the commissaris said, "is no good. It provokes unrest. Take this Douwe Scherjoen, for instance. Would he ever have become quite that mean and irresponsible if he had been allowed to keep a reasonable share of his profits? And could he have practiced usury if you fellows hadn't squeezed the citizens to the point where they had to borrow at such ridiculous rates?"

"Well now," Verhulst said, "if you take that angle..."

"We're filling in time here anyway," the commissaris said. "We might have a little discussion. Do you ever think about your work, or do you merely do as you're told?"

"You wouldn't be Frisian?" Verhulst asked. "I've heard talk like this in these out-of-the-way regions before."

"I was born in Joure," the commissaris said.

"And you left," Verhulst said. "Very clever of you. The colonial life didn't suit you?"

"You're joking, aren't you?"

"Do you see any difference? We used to have our colonies in the Far East and exploit our plantations. Now we still have Friesland, same thing again. Reclaimed wastelands that supply us with crops. The backward tribes supply us with labor. I'm from The Hague, myself."

"Have you been suffering from mental troubles for a while now?" the commissaris asked.

Cardozo charged out of the poplar grove. "Now what?" the commissaris asked. "What's that mess on your head? Don't rub it, it's dripping into your eyes already."

Cardozo stamped his foot. "Heron shit."

"I did have a problem," Verhulst said. "Aboriginal-related. It comes back to me when the government sends me here. I've always served the State. I majored in colonial law, but when I was given my papers, our only foreign colony was New Guinea, populated by wild men. I became a district officer out there, and as soon as I arrived the villagers wanted to hunt some heads. Their grinning top pieces flew all around me. My pith helmet got smudged by their blood. I needed intensive treatment for some years, but eventually I was cured."

Fluid heron droppings had reached Cardozo's delicately shaped nose.

Verhulst jumped up and covered his mouth with his hand-kerchief. He ran away. His car was heard to start up. "Good," the commissaris said. "That was one way to get rid of the boorish lout. Nice job, Cardozo."

Cardozo was tearing at his hair. "Help. This shit burns."

The commissaris dragged him to a pump and energetically worked the handle. Cardozo kept his head in the spouting water. Mem Scherjoen put her bicycle against a fence. "What happened to the poor lad?" She came closer. "Oh, I see. Douwe once had that trouble too. He immediately wanted to shoot the herons, but I wouldn't let him. Come along, dear, there's a shower inside."

Cardozo disappeared into the bathroom. The commissaris was given tea in the kitchen. Mem Scherjoen fetched a suit that had belonged to her husband. Cardozo showed up again, in a black corduroy outfit with silver buttons and a collarless striped shirt. The commissaris applauded. "A living portrait by Rembrandt, Cardozo. Very striking. 'The Jewish Poet.' It's in the Rijksmuseum. He's pictured standing on red tiles, with the light coming in from behind, just like you now. Oh, perfect."

"You look great," Mem Scherjoen said. "And don't you have nice hair!"

"I used all your shampoo," Cardozo said.

"Splendid." Mrs. Scherjoen buttered slices of spiced cake. She poured more tea. Cardozo sat on a stool.

"About your husband," the commissaris said. "We're police officers. We're very sorry about what happened, but please excuse us, we do have to ask questions."

"Douwe," Mem Scherjoen said, "was not a good man."

The commissaris waited.

"But I will miss him," she said.

"You married early?"

"Oh, yes," Mem Scherjoen said. "We were together for ever and ever. When I dream about Douwe now, he's my child or my friend, and I'm his, and not always his girlfriend either. Such strange dreams, but they're all real, and Douwe always makes trouble. I take the good side and he tries to keep us down, but we're always connected, that part does not change."

"Do your dreams end well?" the commissaris asked.

"Not what I saw last night," Mem Scherjoen said. "I was his mother again, but I got sick and died and he tried to crawl after me, but I couldn't take him with me."

"And in the other dreams?"

"We're walking somewhere, holding hands, or we're yelling at each other in some kitchen."

"Not this kitchen?"

"No, in a log cabin it seemed, on a hilltop. We were poor at that time."

"Who started the trouble?"

"Douwe," Mem Scherjoen said. "He broke my last plate."

"You were yelling too?"

"Not so much," Mem Scherjoen said. "I always loved him and he always wanted to make sure I did."

"He made you sad?"

"Yes."

"Did you want to punish him?"

"No," Mem Scherjoen said. "I only wanted to make up for the misery he caused others, but he was too active. I didn't want him to drag us down so much."

The commissaris waited.

Mem Scherjoen's silver-gray hair changed into a halo, speckled with the glowing light that poured through the kitchen windows. Are we really being taken back, the commissaris thought, to the images of the Golden Age? He rubbed his hands with pleasure, but then a cloud interfered and Mem Scherjoen was just another old lady and Cardozo was an actor, getting used to a costume that didn't quite suit him.

"Now that I have Douwe's gold..." Mem Scherjoen said. She was interrupted by the commissaris's cough. "Gold?" the commissaris asked in a strange, high voice.

"Yes," Mem Scherjoen said. "It must be in the house here. Douwe always waited until I had gone to bed, and then he rummaged about. He was always bringing in gold."

"Gold?" the commissaris asked again, in the same surprised voice.

"Little slices," Mem Scherjoen said, extending her index and little fingers to indicate the size of little gold bars.

"Are you a good shot?" Cardozo asked.

"Yes," Mem Scherjoen said proudly. "I learned to shoot during the war. The British dropped an instructor who lived in our loft, on my parents' farm. He put up a range for us. With a rifle you had to pull the bolt, but the pistol was easier.

You just cocked it once. We were close to a sawmill, and
the howling of the saw blocked all the noise."

"The Mauser was yours?"

"The Germans left it," Mem Scherjoen said. "Some German troops later camped in our field. They got away just
before the liberation. I found the Mauser in one of their
tents."

"Shouldn't you have handed it in?"

Mem Scherjoen smiled and shrugged.

"Did Douwe fight the Germans too?" the commissaris
asked.

"Not at first," Mem Scherjoen said. "He was selling them
supplies, but they beat him up because of some rotten potatoes, and talcum powder mixed with gravel to put into their
shoes."

"Did he revenge himself?"

"He was never too courageous."

"That night," Cardozo said, "the night your husband was
murdered, you were in Amsterdam."

Mem Scherjoen was still smiling. "Yes, I stayed with my
sister, but I didn't shoot him. How could I have done that?
I never shot anyone. During the war I transported contra-
band. All the killing was for the men."

"Times have changed," the commissaris said. "Women
are active now, they're motorcycle cops and jet pilots and
submarine captains."

"I'd rather take care of retarded men," Mem Scherjoen
said. "Douwe was a little backward too. He never wanted
to learn. I thought of taking them into the house here. Wouldn't
that be nicer than some cold institution? They could play in
the garden and I'd cook for them. Douwe was quite fond of
my cooking."

"Would you have a photograph of your husband?" Cardozo asked.

Mem brought out an album. "Snapshots. I took them when
he wasn't looking."

Cardozo and the commissaris saw Scherjoen wandering

about the rocks in the herb garden, feeding ducks in the pond, digging in the vegetable garden. Mem Scherjoen looked over their shoulders. "He did have his moments."

"May I borrow this?" Cardozo asked. "I'll return the album soon."

"Certainly." She cut more cake. The commissaris and Cardozo chewed slowly. Mem said that an inspector from the Tax Department had been around, but that she hadn't looked for the gold yet and wouldn't hand it over once she found it. "I was thinking of taking it to Switzerland. Change it for money. Then maybe bring the money back? Surely I could get around this Mr. Verhulst?"

"Did you tell him there was gold here?" the commissaris asked.

"No, I didn't."

"If you bring it in as cash and keep it out of your bank account," the commissaris said, "the tax hounds will never know. You might have a meeting with your accountant. Was Douwe's life insured?"

"Yes," Mem Scherjoen said. "Amazing, I never thought he would have bothered. The check will be enormous."

"Will it cover the mortgage?"

"There'll be a good bit left over."

"Your accountant will advise you to invest the difference and live off the income. If you do that, the gold will be extra."

"Isn't that nice?" Mem Scherjoen asked. "I can take care of a lot of retarded men."

"But how will you take the gold out of the country?" Cardozo asked.

"Gyske will help me. She has a good car."

Mem walked her visitors to the Citroën, and waved as they drove away. "Mem has the same eyes as you," Cardozo said. "A soft shade of blue, very rare, I never saw it in another person. She could be your sister. Same character, I imagine. The dove and the serpent."

"What's that?" the commissaris asked.

"Innocence of the dove? The devilish insight of the serpent?"

"Please," the commissaris said. "You can spare me your callous observations." He sucked on his cigar. "But let's see now. Devilish, eh? Shoot down her own man, burn the poor fellow, and ask us for advice about how to save the spoils. Suspect may be suffering from a mother complex. Wants to assuage her guilt by taking care of surviving suckers."

"She isn't stupid," Cardozo said. "And she's got guts. Motivation, opportunity, ruthless goal-setting, it all fits better and better. Will we be searching the house soon? The gold should be found. When we dump a load of gold on the judge's table, he'll be impressed by our charges."

"We'll give her a little time," the commissaris said. "And then I'll phone. I'll have to obtain her sister's number, check out the alibi, see what I can turn up next."

"Won't the Tax Department be happy?" Cardozo asked. "We'll all be delighted. Once again the State will win."

"But a delightful lady," the commissaris said. "Don't you agree? Such a dear woman. What do you think?"

"That I'm hungry," Cardozo said.

"Are we going the right way?" the commissaris said. "All the signs are pointing east. Isn't Leeuwarden to the north?"

"There's an officer on a motorcycle following us," Cardozo said.

The motorcycle cut off the Citroën. A corporal got off and saluted.

"We're headed for Leeuwarden," the commissaris said.

The motorcycle showed them the way. It stopped again. "Can't take you any farther, sir," the corporal said. "I'm State, and we're getting into the territory of the city. If you have a moment I'll radio for assistance." He detached the microphone from his radio. "Municipal Headquarters? Over."

The corporal spoke Frisian. He seemed to have trouble making himself understood.

"Don't they all speak the language here?" the commissaris asked.

"Some don't," the corporal said. "We have our traitors. They insist on using Dutch. Some of us believe there are too many languages in the world. They'll have us all speaking Russian soon." He bellowed into the microphone again.

"Now what?" the radio asked in Dutch.

The corporal sighed. "Very well. The silver Citroën. On the ringway, milepost twelve. Send out a car and pick up colleagues from the Netherlands."

"You are *in* the Netherlands," the radio said curtly.

"Will you send a car?" the corporal shouted, getting red in the face.

"Understood," the radio said, and chuckled.

||||| 16 /////

"I OFTEN SURPRISE MYSELF," DE GIER SAID. "OUT ALL DAY and I still come up with a good meal. Look at this spread. Fresh-fried sole, smoked eel on bread that I'm about to toast, personally whipped cream, and hand-cleaned strawberries. Maybe I'll still have time to toss a salad. And you just bumble about. The complete nonachiever. You could help, maybe."

"Lay the table?" Grijpstra asked. He pulled open a drawer in his search for a cloth. But he used too much force, and the detached drawer, filled with kitchen tools, fell on his toes. Grijpstra hopped out of the kitchen, uttering a string of four-letter words.

De Gier followed. "You sure you're Frisian? Frisians are not supposed to let themselves go like that."

Grijpstra sat down and took off his shoe.

De Gier lay on the couch and picked up his novel.

Grijpstra breathed heavily.

"'You're an asshole,'" de Gier read. "Not you, but the male hero in this book. He's addressed by his wife. She's called Martha again. I would say that their relationship is troubled because she'll never let him have his say. If she did, she might see what he doesn't understand about her attitude. If she did, the book could end well, but maybe that's bad literature." De Gier struggled free of the cushions on the couch. "Why can't anybody ever be happy? It's the same here in this province that's so superior to the rest of the country. Mem and Douwe, Gyske and Sjurd, and Sjurd's nephew's girlfriend just broke the engagement. The disharmony between spouses and lovers is about as bad as what we're used to at our end. Misery all over."

Grijpstra had put his shoe on again and was on his way to the kitchen. "Happiness," the adjutant said, "is maybe not what we should be after."

"Happiness," de Gier said, "is a white toy rabbit with a red ribbon around its fluffy neck. I never liked the idea either. How did you fare with Pyr, Tyark, and what's-his-name?"

"Yelte," Grijpstra said miserably.

"What a deadpan face you have," de Gier said. "I've always admired you for the way you never let on. The suspects have quite normal names, I'm sure. You made up those weird names to make sure I wouldn't interfere."

"Real names," Grijpstra said. "And you," Grijpstra shouted, "why don't you keep out of this, eh?"

"I'm your friend," de Gier said. "We're living together. I'm being sympathetic. I worry about your welfare. You're doing too much, and you should learn to relax. Why are you so busy?"

"Shouldn't I be busy?" Grijpstra asked. "In my Frisian jersey? Under my Frisian cap? Shouldn't I be visiting those human sheep? That bleat up front and rattle in the rear? Because their shit is never wiped and dries out in their ass hairs. Yellow-eyed, brainless throwbacks, happily hiding in their inbred stupidity."

"Rattle?" De Gier jumped up. "I'll be back in a moment."

He came back with the rat. Eddy had collapsed on de Gier's hands; his tail and legs hung down.

Grijpstra had found the tablecloth and was shaking it out of its folds. "Hi, Eddy."

Eddy's pink nose trembled.

"Listen." De Gier's nose pointed toward Eddy's chest. Grijpstra bent down. "You hear it?"

"Rattling again," Grijpstra said. "Cats purr. Maybe it's okay, but he looks sick to me."

Eddy was carefully dropped on the couch. Grijpstra stroked the rat's back. De Gier brought cheese. Eddy struggled up and grabbed the cheese.

"Back to my role," de Gier said, "of loving sharer of whatever you're not getting together these days. What did Pyr, Tyark, and Yelte tell you today?"

"They called me *amtner*. They accused me of *rabberij*. And they claimed to know nothing."

"Your terminology is not quite clear."

"I thought you had mastered the lingo." Grijpstra raised his voice. "I thought you were the scholar."

De Gier checked his dictionary. "*Amtner* merely stands for 'official' but *rabberij* means slander."

"And *belesting*?"

"Ah," de Gier said, "that'll be 'tax.' It's clear to me now. Were you trying to upset the suspects, hoping that they might give themselves away in anger?" De Gier put the little book away. "The usual technique? If you were accusing them of tax-free and therefore illegal transactions, you may have scared them." De Gier shook his finger. "But you didn't apply your method right, for you still know nothing."

"FYUU," Grijpstra shouted.

"You'll hyperventilate," de Gier said kindly. "Control your breathing."

Grijpstra's face became redder.

"Fyuu?" de Gier echoed angrily. "I'm only trying to help, and you just make sounds." He picked up his novel. "Here. She—Martha again—is complaining that she's out of the regular world." He dropped the book. "What is she telling us? That she can no longer make contact with the others. The unhappy woman doesn't know that others are just as helpless as she is. What have others ever done for anyone? Where is my Hylkje? She should be here. Didn't she promise to be here for dinner? Last night she stimulated me sexually for hours, and then when the moment came, she took some drunken bum to her bed."

"'The Man, the Marionette,'" Grijpstra said triumphantly. "Title of a play on TV. You remind me of the hero."

De Gier's mouth opened slightly.

"Watch some TV sometimes," Grijpstra said, "then you won't have to gape at me. The play showed what it will be like once men have lost, seen from the winning female point of view. Swedish, of course. Subtitled and tragic. Everybody goes gay!"

Eddy rattled softly. "Not now, Eddy." De Gier caressed the rat.

"My wife liked that play," Grijpstra said. "I liked it too, for I finally saw how we are humiliated. And once I got that—it was quite transparent, really—I began to behave in an opposite way from what she expected. She eventually left me, and I was free."

"Hylkje is not gay," de Gier said, "and neither is your wife."

"No?" Grijpstra asked triumphantly. "So why does Hylkje go about dressed in leather? Any why does she subdue the male image of the motorcycle?"

"So every woman choosing a heretofore male profession is homosexual?"

"Funny voice, too."

"Watch it now," de Gier said. "But you're right, she does have a funny voice. Bisexual, perhaps?"

"I don't care what they are," Grijpstra said. "They can pervert the codes to the hilt. The law allows for aberrations, and we don't have to bother. But there is one taboo left," Grijpstra shouted. "Murder! And we're the Murder Brigade."

"They should be careful with fire, too," de Gier said. "Arson is another taboo. Arson is worse, for the country is short of homes. There are far too many people. If murder were allowed, the population would decrease, a healthy balance would be found, and..."

"So unhappiness is our fault," Grijpstra said sadly.

The doorbell rang.

"You open up and apologize," de Gier said. "Such a well-mannered girl, arrived right on time, unaware of your slander. Hylkje is normal, healthy, attractive, and under the spell of my charm. Why don't you ever use charm? No wonder Pyr, Tyark, and Yelte didn't respond."

"Evening, sir," Grijpstra said in the corridor. "You're just in time for dinner. And who may you be?"

"It's me," Cardozo said.

"Are there local festivities?" de Gier asked when Cardozo came in. "Are we required to dress up in Frisian garb?"

"A pox on you," Cardozo said, and turned to leave.

The commissaris's small hand grabbed Cardozo's wrist. "Stay here." Cardozo pulled a little. "I don't want to be laughed at, sir."

Grijpstra and de Gier were pointing at Cardozo, laughing and slapping each other's shoulders.

"Enough," the commissaris said. "It's time for an official meeting. And dinner meanwhile. We brought the alcohol." He produced small bottles, wrapped in linen, out of his pocket. "Present from Chief Constable Lasius of Burmania, a most helpful nobleman who gives them out to tourists."

De Gier tore the linen bags containing the bottles, and Grijpstra unscrewed the caps. Cardozo found glasses. The commissaris raised his. "To Cardozo, who can report first."

Cardozo talked.

"Are you done now?" de Gier asked. "The business with the herons is clear, but how did the Chinese in front know about the Chinese to the rear?"

"Sir?" Cardozo asked.

The commissaris laid out his theory for them. "I can't prove any of this," he added, "for all parties are dead. Whether I'm right or wrong, I suggest that Wo Hop, provided his papers are not in order, leave the country forthwith. We can see what happens later. We just might have some peace."

"But how could they presume that the police are corrupt?" Grijpstra asked. "That if one of us cycles on a dike, he carries heroin in his lunch box?"

"The papers keep accusing us," de Gier said, "so the public believes the lies."

"Your turn," the commissaris said.

"I'm not in on this," de Gier said. "Not being Frisian, sir."

"Grijpstra?"

Grijpstra reported.

"Same with my investigation, so far," the commissaris said. "Mem Scherjoen is a first-class suspect. She won't admit that fact. Neither do your sheep dealers. They shouldn't volunteer information at this point, for they know we have no tangible evidence. All we can do is inquire politely."

"While Cardozo cycles through death and damnation," de Gier said.

"Shouldn't you keep out of this?" Cardozo asked.

"Sir?" Grijpstra asked. "How did the Arrest Team know that Cardozo would be cycling through death and damnation?"

"They didn't," the commissaris said. "Remember the Indonesian revolutionary immigrants who ran berserk in the east of the country one pleasant Sunday not so long ago? The local State Police came marching by, on their way to some festival. Luck favors us at times. Fate won't let us lose forever, for if it did, we would give up and there would be nothing for Fate to watch. You should have seen the aggressive exhibition on the dike today. Supermen in combat clothes firing their futuristic weapons. If I dared to tell my wife, she'd never let me out again. War in a galaxy of a parallel universe. A commander knocking off foreign peons without the slightest emotion. A machine-man, an inhuman computer. Automatic horror released by secret training camps spawned by our own organization. A most effective and interesting show." The commissaris held up his glass. "Not that I liked it."

"No," de Gier said, his voice muted by enthusiasm barely controlled.

"Doesn't the idea 'proportion' figure largely in our laws?" the commissaris asked, emptying his glass again. "What will Bald Ary and Fritz with the Tuft be thinking when they're jumped by mechanical humanoid destruction from all sides at once? Their successors will adapt to the situation we are creating and attack in army strength, supported by missiles.When the punks attack in Amsterdam again, they'll be in armored vehicles."

"Really?" de Gier asked, slowly rubbing his hands.

"Get away," Grijpstra said. "You, of all people. One drop of blood and you faint away."

"Me?" de Gier asked, jumping from the couch, grabbing a machine gun from the air, and mowing down all available criminal elements. "Me? I'm a warrior. Aggression is in my genes. Times have been too soft for a long while now. The knight, the samurai, the mercenary are in me. Tanks in the streets. Submarines in the canals. Howling crowds attacking Headquarters. The last fight, with my back to the last crumbling wall. The life of the hero."

The doorbell rang, and de Gier answered it.

"Hello, Hylkje," de Gier said. Hylkje thought that Cardozo looked funny too. She sobbed with pleasure in de Gier's arms. She doubled up when he stepped back. She dried her eyes.

"I'm off," Cardozo said. Grijpstra's hand dived down. Cardozo fought in Grijpstra's grip.

"I'm sorry I had to laugh," Hylkje said. "Wherever did you get that suit?"

"Mem Scherjoen gave it to him," the commissaris said. "From Douwe's legacy."

Cardozo had to explain about the herons again. Hylkje blew her nose furiously. Her eyes sparkled above her handkerchief. "Think of something else," de Gier said. "It'll probably pass."

"I just came from Dingjum," Hylkje said. "After riding the dike on patrol. Lieutenant Sudema has demolished a good part of his house. Gyske came back from visiting Mrs. Scherjoen." She looked at the commissaris. "You don't seriously suspect Mem?"

"A mere formality," the commissaris said. "A technical possibility, however slight."

"Gyske says," Hylkje said, "that it would be absolutely impossible for Mem to hurt anyone at all."

"So says Gyske," the commissaris said. "But Mem's motivation might be just fine. Perhaps Mem would be interested in protecting the world against the type of evil that someone like her husband is likely to commit. In our literature such cases are known, in studies on extenuating circumstances. I remember the case of the American father of a psychopathic small daughter who—in Massachusetts, I believe—was killing off her teachers. The child was, unfortunately, a genius in evil. Only her father knew she was the killer, and he murdered his own child to prevent further trouble."

"Didn't he give himself up?" de Gier asked. "Is Mem Scherjoen giving herself up?"

Grijpstra kept coughing. "Sorry," de Gier said. "I'm out of this, but I couldn't help being curious. Sorry, Adjutant."

"Gyske says," Hylkje said, "that Mem loved Douwe dearly. You're all men, you cannot possibly identify with a woman in such a relationship."

"The female attitude is changing," the commissaris said.

"Only lately, sir. Mem is from the past."

"Dinner?" the commissaris asked.

De Gier fried the soles, flipping them over with smart flicks of his fork. The crunchy fish were served in a ring of fresh lettuce. There was a tomato salad, with a dressing flavored with herbs from the garden. The commissaris ate the last golden fried potato. Cold beer foamed.

De Gier brought out strawberries, under a cloud of whipped cream.

"You're good," Hylkje said.

"The sergeant lives alone," the commissaris said helpfully.

"In contrast," Grijpstra said, "to all of us who fail in marriage or are manipulated in other unfortunate relationships, de Gier lives well. He may not be a Frisian, but he's still an example."

"Exactly," sneered Cardozo. "Who needs women, anyway?"

"Because I laughed?" Hylkje said. "Because *you* looked funny?"

"Yes," Cardozo said, "for I had been laughed at already, and I wouldn't expect a woman to sink that low. Maybe I'm an exception too. I began by adoring all women. I'm still young, my views could change again. I'm not saying you're all bad. No, I won't go that far yet."

"He's weakening," Grijpstra said. "Keep it up, Cardozo."

"So how far would you like to go?" Hylkje asked, adjusting a golden lock. Her eyes had grown larger. Her lips were moist. She sat up straight. Her bosom pointed at Cardozo.

"To get back to our subject ... " the commissaris said.

"Yes, what shall we do now?" Grijpstra asked.

"Please tell me," Hylkje said. "Soon I'll be too old for the motorcycle brigade, and I'm planning to apply for a position as a detective. Do you have a plan, sir?"

De Gier brought the coffee in.

"Patience," the commissaris said. "Perseverance. No loss of enthusiasm now. Arrange our facts. Connect all causes and effects and study the points where the lines meet. Ignore what doesn't make sense, and keep working on what will hold under scrutiny. I see only four connections so far. We have one abused spouse and three conflicts of commercial interest. What else can be observed? The bizarre aspects of the murder? Why did the killer go to so much trouble once the opponent was destroyed? Would an older lady like Mem

Scherjoen drag her husband's corpse through winding alleys? Does mere loss of cash provoke sadistic hatred? Are we right in paying so much attention to three rustic types who smoke pipes under chestnut trees after their work is done? Let's have your opinion, Sergeant."

De Gier shrugged in defense.

The commissaris looked at Hylkje. "Would Frisians be likely to misbehave in such a flagrant manner? Why the urge to totally destroy the enemy? How do you see your own people? As noble, straight, honest, industrious, moral, God-fearing?"

"Oh, yes, sir."

"There's much clear light here," the commissaris said, "so the shadows will be dark. Darkness is part of our being. The part that we hide in shame is always active too."

Hylkje supported her chin with clasped hands. Her long eyelashes protected her staring eyes. "You put things so well."

"Well . . . " the commissaris said shyly.

"And then?"

"Darkness," the commissaris said, "is tolerated in Amsterdam. Tolerance makes evil show itself. Once our bad sides can be seen, we may learn to live with them, up to a point. I postulate that Frisians tend to hide their shadows. When the shameful aspect is masked and repressed, we may expect considerable tension. Our evil will do everything to break out of our discipline, and then, suddenly . . ."

Hylkje looked at de Gier. He placed empty cups on a tray. His shoulder muscles bulged easily under the thin cotton of his tight shirt, which tapered down to his narrow waist. His long, supple fingers grasped the ear of a teacup tenderly. As he carried the tray away, his arm brushed past Hylkje's hair.

"I see what you mean," Hylkje said. "The pushed-down immoral desire will have to break free, and if you hold it down too long, because there's no opportunity to let it go, or you're just too busy—well, I really wouldn't know what sort of terrible explosions could possibly take place."

"Exactly," the commissaris said, "and that's why I suspect that *here*, in this most moral and clearly healthy Frisian mindscape, the causes can be found that led to the horror in the Amsterdam Inner Harbor. Scherjoen was abusing his fellow Frisians. I hear he provided loans against unbearable interest. We can add that sin to his other misdeeds. Who can fathom Mem's continuous suffering? Desperate mothers at her door, dragging starved kids? And her husband to blame?" The commissaris got up. "I need a phone."

Grijpstra took him to the other room.

"What will you be doing tomorrow?" Hylkje asked de Gier.

"I want to visit the market."

"The cattle market? It starts at five A.M."

"I'm getting older," de Gier said. "Older men need less sleep."

"You can sleep late for another week," Cardozo said. "Bald Ary and Fritz with the Tuft aren't supposed to attack until a week from Friday."

"And our side will be exercising," Hylkje said. "The Municipal Police are to set up a command post. State Police will bring in communications gear. There'll be technicians from The Hague. Students from the Police School will be blocking the roads."

Grijpstra had come back. "You don't want to be in the way of all those good people, Sergeant."

"Please," de Gier said. "I'm an interested tourist. *Couleur locale*. I've never had a chance to visit this picturesque province before. And maybe I can find some food. A sheep may be crushed, or I'll find a lost piglet. I have some recipes for stew."

Smiling, the commissaris came back into the room. "Mem Scherjoen does have a dear voice. It's all agreed. Tomorrow afternoon we'll search her house, and in the morning I'll be visiting her sister in Amsterdam. A certain Miss Terpstra." He checked his watch. "My wife is expecting me. Are you coming, Cardozo? I'll drop you off at home, and maybe I can talk to your brother about his bike."

"I'll drive ahead in my Deux Chevaux," Hylkje said, "so that you won't miss the dike, and then I'll come back here."

De Gier washed up. Grijpstra checked on Eddy. He reported to the kitchen. "Rattling again. Doesn't seem well. I'll try some more cheese."

Hylkje came back. De Gier opened the door. "Come upstairs for a moment."

"Won't it be better at my apartment?" Hylkje asked. "We won't be bothering the adjutant, and I don't have flowered wallpaper. Counting the roses may distract."

"Don't be so singleminded." De Gier led the way.

Eddy was rattling in the sawdust of his terrarium.

"Too warm here, maybe?" Hylkje asked. "Shall I open a window?"

"Won't eat any more cheese," Grijpstra said, gently scratching the rat's head.

"This is no good," de Gier said. "We're supposed to look after the little chap. He might be dying on us, and we'll get all the blame. I'll phone the Oppenhuyzens."

"Sorry to bother you, ma'am," de Gier said into the phone. "I know it's late, but your rat is unwell."

"He rattles," de Gier said.

"No, it's worse than that, and he's just lying about. Could you come and fetch him, do you think?"

"Yes, ma'am. I'll let you know."

He put the phone down. "She says Eddy's a comedian. He'll be all right in the morning. Needs attention and rest." De Gier stretched. "Who doesn't?"

"Come along," Hylkje said. "You need attention too."

De Gier yawned. "Ran about on that island a lot. I'm not used to the fatigues of nature."

"I'll wake you up in time for the market," Hylkje said. "Coffee and a croissant."

Grijpstra lumbered off. De Gier stood there thinking. Hylkje rose up on her toes and put her arms around his neck.

"You heard what the commissaris said. If I keep repressing my evil longings, something horrible might happen."

"I'm not a Frisian," de Gier said. "You'll be disappointed."

Hylkje smiled softly. "I do like the commissaris. I just read a novel about an old gentleman who was picked up in a bar by a starving young woman. He took her home and kept being polite and he never hurt her and took care of all her needs."

"The commissaris is happily married," de Gier said. "When that sort of thing comes up, I usually replace him."

"That girl was rather forward," Hylkje whispered. "Do you think I am too?"

"You?" de Gier asked. "I've approached you in every way I know of, and you still haven't given in."

"Enough stalling," Hylkje said, and pulled him to the door. "You come with me."

⑾⑾ 17 ⑾⑾

CORPORAL H. HILARIUS CRIED THAT NIGHT, AND NOT because Sergeant R. de Gier hadn't performed as well as could be expected. Hylkje, after pushing Durk the rabbit off the bed, wept—de Gier thought he could describe the steady flow of tears as weeping—because she didn't have to pretend that she was tough. She said so herself.

Durk bounced about the floor, dropping neat round turds, while de Gier watched.

"And you're so well-mannered." Hylkje said that, too.

"Me?" de Gier asked. "Have you gone out of your mind? Wasn't I manly, dominating, hard as steel?"

"You were," Hylkje sobbed, "but that's something else, you did a good job, and at your age."

"You wouldn't mind if I slept a little now?" de Gier asked. "I'm just a trifle tired."

"And you're a good cook," Hylkje sobbed. "And you don't have a temper and there's nothing about you that puts me off. I like you better than Durk. Can't we stay together forever?"

De Gier slipped away and woke up in the office of a bank. He was signing mortgage papers, at interest that would absorb half his wages. "Sign here," the bank director said. "We'll insure your life, too. Nothing can happen to you now. You'll be happy, sir, forever."

De Gier groaned.

"Say something," Hylkje sobbed.

De Gier was awake. "I have commitments. I have to follow the commissaris around and catch him when his legs give way. I keep Grijpstra out of trouble. I feed Tabriz and rub medicine into her fur. Tabriz is going bald on the belly."

"You're living with her?" Hylkje sobbed. "What is she? An ape?"

"And I grow weeds on my balcony," de Gier said, "that I have to watch, and there's the flute to be played and books in French to be misunderstood." His voice ebbed away.

Hylkje rubbed his back. "You're such a darling."

The darling slept. He snored and was shaken by the shoulders, for Hylkje had no need to listen to his bubbly snoring. She left the bed and tripped across the room on high-heeled slippers. She poured boiling water on a coffee filter. The steady dripping was putting de Gier back to sleep. He lived in a big house now. Hylkje watered roses in the garden, but there was a big bald man in the kitchen hitting a drum, with powerful swings that made muscles bulge on his bare arms. The house changed into a slave ship. De Gier was rowing. The bald man had a whip that lashed out.

"Sit up," Hylkje said. "I have cognac too. Drink your coffee, dear."

"Isn't it cozy here?" Hylkje asked when she sat next to him again, with Durk cradled in her arms.

"Fortunately not," de Gier said. "At home it used to be cozy, on Sunday afternoons. Dad made us listen to radio concerts or we were taken to the zoo, to watch sick animals staring at us from cages. I used to throw rocks at the attendants. They would beat me up when Dad wasn't looking."

Corporal Hilarius pushed out her lower lip. Her eyes were asking. "Nice lip," de Gier said.

"Shall we kiss again?" She caressed his hair. "Maybe I don't understand men. Don't you want to be cozy?"

"I never understand women," de Gier said. "Good for me, maybe. Understanding may leave big holes."

The room had a slanting roof, with a skylight showing a slow-moving sickle moon. Hylkje's body took on a creamy white tinge. De Gier nudged Durk away and drew a triangle, beginning between her breasts and ending under her navel.

"What are you doing?"

"If I blow on your bellybutton now," de Gier whispered, "you'll be mine forever."

"Don't. Please. I don't want to be possessed."

"I must," de Gier said sternly. He blew, but first wiped the triangle away. "A black witch doctor taught me the spell. A dark secret obtained during the course of my duty."

"Why did you wipe out the triangle before you blew?"

"To make sure the spell won't work."

"You don't want me to be yours forever?"

"What do I want?" de Gier asked loudly, "with a female warrior who fights for liberty on the good side of the line? I'm too one-sided already. You'll limit my inquiry."

"I put men off," Hylkje said, "because I dress in leather and ride a motorcycle. I can get you one too. We'll race down the dike forever, for the true dike never ends, and we'll go faster and faster."

"To where?"

"We'll never get to 'where.'"

"You're sure now?" An odd thought started up in a corner of de Gier's mind. A thought to do with nowhere. He tried to catch the thought, but it was riding a motorcycle down a moonlit dike. He kept missing it, which was a pity, for he wanted to crash with the thought, evaporate, share its disappearance. Durk knocked the coffee out of his hand, but he didn't notice.

The alarm clock tore at the silence in the room. Hylkje's hand aimed for it, but smacked de Gier's cheek instead. He fell off the bed, rolled on the floor, pushed himself up, tripped over Durk, jumped up again, and assumed a proper defensive position.

"Hoo," Hylkje said. "That's nice. I like the way you dangle. Don't move now. You must be good at judo."

"Not too good," de Gier said. "Some must be better. I'd like to meet them sometime." He wandered about the room, looking for his clothes. A thrush began its early-morning cantata above the skylight. Hylkje put the coffee on, singing softly.

> *"Ubele Bubele Bive*
> *Ubele Bubele Bix*
> *Stay home, dear wife,*
> *It's only a quarter to six."*

"That late?" de Gier asked.

"It's a quarter to five," Hylkje said, "but it's later in the song. It's a Frisian song. The man sends his wife to work, but he also wants her to stay home to fix breakfast. If you stay with me, you can stay in bed all day. I'll do all the work."

"Good," de Gier said. "But I sometimes have ideas. Like now. I have the idea to go to the cattle market. They're bad ideas, but I can't get rid of them."

"You're so talented," Hylkje said, bringing him his coffee. "You're good with women. Why don't you start a brothel? Exploit silly women?"

"Brothels have regular hours," de Gier said. "I'd feel tied down."

"I'll help you get women," Hylkje said. "You can have my three sisters. They watch TV in stained housecoats now, and have curlers in their hair. With some discipline they would be quite attractive."

"Maybe the commissaris was right," de Gier said. "Once evil is released here, it's ready to take on anything. Let me consider your proposal, but first you can take me home."

De Gier sneaked through the corridor of the house in Spanish Lane. Grijpstra sneaked through the corridor too. Grijpstra's pistol protruded from the pocket of his pajama jacket. "It's you," Grijpstra said. "I've been threatened all night, and then I heard a creepy noise. Did you have a pleasant night?"

De Gier shaved and showered. Grijpstra brought coffee. "Who was threatening you?"

"Women," Grijpstra said. "All Frisian women were after me. Wanted to punish me for what I did to my wife. Hylkje was in charge, assisted by Gyske, and that Mem Scherjoen wanted me too."

"You were pretty good to your wife," de Gier said. "It wasn't your idea that she should leave and you're paying. Anything else happen in your dreams?"

"There was Douwe's skull," Grijpstra said, "and Eddy rattled inside it. And then the shuffling in the corridor, but that was you."

"Fears," de Gier said. "I'm not having them because I'm on holiday now. Having Hylkje around helps. Good company, don't you agree? If it wasn't for Douwe's skull, I would never have found her. When I saw that skull, I thought it was trying to get me somewhere, but I had no idea the place would be pleasant."

"I'll work," Grijpstra said. "While you're running about."

De Gier ran down the stairs and out the door. He drove the Volkswagen to the cattle market. He had no idea where the market was located. I'm glad, de Gier thought, that I'm a sleuth. An ordinary man would be quite lost, but I find this cattle truck and follow it to my destination.

"Hello," a policeman said in the parking lot of the market. "Lost, are you? If you can wait a minute, I'll get a car and show you the way. Where would you like to go?"

"You know me?" de Gier asked. "How come everybody here always knows me?"

"Couple of nights ago," the policeman said. "You were having a beer. Making a pass at Corporal Hilarius. My name is Eldor Janssen."

"Right," de Gier said. "You were the cop who came to

make sure that the café would close, but it didn't. I don't want to go anywhere. I'm here because this is where I want to be." The constable directed him to a parking place between large trucks that had just dropped their loads. They walked together to the hall.

"You're not a Frisian?" de Gier asked. "You've got a normal name."

"I'm Frisian," the constable said. "Names mean nothing. Just pay attention to the way people look. We came out better. The pure Frisian soil. Ha ha. You've heard that before?"

"You're too tall," de Gier said. "I don't like that much. I'm supposed to be tall, but here I keep looking up."

"I won't say that we're a super race," the constable said.

"I heard that joke too," de Gier said. "That's all you have here? Two jokes? Neither of them particularly funny?"

"That's our trouble," Eldor said. "We're too serious. That's why nothing ever happens here. We're slow and we're square, that's why our new building is a cube. I've been on duty for three consecutive nights, and I arrested one pisser."

"To piss is illegal?"

"It is when they piss against a squad car," Eldor said. "I told the subject and he drew a knife. I took it away and returned it the next morning. An expensive knife."

"You didn't make a report?"

"After he had spent the night in one of our cells? Ever seen our cells? Even the rats won't stay there."

"I'll send you Eddy," de Gier said. "He likes to show off. He might lose his habit."

"The rattle-rat?" Eldor asked. "I know Eddy quite well. I used to visit the house where you and your mate are staying now. Adjutant Oppenhuyzen is the local champion at checkers. I always lost, so I stopped going. He won because he made me nervous, I think. Feeling his cheeks all the time and twisting his face. And then, some other evening, he seemed over-relaxed. Most amazing. The rat got on my nerves too. It would run about and suddenly drop on its side and

rattle. A depressing household. I didn't like Mrs. Oppenhuyzen, either. A woman in bad taste. Not her fault, I'm
sure." Trucks blew their horns behind them. "Maybe I'd
better do some work," Eldor said. "I'll look you up later."

De Gier walked into the hall. A man in a frayed linen coat
pulled at a cow. The cow pulled in the opposite direction.
"Turn!" the man shouted. De Gier didn't know *what* to turn.
"Her tail!" shouted the man. Another man showed de Gier
what to do, by grabbing hold of the cow's tail and twisting
it gently. The cow changed her mind and walked ahead,
limping with one leg.

"What's wrong with her?"

"Wrecked."

"?"

"Sick," the man said. "We're the checkers. We catch all
the wrecks. They can't be sold here. The dealers are always
trying to cheat each other, so they pay us to take out the
wrecks. We earn a lot of money."

The cow was tied to a fence. There was a sign above the
fence reading WRECKED CATTLE.

De Gier ambled about. One large truck after another
dropped its rear door, and hundreds of cows ran down, pushing each other. Farmers and their assistants clattered their
wooden clogs on the cobblestones. Most of the cows had
their tails raised and were dropping manure. Animals and
men had trouble staying upright. The layer of semiliquid
droppings grew steadily. Trucks rumbled off and were immediately replaced by others. New troops of cows tumbled into
the building. The steady lowing was punctuated by shouts.
A bull, released from a van, stopped and scratched the mess
underneath with its pointed hoofs while it lowered its large
head. Steam shot from its widened nostrils. The bull rumbled
inarticulate threats. A rope had been attached to its horns.
The bull's owner jumped from the van and grabbed the rope.
The bull's roar drowned the clamor in the hall.

"Watch it! Watch it!" shouted farmers, assistants, and
checking officials. The bull lumbered forward and began to

run. The owner followed, skiing on his rundown clogs, sending up a double spout of splashing shit. People and cows pushed out of the bull's way. De Gier jumped ahead and clawed a grip on the rope. Ahead, the farmer slid along, hanging back. The bull crossed the entire hall until it thundered into the rear wall. De Gier braked on his heels. The farmer slid to the side and back again, coming to rest against the heaving chest of the bull. He tied the rope to a railing. His arm linked into de Gier's. "A drink?" the farmer asked. "To calm our nerves?" asked de Gier. "What nerves?" the farmer asked. "It's drinking time. I'll sell the bull later, there's no rush. Splendid animal. Put up a good show."

"A good show of what?"

"Got himself into the exact spot where I wanted him," the farmer said. "The bulls are kept in the rear. Weren't we there in a jiffy? A tame bull will take hours to cross the hall."

The bar was on a raised floor in the back of the hall, commanding a view of what went on below. A thousand sheep were driven into the hall, bleating nervously, darting to and fro between the fences.

"Coming to buy?" the farmer asked.

"Only to look."

De Gier finished his drink, and the farmer pulled out his purse, which had been tied around his neck. "You're well provided," de Gier said. The farmer flicked thousand-guilder notes under a dirty nail. The purse was hidden under his black silk waistcoat again. "About a quarter of a million," the farmer said. "I expect fifty thou for the bull, which is about right. I need three hundred thousand to buy cows today."

"I could retire on that," de Gier said.

"Not much at all," the farmer said, "but it's more than I usually carry. You see the fat man over there, with the green cap? That's Kryl. Kryl will be buying for a million in a minute. And Wubbe, over there, the man with the beard and the silver knob on his cane? He'll be spending two million if he can find the right beasts."

De Gier shook his head slowly. "And they've got all that in cash?"

"They won't be paying taxes," the farmer said. "We don't like that here. If you pay through the bank, the government is watching. Signing papers." The farmer waved all thoughts connected to signed papers away. "That's good for the likes of you, who live below the dike. Keeps you busy, I'm sure. The busier you are, the better. You were so busy that you didn't watch out for the plague. Lost your cattle, and we'll be selling you new stock. We don't mind making a profit."

De Gier excused himself, for he had just seen Bald Ary and Fritz with the Tuft, admiring cows in the hall below. Easily recognizable from the photographs de Gier had studied, both suspects strolled about at ease, as lithe as lethal predators in a prairie filled with juicy wildlife waiting to be pounced upon. How wonderful, de Gier thought, that I can watch this, and follow at my ease, and have nothing to do with any of it.

"Cattle plague," Ary was saying. "Why doesn't anybody ever tell me anything? So there'll be a lot more trading today. And we never prepared."

"Another serious mistake," Fritz said. "Today is the day, not next Friday. And we haven't dressed for our parts."

"The successful know how to control a given situation," Ary was saying. "I say the hell with caution. We'll do it today. This is our luck, let's grab it."

De Gier was gone. Where were the colleagues? Everybody around wore linen coats and caps and were minding their business. De Gier ran outside.

Eldor Janssen was herding trucks that tried to squeeze through the wrong gate. Eldor wouldn't give way. The trucks backed up.

"Eldor," de Gier shouted, "they'll be doing it today, this Ary and this Fritz."

"Can't be," Eldor said. "I spotted them too, just now. We have their photographs up in our cube. Today they're supposed to be scouting, and they'll be back next week and *then* we'll take care of them."

"Today," de Gier said. "Because of the vast volume of trading that's going on. There's more loot to be grabbed. Where is your command post?"

"Aren't they clever fellows?" Eldor asked. "All the cars that belong to the Arrest Team are parked in the rear, where they can't get out. I've been directing trucks that way."

"Get the trucks out. Find me your chief."

Eldor said, "The command post is next to the bar. The chief constable is in charge. He's a nobleman, you'll recognize him at once. He's so straight that he leans backward."

"Now look at that," de Gier said, pointing at Ary and Fritz, who were buying dustcoats at a stall. "They're about ready."

"Sergeant," the chief constable said. "Not today. Out of the question. Please. Do go away."

"Should I talk to the suspects?" de Gier asked. "Tell them to go home and try again next week? When you're ready?"

"This is only an exercise," the chief constable said. "The communications gear hasn't even been connected."

The commander of the Arrest Team reported.

"You too?" the chief constable asked. "Not today, that's final. We'll do a good job or we'll do nothing at all."

"My cars are blocked," the commander said. "I have no idea what car the suspects will be using, or which way out they're expected to take. I need an open range so that I can use fully automatic fire."

"War tactics?" the chief constable asked. "Here? In my city?"

"Wherever you like," the commander said. "I don't care where I direct my fire. I'll blow suspects to smithereens in any location you will be good enough to suggest. Violence will be used."

"No violence," the chief constable said. "Violence is to be prevented at all costs."

"So why call us in?" the commander asked.

"Listen here, colleague," the chief constable said. "The suspects will commit their armed robbery and subsequently escape, according to our plan. We know what they look like, and they'll be arrested later on."

"*What*?" the commander said. "No, sir, they'll be liquidated with minimal delay."

"All of this still has to be looked into somewhat," the chief constable said.

"Sir?" de Gier said. "The suspects are walking over there. Two dangerous and armed criminals. They've just picked up their weapons from their car. The robbery"—de Gier raised his hand slowly—"will begin ... about ... *now*."

"That's all very well," the chief constable said, "but this is not the right time at all. Peak hour. Here we are, hampered by cows milling about, and the streets are clogged with daddies driving to work and mommies walking the kids to school."

"So what?" the commander asked. "We'll barrel right through any obstruction. That's the way we're trained. *Whap*, another bicycle flattened, *kerblam*, another car on its side. All our arms will be aimed at the escapees and our engines will growl with uncontained fierce energy. In cold blood my men will handle their supermodern equipment."

"This is not really the way I'd been visualizing proceedings," the chief constable said.

"Should I follow the suspects a little?" de Gier asked.

"If only I could warn someone," the chief constable said.

Ary and Fritz drank coffee in the bar. De Gier was at the next table, one ear freed from his exuberant curls.

"This coat is too large for me," Fritz said, "and the clogs are too small. Did I become a successful gangster to clobber about on clogs?"

"This cap is oversized," Ary said. "It keeps tipping into my eyes. It'll be hard to see what I'm doing."

"Why didn't we know earlier?" Fritz asked. "I know just the right atelier that supplies wigs, mustaches, anything. Good thing we brought our guns."

"Our clients are getting sozzled," Ary said. "Shall we have one for the road?"

"Just one," Fritz said.

The waitress brought them Frisian jenever.

"This isn't nice," Ary said. "It reminds me of my Mary's tea. Would it be some health drink?"

"It'll stop your cough," Fritz said. "Okay, here's the plan. Money doesn't change hands in the hall below, I've noticed that. Bills are settled up here. You can see it for yourself. Look down there, over to the right. See the two farmers slapping each other's hands? The one rustic keeps walking away and the other doesn't stay close either, but they keep meeting once in a while."

"Crazy show," Ary said. "Now they're both complaining to their cows. As if the silly beasts care about what prices they'll be fetching."

"It's all for entertainment," Ary said. "At this stage it is. Now. Right. They slapped for the third time. Third time counts. Now one has to collect money, and he'll be doing it here. Once most of them have come into this bar, we'll start our action. There are only two doors. You take one and I'll cover the other. Guns at the ready. The first shot will be a blank, just to show them what's what. Bit of a bang. You're with me so far? Then we move in and grab their purses table by table?"

"The purses are attached to their necks."

"We'll yank them off. Purses into our bags. As soon as the bags are filled we'll be on our way. Into the car and gone."

Fritz looked about him. "Still too few customers in here. Maybe we can use another herbal beverage for our health. Miss?"

"Here's how," Ary said. "How," said Fritz. "We Indians are winning."

De Gier walked through the hall. The chief constable ran by. "Sir?" de Gier said.

"Not now," the chief constable said. "Try someone else.

Any man with a red necktie is a cop," The chief constable jogged off.

A red necktie came by. "Hello?" de Gier said. "Anyone in charge here on this lower level?"

"In charge?" the man in the red necktie asked. He draped his arm around de Gier's shoulders. "I bought the sexiest cow, spent my last penny. I'm so tired, but I'm exuberantly content."

De Gier stared at him.

The man repeated his statement in Frisian.

"I don't speak your language yet," de Gier said, "but I can read it somewhat. I've been reading about a lady called Martha who detests all her men. I'm really after the chief cop in the hall now. Would you mind pointing him out?"

"I left my chief at home," the man in the red necktie said. "And later today I'll be going to Amsterdam. To hire a better-looking chief, but she won't be as attractive as my cow."

De Gier ran off. The chief constable had found the commander of the Arrest Team. Both men were shaking their fists. "It can start any minute now," de Gier said.

"I say grab them here," the commander said.

"Without using your guns?" the chief constable asked.

"What's the matter with you?" the commander asked. "You want suspects to be shooting at my men? They're trained to attack, they can't defend themselves."

"Why don't you have your men shoot suspects beyond the city limits?" de Gier asked.

"Who is this character?" the commander asked the chief constable.

"It'll be quite an adventure," de Gier said. "If you open fire here, you're not granting yourself a speedy pursuit. Haven't you been equipped with fast cars?" He pointed. "Look, they can get out now, the trucks have gone. If the chief constable here lets the suspects get away, you can catch them in open country—or not, of course, if your cars are too slow."

"Too slow?" the commander said. *"Too slow?"*

"What you might be doing outside my limits," the chief constable said, "would not be without my blessing."

"Good country here," de Gier said. "Nothing but narrow, curvy dikes. If you push suspects off the road, they'll land in a moat. Unarmed submerged combat, just the ticket for your men."

"We're trained with knives too," the commander said.

"Knives," de Gier said slowly. "I can see it. Fritz and Ary hiding in the reeds, you and your men crawling noiselessly closer, still closer. Glistening steel between your teeth, and then, *whish*."

The commander grinned, "You're my sort of fellow. Would you be from Amsterdam?"

"Yes, sir."

"One beautiful day we'll invade that city. Rub all black faces into the gutter. Push the furry Far Eastern monkeys up a gable. Liquidate the foreign gangsters. Hunt punks and pimps into extinction. Won't be long now, I bet."

"You think so, sir?"

"Not with the way you're not doing things. Go on selling your services to the enemy. Let misery take solid root. Then we'll be called and we'll clean you all up."

"Right, sir," de Gier said. "I can hardly wait. If you'll excuse me now, I'll go and watch the suspects again. I'm only an observer, I'm not in on this at all."

Breathing deeply, de Gier strolled along. In the past, he thought, a scene like this would have irritated me considerably, but now I know better. It's a matter of tolerating all-pervasive stupidity. The individual cannot change the ignorance of the powerful group, but he can learn to go alone and follow his chosen path. By manipulating my private fate, I will rise to dizzy heights and enjoy myself on the way. Live the good life. Like now, for instance, I think I'll have a snack.

He leaned against the front of a stall. A young woman in a spotless white coat leaned toward him. De Gier ordered fried sole on a bun. Up in the gallery he could look down on the hall. More farmers were slapping hands with each other. What do I see here? de Gier thought. Small-minded greed preyed on by evil. Amused, I follow fateful events that I'm quite free of myself.

"Coffee with it?" the young woman in the white coat asked.

De Gier nodded, from far away, for he was soundlessly moving, at speed, in empty space. Yes, why not, some nice fresh hot coffee.

"Hi," Eldor said.

"And a nice day to you," de Gier said cheerfully.

"Anything happening yet?"

"Any minute now, dear Eldor." De Gier smiled. "Shots will crack in a moment, or one shot to be exact, and it'll be a harmless blank. Further shots might make corpses."

"Get away," Eldor said. "Corpses in Friesland? I've been a cop six years, and the worst I've ever seen was a husband arguing with his wife. I've also seen cars go against traffic on a one-way street, but that's because of the way we've arranged our transport here. I don't even write a ticket when I see it happen."

"In Amsterdam..."

"Yes, sure, in Amsterdam," Eldor said. "But my wife won't let me work there. My wife is a good woman. My kids are good kids. I'm good too. Just look at me."

Eldor Janssen towered above de Gier. His freshly laundered uniform was an artful combination of pure blues, framing six foot six of rugged manliness. Eldor's eyes reflected an unpolluted, ever-present sea.

"What do I see?" de Gier asked.

"Goodness," Eldor said, "is too one-sided for me. I wouldn't mind being bad, but that's impossible in these parts. Ride a horse into a church and rape the bride, I wouldn't mind that. Or be a pirate, swinging through rigging, flashing a curved sword, or astride an old-model Harley-Davidson, in smudgy leather, with 'Fuck You' painted on the back of my jacket."

"Really," de Gier said. "Eldor!"

"I just want to be courageous," Eldor said. "On the right side, if need be."

"Good hasn't won yet," de Gier said, "and as long as it hasn't, there is still much to do."

"It has won here," Eldor said sadly.

The farmers began to climb the stone steps to the bar.

"Watch it now," de Gier said. "The suspects should be taking charge of the doors."

"You're sure now?"

"I have never," de Gier said, "been more sure of anything than that that bastard over there, with the dusty curls under the edge of his cap, is Fritz, and the other bastard over there, in the shiny wooden clogs and the dustcoat with the sleeves rolled up, is our Ary. They each have a hand in a pocket, holding a gun, and they have other hands out to hold on to their bags."

"I'm not to go inside," Eldor said. "The chief constable told me just now. My uniform might just possibly excite the suspects."

"Oh, I don't know," de Gier said. "They're professionals, they won't be easily upset."

"Our instructions," Eldor said, "tell us clearly that in a situation like this, we cannot even think of drawing our guns. Three hundred fellow beings pushed together in a bar, and there I would be, maybe firing hard-hitting, long-range rim-fire bullets. The bullets will penetrate the guilty party and all the not-guilty parties behind him too."

"You stay right here," de Gier said, "where nothing out-of-the-way can happen."

A shot cracked, followed by sudden silence, then by the screaming of waitresses and the melancholy lowing of the cattle below. Eldor considered, his hand resting on the butt of his gun. "Maybe I'll just take a look," Eldor said softly. De Gier walked along. Fritz came hurtling out through one of the bar doors, revolver in one hand, filled bag in the other. Eldor pushed himself through the door and the human cluster behind it.

Ary, interrupted in saying good-bye to his victims, looked around. "No cops here, get out."

Eldor towered quietly, his eyes ablaze with cold blue power.

Ary's revolver indicated a moaning waitress. "You want me to do away with this poor innocent woman?"

Eldor's silence persisted.

"You don't," Ary said. "So here we go, the poor woman and me. Get going, miss."

"Just a moment," Eldor said.

"Listen, cop," Ary said. "I'm serious. You really want me to do away with this lovely lady?"

Eldor's finger pressed the spring in his holster. The gun jumped into his hand. Eldor's arm rose slowly. His pistol's barrel pointed at Ary's nose.

Ary's revolver pointed at Eldor's wide chest.

"You," Ary said, "or me."

"I," Eldor said, "or you." His other arm rose and supported the mighty hand that held his pistol.

"You're making me real nervous," Ary said.

"Put your gun on the floor," Eldor said.

"So what have I got to lose?" Ary asked. "Think of yourself, dear fellow. A young man with a beautiful wife and cute kiddies playing at her feet. Your career, officer, consider it while you still *can* consider."

"I'm going to count now," Eldor said. "Starting with *one*."

"You," Ary said, "are making a serious mistake."

"*Two*," Eldor's bass voice sang melodiously.

Ary lowered his revolver.

"Put it down," Eldor said. "Don't drop it. I'm counting again. *One*."

Ary's gun nuzzled Eldor's knee.

"*Two*," Eldor sang.

Ary squatted and placed his gun on the floor.

Everybody around them cheered and applauded.

De Gier ran away, through the door, across the gallery, down the stairs. He sped athletically through the hall. He crossed the parking lot. He came to a stop. Two cars, their noses mashed into each other, were silently watched by tall, unhappy-looking men. All the men were heavily armed.

"A little accident?" de Gier asked the commander.

"Always an extra problem," the commander said. "How can one ever take all possibilities into account? Some idiot truck, complete with trailer, suddenly shooting off toward the gate. All my routes blocked at once. Car number three, supposedly swerving to the right, totals car number one, which supposedly is the pivot of my pursuit."

"And Fritz?" asked de Gier.

The commander waved a tired arm at the gate. "A most unfortunate concurrence of unpredictable circumstances. My car in the middle, pushed out of its course by the truck and trailer, makes a sudden sharp left, and one of my men, ready to shoot, falls on the door handle. The door opens. My man falls out. Fritz, in his Mercedes, coasting toward the gate too, sees the pistol in the hands of my man."

"You had five cars," de Gier said.

"Three are in pursuit now," the commander said. "But where is the beauty of a well-planned attack, if two-fifths of my power falls away at the start? If it could only go right once, just once. Why do I always have to improvise within the first five seconds?"

De Gier found his Volkswagen and drove into Leeuwarden. The streets were busy. Somewhere ahead, in the core of the city, sirens chanted sadly. Threatened by two lanes of oncoming traffic, the Volkswagen found refuge on the sidewalk. A policeman approached. "Lost, colleague?"

"Looking for those sirens."

The officer listened too. "Would be close to the railway station. Take the next alley to the right, and never mind from then on. Just go straight, can you do that?"

De Gier made the Volkswagen bounce along the pavement and took the first right. The alley was marked as a bicycle route. Ignoring further signs, de Gier took a one-way bridge from the wrong side, broke through a red and white checkered partition that bordered a parking lot, and roamed about between long lines of silent cars. A Mercedes sports car appeared, and the car's pursuers, racing along in two sleek Ford convertibles. The Volkswagen jumped ahead and tried to follow the chase.

Around and around and around.

Monotonous, de Gier thought. The Volkswagen began to weaken. De Gier noticed an open parking space, and filled it. The Mercedes aimed for the bridge, but a Ford tried to cut it off. The military policeman in the rear seat emptied a clip from his Uzi. The weapon spat rapid fire just before Mercedes and Ford ripped off each other's fenders, went out of control, and began to destroy parked cars. De Gier approached the final scene on foot. The Ford's driver rested his bleeding head on the steering wheel. The Ford's horn howled tragically. "*Yayhay*," the other policemen, jumping from the Ford, were shouting while they leaped at the stalled and silent Mercedes from three sides. The Uzi chattered again. De Gier reached the Mercedes too.

"Huh?" the military policemen asked each other.

De Gier looked into the car. "You took his head off," he said quietly. "No head." De Gier sat down, for he was tired now. He preferred to lie down, and stretched himself on the tarmac.

"Everything is fine," a kind voice said.

De Gier thought he might want to sit up now for a bit, but he couldn't, for he was strapped down.

"Won't be long now," a kind voice said.

Isn't the world a friendly place? de Gier thought.

He woke up a few minutes later and heard Grijpstra's voice.

"Can I have him now?" Grijpstra asked.

De Gier noticed a sour taste in his mouth.

"He threw up in the ambulance just now," Grijpstra said. "Otherwise he's fine. Truly. I've known him for maybe twenty years. The sergeant can't stand blood. If he sees blood he throws up."

De Gier stumbled against Grijpstra's arm. "Fritz had no head." He burped.

"So they were saying," Grijpstra said. "But it isn't too bad. Sprayed fire, they call it. The bullets spread, formed a cloud, cut down everything in their way. And that Fritz was no good."

The Volkswagen waited in the hospital's driveway, with a bashed-in front end.

"Did I do that?" de Gier asked.

"It was me this time," Grijpstra said, "but it's all right. Bit of confusion out there. I found the car, and you had left the key. I wanted to save our faithful companion, but one of the Arrest Team's vehicles was still tearing about, and the ambulance came for you. Not a clear situation. You know a colleague by the name of Eldor Janssen?"

"A great man," de Gier said. "An example to us all. A true Viking, Adjutant, they still have some here, I believe. If only there were more of them."

"Sure," Grijpstra said. "Well now, that Eldor has a wife and she also wrecked a Volkswagen, her own, but the front end is okay. She's giving it to us."

"When I looked in on Fritz," de Gier said, "there was still some movement in there. Maybe Fritz wanted to tell me something, but he was short of his head."

"What were you doing there, anyway?" Grijpstra asked. "The confrontation was planned for next week. Here I am, doing everything possible to keep you free of what's going on, and you're out there in a hail of bullets."

De Gier had been bedded down on the couch. Grijpstra brought tea.

"Was I out a long time?"

"The doctor said you were asleep," Grijpstra said. "He thought you'd been overdoing things a bit."

"I fainted."

"You did not, you know," Grijpstra said. "First you ran about all day on a tourist island, and then you spent a hectic night with Hylkje. A visit to the cattle market after that. You had worn yourself out."

"I'm tired now," de Gier said.

"Rinus?"

De Gier mumbled.

"You're not doing something sneaky, are you now? Remember our arrangement? This is my project. Rinus, are you with me?"

"So tired," mumbled de Gier.

⦚⦚⦚ 18 ⫼

"I NEVER THOUGHT OTHERWISE," SAMUEL CARDOZO SAID, "and it couldn't have gone any other way."

Simon Cardozo was trying to carry the bicycle's remains up the steep and narrow stairs.

"You wouldn't be expecting any help, would you?" Samuel asked. "Why bring up this mess, anyway? Leave it outside with the other garbage."

"Shh," Cardozo said. "I'm not alone."

"Evening, sir," Samuel said to the commissaris. "Didn't see you. Sorry about that. A bit dark on the staircase." The commissaris pushed, Simon pulled, Samuel pulled a little too.

"Not in my kitchen, that scrap," Mrs. Cardozo shouted. "Oh, hello, sir. Nice of you to visit us. Would you like some coffee?"

Samuel had a friend with him. "Are you the famous commissaris?" the friend asked. "I read about you. About the bribes and so forth, but that wasn't your department, that's what you said to the journalist."

"How are your legs these days?" Mrs. Cardozo asked.

"Better," the commissaris said. "Thank you. I've been given exotic herbs for my bath. Samuel, I'm sorry about

225

your bicycle. We brought in what's left because your brother says you're handy. You think the bike can be fixed?"

Samuel bowed over what had been put against the kitchen table. "The frame is gone, and the wheels are beyond repair too, buckled, very buckled, and the pedals—these must be the pedals—and the handlebars, where are the handlebars? Maybe I could do something with what's left. The chain seems okay—no, the chain is broken."

"I'm sorry," the commissaris said. "The police are thrifty these days, but I would be delighted to buy you the new bicycle of your choice."

"Sir," Samuel said, holding up his hands. "Sir. Please."

"Don't do it, sir," Simon said. "My brother is a member of the Socialist Party. The purpose of his life is to serve others, right? Samuel?"

"Mrs. Cardozo," the commissaris said, "your Simon has been a true hero again, I came to tell you that. You should be proud of him."

"Is that right?" Mrs. Cardozo asked. "Oh, sir, I was so pleased when my Symie was able to become a detective. When he was still in uniform, I always worried so. When he's in regular clothes he can always get away. I keep telling him that. 'Simon,' I say, 'I'm telling you, me, your mother, for one heroic deed and one guilder and seventy-five cents, no respectable café will serve you a cup of coffee.'"

"I wasn't heroic," Cardozo said. "I was hiding in a ditch and out of reach. Nothing could possibly have happened to me. The commissaris was around, and the Military Police, and all the bad guys were mowed down in the end."

"You were shooting?" Samuel's friend asked. "I thought a commissaris never used a gun. They just like to travel a lot. I read that in the paper. It said that commissarises travel to the ends of the earth, using special funds. Tax money well spent."

"I had forgotten my pistol again," the commissaris said. "The new model is too large for me. I don't want to keep leaving it at home, but unconsciously I never seem to take it along." He scratched his chin. "What do you do for a living?"

The friend made manikins.

"To play with?"

No, the friend was employed by Madame Tussaud's Museum of Wax Manikins.

"Mother," Samuel said, "why is Simon wearing that weird suit?"

"*Now* he notices," Simon said. "I could paint myself green and he would notice next week."

"I think you look cute," Mrs. Cardozo said. "When you were little, I made you a suit out of corduroy once. You were such a little darling, and I always washed your hair. It used to shine, just like it does now. Oh, my little Symie."

"A mishap," the commissaris said. "He was covered with the stuff."

Mrs. Cardozo's eyes grew round. "Blood? Was he bleeding?"

"Shit," Simon said. "Frisian."

"What were you doing in Friesland?" Mrs. Cardozo asked angrily. "You should stay away from the country. I raised you in the city. The country smells. Stay here where you belong."

"And who do the cute clothes belong to?" Samuel asked.

"To a corpse," Cardozo said angrily.

"A corpse's suit," the commissaris said thoughtfully to Samuel's friend. "Tell me, young sir, are you good at making those wax figures that Madame Tussaud's exhibits?"

"I'm gifted that way," Samuel's friend said. "I've just finished the Libyan colonel, and our prime minister, but I'm not happy with our top official. He's a good guy, and I prefer to make the other kind, I'm good at showing up evil."

"Good at evil," the commissaris said thoughtfully.

"I'm working part-time," Samuel's friend said. "Madame Tussaud's thinks that there's enough horror about nowadays."

"And you're an idealist too?" the commissaris asked, "like your friend Samuel, I mean?"

"Certainly," the friend said. "Labor Party, that's me, but I don't labor much these days. Through no fault of the party. It's the reactionaries again."

"Yes," the commissaris said. He got up and shook the friend's hand. He sat down again. "I do admire idealism."

"How do you mean that?" Samuel's friend asked.

"I mean," the commissaris said, "that in these difficult times we are short of funds. The funds you kindly mentioned just now have all been spent. If we upholders of public order ask for help these days, we cannot pay for such service."

"I gathered you were aiming that way," Samuel's friend said. "What can I do for you? I would like to perform some labor."

"Cardozo," the commissaris said, "let's see that album with the snapshots of Scherjoen."

Cardozo brought the album and opened it on the table.

"Nice old bird," Samuel's friend said. "Much too nice for what I'm gifted for."

"Not so nice," the commissaris said. "Look a little closer. What we have here is an evader of taxes and a usurer at thirty-percent interest. If you...." The commissaris smiled warmly and went on, "But this may be quite a tricky project—if you feel you can't do it, you can say so at once—if you could distill the evil from these images and dress them in the suit that Simon is wearing right now, and if you used, instead of a proper head, a burned skull that we'll provide you with, and if you found some skeleton hands that could extend from the jacket's sleeves, and if you made those hands hold something—what, I don't rightly know now, but we may think of a suitable object..." The commissaris felt his chin.

"Yes," Samuel's friend said. "Absolutely. The very thing. I can do it. I want to do it. You have some goal in mind?"

The commissaris asked if he could smoke. Mrs. Cardozo nodded and shivered. "How terrible, sir."

"It has to be terrible," the commissaris said. "You see," he pointed at the album, "this man may not have been a likable gent, but he was cruelly murdered, and we have four suspects, but nobody is talking. I'm not saying that the suspects are not as innocent as they profess to be, but I would like to be sure. If they escape from our grasp, we'll look for something else, but at the point where we are now, the four suspects are in my way."

"You plan to shock them loose?" the friend asked.

"I don't like the method," the commissaris said, "but I don't like any method in our branch. Threats, manipulation, interference with liberty, all our tricks are the same, in essence. A quick shock might be best."

"So my manikin has to be nasty," the friend said. "I can use lights? Some movement? I do have some skills. Do I have some time? Can I do a good job?"

The commissaris looked at his watch. "No hurry. Can you deliver by tomorrow?"

The friend shook his head sadly.

"Don't put yourself out," the commissaris said. "All we need is an impression, a glimpse, nothing fancy."

"Tomorrow," the friend mumbled.

"You can come with us now," the commissaris said and got up. "The skull is at Headquarters. Cardozo will give you the suit, and I'll make sure you have a room in the building where you won't be disturbed. Tomorrow afternoon I'll bring in my suspects. Four little meetings, and we're all done."

"I need help," Samuel's friend said. "And we need something bad that our creation can hold out to the audience. Can you think of something? Simon?"

Cardozo leered and rubbed his hands.

"My Symie," Mrs. Cardozo said. "Did I bring you up for this?"

"Heh heh," laughed Cardozo.

||||| 19 |||||

"MISS TERPSTRA," THE COMMISSARIS SAID, "I'M TRULY
sorry to disturb you, but it's sometimes necessary to inconvenience people when we're facing a horrid crime. I hear
your sister stayed with you during that ghastly night. Was I
informed correctly?"

Miss Terpstra did look a little like Mem Scherjoen, but
she had to be less intelligent, the commissaris thought. The
cause would be in the arrangement of the Terpstra genes, in
the way the microscopic seeds of father and mother had
embraced each other a long time ago. He thought of his
brother, who looked rather like him, and had grown from
the same genes as his own, but in quite a different combination. My brother is very intelligent too, the commissaris
thought, but he makes a different use of his brilliant mind
and merely became rich so that he could retire in Austria,
buy himself a chalet, and pour rare wines for his friends. In
my case the genes mixed in a more useful manner, for I serve
humanity and pay no attention to personal comfort. Intelligence can be applied stupidly too. It's all so tricky, and no
one, perhaps, can be blamed. Human development is probably terminally determined at the moment of conception.
But my brother and I share the same arrogance, the com-

missaris thought, for we both assume that we really matter, a basic mistake that's not simplifying our lives.

Miss Terpstra's face was sharper than her sister's, and her attitude decidedly stiffer. Her apartment in the dignified eastern suburb of Amsterdam was furnished with a straight simplicity at odds with two pairs of porcelain dogs that faced each other on the windowsills. The dogs mirrored each other. "Lovely little dogs," the commissaris said, for Miss Terpstra said nothing.

"You think so?" Miss Terpstra asked coldly.

"In excellent taste," the commissaris said. "You collect porcelain dogs?"

"I brought them from Ameland," Miss Terpstra said. "My great-grandfather started the collection, the whoremonger."

The commissaris let that go for the moment. He meant no harm, as his servile attitude showed. His wife had dressed him extra carefully that morning, because she was sorry. She knew that her worrying did not ease his life. "I do have to work," the commissaris had said that night, in his sleep. "What else can I do?" he had asked while asleep. She had kissed him, for of course there *was* enough else for him to do. Couldn't he play with his turtle in the garden? Or pick up garbage in the park? Or go on a journey with her? Did he have to protect society against itself? Miss Terpstra was softening too, for she hadn't had a male visitor in several months, and this one looked exceptionally neat, in his tasteful light gray summer suit, with the antique watch chain spanning the slight bulge of his stomach, and the well-arranged hair, the neat, sensitive hands folded in his narrow lap, and the cultured way in which he expressed himself. Could she possibly like this man? Miss Terpstra asked herself.

"Tea?" Miss Terpstra asked the commissaris.

He was given a cup. "What is the connection," the commissaris asked, "between porcelain dogs and whores?"

"They were captains in the whaling fleet," Miss Terpstra said, "those grandfathers and great-grandfathers of mine, and they had the best houses on the island, with specially designed gables made of imported bricks, so that everybody could see how important and wealthy they were."

"On Ameland," the commissaris said.

Miss Terpstra nodded. "And they all abused their wives. Women accepted that in those days. They don't now, as you must know."

"Yes," the commissaris said softly.

Miss Terpstra slapped the TV next to her. "I see it in there. Last night again. Did you watch the program? The lesbian communist and her forward ideas?"

"What?" the commissaris asked.

"Yes," Miss Terpstra said happily. "We women are taking over. They can't bed us anymore, those men, they've lost our greatest gift." She spoke faster. "You know what my forefathers used to do?"

"They visited whores in those long-gone days?"

Miss Terpstra's face hardened. "The habit still goes on."

"No," the commissaris said. "Maybe a long time ago. I never planned it, but it was made so easy."

"Bah," Miss Terpstra said. "To make use of the weakness of a humble minority."

"And the dogs?" the commissaris asked.

"A despicable minor habit of the time," Miss Terpstra said. "The whalers used to visit London, before returning to our island. And afterwards the whores would give them those dogs."

"Ha," the commissaris said. He slapped his hand over his mouth. "I beg your pardon, Miss Terpstra; as a sentimental reminder, you mean?"

"Yes, so that they would come again and fetch the dog's twin. You had that type"—she pointed at the larger variety, with a golden neckband—"and there was one size smaller, the one over there, and the tiny little ones, in case my forefathers insisted on discounts. And then they would bring the miserable little beasts home and give them as presents to their wives. Well? What do you think of that?"

"Disgusting," the commissaris said.

"Men," Miss Terpstra snarled. "Douwe was no exception—poor Mem—but now we're nicely rid of him."

"And Mem spent the evening with you? The night as well?"

Miss Terpstra understood. Her voice cut through the small room. "You're thinking...?"

The commissaris retreated into an expressive silence.

"You're really thinking...?"

The commissaris smiled.

"Do you think"—Miss Terpstra's sharp icy voice became a dagger that penetrated between the commissaris's eyes—"that I—I—would tell on my own dear sister, even if she had happened to leave my apartment for a single second? That I, the doormat on which uncouth types like you have been rubbing their soiled boots for generations—that I, the abandoned, uncared-for, ignored, insulted..."

She rose slowly. One of her hands held on to her Adam's apple, the other stretched toward the door. "Leave!" Miss Terpstra shouted.

"Good-bye, Miss Terpstra," the commissaris said.

⁄⁄⁄⁄ 20 ⁄⁄⁄⁄

"How did it go with my sister?" Mem Scherjoen asked.

The commissaris mentioned the porcelain dogs. "Yes," Mem said, "I inherited half of those mongrels, but I didn't like them much." She giggled. "Poor Jenny. Do you know that she's always cutting *Playgirl* pictures?"

"What does she cut?" Cardozo asked.

"There are photographs of gentlemen," Mem said. "Jenny likes to remove their equipment."

Cardozo's eyes grew, and his mouth shrank.

"She doesn't mean badly," Mem said. "She only thinks she does. Jenny hasn't developed much in her relationships with men. Men are just a little different—the same in a way, but turned around, I think." She led her visitors to the sitting room downstairs. "Are we going to have our search now, at last? I'm so glad you want to help me. I kept planning to look around myself, but it seemed like such an effort."

Cardozo apologized for not having returned Douwe's corduroy suit yet, but he told her he had dirtied it a bit and it was now at the cleaner's. Never mind, Mem said, he could keep it if he liked—although maybe not, for later, when the retarded men would appear, one of them might need it. "Some small-sized fellow," Mem said kindly.

Cardozo wandered about the large room. Above a window filled with flowering vines, leatherbound books were arranged on a shelf.

"Antiques," Mem said. "Religious works. My forefathers used to read from them on Sundays. Douwe wanted to sell them. He didn't like God, because God kept loving him, but I said the books were increasing in value, so he let me keep them."

Mem fetched a small stepladder from a cupboard, and Cardozo climbed it. He picked up a book and read the title. *Divine Quarterly, Part III*. He turned leaves and read, *Release us, dear Lord, from the slavery of adoring images of heathen. Save us from the foreign tyranny, let peace and unity amongst us last forever*.

Cardozo put the book back and took another. "Aha."

"Aha," the commissaris said.

"Aha?" asked Mem.

"We're always finding things in books," the commissaris said. "They're fashionable hiding places today. Widely advertised so that all burglars may know. They're hollowed out and made to contain jewelry, money, small firearms, dirty pictures."

"And slabs of gold," Cardozo said.

"Pass me all the heavier books," the commissaris said. Mem opened the books. "Really," Mem said. "That Douwe. Cut holes in the pages. And these books were supposed to be mine."

"But you knew, didn't you?" the commissaris said, watching Mem take the gold out and stack it neatly.

"In a way," Mem said. "I heard him doing things here at night, when he thought I was asleep. He'd take out the stepladder and hit chairs with it. I get dizzy when I stand on heights."

"So you asked us to climb the stepladder."

"I thought you wanted to do that," Mem said.

"Here," Cardozo said. "The administration of his money-lending business, on loose sheets stuck between the pages of this picture Bible. All the amounts are ticked off, so they must have been paid."

"Yes," Mem said, "I put a stop to that. I couldn't stand it, bothering poor people like that."

"And Douwe obeyed you?" the commissaris asked.

"I would have left him," Mem said firmly. "It was the only time I said I would. Douwe would have had to hire a housekeeper, and they're expensive these days."

The commissaris read the title page of a picture Bible aloud. "'The wicked will be carried off by death, but he who loves his neighbor continues to live, even in death.'"

"Douwe never read," Mem said. She sighed. "It's so clear, why didn't he ever understand?"

"I'm not religious, Mem," the commissaris said. "I can never follow spiritual literature. What do you think the text means?"

"Look at the illustration," Mem said. "Here. See? This is death in life."

"Those little fellows must be devils," the commissaris said, adjusting his spectacles. "My, what are they doing to that unfortunate fellow? They're pumping him full of some fluid, through the navel, oh, the poor man."

"They're pouring something into his anus too," Cardozo said.

"Using a funnel. Boiling oil, I suppose. And here, look at this, Cardozo, worms with sharp scales that are crawling into the unlucky chap's ears."

"Douwe had all that in life," Mem said. "Eczema in his ears, it itched and made them swell up inside, and he always complained about food thumping his stomach and his hemorrhoids. Terrible. They'd get infected and he'd bleed through his pants."

The doorbell rang loudly. Cardozo peeked through the vines. "The enemy, sir, ready to pounce."

Mem peeked too. "Mr. Verhulst. He telephoned earlier. I'd forgotten all about it."

"Keep him talking outside," the commissaris said. "Cardozo, replace those books."

Verhulst lumbered into the room. The commissaris reclined in an easy chair. He held up a limp hand. "Glad to see you, I'm sure," Verhulst said. "Are you getting somewhere?"

The commissaris pursed his lips.

"Restored to your previous form, I see," Verhulst said to Cardozo. "Boy, did you look a mess. Those herons are a plague. Feathered varmints, what do we need them for?"

Cardozo pursed his lips.

"Mrs. Scherjoen," Verhulst said, "I'll be brief and to the point. Your husband embezzled a fortune from the State, which is a sin and prohibited by law."

Mrs. Scherjoen put up her hands in consternation.

"Some laws need changing," the commissaris said.

"I need your professional help here," Verhulst said. "This is no time for moralizing." He turned back to Mrs. Scherjoen. "That fortune needs to be returned. To me." He tapped his case. "I'll give you a receipt and you may hear from us. There should be fines, but if you cooperate now, I'll see what I can do."

"We're working on a murder here," the commissaris said, "and you're in my way. Why don't you leave? You'll hear from me once my inquiry has ended."

"Sir," Verhulst said.

"Sir," the commissaris said.

Cardozo held up his police identification. "Mr. Verhulst, I order you to leave this house at once. If you stay, you're trespassing, and I'll reluctantly arrest you."

Gravel flew from the tires of Verhulst's car. The commissaris peeked through the vines. "Now," Cardozo said.

"What happened to the gold?" Mem Scherjoen asked. The commissaris pointed at his chair. He rubbed his bottom. "I'm glad he left. Good work, Cardozo."

"Will you confiscate it now?" Mem Scherjoen asked.

"No. I think you should remove it. Although..." The commissaris thought. "Maybe you should wait a day or two.

Let's say the day after tomorrow, once we've closed this stage of our investigation. Yes, that'll be best."

"I'll have to wait for Gyske, to help me change the gold into money in Switzerland," Mem Scherjoen said. "She can't leave just now, for the lieutenant is still wrecking their house, and his mind isn't clear. Alcohol and Valium, and he has a need to talk."

"What do you think about their problem?" the commissaris asked.

"It isn't serious," Mem said. "Everybody knows it and the lieutenant will find out in time."

"So it'll be all right again?" the commissaris asked.

"Better than ever before," Mem said. "I'm doing what I can. Gyske isn't too patient, and she works half-days, and the kids and all. She's too busy to put up with his rambling. I don't mind listening to Sjurd at all. He keeps holding forth about the shelf in the cupboard." Mem tittered. "Wouldn't it have been nicer if Gyske had used a bed? There's too much guilt here; I think sometimes it prevents us from enjoying ourselves."

"Well?" Cardozo asked in the car.

"No," the commissaris said. "Or yes, maybe. I wish I were a woman at times. It's about time we hired some female detectives. What do you think, Cardozo?"

"What do you think of my mother?" Cardozo asked. "Tell me the truth. I can take it, I think."

"I think she is a dear, caring soul."

"And a good cook," Cardozo said. "Very patient with Dad and us. We had rats in a cupboard. Dad was going to kill them, but he didn't in the end. Samuel volunteered. He spent some time in the cupboard. Everything was very quiet and then he came out. I went in too. The rats were looking at me. Then my mother grabbed a poker, and wham, wham, wham."

"Ferocious, eh?" the commissaris asked.

"Ferocious," Cardozo said. "Mem is a mother, but she

has no children of her own. All people are her children. And now this big filthy rat turns up and harms her kids."

"Yes," the commissaris said. "Listen here, Cardozo, that rat was Mem's own husband. She took snapshots of dear Douwe and pasted them in her secret album. Douwe was her child."

"You asked what I was thinking," Cardozo said. "So there is this big nasty kid and he harms all the other kids."

"When she told him to stop lending money at thirty percent, he stopped."

"The sly bastard," Cardozo said. "He thought of something worse and was about to try it out. Mem found out. Wham."

"Possibly," the commissaris said. "But there are other explanations that might fit the facts. Let's start by frightening Mem. If she's playing a part, she'll have to drop her mask. You know, Cardozo..."

Cardozo looked over his shoulder. "Do you know that a Land Rover is following us? Blinking his lights?"

The commissaris checked his mirror. "So he is."

"His flashing lights are on too," Cardozo said. "I think he's ordering us to pull over."

"Not now," the commissaris said. "Hold on, Cardozo." The Citroën suddenly lurched forward.

"They only want to help us," Cardozo said. "We've lost our way again. We're going west instead of north."

The Citroën screamed through a curve, then unexpectedly swerved off the highway, followed a dirt track, swerved again, and went through some shrubs. The Land Rover sped on, swishing its lights stupidly, crying sadly with its siren.

"You know, Cardozo," the commissaris said, "it's all a matter of conscience. The law that we have been inventing tries to standardize our conscience, but it hasn't been doing too well. There are all sorts of consciences. Some rise above the average measure."

The Citroën drove back to the highway. The Land Rover, hidden behind a hedge, suddenly reappeared.

"Aren't they clever?" the commissaris asked. The Citroën changed into a hazy silver line streaking past dark green meadows.

"Suppose," the commissaris said, "that I have a higher conscience. If I had one I might, from my dizzy level, decide to leave Mem alone. Practically, it would be easy. I could withdraw, claiming lack of proof, or I could write an ambiguous report that the public prosecutor would lose at once. But"—the commissaris thumped the steering wheel—"I first have to know what has been going on."

"Irrational female goodness," Cardozo said. "You should have seen my mother exterminate those rats. Complete, utter destruction, and only because she assumed that rats spread disease and that we might get sick."

"Not that *she* might get sick?" the commissaris asked.

"My mother never gets sick," Cardozo said.

The Citroën found the speedway leading to Leeuwarden. The commissaris blew his horn at road hogs who got in his way. The speedometer needle hung right over. "A dilemma," the commissaris said. "Not uninteresting. Look, there's the capital of this fair land."

"Now what?" Cardozo asked, for the Citroën had pulled up on the shoulder.

"I always lose my way in the city."

"That Land Rover gave up on us, sir."

"We're Frisians," the commissaris said. "Don't tell me what we will or won't do. I was born in Joure."

They waited for a while.

"Cardozo," the commissaris said. "Have you considered Mem's guilt, whether she killed Douwe or not?"

"I don't think I'm following you now," Cardozo said.

"Am I expecting too much again?" the commissaris asked. "Are you too young to comprehend? Maybe you're unaware that men live by the power granted them by women. Now suppose that power is deliberately withheld. Say that one particular woman tells her man that he's gone too far, that she'll have no more, that he'll have to live without her love.

What happens then? Wouldn't the man stumble and no longer be capable of defending himself against normal hostilities aimed at him by his environment? Mem told Douwe to go it alone, and he immediately fell down? Oh, hello, Sergeant."

"At your service," the state policeman said, bending down to the commissaris's window. "Just for the record—or off the record, rather—you shouldn't park here."

"I'm sorry," the commissaris said, "but I wonder if you'd mind directing us to the headquarters of the Municipal Police?"

The sergeant got back into the Land Rover and drove off slowly.

"I'm tired," the corporal next to the sergeant said. "You've no idea how these Amsterdam colleagues are tiring me. I do hope they crack their case, for I can't put up with them much longer."

The sergeant drove the Land Rover.

"Don't you speak Frisian anymore?" the corporal asked.

"You're disturbing my thoughts," the sergeant said. "I am thinking in Dutch. Just like they're doing. To try to follow them. Maybe, if I think with them, I can figure out what they're doing and why."

"Shouldn't you have turned off here?" the corporal asked. "We've passed the cube."

"We'll keep going," the sergeant said. "This highway circles the city. We'll have another chance."

"Sir?" Cardozo asked half an hour later. "Please turn off now, or we'll miss police headquarters again."

The Citroën turned off. The Land Rover drove on.

"Did I do it again?" the sergeant asked.

"Thanks," the corporal said. "I hate to go crazy alone."

⫸ 21 ⫷

"Do you keep losing the way here too?" Cardozo asked de Gier in the house in Spanish Lane.

"Where's the commissaris?" Grijpstra asked.

"At local headquarters," Cardozo said. "He gave me the car, for I have to return to Amsterdam. He'll be taking the train later. I just dropped in to hear whether anything's going on with you. Any information I can use?"

Grijpstra stretched on the couch under the flowered wallpaper, stared at a ceiling tile that was coming loose. "Cardozo works according to plan. He's ticking off moves. He's following a line of action." He pushed himself up. "What will you do in Amsterdam?"

"Make a manikin," Cardozo said, "or rather, I'll help. Reconstruction of the corpse and then bringing it to life. Ah, Adjutant?"

"I haven't lost the way here yet," de Gier said, sipping tea, flanked by fuchsias, legs crossed, little finger raised. "I think the adjutant and the commissaris are suffering from the past. Their roots are here, and they keep tripping over them. You and I don't have to carry memories. Our innocence keeps us right on course."

Grijpstra grunted.

"Adjutant?" Cardozo said.

"If only they had said something," Grijpstra said. "This Pyr, Tyark, and Yelte. Never mind what. Any sort of statement. I would have checked it, found it to be untrue, and I'd have seen them again, clobbered them with my clout. Their fear would have delivered them into the hands of justice. But if they say nothing...,"

"You could have made an effort," de Gier said. "The language is easy enough. I have a dictionary. 'Dead' is *dea* in Frisian. You could have started at the end. 'Not' is *net*. You keep saying *net*, and they may come up with the truth."

"*Net dea*?" Grijpstra asked. "But Douwe *is* dead."

De Gier looked at Grijpstra over the edge of his cup. "Do try and follow me on the intellectual level. Go on, you can do it."

Grijpstra got up slowly. He was lowering his head.

"Adjutant?" Cardozo said. "I'm glad you mentioned Pyr and the other two. I almost forgot. The commissaris wants you to visit them again and invite them to visit Headquarters in Amsterdam tomorrow at five P.M. There'll be a confrontation. Can you make sure they'll be there?"

Grijpstra fell back on the couch. "Not again? Again the narrow dikes? The silence? No, I won't."

"Of course you will," de Gier said. "You'll enjoy it, too. You'll be working toward the subtle solution of another tricky case. Patience and perseverance. You've seen it before. We're ready to give up, but we keep pressing, and then over they go. The suspect's knees wobble, his head sags to the side, spittle drools out of the side of his mouth, his hands fall down, and the truth drops out. Crime and punishment, the balance we fight for, and there you are, holding the flaming sword."

"Yes," Grijpstra said. "Maybe. But do they admit guilt? Are they ever sorry?"

"Of course," de Gier said. "Have you ever met anyone who really *liked* evil? Or committed it on purpose?"

"Yes," Grijpstra said. "All suspects are evil by nature."

"Come off it. Did they have a choice? Weren't circumstances forcing them? Did they ever plan? Dragged by fate, they were, and you'll be dragging them to prison. And we're dragged too. We splash about in the current and we think that we swim, unless you accept that we're all quite helpless."

"Except for yourself."

"Me included," de Gier shouted, splashing tea on his trousers. "Everything's included. Think back, think ahead, you'll never get out."

"You don't belong in the police."

"I don't want to belong anywhere," de Gier said. "That's why I'm enjoying this case. For once I'm supposed to be excluded."

"I don't think you are," Cardozo said.

De Gier sat down and stared at the floor. Grijpstra stared at Cardozo. Cardozo stared at Eddy. The rat had been asleep on a chair, lying limply on his side. He now struggled up and looked over the edge of the seat. Cardozo helped him down to the carpet. Eddy dragged himself along, trailing his tail. "Is he sick?" Cardozo asked.

"Showing off again," Grijpstra said.

Eddy stood up against Cardozo's leg. His red eyes bulged. The dry little hands held on to the edge of Cardozo's sock. "Whee," Cardozo said.

"He won't hurt you. Why don't you pick him up?" de Gier said.

Cardozo reached down gingerly. Eddy let himself be scooped up, sighing his pleasure, baring his long teeth. Dark red veins crinkled through the almost transparent skin of his ears. Cardozo's finger scratched the rat's pink belly. "Cute," Cardozo said. Eddy rattled weakly. His mustache drooped and a spasm shook the small body. "Wha," Cardozo said, letting go. The rat fell on the floor. Cardozo squatted. "Now what did I do?"

"He's still moving," Grijpstra said. He squatted too. "And rattling."

De Gier crawled after the rat. "Rats don't live long, I think. Maybe he's old. Are you old, Eddy?"

Eddy waved a leg.

Grijpstra groaned and got up. "The death rattle, perhaps?"

"Just our luck," de Gier said. "We always come in at the end."

Grijpstra telephoned. "Mrs. Oppenhuyzen? About your pet again..."

"I think he's dying."

"You have no car?"

"Your husband isn't with you?"

"You would like us to bring him to you?"

"Yes, ma'am. Will do."

He hung up.

"You're going to your loved ones," de Gier said to Eddy. He fingered the trembling little head. "And then maybe you'll go altogether. To a better afterlife. Swings and music, choice cheese, rodent sex. You'll have a great time."

"You take him," Grijpstra said. "The move isn't case related. And I want dinner. You cook the dinner too."

De Gier brought in mussel soup and fresh bread. Grijpstra snorted his way through several helpings. "Good," said Cardozo. "Subtle flavor."

"Frisian, of course," de Gier said. "The recipe was in the paper. Curry, flour, cream, and stir well. The mussels are fresh, compliments of the Military Police."

"Did you see them again?" Grijpstra asked.

"Thought I'd drop in for a chat," de Gier said. "They were having their coffee and cake, off the mahogany table. Told me a good tale. Very exciting, their daily routine. Some copper was stolen from the islands, property of the military. Amazing. This morning the copper turned up again. And then there was this deserter that they were hunting, but he turned up by himself too, and he'll be let off. There's too much manpower, the Air Force is automated. The less men about, the better."

De Gier cut bread and passed the butter.

Grijpstra and Cardozo weren't listening too well.

"Like the bread?" de Gier asked. "Lieutenant Sudema baked it himself. I visited him too. He's done with the wall and has replaced it with three posts from Ameland. His nephew brought them in, in the Military Police patrol boat, but that boat isn't really theirs, it belongs to the Wet Engineers."

"More soup," Grijpstra said.

"Yes," de Gier said, "and the Sudema wall will go up again. He's been given some bricks by the Water Inspection. The bricks were brought in by the Game Warden Department; he exchanged them for tomatoes. The tomatoes will end up with the Navy, who'll send an Army truck to his greenhouse, a truck temporarily registered with the Municipal Police."

"More bread," Grijpstra said.

"It'll take time," de Gier said. "Sudema is distracted. Keeps kissing his wife. Embarrassing. I had to watch it."

"What are you really doing?" Grijpstra asked, cleaning his plate with the last crust of bread.

"Too much," de Gier said. "Coffee, Adjutant? You can do the dishes, Cardozo."

Cardozo had to go. De Gier waved as the Citroën left the street. Grijpstra did the dishes.

The doorbell rang.

"Hello, Hylkje," de Gier said.

"I'm not going," Grijpstra shouted from the kitchen. "I've got to see Phyr, Tyark, and Yelte. You take the rat."

Hylkje and de Gier went to look at Eddy. Only the rat's nose moved. Hylkje touched one of Eddy's feet. She let go quickly. "Cold."

"Warm them," de Gier said.

"I'd rather warm yours," Hylkje said. "In your bed in Amsterdam, the one you told me about, with the brass ornaments on each side. I'll come and visit you from time to time. I won't stay. No commitment. I'm not after you at all. Maybe you think that, and are trying to keep your distance, but there's no need. I'll bring coffee and my filter machine, and Sunday evening I'll be off. No aftermath. Nothing."

"Promise?" de Gier asked.

"Promise."

"Not me," Grijpstra shouted from the kitchen. "You take Eddy. You used every pot in the house to make a pint of mussel soup. I'll be here for hours."

"My apartment faces a park," de Gier said. "I'll take you for a walk. We can feed the ducks."

"How romantic," Hylkje's eyelashes fluttered.

"I've got to go to Dinjum too," Grijpstra shouted, "to tell the lieutenant where I hid his pistol. I'll be busy all night."

"I'd like some romance tonight," Hylkje said.

"We'll combine all our duties," de Gier said, "and construct activity that provides optimal satisfaction for all parties concerned. Eddy has to go to Engwierum. Grijpstra needs the Volkswagen. There's a full moon tonight. You have your Deux Chevaux. This is beautiful country. You want to be romantic. You and I will go for a drive. Everything fits in."

"Eddy's death too?" Hylkje asked.

"Of course," de Gier said.

De Gier picked up Eddy, moving both his hands slowly under the small body.

"You did that at the right moment," Hylkje said. "You knew I was ready to beat you up. I can't stand that cold logic of yours and the way you make others fit into your plans. You're inhuman. What am I to you? Something that you can combine?"

De Gier took Eddy into the kitchen to say good-bye to Grijpstra.

"You abuse me," Hylkje hissed in the car.

"I use you," de Gier said warmly.

"I'm not going to be forced into anything," Hylkje said.

"I'm merely making use of your desire," de Gier said, "like you use mine. What's wrong with that? Isn't there mutual benefit?"

"Oh," Hylkje whispered hoarsely.

"I do like your voice," de Gier said.

Eddy rattled, shook, and slackened in de Gier's hands.

"Eddy is all used up," de Gier said.

⑉⑉⑉ 22 ⑊⑊⑊

"POLICE?" MRS. OPPENHUYZEN ASKED WHEN SHE OPENED the door.

"Now that you mention it," de Gier said, "I had forgotten, but I am. And Hylkje too, she's with the State Police. We came to deliver the dead."

That was crude. It's no time to be flippant when you're handing someone a dear dead pet. De Gier felt sorry, but he didn't like Mrs. Oppenhuyzen, there was that too. He realized why. Mrs. Oppenhuyzen's dress was printed with the same flower pattern as the wallpaper in her city house. Mrs. Oppenhuyzen was a printed rose. De Gier was familiar with this type of woman, familiar but uncomfortable, for they don't look good and they live drably. Was this the egocentric argument that forced him to live alone? But I like to be alone, de Gier thought. Alone with Tabriz, and Grijpstra over for coffee once a week, and maybe Hylkje for a weekend but no commitment, a promise is a promise.

"Please come in," Mrs. Oppenhuyzen said. "I'm sorry Eddy kept causing trouble, and that you had to come all the way here."

De Gier had to bend over so as not to hit his head against a brass Chinese lamp in which four sharp-tailed dragons held up the bulb. Walls and ceiling were made out of sheets of pressed sawdust covered with peeling paint. Mrs. Oppenhuyzen's ample shape swung ahead. De Gier still carried dead Eddy.

"Oh, dear," Mrs. Oppenhuyzen said, "nothing but trouble."

He remembered an aunt of his, who also wore flowered dresses and liked to complain, whom he had visited once and never again. He couldn't have been more than three years old at the time, and she had lived in some suburb, surrounded by knickknacks from the Far East, where her husband had been a soldier. He had escaped halfway through the visit, and was found by strangers and taken to a police station, where he forgot his name out of spite.

Mrs. Oppenhuyzen directed them to plastic camping chairs, mumbling, biting a finger, and adjusting her hair, which was tied in a bun that had become undone. "I don't really want him," she said, nodding toward Eddy. "He belongs to Sybe, you see. A holiday doesn't mean anything to my husband. He's always working, he hardly comes here. I was to go first and Sybe would bring Eddy later, but he never did."

"Your husband works during holidays?" de Gier asked.

"He's always about," Mrs. Oppenhuyzen said, "except when he's in pain."

"What's his ailment?" Hylkje asked.

"Trigeminal neuralgia," Mrs. Oppenhuyzen said.

"Something with nerves?" de Gier asked.

"A pain," Mrs. Oppenhuyzen said. "In his face. The triple facial nerve, you know? There are two varieties of the disease. One is hopeless, they say, for they don't know what it is, and the other has to do with infection." She worked on her hair bun. "What do I know? That's what the doctor says."

"From which variety does your husband suffer?" de Gier asked.

"Sybe has the hopeless kind. Can't be cured at all. Sure,

he can eat aspirin but that gives him a pain in his tummy that isn't nice either."

"The poor man," Hylkje said.

"So you are police too?" Mrs. Oppenhuyzen asked Hylkje.

"Yes," Hylkje said. "A colleague of your husband's."

"But you're State Police," Mrs. Oppenhuyzen said. "We have State Police here, in Engwierum. It's such a small village, there's no Municipal Police."

"Right," Hylkje said.

"And you are Municipal Police," Mrs. Oppenhuyzen said to de Gier.

"From Amsterdam, ma'am. I'm with the Murder Brigade."

"I see," Mrs. Oppenhuyzen said. "Well, Sybe isn't here. He did come in earlier on, for his face hurt him again. I got him some cough syrup, the codeine helps somewhat. Our doctor doesn't want to prescribe codeine, but you can always buy cough syrup over the counter. It nauseates him, but it does lessen the pain."

"And where's your husband now?" de Gier asked. "I would like to tell him about Eddy. It's a bad thing that Eddy had to die while we were taking care of him. I fed him the cheese you said he likes, and bathed him a few times, but he wasn't getting any better. He kept rattling on us."

"Would you like a drink?" Mrs. Oppenhuyzen asked. "Sybe has just stocked up. He likes to drink when he's in pain."

"We came by car," Hylkje said.

"No, thank you," de Gier said. "So where's your husband now?"

"In Bolsward," Mrs. Oppenhuyzen said. "He had to see Mr. Wang. You know your way about in Bolsward?"

"My aunt lives there," Hylkje said.

"In the new part of town," Mrs. Oppenhuyzen said. "A Chinese restaurant. Such a lot of trouble with the Chinese nowadays. Sybe doesn't want them here, but they keep coming from the south. He helps them with their papers."

"What sort of car does your husband drive?" de Gier asked.

"A Saab."

"Saabs are nice," Hylkje said. "My father was going to buy one, but then he heard the price."

"Ours is very old," Mrs. Oppenhuyzen said. "It doesn't work very well these days. Sybe prefers to drive his police car, but he can't do that now, for he's on holiday."

"I hope we're not causing you any trouble," de Gier said. "We kept your house in good order. I used some of your flour today, I needed it for the soup, but I'll replace what I took. We also picked some herbs from your garden. I hope you don't mind."

"No," Mrs. Oppenhuyzen said. "Sybe and I weren't quarreling because the chief constable wanted you in the house. It was the pain again. I should have more patience, but Sybe keeps going to Amsterdam, and he smells when he comes home. It's irritating. All that pain." She swept her hands about as if she were chasing insects off.

De Gier was sorry he wasn't sorry. It must be a curse to live with a spouse who's forever in pain.

"It must be nice out here," Hylkje said. "I can hear the sea."

"The birds sing in the morning," Mrs. Oppenhuyzen said. "I have a bit of a garden. The vegetables are going well this year."

De Gier smiled. "You've been to Singapore?" he asked.

"Because of the needles," Mrs. Oppenhuyzen explained. "There are doctors there who insert needles. Sybe looked like a porcupine, stuck full of needles."

"Acupuncture," Hylkje said. "It's supposed to be most effective. The Chinese know about medicine, they have practiced for four thousand years. In the West, medicine is still new."

Mrs. Oppenhuyzen said that acupuncture had done nothing for Sybe.

"What gave you the idea to go all the way to Singapore?" de Gier asked.

"Sybe has this friend," Mrs. Oppenhuyzen said, "Mr. Wang. He's with him now. Such a nice man. Mr. Wang said we should go."

"An expensive journey?"

"Oh, yes."

"Enjoyable?" Hylkje asked.

She was glad to be back, Mrs. Oppenhuyzen said. All those Chinese. There were brown people out there too, and some white people even, but the needle doctor was Chinese, so they had to stay in the Chinese quarter, in a boarding-house, and they ate noodles for breakfast. One evening all the streets exploded; she thought there was a war.

"There wasn't?" de Gier asked.

"No. Fireworks, but I didn't like it at all. After that I wouldn't go out anymore, and we still had to stay, for the return ticket wasn't valid yet. And my stomach, oh, I was always in the bathroom. Squid doesn't agree with me at all."

"And your husband's pain didn't get better?"

"No," Mrs. Oppenhuyzen said. "That triple nerve is so sensitive. Every time he yawned or coughed it started again, such a terrible pain."

"The poor man," Hylkje said.

"We won't bother you any longer," de Gier said.

Mrs. Oppenhuyzen picked up Eddy and walked her visitors to the front door. "Mr., uh . . ."

"Yes?"

"Look, I'm sorry," Mrs. Oppenhuyzen said, "but I don't know what to do with a dead rat. He belongs to Sybe, and Sybe isn't here. Can't you take him with you? I'll tell Sybe Eddy died and that you buried him somewhere."

"What are you going to do with the rat?" Hylkje asked. "Throw him out? That's not very hygienic."

De Gier dropped Eddy on the rear seat. "Don't know yet. I'll think of something. Bury him in the garden?"

"What are you planning?"

"I thought we would just keep going," de Gier said. "We always keep going. We usually figure it out in the end. It doesn't matter if I'm in on it or not, I'll just keep watching from the side."

"With us," Hylkje said. "What are you planning with *us*?"

"How did you like Mrs. Oppenhuyzen?" de Gier asked.

Hylkje shrugged. "Another stupid woman. Married a fool who likes to visit whores. Can't even stay home with her when they're on holiday. Stinks of perfume when he comes to pick up clean clothes."

De Gier's head hung to the side.

"You wouldn't be asleep now?" Hylkje said.

"I'm thinking," de Gier said. "I think better when I'm asleep. No new impressions to distract my line of thought."

"Are you thinking about us?"

"Not really," de Gier said.

"Think about us."

"What do you want me to think?" de Gier asked. "You're a modern woman, equalized and all. You're enjoying your self-won freedom."

"I wouldn't mind having your baby," Hylkje said. "A stupid fat baby, with shrimpy toes and a big mustache."

"Fat?" de Gier said, raising his head. "Grijpstra is fat. You'll have to change direction."

"All babies I dream about are fat," Hylkje said. "Don't you want a baby?"

"Sure," de Gier said. "But this planet is too small. It's uncomfortable here. I hadn't planned on coming myself, but something went wrong again. If I cause babies, they'll grow up and blame me. 'Why, Dad?' What will I say?"

"I can explain it to them," Hylkje said. "I'll get them little motorcycles, they'll have a good time."

"Can I borrow your car when we're back in Leeuwarden?" de Gier asked. "I want to go to Bolsward."

"Why?"

"I never really know why," de Gier said. "Whenever I

think I have the answer, it's the answer to the wrong question. Just let me go to Bolsward. I won't be long. You'll have your car back before you go to work."

"It's some distance, you must be tired." She parked the car. "Stay here with me."

"It can't be far," de Gier said. "That's what I like about this country; everything is just around the corner. You talk about wide spaces, but they're highly illusory. Just a few square kilometers and a few ponds here and there."

"Yes, you're much bigger than me," Hylkje shouted. "You're a gigantic Dutchman and I'm a provincial dwarf. Get back to your real world below the dike, to your filthy whores. Leave me alone." She jumped out of the car.

"'Bye, Hylkje." The Deux Chevaux swung away. Its noisy engine drowned Hylkje's screams.

ⅢⅢ 23 ⅢⅢ

THE CHIEF CONSTABLE WAS ABOUT TO GET INTO HIS CAR.
"Hello, Mr. Lasius of Burmania," the commissaris said. "I
came to report on our inquiry, about how we're doing—or
not doing, to put it correctly."

"Hello," the chief constable said. "Care to join me? I'm
off to the pub. I'll be doing something useful later on, but
there's some time to fill pleasantly." He checked his watch.
"About an hour."

The commissaris made himself comfortable in the new
Volvo. "Some good action tonight?"

"Unfortunately." The chief constable frowned. "Internal
trouble that's beginning to stink up the outside. A rotten
apple in my basket."

"A colleague?" the commissaris asked. "What's the nature
of the charge?"

"Not really a charge," the chief constable said, "although
if there were one, it might be called corruption. Caused by
loving kindness, one might say, but even so, we can't have
that in the police. We're not the Salvation Army. What do
you think?"

The commissaris looked fierce.

"In Amsterdam, of course, you are more tolerant," the chief constable said.

They left the car and crossed the square. "Such delightful peace," the commissaris said. "Such architectural beauty." He waved at the quietly impressive buildings. "A simple style, but majestic all the same. Rather amazing to find that in a province."

"I wouldn't call Friesland a province," the chief constable said. "It's more like a state."

"Why not?" the commissaris said. "That explains the stately buildings. You're right, of course. I was born in this state, in Joure."

"The boss himself," Doris said, and bowed. He moved quickly from behind his counter and brought a barstool. "Sit down, sir. The little gent is your guest?"

"He is, Doris," the chief constable said.

Doris brought up another stool. Cold beer foamed in tall glasses.

"To Friesland," the commissaris said.

"To Friesland," all the customers said loudly, too loudly, perhaps. The sudden silence was broken by the commissaris.

"My murder," the commissaris said.

"You still haven't got a clue," the chief constable said. "I know. Your theories are off. They'll be off for as long as you hang around here, but please stay if you like. We'll be as helpful as we can be. Haven't we been helpful? You must have noticed."

"Let me tell you about my murder," the commissaris said.

The chief constable lit the commissaris's cigar. "One of my men stumbled, I don't like to see that. I'll talk about it a little, maybe it'll relieve my feelings. Adjutant Oppenhuyzen, you've heard the name?"

"The kind colleague who lent his house to my detectives?"

"The very man," the chief constable said. "He's in charge of our Aliens Department. A good man at heart. But he's gone too far."

"Where did he go?" the commissaris asked.

"Two more, Doris," the chief constable said. "Oppenhuyzen can't say I didn't warn him. I don't mind Chinese, they have to be around too. I saw an exhibition of Chinese art a while ago, and I can't say I was not impressed."

"I like Taoism," the commissaris said. "That's Chinese too. It's about nothing. It says that nothing matters. That nothing has always been, will be forever, that our activity leads nowhere, that we never have to do more than nothing, that while we do nothing, nothing will be rediscovered. That's Chinese, I like that."

"Their cooking is good too," the chief constable said. "Mrs. Oppenhuyzen can't cook—I had dinner once at her house—perhaps that's why the adjutant is so fond of Chinese. But whatever his reason may be, his activity is unacceptable."

The commissaris's eyes didn't focus.

"Whatever my adjutant's motivation," the chief constable said, "I can't accept his supplying illegal aliens with papers. Complaints are reaching me from everywhere. Unsavory individuals cannot be sent out of the country because of my adjutant's good deeds. I'll just have to stop him."

"Tonight?" the commissaris asked.

"I had Oppenhuyzen followed," the chief constable said. "He'll be in Bolsward now, with his friend Wang, a restaurant owner. Wang is a fine old man, born and bred in Friesland, but you know how the Chinese work, they abuse their residents here, through their infamous Triads. Wang will be a member too, or he'll lose his venerable head. Tough types. We just had that battle on the dike."

"Gang warfare," the commissaris said. "Without survivors. Not a bad thing in itself, self-inflicted extermination, but does it have to happen here? While I am watching?" The commissaris blew ashes off his sleeve. "I found the sight somewhat upsetting."

"I couldn't agree more," the chief constable said. "All Oppenhuyzen's fault."

"The adjutant is handing out resident papers in Bolsward?"

"For the very last time," the chief constable said. "Doris, I'll have my check. I'll be meeting my men at headquarters now. We'll be taking four cars and a bus. All suspects to be arrested, and Oppenhuyzen on indefinite leave."

"The more elegant solution," the commissaris said. "We don't want an inquiry by Central Detection. That's really endless trouble. It gets into the papers, too. I've been through that. My wife didn't like it, either."

"You'll be losing your way again," the chief constable said. "Would you like me to get someone to direct you? Anything at all, just specify your request."

"I'll be going with you to Bolsward," the commissaris said.

The Volvo, lead car of the convoy, sped through the quiet night. The chief constable handled the wheel in silence. His noble profile expressed powerful activity. He concentrated on the job ahead.

"I'm not saying," the commissaris said, "that my method is in any way scientific, but we do develop intuition in our line of work, and everything else having failed, I've allowed myself to listen to the inner voice. Not entirely without reason, as you may safely assume. Do I really overreact if I find a connection between Scherjoen's death and his native soil? The man's existence in Friesland was blackened by evil. I haven't been able to interview anyone who had a good word for Douwe. If I keep stumbling along in my chosen direction, I just have to trip over the killer."

"I don't like doing this," the chief constable said. "Oppenhuyzen is essentially a good man, and he's been tortured by excruciating nerve pains. There seems to be no cure for his ailment."

"Weakness," the commissaris said, "attracts evil. I do have four suspects. Three men weakened by greed, and a lady whose very lovingness may have made her slide into darkness. In a way I favor Mem, because if she committed evil she meant it for good."

"Lately I have suffered from toothache," the chief constable said. "When it hurts, I'm not myself. My poor adjutant has been in pain for years, although at times he seems to have fought it successfully. He sometimes seems at peace."

The radio came to life. "Sir, next turn off the highway and then a sharp right will take us to the new quarter. The restaurant faces the boulevard."

"What did he have to gain?" the chief constable asked. "Free cognac and expensive cigars? He paid for that trip to Singapore himself, I'm fairly sure. Or are things worse than I dare to think? A bank account in Switzerland, maybe? I hope we won't be turning up any hidden surprises."

"Sir?" the radio said. "Next block. We'll be hanging back now. There are no exits on the side. If we set ourselves up at the rear of the restaurant, we can catch them if they try to escape."

"Very well," the chief constable said. "Prepare your weapons. No hesitation while arresting the subjects. I want the crew of car number two to back me up. All others watch the rear."

"Understood," four voices answered.

The shopping center was guarded by two high apartment buildings. The Volvo parked. The commissaris got out. He waved at a passing Deux Chevaux, of a bright orange color. The occupant waved back.

De Gier got out of the Deux Chevaux. The commissaris introduced the sergeant. "A coincidence?" the chief constable said. "Will you be coming with us?"

"If you please," de Gier said.

"I was addressing your chief," the chief constable said. "I'd rather have you wait outside. You can expect Chinese suspects. The two men over there are mine, and the two over there are mine too. Please introduce yourself to them. I'm a little short of time now."

The chief constable walked into the restaurant, followed by the commissaris. There were no clients seated at the tables, but young Chinese surrounded the bar.

"Police," the chief constable said loudly. "Checking your residence permits. Your papers, please."

The Chinese in the rear backed off, and the Chinese in front approached, running around the chief constable and the commissaris. They came back again, trying to get away from the policemen now appearing at both sides of the large room. One man remained at the bar, neither young nor Chinese, a fairly heavy man with a rather red face. He wore a tweed suit. "Evening," the man said.

"Evening, Adjutant," the chief constable said. "I had hoped not to find you here. Stay where you are, never mind what goes on."

Behind the bar, an old Chinese smiled at the confusion. The commissaris slipped behind the counter. The old Chinese offered his hand. The commissaris shook it. "Wang," the Chinese said.

"A good evening to you, Mr. Wang."

The young Chinese were shouting at the policemen.

"What are they saying?" the commissaris asked.

"'Rotten egg,'" Mr. Wang said.

The young Chinese made fast beating and kicking movements, turned rapidly on their own axles, breathed sharply in and out. The policemen were quiet behind their drawn guns.

"What are they doing?" the commissaris asked.

"Gymnastics," Mr. Wang said. "Karate. Like in the movies. You know that type of movie? *'Sah! Toh! Wah!'*"

"I hardly ever go to the movies," the commissaris said.

"They say that when they fight," Mr. Wang said. He blew and hummed simultaneously. "Never heard that sort of sound? They do that too, when participants close in on each other."

The young Chinese were humming and blowing.

"And where does that get them?" the commissaris asked.

"When they do it in the movies," Mr. Wang said, "they're paid."

"You're under arrest," the chief constable said loudly. "All of you, turn to the wall and put your hands behind your necks. Right away. Hop."

"Hop isn't here," Mr. Wang said.

"Your Dutch is impeccable," the commissaris said.

"I was born here," Mr. Wang said. "I don't want to be Chinese anymore. I prefer to be nothing."

"Weren't you nothing from the beginning?" the commissaris asked.

Wang reached for a bottle of cognac and two glasses. "Are you a Buddhist?"

"You're not right in the head," the commissaris said. "A Buddhist is something. Why should I be anything at all?"

Wang poured the drinks. He gave the commissaris a glass. "I beg your pardon. Your very good health."

"I beg your pardon too," the commissaris said. "*Your* very good health."

The chief constable was accepting the weapons found on the young Chinese. "Would you like a bag?" Mr. Wang asked. Two revolvers, a pistol, and six knives were pushed into a white plastic sack. The chief constable put the bag on the counter and looked at Adjutant Oppenhuyzen. He put out his hand. "Your weapon, too, and your identification. Apply for leave in writing. It'll be granted, for the rest of your years, forever, amen, Adjutant."

Oppenhuyzen gave him the requested objects.

"Go," the chief constable said, "and never be seen again."

Oppenhuyzen smiled inanely, pushed himself off his stool, said "Good evening" dreamily, and wandered to the door.

De Gier came in after the suspects had been led out. Eddy rested on the sergeant's hands.

"Away," the chief constable said. De Gier turned about. "Not you," the chief constable said. "I meant the rat. What's a dead rat doing here? Did you find him outside?"

De Gier turned about again. He offered the rat to the commissaris.

"For me?" the commissaris asked.

"For Douwe, sir. Didn't Cardozo say Douwe still needed a gift to present to your suspects?"

"Would you like a bag?" Mr. Wang asked.

Eddy was shoved into white plastic.

"Friend of yours?" Mr. Wang asked.

"Yes," the commissaris said. "Sergeant de Gier. He'll go far, I keep thinking."

"I meant the rat," Mr. Wang said.

"In a way," the commissaris said. "I haven't known him all that long, and I already have a friend, a turtle, who lives in my rear garden. I rather prefer quiet friends. Eddy liked to rattle. I didn't take to the sound."

The young Chinese were shouting on the parking lot. "'Rotten egg,'" Mr. Wang said. "Their conversation is monotonous. I hope to be without it for a while."

"Coming?" the chief constable asked the commissaris.

"I should go back to Amsterdam," the commissaris said. "Rinus, you take me. Cardozo has my car. And then you can drive back to Friesland. You'll be off tomorrow again, and can sleep late."

The commissaris thanked the chief constable for the adventure and Mr. Wang for his hospitality. He carried Eddy in his bag to the Deux Chevaux.

De Gier waited for the question that wasn't coming, for the commissaris was asleep.

"You're home, sir."

"What?" the commissaris asked. "Right." He got out. De Gier took him to the door of his house and handed him Eddy in the bag.

"Thank you," the commissaris said. "Have a good trip back, Sergeant."

⫸ 24 ⫷

MODERN SCIENCE HAS DEVELOPED A TYPE OF GLASS THAT is transparent on one side and mirrored on the other. The invention benefits detection. With a suspect on one side and a detective on the other, much that was hidden becomes instantly clear. A wall of this type of glass divides two rooms in Amsterdam Police Headquarters. On the suspect's side of the glass wall, much work was done that day, observed by curious eyes hidden behind the mirror. Cardozo and the Madame Tussaud friend didn't know that Adjutant Grijpstra watched their movements. They could have known, but they were too busy creating. True creation, the Madame Tussaud friend explained, reconstructs reality. Modern reality may be of divine origin, but once the thing is done, the artist gets his chance in duplication.

Grijpstra didn't hear that, or he would have frowned. The adjutant smiled, for he was listening to jazz through earphones connected to a box. He had the box because Jane wanted him to repair it. The box only needed new batteries, and a cassette that Grijpstra happened to find on de Gier's desk. He now listened to a jazz mathematician on piano— nameless, for the sergeant had left the label blank. Grijpstra smiled because it wasn't often that luck reached him from several sides at once. The beautiful constable and the perfect music met in his mind, housed in a rhythmically wobbling head. Let it all come to me, Grijpstra thought, and not by my own effort, and while it does, I can watch those two jokers. While I do nothing myself, all the mysteries are clarified, beginning with the riddle of Douwe Scherjoen's being.

"Yahoo!" and "Whee!" Cardozo and the Madame Tussaud friend shouted while they worked on their tangible expression of the dead man's dark side. Their diligent hands stapled strips of black cotton material to wooden sticks, hinged so that they would move at the pull of a string. Douwe could already sit down and get up. He also had to take a step forward while stretching out his hands, and the hands, emerging from cotton cuffs, were to give the visitor the gift. The gift, sent by the commissaris, waited in its plastic bag. As the bony thumbs kept slipping, the Madame Tussaud friend experimented with wires meant to hold joints together while Cardozo worked on the lights, which hung in the corners of the room and were able to turn and flash.

"A sudden impression," the Madame Tussaud friend said. "It has to work for only a single moment."

Grijpstra's jazz cassette had come to the end, and the adjutant now listened to the artists' dialogue, picked up by microphones and amplified on his side of the glass.

"Never mind Douwe's bright side," Cardozo said, closing the album that he had been studying before. "Let's show him at his worst, chill the visitor with pure nastiness."

"Too abstract," the Madame Tussaud friend said. "They won't believe it. We'll make Douwe beg for forgiveness. Let's give him a pathetic touch."

"Revenge?" Cardozo asked. "He's a ghost now, without peace. He's still a businessman, too. He'll suggest a fair exchange. They can have dead Eddy, and in return they find Douwe's killer."

"Who wants a dead rat?"

"Okay," Cardozo said. "He's threatening them. A dead rat is revolting."

"Death," the Madame Tussaud friend said, "that's what we have to work on. The death of Douwe's burned skull, the black holes of his eye sockets, the limp corpse of the rat, tail and feet hanging down, the end of everything."

The artists took time off, to roll cigarettes, suck smoke, reflect on their intentions. "Frighten them, okay," Cardozo said. "But they've got to feel sorry for him, too. And for themselves, that they reduced him to this state. The murderer is among them."

The Madame Tussaud friend jumped up. "Let's make him more pathetic."

Douwe sat down and got up again, stepped forward slowly. They bent his spine, slowed the movement of the arms, turned the skull to the side, flashed more sudden light.

"Please," Douwe begged, "please help me. I never killed anyone, the punishment was too cruel, fill in the gap, show your guilt, please confess."

He's asking for compassion, Grijpstra thought, that's better. He wants help. We all want help. We're weakly human. I'm seeing myself now, I'm as damned as Douwe, I'll be damned if I don't want to help him. They're doing a good job.

"Done!" Cardozo and the Madame Tussaud friend shouted. They had pressed a flat black cap on Douwe's skull, and beyond that final touch, there was no more to be done. The skull's reconstruction had succeeded. Only the top part, with the grinning sockets, had been Douwe's property once; the wired-on lower jaw had been picked up in a forgotten corner of the police laboratory, but that the two halves didn't belong together was satisfactorily smoothed over by the shadow of the cap's visor, strengthened by pulsating light.

Cardozo & Co. entered Grijpstra's room. "I didn't know you were here, Adjutant," Cardozo said. "What do you think?"

"Not bad," Grijpstra said.

"You hear?" Cardozo asked.

"Who needs praise?" the Madame Tussaud friend asked.

"The adjutant never approves of me," Cardozo said.

"They weren't *your* efforts so much," the Madame Tussaud friend said. "All you did was hand me tools. But that's fine, you were useful in a way."

The commissaris came in. Cardozo went back to the other room and brought Douwe to life by pulling strings. Douwe got up and offered the dead Eddy. Eddy's eyes glowed a sparkling red in the suddenly switched-on light.

"Really," the commissaris said, "aren't we overdoing this a trifle? I hadn't meant to go quite this far. No. Not at all."

"Okay?" Cardozo asked, rushing into the room.

"Your chief isn't sure," the Madame Tussaud friend said. "Will you be canceling the performance, sir?"

The commissaris shook his head. "I don't want to waste your work."

The telephone near Grijpstra's hand rang. He picked it up. "The reception desk downstairs, sir. Suspects have arrived."

"Go down, Adjutant, and fetch them, one by one. Pyr, Tyark, and Yelte first. Don't go in yourself. Pull the door closed after them, and come here."

Pyr entered the room. Of all the suspects, he resembled Douwe most. Pyr was small and bent forward. What Pyr said, when Douwe offered him Eddy, wasn't Frisian, but the prehistoric scream of those who are suddenly faced with the ultimate threat that life can offer, as the commissaris explained later, yanking his own watch chain until it broke. "Pyr saw his own being," the commissaris explained.

"*Trrruahahahahee*," Pyr screamed, according to the tape that preserved the sounds of the interrogation room and was played back after the suspects had left.

After that scream, Pyr understood that he was in the presence of a lifeless puppet made of cloth and sticks, nothing to get upset about. Pyr wandered about the room, guiltless but shaken, as could be expected. Grijpstra fetched him and took him to another room. The commissaris casually dropped in. Pyr, angry now, swore in Dutch.

"Mr. Wydema," the commissaris interrupted. "I'm sorry we had you come all this way for this, but I wanted to save you the trouble of endless interrogation."

"You don't have any proof at all!" Pyr shouted.

"Tell me," the commissaris said, "the sheep that you export, do you know their eventual destination?"

"Turkey!" Pyr shouted.

"You collect the money over there?"

Pyr had been to Turkey.

"You ever spend any money there?"

"On what?"

"On purchases? Products? Something to bring back?"

"From *Turkey*?" Pyr asked. "What have they got out there? Flies? Old women? Holes in the street?"

Pyr was sent back to Friesland. Tyark Tamminga was sent to Douwe. Tyark, a tall, wide-shouldered man, had to cry a little. He threw his cap on the floor and staggered to the door. The door was locked. Tyark pressed himself against the wall of glass and had to be pried loose by Grijpstra.

"I'm sorry, Mr. Tamminga," the commissaris said, "that we had to bring you in for this, but..."

"Douwe is in hell," Tyark said, "with a rat. I should have known."

"Why, Mr. Tamminga?"

"But I didn't want to know," Tyark said. "I never like to think about things like that. When they die, they're still somewhere. I'll be too, one day."

"In hell?" Grijpstra asked. "What did you do that you deserve hell?"

Tyark shook his head.

"Do tell," the commissaris said. "Something bad?"

"Yes," Tyark said. "I'm rude to my farmhand. And Ushe's dog, he kept stealing and losing my clogs. I shot him for that, but that's years ago."

"Ushe is your wife?"

"Yes," Tyark said. "That's where I'll go, to hell, with a rat."

Tyark left for Friesland.

Yelte Pryk wasn't grateful for Douwe's gift, either, but he kept minding his manners. Yelte raised his hand to greet Douwe. The hand touched Eddy's tail. Yelte stumbled and groped about the room, illuminated by the spotlights.

"I'm sorry, Mr. Pryk," the commissaris said, "that we had you come all the way from Friesland..."

"Douwe pulled me out of the moat," Yelte said.

The commissaris nodded.

Very nice of Douwe, Yelte said. You can be most mistaken in judging others. Yelte's van had slid off the dike, and Douwe happened to come along and pulled him out. Douwe burned out his clutch, and Yelte had expected to be asked to pay, but Douwe never mentioned the expense.

"So you rather liked Douwe?" the commissaris asked.

Yelte wouldn't go as far as that. Some honesty must be held on to. But Douwe in hell, with rats, that was a bit much. Poor Douwe.

Yelte was sent home.

The commissaris went down to fetch Mem Scherjoen. He opened the door of the room and waved her in.

"Douwe?" Mem asked softly.

Douwe offered Eddy.

Mem was about to accept the rat when her arms dropped down. "It'll be all right," Mem whispered. "Wait for me, dear. I'll be along and I'll get you out. We'll start all over."

Douwe tried to give her the rat again.

Mem turned away.

"I'm sorry, Mrs. Scherjoen," the commissaris said.

"We'll be together again," Mem said. "Douwe'll have to learn. I'll never give up. I'll always be with him. I wish I could help the other one, too."

"Which other one, Mem?"

"Douwe's killer," Mem said. "He's having a hard time now. And he's alive, maybe that's worse. Can't you make it easier for him, a little?"

"As long as he won't come forward," the commissaris said, "I may have to wait."

"You might go to see him."

"Yes," the commissaris said. "I'll be doing that soon. Did you come by train? Shall I give you a ride back?"

"That would be nice." Mem touched the commissaris's arm. "You didn't really frighten me. I dream about Douwe, and he does look strange now, very much like what you just showed me in that room. No peace for Douwe yet. Once I can take care of the retarded people, things should get better."

"They will," the commissaris said.

"And if you help the other one, we'll all be doing what we can."

"Absolutely," the commissaris said. "I'll start working on that at once."

///// 25 /////

DE GIER LET GO OF HIS BOOK, SWUNG HIS LEGS OFF THE couch, and grinned at Grijpstra and Cardozo.

"Dinnertime," Grijpstra said. "Cardozo is hungry too."

De Gier covered his eyes with both hands.

"Food!" Grijpstra shouted.

"Food?" Cardozo whined.

De Gier was back on the couch. "I'm so slow. Why didn't I understand?"

"Go on," Grijpstra said. "Serve dinner. *We* worked all day. We've been looking forward to dinner all the way up the dike."

"Of course," de Gier said. He held up the book. "This woman, who calls herself Martha, also wants to kill her men, and at times she does it, too. All her stories have the same basic subject, and I kept wondering what could be at the bottom of all her troubles."

"No sole," Grijpstra said. "No noodles with tomato stew, no mussel soup. Not the same thing over and over again. An Eastern dish this time, I thought."

"With a hot sauce," Cardozo said. "We earned a good meal. We were at it again all day while you were sitting on your butt."

"And this Martha," de Gier said, "is considerably more intelligent than all the men she's married to in her tales, but because they only make her slave, her intelligence hardly shows. The men fart around and then they show up at home and force her to do heavy work, and whatever she comes up with isn't good enough. She has no chance of ever accomplishing anything, so she doesn't, and they aren't pleased and yell at her."

The doorbell rang. De Gier threw the book down and went to the corridor.

"Evening," the commissaris said. "I had a hard day. I'm sure you prepared a tasty meal. You can bring me a drink first. Why do you look so sleepy? Have you been napping all day again? The house is a mess."

"But it wasn't Mem," de Gier said. "If I had finished Martha's stories earlier on, I might have accused Mem. These Marthas don't really kill their husbands, they escape into fantasizing. In the future they just might kill us, but under present conditions they still depend on us. Or they think they do, which comes down to the same thing. Poor souls."

"I don't know what you're talking about," the commissaris said from the recliner, "and frankly I don't care. Can I have that drink?"

"No drinks," de Gier said. "No dinner. The stores are closed. Anyone care for a Chinese meal?"

Cardozo shuddered.

"Nothing Chinese for poor Cardozo," the commissaris said. "He might be reminded. Whip something up, Sergeant, it's the very least you can do."

"The kitchen is cleaned out, sir. I thought the case was all wrapped up."

"You can't know that," the commissaris said.

"De Gier has been working on the sly," Grijpstra said. "I suspected that from the beginning. Against my strict orders. He's had all sorts of help, too. Hylkje couldn't do enough for him. The sergeant has been slithering in and out of the local scene and has kept all available information for himself."

"You mean you still don't know?" de Gier asked.

"I want dinner," Grijpstra said.

"And you?" de Gier asked Cardozo. "You're still after your sheep-buying sheik? What was his name? Hussain bin Allah?"

"I want dinner too," Cardozo said.

"My treat," the commissaris said. "At the first place we find, but it can't take long, for I still have to go somewhere."

"It's not too hard to find," de Gier said, pulling french fries from a paper bag. "You head for Dokkum, turn at Britsum, and make sure you don't miss Ee and Metslawier."

"You don't know where I'm going," the commissaris said.

"What's de Gier saying?" Cardozo asked, chewing his hard-boiled egg.

"He's speaking Frisian again," Grijpstra said, pulling plastic wrap off boiled meat. "He's linguistic."

"I learned some good Frisian last night," de Gier said. "Poetic too. Hylkje taught me. She acted it out, too. Want to hear?"

"Showoff," Grijpstra said, then turned to Cardozo. "I hope you see that now. He's not a good model for you. Real heroes never have to show they are special."

"And he wouldn't even cook us a meal," Cardozo said. "How could I ever want to imitate him? He really fell through on this case. He blinded me for too long. This egg is old."

The commissaris paid. "Got to go now."

De Gier followed him. "You'll lose you way, sir. It'll be dark in a moment, and all those dikes look alike."

"Come along, then," the commissaris said.

The commissaris looked over his shoulder. "Another Land Rover." His fists hit his knees. "Ouch. No. I won't have it. Get rid of them, de Gier. You're a good driver. Let's see what you can do."

De Gier stopped just before the village of Metslawier. The Land Rover parked ahead. "Evening," the sergeant said.

"I know the way," de Gier said. "I swear."

The sergeant saluted and marched off. "Well?" the corporal in the Land Rover asked.

"A legend doesn't have to be true."

The corporal, a man from The Hague, recently transferred but able to speak Frisian quite well by now, said that legends must be true, just because they *are* legends. "You're a religious type, aren't you?"

"Like any Frisian," the sergeant said.

"So they must be lost. Your faith supports you in believing they are. We showed them the way. We'll tell all the colleagues, and they'll all be happy."

"I was happy before this came up," the sergeant said, "and I'm still happy. Policemen from below the dike are morons, whether they've lost the way or not."

"I just wanted you to keep on being happy," the corporal said. "This is paradise, is it not? As soon as doubt comes up, we have to crush it."

"You haven't lost your way here yet?" the commissaris asked in the Citroën.

"No," de Gier said, "but then it was all made easy for me."

"Because you weren't in on it?"

De Gier took the turn toward Ee. "A little question, sir. Did you intentionally place me in an outside position?"

"Now whatever makes you think that?" the commissaris asked. "Don't put me on a pedestal, how many times haven't I said that to you? You've always wanted to change me into a legend, but legends are always lies. Sane doubt, Sergeant, will serve you better than creating idols to populate your little heaven."

"I don't believe you," de Gier said. "Whatever you do has to be intentional. You push someone out and he immediately starts to prove himself, and since he isn't part of the team, he has to approach the problem from a different angle, as you wanted him to."

"And I'm admiring the proceedings of that free individual?" the commissaris asked. "Stop carrying on so, Sergeant. Have I, anywhere during this inquiry, asked you what you might be doing?"

"You didn't have to," de Gier said. "You're a good observer."

"There you go again," the commissaris said, "although it's true that we are now both headed in the right direction."

"Before we get there," de Gier said, "you might give in. Talk to me now, and you'll be in a better position when you try to trap the man. But maybe you don't need to give your game away now. Are you still testing me?"

The commissaris stared sadly at low houses clinging to the dike. "Who is the Frisian here? Don't be stubborn, Sergeant. I'm not testing you in any way. All I want to do is meet with the suspect and get back to Amsterdam to see if I can get some rest."

"Ha," de Gier said. "The suspect can't be arrested. We'll be grabbing thin air. Isn't this a wasted trip, sir?"

"Now why can't we grab Adjutant Oppenhuyzen?" The commissaris smashed a nonexistent fly between his hands. "We'll make him confess, that's easy enough, contact the Super Police in The Hague, and Central Detection will be here in a jiffy and nab him. True?"

"Not true," de Gier said. "I think you're testing me again. This, sir, is Engwierum. The adjutant's summer shed is on the next street on the right, at the end, facing the sea. Shall we go?" He parked the car.

"Hmm," the commissaris said.

"You prefer me to park in front of the suspect's house?"

"I lose," the commissaris said. "You're right. I can't arrest him."

"So why are we visiting the poor fellow?"

"I lose again," the commissaris said. "It might be better if you'd fill me in first. What do you know, Sergeant?"

"After you," de Gier said. "You made me set myself up by coming along. I give in. Won't you tell me first what you found out?"

"Very well," the commissaris said, "but let me lose a little. Answer this question. How wealthy is the adjutant?"

"He isn't," de Gier said. "Oppenhuyzen drives an old Saab. He doesn't dress well. You've seen his house in Leeuwarden in Spanish Lane, paid for out of his wages, furniture and all. The summer house is constructed from pressed sawdust sheeting."

"Would he be stashing money in a foreign country?"

"Not the type, sir. Mrs. Oppenhuyzen doesn't like to travel, and the adjutant doesn't strike me as an adventurer either."

"No money in an old sock?"

"I don't think so, sir."

"Suspect visits prostitutes," the commissaris said, "according to Cardozo. So he does. So what? Once in a while, maybe. It's not a costly habit."

"Sir," de Gier said, "I'm positive Adjutant Oppenhuyzen never accepted bribes in cash. He went to Singapore at his own expense, to visit a needle doctor. He and his wife stayed in a boardinghouse. The doctor was a friend of Wang's, the restaurant owner we met last night. A good guy, I'm sure."

"Mr. Wang impressed me," the commissaris said. "He knew what I was talking about. He must be a sage."

"Are you a sage too, sir?"

"Hmm," the commissaris said. "Don't get too clever, Sergeant. Attack is easy."

"Well, maybe the suspect did accept something," de Gier said. "But I'm sure the Triads didn't pay for his Singapore cure."

"Did the cure work?"

"No, sir. But Oppenhuyzen did, from time to time, have periods when he suffered no pains."

"You can switch the engine off now," the commissaris said.

They walked the rest of the way. "At times there was no pain," the commissaris said, "so we may presume that the suspect could, on occasion, procure a strong drug. Heroin is the best painkiller known to modern medicine. Continuous and excruciating pains in the face are often diagnosed as neuralgia, perhaps an incurable disease. Morphine will do away with the pain, but our doctors don't like to prescribe the drug, and if they do, the quantities are always too small."

"He could have used a bullet," de Gier said. "Bullets are often better."

"You're too young," the commissaris said, "but you're excused. I would have made the same comment twenty years ago. Strange, don't you think? The more energy we have, the more suicidal we seem to be."

"I don't know any better," de Gier said. "Sorry, sir."

"Neither do I, Sergeant, but at my age the doubt is more subtle. To wish suicide on another seems silly to me now."

"I said I was sorry, sir."

"All right, all right," the commissaris said. "Oppenhuyzen accepted heroin to relieve the pain that drove him crazy, in exchange for settling papers and giving advice and general help to a foreign criminal element. Unacceptable, but very easy to understand."

"If you'd be good enough to tell me what you plan to do now," de Gier said, "my spirits might rise. The chief constable has already sentenced the adjutant to official leave for the duration. I don't see how you can go any further. Interrogating an officer from another police corps is illegal, unless you are accompanied by his chief." He looked over his shoulder. "Is the chief constable of Leeuwarden about, by any chance?"

"There's no flaw in your reasoning," the commissaris said. "But now tell me how you found the connection between Oppenhuyzen and Douwe Scherjoen."

"Turkey," de Gier said. "I suspected Mem Scherjoen and that fellow Pyr and the other two sheepy types. In every case the motivation would be revenge. Mem was tired of being abused, and Pyr and his mates were attempting to save their business. Grijpstra was working on the cattle dealers, and you were all set to give Mrs. Scherjoen a hard time."

"And what were you doing?" the commissaris asked.

"Thinking of Turkish heroin," de Gier said. "Until recently, most heroin came from the Far East through the Hong Kong and Singapore Triads, brought in by so-called nephews of legal Chinese who had been here for generations. They forced their 'uncles' to put them up, hide their heroin, feed and lodge them for free. Many of the local Chinese have restaurants. Some of the restaurants are good, but Wo Hop's place in Amsterdam, where Cardozo entered in innocence, must be a Triad hangout."

"Yes," the commissaris said, "and I wonder why that place hasn't been raided by us. Protection?"

"Yes, sir."

"Yes," the commissaris said. "But you can't be sure."

"Sure enough," de Gier said. "And when I'm back, and you'll be helpful enough to place me off side again, I could look into that protection."

"A thought," the commissaris said.

De Gier stopped and rolled a cigarette. "Now, Douwe was described to me as a most evil man, when I stumbled into an acquaintance while I sniffed around in Leeuwarden, looking for heroin. Douwe also made private loans, at killing interest."

"That upsets you?"

"Oh, yes," the sergeant said. "Sucking the hopelessly lost?"

"That's bad," the commissaris said.

"The Chinese were short of heroin, but they controlled the retail market. If they couldn't get it from their own contacts anymore, because of the frenzy with which immigration and customs are now pursuing all suspect couriers, they could still obtain supplies elsewhere. The Middle East manufactures heroin from homegrown opium. We also watch the Turks. Douwe is no Turk. He sells sheep to Turkey. Turks owe him money. What if he was paid in heroin? I imagined Douwe bringing the drug in."

"Right," the commissaris said. "After a while I thought of that possibility too, but you were far ahead already."

"But you were working on Mrs. Scherjoen," de Gier said. "There's only so much time. Although, to be sure, I couldn't see what you were hoping to bring about. Would you have arrested a nice widow?"

"Look here," the commissaris said. "I've got to do my job. I'm hopelessly curious, too."

"You gave her a fright," de Gier said.

"I did not, Sergeant. Mem was innocent and never budged. I thought she was guilty because she might have discovered that Douwe was selling heroin and had meant to put a stop to that, but she never knew about that part of his activity."

"Could she have killed her own husband?"

"Yes," the commissaris said. "She's a most admirable lady who lives by her conscience. You don't see that too often."

"Shot and burned her own husband?"

The commissaris nodded. "Absolutely, and her sister would have helped, another suspect meeting all my requirements. Mem is an idealist, Miss Terpstra is a perfect terrorist."

"So you see," de Gier said, "you were distracted. I couldn't be, all I had was one direction. I was lucky, too, for Lieutenant Sudema stumbled my way. Sudema had some ideas, subconsciously perhaps, and he had to get real drunk to be able to express them, and even then he would merely hint. He sent me to his nephew, a Military Police private who was picking up a deserter on Ameland, who had dealings with Scherjoen."

"A full report, please," the commissaris said.

De Gier reported.

"Has the copper been returned?" the commissaris asked.

"Yes, sir. That wasn't a real theft, but more like a traditional adventure that islanders go in for, to earn the respect of their peers. The deserter told me all I needed to know. Scherjoen would be bringing in heroin on his own account.

He must have sold to Wo Hop, who was making most of the profit. Scherjoen wanted all the profit. He may have planned to sell his next import directly to users, or perhaps he had already sold retail, in Amsterdam of course."

"You were definitely ahead of me," the commissaris said. "Well done, Sergeant. I imagined Scherjoen in the power of the Chinese gangsters and struggling to get free, as you did, but you had some facts."

"Chinese gangsters do not shoot us Dutch," de Gier said. "They *do* shoot each other. If they hit us, their position weakens further, for we become nervous, refuse to cooperate, and get at them even more. Wo Hop forced his flunky, Oppenhuyzen, to do away with Scherjoen."

"In exchange for more medicine," the commissaris said. "Last night our suspect had heroin up to his ears. Did you see how he reacted when his chief sent him off?"

"I did," de Gier said. "Let's hope he still has some left. He must be under heavy tension. Hylkje and I delivered dead Eddy here last night, and Mrs. Oppenhuyzen kept thinking we had come to arrest her husband."

"Report on that visit."

The commissaris listened.

"Why," de Gier asked finally, "didn't you ask me last night what I was doing in Bolsward, sir?"

"Childishness, Sergeant. I wanted to see if I could figure it out myself."

"You were testing me."

"Please, Sergeant."

"You still want to call on the suspect, sir?"

"I'll have to," the commissaris said. "More childishness. Cardozo's prank with the ghost of Scherjoen slipped completely out of control. I had no idea what horrible artwork those two young jokers might be capable of. My legs were shaking when they popped the result on me. I had meant to bring about a slight shock, but the muses of hell must have inspired Cardozo's effort."

De Gier thought. "Mem Scherjoen?"

The commissaris nodded behind the glowing tip of his cigar.

"She wants you to bring her Oppenhuyzen's scalp?"

The commissaris sighed. "If only that were true. I would have refused. No, Sergeant, I promised to help the poor fellow."

De Gier looked at the sky.

"He won't help," the commissaris said. "Direct your prayers at yourself."

"I wouldn't know how to fix this either," de Gier said, and rang the doorbell of the small summer house.

"You really want to bother Sybe?" Mrs. Oppenhuyzen asked. "He's in pain. Isn't it rather late? Are you a policeman too, sir?"

"Yes," the commissaris said, stamping out his cigar.

"Central Detection?"

"No, ma'am, I want to be of help."

Mrs. Oppenhuyzen shook her head. "Well, come in, then." She took them to the sitting room, pointed at the plastic chairs, and went upstairs.

Adjutant Oppenhuyzen came downstairs, fumbling with the cord that closed his housecoat. "Sorry, sir. I'd gone to bed."

"You're not feeling well?"

The adjutant sat down slowly. "It's not too bad now. I took my medicine."

Mrs. Oppenhuyzen sat down. "Offer the guests something," her husband said.

"In a minute." She held his hand. "I want to be with you."

"I know what medicine you're using," the commissaris said. "It'll be unavailable to you from now on."

"Oh." Mrs. Oppenhuyzen squeezed her husband's hand. "Don't say anything, Sybe."

"It's all right," the adjutant said. "They're colleagues."

"Shut up. Please."

"Your husband can say anything he likes," the commissaris said. "We can't press charges."

"Make some coffee," Oppenhuyzen said. "I'll call you in a moment. I want to discuss something with the gentlemen."

Mrs. Oppenhuyzen began to cry. De Gier jumped up. "I'll go with you, ma'am. I'm good at making coffee."

"No," Mrs. Oppenhuyzen said. The door banged behind her.

"It was you?" the commissaris asked.

"You mean the business with Douwe?"

"You used your service pistol?"

"Let's say I did," the adjutant said. "There's still no proof. I've read the reports. The bullet wasn't found, and the skull had been damaged by fire."

"You burned the body yourself?"

"Yes," the adjutant said. "The Chinese had the dory ready, but they left too little gasoline. The corpse should have disappeared altogether. I went to see Wo Hop, but he didn't have any more gas, and my face was hurting again. I hadn't used my medicine that night, it always makes me slow."

"I see," the commissaris said.

"I botched the job," Oppenhuyzen said. "I didn't know Douwe personally, or I couldn't have done it at all. Not a good man, was he?"

"Rather not," the commissaris said.

"I never accepted any money, sir."

"There is a doctor in Amsterdam," the commissaris said, "who specializes in your disease. You won't believe me, but he's Chinese too. Still a young man, got his Ph.D. in the treatment of neuralgia."

"I've seen all the specialists," Oppenhuyzen said. "I have the incurable variety. When the pain starts up, I go crazy, I'll take anything that's around, but only heroin helps, it plucks the pain away. If only the doctors would prescribe the drug, but they're too worried about addiction."

"Are you addicted?"

"I don't think so," the adjutant said. "A while back, the

pain left me for a few weeks and I never even thought of the drug."

The commissaris tore a page out of his notebook and wrote down the name and address of the Chinese doctor. "Give him a try. Do you have any plans for the future?"

"None," the adjutant said. "You heard what the chief said. I'm on sick leave until I'm old enough to retire. Maybe I'll fix my house up, the house in the city. This one will fall apart if I touch it with a hammer."

"You're not planning to apply for an interview by Central Detection?"

"No," the adjutant said. "I can't be arrested on my confession alone. There's no proof. No witnesses will ever show. The Chinese who brought the boat and the gas died on the dike. And what about my wife? Shouldn't I look after her?"

Mrs. Oppenhuyzen brought the coffee in.

"I told them," the adjutant said. "It's all right."

"He mustn't give himself up," Mrs. Oppenhuyzen said. "That Douwe wanted to bring poison in. It corrupts young people. But it never bothered Sybe. It's good medicine, but it should be strictly controlled."

"I shouldn't have done it," the adjutant said. "There are some who take bribes, but that's no excuse. I've always tried to be honest. I should have talked to the chief. Douwe took a lot of money from Wo Hop to finance a big import from Turkey, but when he brought it in, he sold it to the junkies himself. Hop doesn't like that."

"Wasn't Douwe afraid of Hop?" de Gier asked.

"He thought Hop would be arrested and kicked out of the country, but Hop has good protection."

De Gier rubbed his hands. "Wo Hop."

"You can't touch him," the adjutant said. "If you go after Hop, you'll have to work in high places."

The commissaris rubbed his hands too. "We might give it a try." He looked at his hands. "Are you sure you don't want to talk to Central Detection? If you do, you've done everything that's humanly possible."

"No," Mrs. Oppenhuyzen said.

The commissaris got up. "And do visit that Chinese doctor. You never know. Maybe it'll work out."

"Thank you, sir," Adjutant Oppenhuyzen said.

"You won't go any further?" Mrs. Oppenhuyzen asked.

"I don't have the authority," the commissaris said. "I came as a friend. Thank you for the coffee, ma'am."

‖‖‖‖ 26 ‖‖‖‖

"WAS EVERYTHING AS EXPECTED?" MR. WANG ASKED.

The commissaris dabbed his mouth with his napkin. "Yes, certainly, a delicious dish of fried rice, Mr. Wang."

"A cognac?"

"Some tea?" the commissaris asked. "Pot of tea and two cups?"

Wang brought the pot.

"Do sit down," the commissaris said.

"Tea," Mr. Wang said, "to celebrate our meeting. I often celebrate with tea." He sat down, poured the tea, and held up his cup. "I celebrated when two of my children were stillborn, and I celebrated again when two others arrived alive."

"They're doing well?" the commissaris asked.

Wang opened his mouth and pointed at his gleaming teeth. "One is a good dentist."

"And the other?"

"He helps to develop warheads of atomic missiles," Mr. Wang said. "In the United States. A genius, that boy. I had tea with him when he finished his studies, and I'll have tea again when his first missile hits a large city."

"Your nephews," the commissaris said, "the young fellows that my colleagues arrested here two days ago, will be expelled, after they've done their time in jail."

Wang sipped his tea.

"And if they show up again," the commissaris said, "which may be soon, for they won't be locked up long, you might want to call me." He presented his card. "Phone me at home, I'm usually in at night."

"I stay away from phones,"Wang said.

"Your Dutch is really impeccable," the commissaris said.

"I was born here in Bolsward," Mr. Wang said.

The commissaris poured tea. "I was born here, in Joure, we're both Frisians."

Mr. Wang laughed. "We're both Earthmen," Mr. Wang said. "We do have a lot in common. Maybe I will phone you after all. Aren't you the commissaris who's often mentioned in the paper? Will you be arresting my nephews here?"

"I'll catch them at Wo Hop's," the commissaris said. "By the way, about Mr. Wo Hop..."

Mr. Wang shook his small, smiling head.

"No?" the commissaris asked. "Would I be overreaching myself?"

"Yes," Mr. Wang said.

"A pity," the commissaris said. "And to think that I'm fighting on the side of Good."

"Maybe that's why."

The commissaris looked about him. Mr. Wang pointed out a green dragon that had been painted on the wall above the bar. The dragon was nuzzling his own tail.

"That's Wo Hop," Mr. Wang said. "Give him time. He'll eat himself."

"He's rather a long beast," the commissaris said. "And he hasn't even taken his first bite."

"Soon," Mr. Wang said.

"Westerners aren't known for the exercise of patience," the commissaris said. "What would you advise me to do in the meantime?"

"Drink lots of tea," Mr. Wang said. He got up and walked

to the bar. He came back with a can. On the can, a picture had been painted showing a turning wheel. At the center a cock, a pig, and a snake were turning spokes.

"My present to you," Mr. Wang said. "There's good tea in the can. Patience tea. You can accept the present. It's worth only a few guilders, and you did rid me of the nephews."

The commissaris studied the picture. "The wheel of life," Mr. Wang said, "moving because of the powers of pride, greed, and mean behavior."

"Will it turn forever?"

"It'll break by itself," Mr. Wang said. "Won't take long now."

The commissaris paid the check.

Mr. Wang walked him to the door.

~~~~ 27 ~~~~

IT WAS SNOWING. THE COMMISSARIS LOOKED OUT HIS WIN-dow. He was rubbing his leg. De Gier stood next to him. "Slithering-about weather," the commissaris said. "Plugged-up-noses weather. We'll have a whole winter of it again. Thaw, quick freezes, mud, I don't feel like putting up with it again. Cheer me up, Sergeant."

"Hylkje?" de Gier asked. "Do you remember the young lady?"

"Yes." The commissaris smiled. "Such a lovely woman, and that huge motorcycle, the Frisian adventure, Sergeant. Some of our better hours."

"She was here for the weekend, sir."

"Aha," the commissaris said. "I'm glad to hear that. You'd better look into that aspect of your life, Rinus. Soon you'll be old and you'll be complaining. She might want to listen to your complaints."

"I can't visualize that," de Gier said. "She can, but I never see it."

"Take her to New Guinea," the commissaris said, "in a flat-bottomed sailboat. Share your great adventure. I waited too long, but you could replace me."

"She told me about Adjutant Oppenhuyzen," de Gier said.

"He's cured of his disease. Do you remember the Chinese doctor that you said he should visit?"

"No?" the commissaris asked. "True? That's great. I'm very pleased. I thought that might work out. The doctor is supposed to be brilliant. He was recommended by my medical friends when I was looking into the possible source of the pain in Adjutant Oppenhuyzen's cheeks."

"Yes, sir. It seems that the adjutant had a chronic infection of the jaw, of which the neuralgia was symptomatic. Symptomatic neuralgia can be cured if the infection is taken away. The doctor had Oppenhuyzen's teeth pulled, then he scraped his jawbones and prescribed antibiotics. The neuralgic pains didn't come back."

"Then he can fix up his house," the commissaris said.

De Gier scratched his bottom.

"That's an irritating habit you have there," the commissaris said. "What's up now?"

De Gier looked out the window.

"You want the adjutant to be punished?" the commissaris asked. "You're not playing guardian angel, are you now?"

"A man commits murder," de Gier said. "We've all agreed that's bad. We've made up laws to punish murder. We've appointed hooligans like me to catch murderers. So why is murder suddenly all right?"

"We've also agreed," the commissaris said, "that we will not convict a man on his own confession if there's no proof that he committed the crime. Cops don't run around catching cops—that's another agreement we made."

"You could have turned the hounds of Central Detection loose, sir."

"Hmm," the commissaris said.

"So where will this all end?"

"In a bad place," the commissaris said.

"I don't see that, sir."

"You see what you see, Sergeant." The commissaris

dropped into his desk chair and made it turn all the way around. "And what does the adjutant see, when he shaves his painless cheeks every morning, the good adjutant?"

"He sees a killer," de Gier said. "Can he live with the killer?"

"He'll kill him, I think," the commissaris said.

▓▓▓ 28 ▓▓▓

De Gier admired the fresh young leaves of elm trees, on the other side of the window. Grijpstra leafed through a file of recent reports. "Spring," de Gier said. "Unbelievable, but it's here. The winter died. Spring will be dying too. Everything does go away after a while, you noticed that, Adjutant?"

"Wo Hop went away," Grijpstra said. "Read this."

De Gier read "'Hop, Wo, born in Singapore...' blah, blah, hm, '...found lifeless on the pavement of Prince Henry Quay...' hm, '...six bullets in chest...' hm, twenty-two-caliber again, Magnum, right." He turned the page. "Ah, here. 'According to witnesses, Wo Hop was approached by two young male Chinese, dressed in sports shirts, caps...' hm."

"A professional job," Grijpstra said. "Shoot the mark down and keep walking quietly, around the corner, gone. We'll never catch them. They were flown in for the contract and immediately afterward raced out of the country. Probably left from Frankfurt or a French airport. They'll be home in Hong Kong by now."

"And who'll take over Wo Hop's Triad?"

"That we'll know soon enough," Grijpstra said.

"Your Chinese is weak," de Gier said.

"I'll pick it up," Grijpstra said. "Frisian was easy enough. Morning, Jane." Grijpstra got up. "The most beautiful cop on the force." He sat down again.

"I don't like that," Jane said. "I'll be complaining about you. You're committing sexual harassment. I am no more than a female colleague, very intelligent too, and I wish to be treated as such. Your flirtatious attitude insults me."

"You're so right," de Gier said. "What did you do with your hair?"

Jane turned around. "You like it better this way?"

"It makes you look mysterious," de Gier said.

Grijpstra began to cough. "You smoke too much," Jane said. "You're polluting our air. I stopped yesterday, but if I have to breathe your smoke, I might as well smoke myself."

"Cigarette?" de Gier asked.

"Just one," Jane said. She lit his with her lighter. "Did you read the morning paper?"

"Not yet."

She came back with the paper. "Weren't you in Friesland last year? Here, read for yourself. A fatal accident, a colleague was the victim."

Grijpstra grabbed the paper from her hands. "Not Hylkje. Stupid girl. Always speeding."

"Not a woman," Jane said.

Grijpstra read aloud: "'Adjutant Sybe Oppenhuyzen, Municipal Police, Leeuwarden,'—that's him—'temporarily on sick leave'—temporarily, ha!—'died because of an accident yesterday.' Ah, I see what the journalist is trying to say, the asshole."

"They're always trying to show us up," Jane said. "That adjutant was on sick leave but he was healthy enough to work on his roof, and he slipped and fell. Hello, Cardozo."

Cardozo placed a shoe box on Grijpstra's desk. "You'll never guess what I have in here, Jane." He carefully lifted the lid with one finger. Jane bent down. Cardozo pulled the string that dangled on his side of the box. A rat's skeleton jumped out of the box. The rat rattled. Jane ran from the room.

"Haha," Cardozo laughed. "Good joke, eh? Samuel's friend and I made this. Remember Eddy? We buried him and dug him up again. The skeleton was in perfect condition."

Grijpstra and de Gier, who had embraced each other, let go.

"I heard him rattle," de Gier squeaked.

Cardozo produced a tape recorder from his pocket.

"Get out," Grijpstra shouted. "Take that mess with you."

"Don't come back today," de Gier shouted.

The commissaris came in. Cardozo replaced the box on Grijpstra's desk. "Watch this, sir."

The commissaris jumped into de Gier's arms.

"Good joke, don't you think?" Cardozo asked. "We worked on it for hours. Very tricky, to hinge all the skeleton's parts. Did you hear the rattle?"

The commissaris's shaking finger pointed at the door.

Cardozo walked toward the corridor.

"Take the box, Constable," the commissaris said loudly.

Cardozo came back and picked up the box.

"You weren't really frightened, were you, sir?" de Gier asked.

"Just testing Cardozo," the commissaris said, lighting a cigar at the wrong end. "Always keep them in suspense. He thought I wouldn't be frightened, so I pretended I was. That'll teach him a lesson."

"I don't quite follow you," Grijpstra said.

"I do," de Gier said. "Cardozo is much too sure of himself. He needs doubt. The commissaris provides doubt."

"Of course," Grijpstra said. "Very subtle, sir. You could have fooled me. You're a perfect actor."

"You two drive me crazy," the commissaris said.

He stalked out of the room.

"Your hero," Grijpstra said.

De Gier closed his eyes. "He has so much to teach."

ABOUT THE AUTHOR

Janwillem van de Wetering's first book, THE EMPTY MIR-
ROR, describes his year and a half in a Japanese Buddhist
monastery. This experience, as well as his adventures on the
Amsterdam police force, gives a special quality to his novels,
including OUTSIDER IN AMSTERDAM; TUMBLEWEED;
THE JAPANESE CORPSE; and THE CORPSE ON THE
DIKE. He is also the author of INSPECTOR SAITO'S
SMALL SATORI, which introduces us to a new cop, and
MURDER BY REMOTE CONTROL, a mystery told in comic
book format. Van de Wetering lives on the coast of Maine.

MURDER... MAYHEM... MYSTERY...

From Ballantine

12   TA-43